THE RACHEL SCOTT ADVENTURES
VOLUME 1

ASYLUM HARBOR
BURN OUT

THE RACHEL SCOTT ADVENTURES
VOLUME 1

ASYLUM HARBOR
BURN OUT

TRACI HOHENSTEIN

THOMAS & MERCER

The characters and events portrayed in this book are fictitious. Any similarity to real persons, living or dead, is coincidental and not intended by the author.

Copyright © 2011 Traci Hohenstein

All rights reserved.
Printed in the United States of America.

No part of this book may be reproduced, or stored in a retrieval system, or transmitted in any form or by any means, electronic, mechanical, photocopying, recording, or otherwise, without express written permission of the publisher.

Published by Thomas & Mercer
P.O. Box 400818
Las Vegas, NV 89140

ISBN-13: 9781612182933
ISBN-10: 1612182933

Asylum Harbor

ASYLUM HARBOR

BY TRACI HOHENSTEIN

THOMAS & MERCER

TO CHASE SATTERFIELD
—STAY INSPIRED

ACKNOWLEDGEMENTS

A big thank you to my first readers: Stephanie Roessler, Michelle Couch, Chase Satterfield, Bud Satterfield, and Debbie Steber.

A special thanks to Sheila Pennington, who answered all my silly questions about the Bahamas, and Joyce Gleeson-Adamidis, who gave me insight into the cruise ship industry. (If I screwed up anything in regards to the Bahamas or cruises—it's my own fault!)

And thanks to Cyndy Krapek, who let me name a character after her. Also to Jane Dystel and team, Kay Keppler, Jeroen ten Berge, and the Amazon team—Andy, Ashley, Jacque, Rory, Jessica—and all the others who worked to make this book the best it could possibly be.

And to my family, for their patience and support. Love you guys!

CHAPTER 1
AMBER KNOWLES'S STORY

My name is Amber Knowles, and I'm one of the thousands of people who go missing every day. The day I disappeared was beautiful, with lots of sunshine and not a cloud in the sky. My parents had dropped me and my two best friends off at the Tampa dock. We planned to take a cruise on the *SeaStar* to the Bahamas. The trip was a high school graduation present from our parents and a chance to let loose before college.

At first, my parents didn't want me to go. They were worried—with good cause, I suppose. You see, my dad is the governor of Florida, and he plans to announce his intention to run for president in the next election. He was concerned about sending his only daughter on a trip without any security. The last thing I wanted was to be followed around by men in black suits, sticking out like sore thumbs. Plus, we had two parents chaperoning the trip. So I fought desperately for that freedom, and my dad finally gave in.

Now, in hindsight, I kind of wish he had sent someone.

The first day of the cruise we set sail for Key West. My best friends, Nicole and Rowan, were just as excited as me to spend a couple of hours shopping and hitting the famous Duval Street. We even managed to score some margaritas at Sloppy Joes. However, the fun came to an end for me that night.

After a nice dinner, we decided to check out the ship's newest nightclub, Aqua. As we approached the club's door, I saw a cute guy in a white uniform with the *SeaStar* logo. He introduced himself as Josh McCain and told us he was a VIP host. I remembered seeing him earlier that day when we were lounging by the pool. Up close, he was even more gorgeous, with brilliant green eyes and a nice smile. He walked us to a private room and told us to let him know if we needed anything.

We hit the dance floor, but after about an hour, I started feeling sick to my stomach. I wasn't sure if it was the alcohol or if I was seasick. Probably a little of both.

"I'm not feeling well," I said as I laid my head down on the edge of the sofa in the VIP room. The velvet felt cool against my skin.

"We'll get you some water," Rowan said. My friends got up from the couch. "Stay right here."

A few minutes later, Rowan and Nicole came back with Josh, who was carrying a bottle of water. "Rowan said you weren't feeling well. I thought this might help," he said sweetly, handing me the ice-cold bottle. "Do you want to go lie down? I can get the ship's doctor for you."

I took a sip and immediately felt my stomach rolling around.

"Hey, you don't look so good," Nicole said.

"Yeah, you're a little green. You want us to go back to the cabin with you?" Rowan offered.

"No, that's okay," I protested, covering my stomach with my hand.

"I can walk back with her. The commissary shop has some medicine for seasickness that I can get," Josh said to my friends.

After a few minutes of encouraging me, I finally gave in and let Josh walk me back. The last thing I wanted to do was hurl in front of my friends and a cute guy I just met.

On the way back to my suite, Josh told me he was from California and had worked with the cruise ship for about eight months. I couldn't help but wonder if he was flirting with me.

I told him I had just graduated from high school and would be attending Florida State University in the fall.

"I plan on becoming a veterinarian, and they have the best program in Florida," I said. "Plus, it's close to home, which my parents like."

What I didn't tell him was what it's like being the daughter of a prominent governor and how it causes me all kinds of stress and problems. A lot of people at my high school were jealous of the life my family leads. If they only knew. It isn't all glitz and glamour. We have skeletons in our closet just like any other family.

We finally got to my suite, which I could tell impressed him.

"Wow, the penthouse suite. You must be someone special," he said.

The penthouse suite costs like eight thousand dollars for a four-day cruise. I wasn't quite ready to let him know who I was, so I ignored that comment for a moment.

"I'm going to change. Be right back."

I went into my room, pulled the pink sundress over my head, and threw it on the bed. A pair of shorts and T-shirt that I'd worn earlier that day were still clean. I put them on with a pair of flip-flops and walked back out to the living area. My stomach was still rolling around, and I now I had a doozy of a headache, too.

"I think I need to lie down." I headed for the sofa and rested my head on one of the pillows.

"Why don't you rest, and I'll call the doctor for you." Josh stood over me, staring at me with those beautiful green eyes.

"I don't want all the trouble. Some Pepto or Tums would be nice."

"We can manage that." Josh got a towel from the wet bar and ran it under the water. "I had trouble with seasickness when I first started working." He put the cool towel on my forehead. "What really helps is fresh air and looking out over the ocean."

"Fresh air sounds good." I followed him out onto the balcony and, stretching out on the chaise lounge, put the cool towel on my forehead. "I'm feeling better already."

"Good. I'll be back in a few minutes with something for your stomach."

The night sky took my breath away. The thousands of stars combined with the twinkling lights from the cruise ship reminded me of Christmastime. I pulled my long blonde hair into a makeshift ponytail and slid off my pink flip-flops, taking a big breath of the salty air.

A strong gust of wind came out of nowhere and tossed a flip-flop over the railing. I stood up just in time to see the shoe get swallowed up in the foamy wake. *Dammit!* I'd just bought those shoes in Key West. *Tonight is not happening for me. Maybe I should go to bed and try again tomorrow.* But I wanted my stomach remedy. Josh had been gone about a half hour and he should have been back by now. When I heard the sliding glass door open behind me, I turned to see Josh standing there.

"Hey there. I thought you forgot me," I said. He had a strange look on his face. "What's wrong?"

Then someone shoved Josh onto the balcony. I didn't see that person until Josh stumbled forward.

I stared in shock at the strange man. He looked familiar, but I was so scared that I couldn't place him. He pointed a gun at Josh's head.

"What are you doing? Are you crazy?" I screamed at this stranger.

"Move it," the man said, pushing Josh farther out onto the balcony. The man was short, stocky, and bald, with a chipped front tooth.

"Leave her alone. She doesn't know anything," Josh said.

"What's going on?" I asked again. "Josh, who is this man?"

"Come on, Amber. Join the party." The man motioned to me with the gun.

It took me a second to realize what the man said. *How does he know my name?*

I stared at him, trying to figure out if I knew him. I pressed my back into the balcony railing, thinking there was no way I was going anywhere with this lunatic.

"Leave her out of this. She had nothing to do with it," Josh pleaded.

"Not my problem. No witnesses." The man raised the gun and pointed it toward me.

Now I really started to freak out. It's silly now to think this, but I couldn't help but wish my dad had sent security with me. I turned around and could just faintly make out what looked like the lights of a coastline. We must have been near our next stop in the Bahamas. I thought to myself, *If I stay, I die. If I jump, maybe I can make it to shore.* My hands shook as I climbed the railing and threw my leg over the side. The wind was picking up again, and loose strands of hair blew into my eyes. I looked down at the ten-story drop into the swirling water below.

"Amber, what are you doing?" Josh asked me as I sat on the railing, leaning toward the water. A look of panic flashed through his eyes.

"Shut up," the man said.

"Look, we can work this out. I'll tell you what you want to know if you just let her go inside," Josh said.

"Don't think so, *Josh*." The man held the gun steady at me. His intense eyes locked with mine.

He adjusted his stance. The icy finger of fear gripped my heart as I looked into the water again. A loud shot rang out into the night, and then darkness rushed up to meet me.

CHAPTER 2

Juan Perez woke up with the worst hangover he'd had in years. The only thing that made it worthwhile was the fat roll of money in his pocket.

He rolled over and looked at the clock. It was almost noon. He couldn't believe his wife had let him sleep in so late. They must have already docked in Freeport because he couldn't feel the motion of the ship or hear the engines anymore.

Juan sat up in bed and took a drink from the water bottle sitting on his nightstand. Last night had been the best night ever. He'd won over three thousand at the craps table. Winning that much money had given him the biggest high he'd ever had. He'd turned his original hundred dollars into three grand and he didn't want to stop.

So he'd moved on to the blackjack table, but his luck hadn't held. Two hours went by like a blur until he was down to his last twenty bucks. How had that happened? He was headed toward the casino bar to drown his sorrows with his last twenty when the slot machine, lit up with flashing red, white, and blue lights, seemed to shout at him. He'd thought, what the hell, and put his last twenty in the slot.

As he pulled the handle, a beautiful cocktail waitress walked by. She wore a black miniskirt, and her breasts spilled out from the top of her tight, white V-neck sweater.

"Hey, you won!" She excitedly pointed to the machine behind him.

He shifted his eyes away from her ample breasts and turned around slowly. Solid bars of red, white, and blue lined up perfectly as the machine's light on top flashed brilliantly and a siren went off.

"Looks like you won five grand. Good job." The waitress gave him a big smile as she walked off, swaying her hips.

The pit boss came by and escorted him to the cashier's office. The manager collected his tax information and doled out his winnings.

Juan had proceeded to the bar, his pockets fat with dough, and bought a round for everyone. Several drinks later he'd realized it was almost four in the morning. His wife, Danella, would be pissed. He'd promised her that he would spend only a couple hours at the casino before turning in. That had been around midnight.

He'd quickly made his way to the cabin. His luck had stayed with him. Danella was sleeping soundly when he quietly let himself in. He'd slipped out to the balcony to get a breath of fresh air before going to bed. He'd leaned against the railing and saw the ship heading to the Bahamas coastline. Just as he was heading back in to snuggle with Danella, he'd thought he heard a small splash. He'd leaned over the balcony and saw a life raft floating away from the ship. Juan remembered rubbing his eyes, thinking he was seeing things. The next instant, the raft was gone.

He must have had too much drink, he'd thought as he went inside. He'd slipped silently into bed and wrapped his arm around Danella. Within seconds, the life raft was forgotten and he was sound asleep.

Now, it was noon, Danella was gone, and he wondered again if he had hallucinated the lifeboat floating away from the cruise ship. He reached over and grabbed his pants off the chair. He felt around in the pockets, but the money was gone. Had he imagined winning the money, too? No. Here was a receipt for five thousand dollars from the cashier's office.

So that solved that. Danella must have found the money while he was passed out and gone ashore to shop. Juan laughed out loud. That was his penance for staying out past his bedtime. His wife would spend every dime.

Juan got up and searched for some clean clothes. He hadn't dreamed the money. And maybe the lifeboat hadn't been a dream, either.

CHAPTER 3

Rachel sat in a vanity room makeup chair, trying to enjoy being pampered. This wasn't her first time in front of a camera, but butterflies still fluttered in her stomach every time she thought about millions of people watching her on TV. In just a few minutes she'd be on the set of *The Today Show* to do an interview with Ann Curry. Rachel's company, Florida Omni Search, had found a missing Boy Scout in the Florida Everglades last weekend. It was a national news story, and she was thrilled to be a part of a successful recovery.

After what felt like an hour under the unnecessarily intense care of the hair and makeup crew, Rachel looked into the mirror. Her normally long and unruly auburn hair was now silky and shiny. She thought she looked younger than her thirty-five years and was amazed at the magic the makeup artists could do.

Kristy, one of the production assistants, came to escort her to the set. She looked like a former fashion model, tall and lean with faded jeans, a white peasant blouse, and brown suede high heels.

"You look great," Kristy said as they turned the corner into the studio.

"Thanks. I'm a little nervous."

"Don't be. You'll do fine. Just remember to take a deep breath and smile."

The Today Show studio was a lot smaller than it looked on TV. There was a news desk on one side of the small stage and a seating area on the other side. Booms, wiring, curtains, and unused props took up the rest of the space. Directly in front of her the crew was putting together the kitchen for the cooking segment that always aired last.

Ann Curry walked onto the set and introduced herself. She explained how the interview would begin and which cameras Rachel should look into and when. Rachel fought off the butterflies and tried to remember Ann's flurry of instructions. The lights dimmed and Kristy made the countdown to going live. The production assistant's bony finger pointed at them with conviction.

"Good morning, we're back with a special guest," Ann Curry said, smiling into the camera. "Rachel Scott from Florida Omni Search is with us today. Rachel played an instrumental role in locating a missing Boy Scout, Casey Daniels, last week. Rachel, tell us a little about how you got involved with search and rescue."

Rachel took a deep breath and smiled into the camera. "I cofounded the organization after my daughter, Mallory, disappeared several years ago." She paused for a second. This was always the hardest part. Mallory had been only three years old when she'd vanished, and even though it had been five years ago, Rachel still felt a lump in her throat every time she thought about her precious little girl. "I became frustrated with the lack of progress from local law enforcement. Hundreds of people are reported missing every day, and there aren't enough officers to help with those cases."

"Your first case was a missing boy in your area."

"Well, unofficial case. I was watching the evening news and saw that a toddler had been abducted from my neighborhood. I contacted his mother, Janine, and offered my support. We not only were able to track down her ex-husband, who had kidnapped her son, but we became fast friends. Janine Jensen and I founded Florida Omni Search."

"What does Florida Omni Search do for families of missing loved ones?" Ann inquired.

"We're a nonprofit private search firm that has over twelve hundred volunteers from all professions, including people who are trained in forensics. We have more resources and equipment than most law enforcement agencies. That's why they routinely call us when there is a difficult missing person case."

"Last Saturday you received a request from the Palm Beach Sheriff's Office to help locate Casey Daniels." Ann recounted the story. "How did you go about finding him?"

"The troop leader knew Casey's last location, so that helped us narrow our search grid. We found Casey fourteen hours later, about seven miles from their campsite."

"The Florida Everglades is a very unforgiving place—the dangerous elements, heat, snakes, alligators. It's amazing that you were able to locate him so quickly."

"The Everglades are definitely unforgiving. The day we searched, the heat index was over a hundred and five degrees. If you go off the beaten path, like Casey had, it's easy to get lost because everything looks the same. Not to mention, the saw grass can slice through your skin."

"What was his condition when you found him?"

"He was dehydrated and scratched up, but otherwise in good shape. I credit his troop leader, who did a great job teaching the boys survival skills and first aid. It was a successful recovery and a happy ending."

"That's great to hear. We're all grateful for what you and everyone at Florida Omni Search do for missing persons and their families. Thank you for sharing your story with us."

"Thanks for having me," Rachel replied.

Ann looked into the camera. "When we come back, we'll talk to Casey and his mom from the hospital in Palm Beach County."

The show had provided a private car to take her back to the hotel, so Rachel graciously thanked the cast and crew and headed back, listening to messages on the way. One was from Drake Reynolds, an FBI special agent, whom she'd worked with on a couple of child abduction cases. Drake headed the CARD (Child Abduction Rapid Deployment) team from Washington. She quickly returned his call.

"We had a case come up that I hope you can help with," Drake told her. "A girl was reported missing last night in the Bahamas."

"What happened?" Rachel asked.

"She was on a cruise, and the crew officials think she may have fallen overboard."

The town car had pulled up to the hotel and she handed the driver a generous tip. She walked into the hotel's grand lobby and sat down on a sofa.

"That's awful. Is the Coast Guard searching now?"

"They've had a cutter and a seaplane out since early this morning, but they haven't found anything yet."

Rachel tried to think if she could rearrange her schedule. "I was just headed to Tampa for the week. I haven't seen my parents in a while. But I can send our Miami crew down there to help with the search. You know Red Cooper will do a super job."

"We really need you, Rachel. As a matter of fact, you've been personally requested." Drake paused. "The missing girl is Amber Knowles."

The name resonated in Rachel's brain. *Amber Knowles.* "The name sounds familiar…" she started to say.

"Yes, it should. She's the daughter of John Knowles." Drake cleared his throat. "The governor of Florida."

CHAPTER 4

As Rachel walked across the rain-soaked tarmac, the wind picked up and made a mess of her long hair. She had gotten to Jersey's Teterboro airport in record time. The governor had arranged for his private jet to take her to the Bahamas, which was nice and saved a lot of time. A flight attendant greeted her and took her bag. The luxurious jet had six supple leather seats, a small kitchen, and conference area. Rachel immediately spotted Drake near the back of the plane and settled in next to him.

"Good to see you again," Drake greeted her. "Thanks for coming. You remember Lee Phipps?"

Rachel nodded her head. Lee Phipps was well dressed in a dark-blue suit with a pinstriped shirt and tie. His black wingtip shoes were shined to a high gloss and his salt-and-pepper hair was slicked back with gel. *He looks like he belongs on Wall Street instead of the FBI*, she thought.

She remembered that everyone called him by his last name. "Hey, Phipps. Didn't take you guys long to get here."

"We were at a training exercise at Quantico when we got the call. Flew straight here to pick you up."

"Bring me up to speed with what's going on." Rachel opened her purse and plucked out a ponytail holder to put her hair up with.

Phipps leaned forward and pulled out a piece of paper from a manila file. "Here's what we got so far: Amber Knowles, seventeen years old, was on a cruise to the Bahamas with two friends when she disappeared yesterday sometime between midnight and two a.m. She was last seen around midnight when she told her friends that she wasn't feeling well and returned to her cabin with a ship's steward. When her friends went to check on her a couple hours later, the cabin was empty. They alerted the crew. The captain ordered a search of the ship. Nothing. He alerted the Coast Guard and the Bahamian authorities. One of the chaperones informed Governor Knowles, and he called us."

Phipps looked grimly at the piece of paper.

"What about the Bahamas police? Are they investigating?" Rachel asked.

Phipps said, "Governor Knowles doesn't trust the local law enforcement agencies to find Amber. He's only too aware of what happened with the Natalee Holloway case. He doesn't want any mistakes. But the actual investigation does fall under the Royal Bahamas Police Force since the cruise ship was in their jurisdiction."

"Since Amber is an American citizen traveling abroad, the FBI can investigate as well," Drake interjected.

"What's happening now?" Rachel asked.

"The Coast Guard has been searching since four o'clock this morning, but they haven't found anything," Drake said. "Once we land in the Bahamas, we'll go straight to the cruise ship and interview passengers and crew members who have come in contact with Amber during the cruise."

"We believe that Amber was last seen with a crew member," Phipps said. "Josh McCain. He was apparently escorting her from an onboard nightclub to her cabin. She'd gotten ill while partying with her friends. That much we got from the phone call from the governor. We'll know more once we get there."

"Any thoughts on Amber's state of mind? You mentioned she was feeling ill." Rachel directed her question to Drake.

"We have confirmation that she was drinking alcohol. I don't know about any medications that she may have taken," Drake answered.

"After my initial conversation with the governor, I think we can rule out suicide. Her friends and family insist she's a very happy-go-lucky girl," Phipps added.

"Any ransom demands?" Rachel asked.

Drake shook his head. "The family hasn't received any."

"Do you have anything on Josh?"

"We're working on it. As soon as we heard Amber was missing, an agent from our Miami office flew straight to the Bahamas. We'll be meeting with her as soon as we land," Drake said.

"We have no leads, but it's early yet." Phipps leaned back and put on his seatbelt as the flight attendant alerted them it was time for takeoff.

A feeling of dread settled over Rachel. She knew firsthand what it was like to have a child disappear. She'd lived that nightmare when Mallory vanished into thin air. It was the unknown that still caused constant pain. What had happened to her daughter? Was she still alive? Was she being treated well? Rachel put those thoughts aside and concentrated on what Drake was saying.

"We heard about your interview on *The Today Show*. Congratulations on a successful rescue." Drake leaned back in his seat and linked his fingers behind his head.

"Thank you. I practically came straight here after the boy was found." Rachel yawned as she said it.

"Why don't you try to get some rest? We'll be in the Bahamas in about four hours, and I want to hit the ground running when we get there," Drake told her.

Sleep sounded good to her. She'd been up since 3:00 a.m. getting ready for *The Today Show* interview. The flight attendant brought her a pillow and blanket. She didn't think she'd be able to fall asleep, but the constant hum of the engines made her drowsy, and eventually, she drifted off.

✦ ✦ ✦

The sun is shining so brightly it makes my eyes hurt. I sit on the porch watching Mallory playing with her dolls. Everyone always said she looked like the Little Mermaid with her long, red, wavy hair and bigger-than-life green eyes. I hear the distant ringing of the telephone.

"Mallory, Mommy will be right back." I run into the house thinking Rick is calling me on his way to the airport. He probably forgot something, as usual. As soon as I get to the phone, it stops ringing. I look at the caller ID. Rick Scott Imports. Just like I thought.

I hit the speed-dial button and look out the window. There's an indent in the grass where Mallory was sitting.

As I drop the phone and run out to the yard, I can hear Rick's voice in my ear saying, "Hello, hello. Rachel?"

A chill runs down my spine.

"Mallory!" I run around the front yard looking for her. Screaming her name over and over. I can't see her. I can't find my baby. "Mallory!" I yell over and over.

She is gone. My baby is gone.

✦ ✦ ✦

"Rachel, are you okay?" Drake asked as he touched her on the shoulder.

She woke with a start. Wiping the damp sweat from her forehead, Rachel took a deep breath and smiled at Drake. "Sorry, I guess I had a bad dream." It had been a while since she'd dreamt of Mallory. When her daughter had first gone missing, the dream was a nightly occurrence. Over the last couple of years she'd had that particular nightmare only once every couple of months. Rachel smacked her lips. She was parched.

"I'll get the flight attendant to bring you some water. We should be landing in the Bahamas in about half an hour." Drake walked to the front of the plane where Phipps was talking on his cell phone.

Once Rachel heard that Amber Knowles was missing, she had to help. She knew the pain of losing a daughter and wondering if she was okay.

The morning that Mallory vanished, Rachel's life as she'd known it came crashing down around her. Rachel had been a successful businesswoman. She'd had her own real estate company and held financial interests in several small businesses around Miami. Her husband, Rick, was successful in his own right. He owned a slew of luxury car dealerships around South Florida and was expanding into the Orlando area. They'd been part of Miami's social elite. Rachel had thought she had everything—a dream mansion, a high-profile career, a gorgeous husband, and a beautiful little girl.

Until she lost Mallory.

After her daughter disappeared, Rachel spent all her time tracking down leads and working with law enforcement to find her daughter. Her business suffered, her friendships suffered, and her marriage suffered. Eventually, Rick filed for divorce.

Rachel sold her business and all the real estate she had accumulated. With the proceeds and the settlement she got from Rick, she amassed a small fortune. She invested most of that money in her new venture, Florida Omni Search. She put together a search-and-rescue team that rivaled that of any top law enforcement agency in the nation. With qualified forensic specialists came top-of-the-line equipment and technology. After Rachel solved a couple of high-profile missing persons cases, she captured the attention of the FBI and other agencies. It was no wonder that the governor requested her assistance with his daughter's disappearance. Rachel was the best of the best.

She raised the shade on the jet's small window and saw emerald waters dotted with a tiny sprinkling of islands. It had been a couple of years since Rachel had been to the Bahamas. Her last trip was just a quick weekend with girlfriends. They'd forced her to come because all she ever did was work, and Janine said they needed a break. It didn't take an expensive therapist to tell Rachel what she already knew: Keeping busy and focused on finding missing people helped hide the pain of missing Mallory.

Drake came back with a cold bottle of water and handed it to her. Rachel took a long drink and instantly felt better.

"Thanks again for coming. I know how busy you've been lately," Drake said.

"Busy is good for me. Although my parents were disappointed that my vacation plans with them were postponed. Dad thinks I work too hard. But what's new?"

"Well, let's hope that we find Amber safe and sound and we can wrap this up fast. Then you can take that vacation."

Rachel looked at Drake. She'd always kidded him that he looked more like a college professor whom cute girls worshipped than an FBI agent whom criminals feared. He was very handsome with his six-foot-tall frame, wavy brown hair, and inquisitive hazel eyes framed with wire spectacles.

"Yes, let's hope."

The plane shuddered as the landing gear went down. She turned her attention back to the window. As they descended, she could see mammoth cruise ships docked along the port and wondered from which one Amber had disappeared from.

Drake's cell phone rang, and he picked up. "Agent Reynolds." He listened for a few moments, then said, "We'll head straight there."

Rachel and Phipps both sensed something was up and looked at him expectantly.

"That was the Coast Guard," Drake said. "They found a body."

CHAPTER 5

The *SeaStar*, over a thousand feet long and ten stories high, was the largest ship docked at the slips designated for cruise liners. Perched on the top deck was a water park with colorful slides and cascading pools.

"This is one monster of a ship," Rachel said, looking up.

"It has fifteen hundred staterooms, three nightclubs, a full service spa, a water park, six restaurants, and a casino," Drake said, sounding like a commercial for the cruise line.

"No wonder my parents take so many cruises. It has everything you need and then some." Rachel followed Drake up the gangway. She'd never been on a cruise, but she heard all about them from her parents. Since her dad retired five years ago, her parents had taken several. Their ten-day cruise to Alaska was the latest.

Rachel tried to smooth the wrinkles out of her pantsuit as they walked into the impressive ten-story atrium lobby. Sunlight flooded in through a massive skylight. The double staircase and glass elevators encompassed the rest of the lobby, which was filled with happy vacationing passengers. Rachel realized that she and Drake looked out of place among the tourists wearing Hawaiian shirts and flip-flops. Special Agent Cyndy Krapek from the Miami field office was waiting in the lobby.

"Nice to see you guys, finally," Cyndy said as she led them through a maze of hallways to the captain's office. "The ship is docked one more night so we have a lot of work to do. They're scheduled to leave tomorrow afternoon and head to Cabana Cay."

"Where is that?" Rachel asked.

"SeaScape is the conglomerate that owns three cruise ships—*SeaStar*, *SeaMist*, and *SeaPrincess*. SeaScape also owns Cabana Cay, which they use as a destination stop for their West Caribbean cruises. It's located about sixty nautical miles south of Freeport," she replied, talking as fast as she walked. With her short blonde hair and athletic stride, she gave off a no-nonsense vibe that Rachel immediately picked up on.

"Can't you hold the ship longer?" They'd need some time to put together a search party. One night wouldn't be long enough, Rachel thought.

Drake explained to Rachel, "When an American citizen goes missing aboard a cruise ship, even if the ship is in international waters, we can investigate. But unless we have evidence of foul play, we can't hold the ship longer than twenty-four hours."

"What about the body the Coast Guard found?" Rachel asked.

"All we know is that the body was male. We don't know if it's related to Amber's disappearance yet," Cyndy answered, stopping outside a secured door. She pushed the buzzer and waited. "The Royal Bahamas Police Force and the ship's security crew are still processing Amber's suite. We'll head there after meeting with the captain."

The captain's office wasn't as Rachel had imagined. It was small and plain, with a desk, bookcase, and round conference table with six chairs. Cyndy introduced everyone to the captain, Antonio Martin, and the head of security for the cruise lines, Edward Schultz.

Captain Martin was in his late forties, short and stocky, with thick salt-and-pepper hair and an olive complexion. He greeted them with a friendly smile.

Edward Schultz was a complete opposite of the captain. He was tall, very muscular, and bald. And scary looking, Rachel thought. He stood scowling next to the captain.

Captain Martin got right to the topic on hand. "We conducted two full ship searches for Ms. Knowles—the first time when the chaperone notified us that she was missing and again when we got into port. She's not on the ship, which leads us to the unfortunate conclusion that she went overboard." He rubbed his palms together.

"Have you had a chance to look through the security tapes?" Drake asked.

"We're looking at those now," Schultz told him. "So far, the last image we have of Amber is from after midnight, when she was escorted back to her room."

"The cameras cover only about half of the cruise ship," Captain Martin quickly explained. "Mostly open areas. Surveillance cuts off at the main hallway to her cabin."

"We'd like to take a look at those tapes before we talk to the witnesses," Drake said.

"We have them right here." Everyone but Captain Martin sat around the conference table while Schultz uploaded the images to a laptop. Captain Martin stood behind Shultz's chair while the video uploaded. After a couple of tense minutes, a grainy picture came up of a nightclub.

"This is where Amber and her friends entered the club," Schultz said.

Wearing a sundress, Amber approached the club with two girls. "We identified the two girls as Amber's friends and cabin mates,"

Captain Martin said as he pointed to the screen. "Nicole Ryan and Rowan Fitzgerald."

"They look like they're having a good time," Rachel commented, seeing the smiles on the girls' faces. "Who are the guys at the front door?" Both men were wearing the crisp white uniform with the *SeaStar* logo.

Schultz cleared his throat. "They are cruise staff members Andy White and Josh McCain."

Rachel focused on the grainy image that showed Amber talking to Josh for a minute before he escorted her inside.

"Are there cameras inside the club?" Drake asked.

"No, just the entrance. The next shot is about an hour and a half later when Amber and Josh exit the club."

"What's the exact time?" Drake asked as he adjusted his glasses and peered at the computer screen.

"The time shows twelve twenty-six a.m.," Schultz answered. He clicked on another image on the screen. "Next camera picks up Josh and Amber walking down the passageway that leads to her suite. The camera range stops about fifteen feet from her door."

Everyone watched the screen as Josh and Amber walked down the corridor. She stumbled a little and he put his arm around her waist. Another *SeaStar* employee, a woman, passed them in the opposite direction. She was followed by a man dressed in shorts and a T-shirt. The woman glanced back a couple times and then passed out of camera range.

"That's the last image of we have of Josh and Amber," Schultz said. "But we still have a lot of tape to go through. It should take us another couple of hours to review all the security tapes during that time frame."

"Who's the employee and guy that passes them?" Drake asked.

"The employee is Consuela Rodriguez. We've already talked to her. She doesn't remember anything out of the ordinary." Schultz paused and looked over at Captain Martin. "We're working on identifying the passenger. There's another suite on the other side of Amber's." Schultz consulted a sheet of paper in front of him. "Mr. and Mrs. Jacobsen are staying in there. They are on our list to interview."

"What's at the end of the hallway?" Rachel asked. "Just past their cabin?"

"There are two doors at the end of the passageway. One leads to a ladder that goes to most decks. The other door is for employees only and requires a passcode to enter. It takes employees to different areas of the ship," Schultz said.

"And Josh has access to all doors on the ship?" Drake asked.

"He doesn't have full access, but he does have access to most of the doors. Employees have different levels of security access depending on their jobs," Schultz answered.

"Can you show us what doors he accessed the night Amber disappeared?" Drake asked.

"I have that printout right here." Schultz pulled out a piece of paper from a folder. "The last time he used his card was seven fifty-six p.m., which was at the beginning of his shift."

"Has anyone interviewed Josh yet?" Drake asked Schultz.

Schultz looked uncomfortably at the captain. "No." He hesitated. "We haven't been able to find him."

CHAPTER 6

"What do you mean, you can't find him?" Drake asked.

"He didn't clock out after his shift last night, and he's not in his room," Schultz said.

"What happened to him?" Drake looked irritated.

"We don't know. All his belongings seem to be in the room, including his passport," Schultz replied.

"What about the other guy who was working with him?"

"We talked to him right after Amber's roommates reported her missing." Schultz still looked uncomfortable. Rachel noticed he kept shifting his eyes toward Captain Martin. But the captain's face gave away nothing. He stood stone-faced. No emotion whatsoever.

"Andy said Josh never made it back to the club. He didn't get worried until Amber's friends came back looking for her. That's when he notified his supervisor, and within minutes we organized a full search of the ship," Schultz commented.

"Andy didn't think it was strange that Josh never came back to finish his shift?" Phipps asked incredulously.

"One of Josh's responsibilities is taking care of the passengers. He's a VIP host. Andy thought he was just taking care of a sick passenger."

"Does Josh have a private room?" Drake asked.

"No. He shares the cabin with Andy." Schultz took a deep breath. "He said that Josh never made it back to the cabin that night, either."

"How could two people magically disappear?" Rachel wondered aloud.

"We're hoping to get those answers once we review all the tapes," Schultz replied.

"The ship was a couple of hours out from the Bahamas when we got the call that Amber was missing. If she went overboard, there's a chance that she survived a fall." Captain Martin looked over at the security chief before Schultz spoke again. "Of course, you know the Coast Guard found one body already."

"We were notified on the way over here. The Coast Guard said the body is a male." Drake paused. "Are you thinking they found Josh?"

"We think he might have been with her when she fell. We just don't know yet," Schultz answered.

"What about the security tapes? Do any of them show an angle from her balcony?" Phipps asked.

"No. There are no cameras on the outside of her balcony. The only cameras we have outside are the ones near public areas of the ship."

"Can anyone identify the body?" Drake asked.

Captain Martin nodded. "We're waiting for the Coast Guard to give us a call when they're ready."

"We haven't been able to locate family for Josh yet," Cyndy added. "Captain Martin gave us the emergency contact for Josh, but no one has called us back."

"Until then, I want to interview everyone who walked down that corridor between the time the girls left their room to the time

Amber was reported missing," Phipps requested. "Meanwhile, let's go check out the cabin."

"Schultz will escort you. The Royal Bahamas Police Force has an officer in the suite now, and we also have security personnel guarding the door," Captain Martin said.

That reminded Rachel of something she wanted to ask. "Did Amber have security with her on this trip?"

Cyndy shook her head no. "Governor Knowles had insisted Amber bring someone, but she talked him out of it at the last minute."

CHAPTER 7

Captain Martin closed the door behind his visitors. He was annoyed with the Royal Bahamas Police Force and the FBI for boarding his ship and conducting a search. Enzo Morrotti, the owner of the *SeaStar*, had already warned him that the DEA was stepping up its efforts to stop drug smuggling. He wasn't the least bit worried that the FBI agents would find anything in their search for this lost teenager. So he was irritated, yes. Worried, not in the slightest.

He ran a smooth operation and only a few crew members knew what really happened when the ship docked at Cabana Cay every week. The ship was specially fitted with hidden compartments that even the most diligent inspection would never discover. The FBI and the girl from the search-and-rescue company could search the ship for the missing girl all they wanted—they'd never find any evidence of foul play, or anything else, either. He'd been over the whole ship himself with a fine-tooth comb.

The situation was unfortunate, but he'd taken care of the problem for good. He thought about the missing girl and Josh McCain. Josh was a hard worker and losing him was regrettable, but this was the biggest run of the month. He wasn't going to let anyone stop him. The *SeaStar* would depart Freeport tomorrow and head to Cabana Cay on schedule. There, he'd load the ship with the largest cargo to date.

This was his seventh trip to the Bahamas on the *SeaStar*, and he'd proven himself. Mr. Morrotti had guaranteed him a huge bonus at the end of this month. He was already thinking of ways to spend the extra money.

"Captain, phone for you." One of the deckhands said over the speakerphone, interrupting his thoughts.

"Captain Martin," he announced with authority.

"It's Charlie. You wanted me to call you with an update."

Martin took the phone off speaker.

"Yes, Charlie, go ahead." Martin hoped everything was under control now. He didn't want any more mistakes.

"We have the couple in our custody and are heading over to the island tonight."

"Very good. No more problems?"

"We aren't getting any cooperation from the guy. But that was to be expected, no?"

"Right. Well, make them comfortable. We'll deal with the situation tomorrow." Martin hung up the phone and checked the video surveillance on his computer monitor. The agents would be back soon. He'd be prepared for them.

CHAPTER 8

"Wow. Amber's parents spared no expense with her accommodations, huh?" Rachel said as they walked into the girl's cabin.

"This is one of four large luxury suites on the ship. The four of them take up this entire penthouse deck. Each has a master suite, with two additional bedrooms, a living room, dining room, and large private balcony," Schultz said proudly.

"How much does something like this cost?" Rachel asked.

"About four to eight thousand," Schultz answered. "They're very popular, mainly with celebrities or large corporations, and book quickly."

As they entered the suite, Rachel saw a large framed photograph of a very handsome man on the wall above a black marble table. He had dark hair, piercing blue eyes, and he wore a suit with a red tie that had the *SeaStar* logo on it.

"Who's that?" Rachel wondered aloud.

"Ah, that would be Mr. Enzo Morrotti. He's the owner of Sea-Scape Cruise Lines," said Schultz. "He's very hands-on when it comes to running the business."

A Royal Bahamas police officer stood guard in the living area. Schultz nodded to him and explained that the police were still processing the area and keeping everyone out until they were done.

The spacious living room contained an entertainment center and a wet bar. Rachel walked down the small passage leading to the master suite. "I assume this was Amber's room?" Rachel asked.

"Yeah. We found her purse and other belongings in there," Cyndy said, pausing outside the doorway. "Plus, the girls staying with Amber confirmed that this was her stuff."

The room was beautifully done with lots of polished mahogany, brass, and marble. The nightstand held a bottle of water and a book. Rachel picked it up and read the title: *Gone with the Wind*. That was also her favorite book. *Good choice*, she thought.

Across from the king-sized bed was a well-lit vanity and small bench. An armoire set into the wall held a huge plasma television with drawers beneath it. In the master bath, black-and-gold marble tiles surrounded the large Jacuzzi tub and ample shower area. Makeup and hair products littered the vanity table. A container of pain reliever and a half-full bottle of water lay by the sink.

Rachel walked back into the living room and into the second bedroom. This room had two twin beds with a pull-down bunk over each. A desk with a lamp on top and double drawers for storage stood between the beds. Clothes lay scattered all over the floor, the beds, and the walk-in closet. The room's private bath had another shower and Jacuzzi tub. The third bedroom had the same layout, except it had a double bed instead of twin beds.

"This place is larger than my town house," Drake said.

"The governor obviously wanted the best for his daughter," Rachel replied. "He probably thought the penthouse would provide more security for her as well."

"Let's look at the balcony." Drake walked toward the sliding glass doors, and Rachel followed.

"When our security crew did the first search, they found Amber's cell phone, a beach towel, and a single flip-flop out here on the balcony," Schultz said. "Nothing else. The police searched again and took photos."

"No signs of a struggle?" Rachel asked.

"One of the smaller tables was overturned, but that is not uncommon with occasional strong winds."

Rachel examined the balcony railing. It was about four feet high and topped with a wooden bar. "I guess it's possible she could have leaned over too far and fallen overboard." She looked up and around the outside of the ship.

"Wouldn't be the first time someone accidentally fell overboard," Schultz quickly agreed.

"What happened to her other shoe?" Rachel asked.

"We didn't find it in the cabin," Schultz answered. "Another reason we believe she may have fallen overboard."

Rachel looked out over the water again. "How tall is Amber?"

"Five foot six, according to her driver's license," Cyndy answered.

"When someone has had too much to drink, it's easy to lose your balance if you lean over too far. It's tragic, but possible," Schultz said.

Rachel was beginning to feel that Schultz was pushing the "she fell overboard" story a little too much.

"Or someone shoved her. Hey, what's this?" She crouched down and pointed to a small, shiny object near the bottom of the railing.

Drake walked up and leaned over her. "What do you see?" He kneeled down and picked up a small gold ring.

CHAPTER 9

"It looks like some kind of fraternity signet ring. Maybe Phi Kappa Pi?" she said, studying the crest.

"No idea." Drake turned the ring to examine it more closely. There were initials carved on the inside of the gold band:

SMG

"I doubt this is Amber's. It looks like a man's ring." Drake took his cell phone out of his pocket. "Let's take a couple photos before we turn it over to the police." He nodded toward the policeman sitting in the living area. "We can show it to the governor and Amber's friends to see if they recognize it." Drake took a few pictures before alerting the policeman to their find.

Phipps walked back into the room. "I just got a call from the governor. He and his wife are on board now, waiting for us in the conference room by the captain's office."

They walked back to the conference room, where Governor John Knowles, his wife Sarah, and Amber's two friends were seated around the table. Looking every bit as powerful as his position claimed him to be, the governor stood as they entered the room.

Over six feet tall with a muscular build, he wore dark-blue trousers and a white button-down oxford shirt with the sleeves rolled up. His red-striped tie was loosened around his collar.

Rachel felt nervous and wasn't sure why. She'd worked with powerful people before when she'd been a successful real estate broker and developer in Miami. She'd met several political leaders in that time, but never the governor of Florida.

He smiled as he held out his hand, immediately putting her at ease. "Thank you for coming, Rachel. This is my wife, Sarah. Please call me John."

She thought the governor looked more handsome in person than on TV. His thick, dark hair had flecks of gray through it, which made him look more distinguished.

Sarah's blonde hair was pulled back in a neat ponytail and her makeup was perfect. She wore a bright-pink Lily Pulitzer sundress with low-heeled sandals. Rachel had expected her to look more disheveled since her only daughter was missing and believed to have fallen overboard, but she knew that people handled stressful situations differently.

"Thank you so much for being here," Sarah said with a strained smile. "This is Nicole and Rowan, Amber's best friends. They were with Amber on this cruise." She nodded to the girls sitting at the table.

Rachel looked the girls over and took in their casual demeanor. They were both dressed in shorts and T-shirts with flip-flops and were strikingly beautiful, although they looked like they'd been up all night—and they probably had. Nicole had short, spiky, blonde hair with pink tips and reminded Rachel of a pixie. Rowan, in contrast, had long, dark mahogany-colored hair that was thick and glossy.

"Before we get started, take a look at this ring. We found it on Amber's balcony. Do any of you recognize it?" Drake handed his cell phone to the governor so he could see the picture.

"No. That's not Amber's. I've never seen it before."

Drake showed it to the girls. They both shook their head. "Not ours."

"Did you remember if Josh was wearing a ring?"

They both shook their heads no.

Drake put the cell phone back in his pocket. He'd already e-mailed the photo to the FBI's tech guys to see what they could find about the symbol. "A previous passenger might have lost the ring. We're trying to identify it."

"We hope that you can find Amber. As you can imagine, this has been a very difficult time for us," Governor Knowles said.

"I know firsthand how difficult that can be. Time is crucial when a person goes missing, and we need to get started right away. Tell us about Amber," Rachel replied, looking at Sarah.

"I'm having a hard time believing that she fell overboard like the cruise officials have suggested," Sarah said.

Schultz shifted uncomfortably in his seat.

"Why's that?" Rachel asked.

Sarah nodded toward Amber's friends. "It was how Nicole and Rowan described the evening."

"Amber gets migraine headaches sometimes that cause dizziness and blurry vision," Governor Knowles said as he reached over and squeezed Sarah's hand. "She told Nicole and Rowan that she wasn't feeling well. If she was having a migraine, she would have taken her medication and gone to bed."

Sarah agreed with her husband. "The migraines made her sick, and the drugs made her drowsy. So she'd have gone straight to bed. I think something happened to her between the time she left the club and the time she got back to the cabin. But what?"

"That's what we want to find out," Drake answered. "Nicole, Rowan, why don't you tell us what happened last night at Aqua?"

"We went there after dinner," Nicole answered. "After about an hour, Amber said she wasn't feeling well and wanted to go back to the cabin." Nicole looked nervously over at the governor. She was obviously scared and intimidated by him, Rachel thought.

"Did she say what was wrong?" Drake asked.

"She was seasick and had a headache. I offered to walk her back, but…" Nicole said, looking first at Rowan, then again at Governor Knowles. "She said she didn't want to ruin our good time."

Governor Knowles leaned forward and put his hand under his square jaw. Sarah stared at the girls intensely, as though this were the first time she'd heard the story, even though Rachel knew the girls had to have repeated it several times.

"How did Josh get involved?" Drake asked.

"Josh was kind of hanging out with us. He got us into a private VIP room and bought us drinks and snacks. When Amber said she was sick, he offered to walk her back," Nicole said defensively. She looked at Rowan for help.

"He was a nice guy. He talked about how he liked working on the ship and meeting new people," Rowan said, trying to help her friend out. "Have you talked with him?"

"Not yet. We're interviewing all the crew members now," Drake said, not letting them know that Josh was missing, too. "What time did you get back to the suite?"

"We left the club around one thirty to go check on Amber," Rowan answered.

"We were concerned about her," Nicole added. She looked nervously at the Knowleses again.

"What did you find?" Drake asked.

"Amber's door was closed. We knocked, but she didn't answer. I opened the door and looked around. I didn't see her," Nicole said. "I noticed the sliding glass door was open to the balcony, and I went out there. One of the chairs and a small table were turned over, and Amber's phone was left under the chaise lounge. When I saw that, I yelled for Rowan."

"I was changing in my room and heard Nicole yelling, so I headed out to the balcony," Rowan added.

"I didn't know what had happened—if the wind blew the table and chair over, or what. I got worried," Nicole said.

"We ran back inside and called out again for Amber. We searched every room." Rowan started crying. "We couldn't believe she wasn't there."

"Then what did you do?" Rachel asked softly.

"We decided to look around the ship for her," Nicole said uneasily. She patted Rowan's hand, reassuring her.

"We thought maybe she'd gone back to the club looking for us since it was so late," Rowan said.

"Did you go there to look for her?"

"Yes. We asked some of the employees who were still hanging around if they'd seen Josh or Amber, and no one had. The other guy who was working with Josh…uh…his name was…"

"Andy," Rowan said.

"Andy. He went with us to look for her. We walked around the pools and the other decks."

"How long did you look for her?" Rachel asked.

"About an hour, I guess. We came back to the room and called Mrs. Thompson while Andy called the captain," Rowan said.

"Mrs. Thompson is one of the chaperones," Governor Knowles said.

"The crew searched the ship and didn't find anything. By then we'd already started docking," Nicole finished.

"Tell us about Josh." Rachel got a notepad out of her bag. "How did you meet him?"

"He was standing outside the club. Amber walked up to him first and started talking to him," Nicole said.

"He was wearing a uniform?" Rachel asked.

"Yes. He told us that he was a club host and asked if we wanted a private VIP room. We said sure, so he took us to one, and then our other friends came. He was really nice," Nicole said.

"Did Amber talk with him again?" Rachel asked.

"Yeah. He left to talk with some other people, but he came back a few minutes later. They sat and talked for a while," Rowan said.

"After dancing with us for a bit, Amber started feeling sick and said she wanted to go back. Josh got her some water, but she was still feeling bad. So he insisted on walking her to her room," Nicole said again.

"And that was the last you saw of Josh and Amber?" Drake asked.

"Yes," Rowan and Nicole both nodded their heads.

"Okay. Let's take a break." Drake stood up.

"We'd like to stay here and help," Rowan pleaded to Governor Knowles and his wife.

"We talked about it and asked our parents. We don't want to leave without Amber," Nicole added.

"When was the last time you spoke to Amber?" Drake asked Governor Knowles.

"Amber called me from her cell phone right before they left for dinner. She sounded fine and said she was looking forward to the dolphin excursion this morning," he answered.

"Did Amber have security on the ship?" Rachel asked. She caught Sarah giving her husband a knowing look that only a wife can give.

"No. I tried to get Amber to agree to security, but she wouldn't budge. She argued that the chaperones would look after them. Amber was about to turn eighteen and wanted some freedom before starting college." Governor Knowles looked over at Sarah. "I wish I'd sent someone anyway."

CHAPTER 10

Enzo Morrotti sat in his exquisite office overlooking the Miami skyline at the SeaScape Cruise Lines headquarters. He ran his hand through his thick black hair, wondering how he was going to handle this unexpected problem.

He had a headache that would not go away. Opening the desk drawer, he popped open the prescription bottle and shook out two little white pills. He put them in his mouth and took a large swig of water.

The last thing he needed was the FBI crawling all over his ship. He didn't like that at all. Not that he was worried they'd find anything. It just added complications.

He had an agreement with the Cubans that had to be fulfilled. Those caballeros still had two more shipments to deliver. The local police he could deal with. He had a guy on the inside here, and they had an understanding. But he didn't have anyone with the feds. He'd have to stay on top of the DEA. And now the FBI investigation.

He pushed the intercom button, and a minute later, his beautiful assistant entered the office.

"Yes, Mr. Morrotti?" Gia leaned across his desk. Her silky blue blouse revealed an abundance of tanned cleavage. A cascade of brunette hair hung below her shoulders, and her hazel eyes stared at him expectantly.

"Gia. Get Assistant Ambrose with the Royal Bahamas Police Force on the phone for me. Tell him I want an update on the missing girl from *SeaStar*." He barked the orders at her. But she didn't flinch. She was used to his volatile moodiness.

"Yes, of course. Anything else, Mr. Morrotti?" Gia asked, giving him a little pout.

"Find some information on Rachel Scott. Her company is Florida Omni Search. Have Simon help you with it."

Simon Goolsby was a private investigator who helped him when he needed the dirt on someone. He heard through his source that Ms. Scott was in town to help with the search. The more he knew about his adversaries, the better.

"Okay. Is that all?"

"Yes." He dismissed her with a wave of his hand.

His eyes followed Gia as she turned and walked slowly out of his office, shutting the door behind her. Normally, he'd be thinking about her nice, curvaceous ass and all the things he'd do to her later. But right now he couldn't focus on anything but the situation with the *SeaStar*.

Should he wait for this thing to blow over, or should he go ahead and risk moving the shipment with the FBI and DEA watching his every step?

He massaged his temples and thought about it. He'd wait for his contact at the Royal Bahamas Police Force to call him back before he proceeded. He needed to find out what the FBI knew about the missing girl before he made his final decision.

CHAPTER 11

After the interview with Amber's parents and her friends, Drake and Phipps split up and tackled the interviews with crew members. Right away, Drake realized that most of the crew wouldn't be very helpful. Either they were too scared of losing their jobs to say anything or they truly hadn't seen anything that would be helpful to the case.

The last person Rachel and Drake interviewed was a cabin steward assigned to the penthouse floor. She served only the four luxury suites and assisted the assigned butler if needed. She was believed to have been the last person who saw Josh and Amber. Consuela Rodriguez was a petite woman with dark hair and eyes. She wore the same uniform with the *SeaStar* logo that Josh was wearing on the videotapes.

Rachel and Drake had decided that she would interview Consuela. Drake noticed that women responded better to Rachel than to him or any other law enforcement person.

"Hi, Consuela, I'm Rachel. We're here to help find the missing girl, Amber Knowles. She was staying in cabin one-o-one C." Rachel handed the steward a photo. "Here's her picture. Can you tell me about the last time you saw her?"

"Last night," Consuela said in a thick accent. "I was delivering room service to another cabin and saw her walking with Josh."

"What time was this?" Rachel looked at Drake. He nodded his head for her to continue.

Consuela answered, "Late." She paused, licking her lips. "Definitely after midnight." Her answer matched the time stamp on the videotape.

"Did you see Josh walk inside the cabin with Amber?" Rachel asked.

"Yes." Consuela answered. She picked at an invisible piece of lint on her uniform.

"Do you remember what she was wearing?"

Consuela shifted in her seat. "A dress. Pink, I think. It was short and shiny."

This was the dress that Rachel had seen discarded on Amber's bed. So she had definitely changed when she got back.

"Did Amber or Josh say anything to you?"

"Josh said hello. That's all."

"How did she seem to you?" Rachel asked.

Consuela seemed to be confused by the question. "What do you mean?"

"Did she act upset or mad?"

"No. But I think she was sick. Josh was holding on to her." Consuela pursed her lips.

Rachel thought Consuela might be worried that she was telling them too much.

"Anything that you can remember would be helpful, Consuela. We need to find her," Rachel coaxed quietly.

"I just saw Josh helping her walk. The girl looked a little pale. That's all I remember," Consuela replied.

Rachel looked over at Drake for help.

He asked Consuela, "Have you seen Josh since?"

"No," she replied.

"Thank you, Consuela. If you remember anything else, please call me," Drake said, handing her his card.

Consuela took the card and put it in the front pocket of her uniform. She looked at Rachel for a minute.

"Is there anything else you want to add?" Rachel asked her.

She shook her head no and walked out of the room.

Rachel and Drake sat in silence for a few seconds.

"She knows something, doesn't she?" Rachel picked up the picture of Amber.

"I think she knows more than what she told us," Drake agreed.

"So now what?"

"We wait. Let's hope her conscience kicks in and she calls me."

✦ ✦ ✦

Consuela left the conference room with a sigh of relief. She headed down the elevator to the crew's quarters to shower and take a quick nap before her next shift started.

She had learned one important thing early on in her career aboard the *SeaStar*: Keep your head down and mind your own business. No curiosity—that was a requirement of keeping a job here. And she wanted the job, even though she worked sixteen-hour shifts with no overtime pay and few benefits. She sent almost all of her paycheck home to support her family in Mexico. Otherwise, they wouldn't have enough to eat.

It was funny. That was one perk for people who took cruises—food was available twenty-four hours a day. Passengers could go to the all-night, all-you-can-eat buffets or order room service. Whatever your tastes desired, the ship had it. Especially if you were one of the penthouse guests.

But something peculiar had happened last night at the end of her shift. She'd gotten a room service call to the Jacobsens' cabin—cabin 101A—the one next to the missing girl's. She'd dropped off a New York strip steak with new potatoes, broiled lobster tails, and two ice cream sundaes. Mrs. Jacobsen signed for the order and thanked Consuela. Mrs. Jacobsen seemed all right, even though she looked to Consuela to be no more than twenty years old.

But Consuela's friend Gladys, who was responsible for cleaning the Jacobsens' suite and taking care of whatever they wanted, said that Mr. Jacobsen spent all yesterday in his suite talking with some of the ship's employees. Consuela thought that might be all right, because the whole staff had been told that Mr. Jacobsen was a friend of Mr. Morrotti, who owned the cruise line. At first she'd thought Mr. Jacobsen was evaluating the employees, or something. But Gladys said that every time she came into the room to clean, Mr. Jacobsen and his guests would get quiet. Gladys heard something about shipments, and Mr. Jacobsen mentioned Josh's name a lot. Consuela didn't want to know any secrets, and she told Gladys many times to be careful about what she said to other crew members. Gladys liked to gossip, and one day it would get her into trouble.

Consuela didn't know Josh that well, and their paths didn't cross that often. But what she did know—she liked him okay. He made a point to know her name and say hello every time he saw her.

That's why the last time she saw him something didn't seem right. She'd just dropped off the Jacobsens' room service order and was heading back to the kitchen when she realized she'd forgotten to get the room service check from Ms. Jacobsen. She went back, and this time Mr. Jacobsen opened the door. When she told him what she forgot, he said, "No problem," and handed her the leather check cover. He yelled to his wife that he was heading out for a minute and walked out behind her.

It was then that she saw Josh and Amber walking down the hallway toward Amber's room. Josh had his arm around Amber's waist—not in a romantic way, but like he was helping her to walk. Consuela thought the girl was sick or maybe had had too much to drink.

Josh said hello to her as they passed, like he always did. But what struck her as weird was that he didn't say hi to Mr. Jacobsen, and Mr. Jacobsen didn't say hello, either. If Mr. Jacobsen talked about Josh so much, wouldn't he know him?

Consuela looked back at them—she couldn't help herself. She saw Josh enter the suite behind Amber.

Mr. Jacobsen was watching them, too.

CHAPTER 12

The smell wakes her up. A smell of bitter coffee and cleaning solution. Something strong, like ammonia or bleach. She opens her eyes and takes a slow look around. She's in a small room with a single dresser and a nightstand beside her bed. The blinds are closed, but a bit of sunlight peeks through. *Is it day or evening?* She isn't sure. She feels pressure on her arm and looks down to see an IV line plugged directly into her vein.

She tries to remember where she is or how she got here. Did she have an accident, and is she in the hospital? *If so, then where is everyone?* Thinking about it makes her head hurt.

She tries to sit up, but her head is too heavy to lift off the pillow. She looks around for a button to push but can't find one.

"Hey. Someone help me." She tries to speak, but it comes out as a whisper. Her mouth is so dry. She needs some water. *Where am I?* She tries desperately to remember what happened. If only her head didn't hurt so badly.

Then she starts to remember.

The cruise ship. She was on a trip with her friends. Key West. Shopping. Drinking margaritas. Getting back on the boat. Going to dinner and then dancing at the nightclub. *Maybe I have alcohol poisoning or passed out and hurt myself. God, my parents will be so pissed.*

If only she could get something cold to drink and something for her head. It hurts so much to think.

Her mind flutters with more images.

Josh. The cute guy that worked at the club. He walked her back to her room. She hadn't felt well. What else? She has a feeling something is eluding her.

She tries again to call for help, but her throat is so hoarse. Looking under the sheets, she sees that someone has put a long white T-shirt on her.

The door creaks open. She slowly turns her head toward the door.

"Ah, I see you're awake. How are you feeling?" A woman with a thick accent walks with purpose into the room. She wears dark-green medical scrubs and carries a clipboard in her hand.

"I need some water. Where am I?" Her voice just above a whisper.

"You're in a clinic. We found you unconscious on the beach. I'll be right back with some water," the woman says.

"Wait. Can I call my parents?"

"They've already been contacted, honey. Just rest now and I'll be right back." The woman leaves the room as quickly as she came in.

Something doesn't feel right about this. But she is too tired to think about it more.

The nurse returns and gives her a sip of water before pulling a syringe out of her pocket.

"What's that for?"

"It's okay. Just something to help you relax a little." The nurse puts the medicine in the IV.

Just as she mumbles a protest, her eyes get heavy and she slips into a deep sleep.

CHAPTER 13

"We ran Josh McCain's name through our database, and he's red-flagged," Drake said.

Rachel and Drake had finished interviewing Governor Knowles, his wife, and some of the ship's crew and then returned to the hotel to examine their notes. Cyndy had arranged for the hotel to provide a conference room for their use while staying there. She stayed behind on the ship with Phipps to review the rest of the security tapes.

"What does that mean?" Rachel asked as she took another sip of coffee.

"There are several reasons why someone's name would be flagged in the system," Drake explained. "Witness protection. Protected informant. The higher-ups at the FBI are trying to find out why McCain is flagged."

"So Josh is hiding from someone?" Rachel said.

"More like Josh is not who we think he is. My guess is that Amber got caught up in something that he was involved in."

Rachel twirled her long auburn hair around her fingers and thought about this for a minute.

"So let's think about the possibilities. Amber meets Josh at the nightclub. Her friends said she was fine after dinner. She didn't get sick until they got to the club. Maybe Josh slipped her something? Like a…What do they call it? Date rape drug?"

"A roofie?"

"Yeah. Maybe he drugged her?"

"So she started feeling ill, and he offers to walk her back. Then he rapes her and throws her body overboard?" Drake continued for her. "No, I don't think so. She had roommates. He couldn't know when they'd come looking for her. And Josh's coworker Andy said there was never a problem with Josh. His supervisor said the same thing. He has an exemplary employment record on file."

Rachel contemplated that for a minute. "Or maybe she had too much to drink. Her parents said she was taking medicine for headaches. Alcohol and medicine don't mix well. She got sick and Josh was being a nice guy and offered to walk her back."

"She could have had a seizure or something and had an accident. Josh got scared and tried to cover it up," Drake added. "But where is Josh?" His cell phone buzzed. He answered and listened intently.

"We have another piece of the puzzle," he said, hanging up. "That was Phipps. The body recovered from the Coast Guard was not Josh McCain. Our dead guy is Danny Pezzini, according to his driver's license that was found in his wallet."

"Who is Danny Pezzini?" Rachel asked.

"Small-time criminal. Two convictions of drug possession with intent to distribute."

"How did he end up in the water?" Rachel asked.

"Don't know. Looks like he was a passenger on the *SeaStar*," Drake answered. "Phipps has a copy of the passenger manifest with Pezzini's name on it."

"That's odd. No one reported him missing?"
"No. He was apparently traveling alone."
"Think he's connected to Amber and Josh?"
"Maybe so. I don't believe in coincidences."

There was a knock on the door and one of the governor's aides poked her head in.

"Governor Knowles is on his way here. He's ready to release a statement to the media."

CHAPTER 14

The front of the hotel was packed with reporters when they stepped outside. Word had gotten out about the prominent governor's daughter who had vanished from a cruise ship. Reporters threw out questions as they gathered before the podium microphones.

"Do you believe that Amber fell overboard?"

"Is the Coast Guard continuing their search for Amber?"

"Have you found any evidence of foul play?"

A pretty brunette reporter with CNN shouted loudest of all. "Is it true the Coast Guard found a body? Was it Amber?"

The media crew quieted down when Drake raised his hand up. "The governor will make a short statement and then we'll answer a few questions."

Governor John Knowles stepped forward and cleared his throat. He had changed into more casual attire with pressed khakis and a light-blue oxford shirt. Sarah was by his side and had changed into another sundress—this one of sunny yellow-and-white-striped seersucker fabric. She wore her blonde hair loose around her face. She stood ramrod straight and faced the camera with a somber look on her face.

"We have reason to believe that our daughter, Amber Knowles, met with foul play sometime after midnight on the *SeaStar* cruise ship." Governor Knowles spoke loudly and clearly. "The FBI, local law enforcement, and Florida Omni Search are working together to locate her. They are expending every effort and using every resource to bring her safely home. We also want to thank all the volunteers who have stepped up to help."

He paused for a second to gather his thoughts. "If anyone knows anything at all about Amber's disappearance, please call the anonymous tip hotline. Amber's mother and I are offering a reward of one million dollars for her safe return."

Governor Knowles turned to look at his wife before continuing. "We beg you, if you know anything, no matter how trivial it may seem, please call. It could be that one small thing that brings Amber back to us. Thank you." He stepped back and turned the podium over to the FBI.

The reporters went nuts, yelling out more questions as Drake stepped up. "Thank you, Governor Knowles and Mrs. Knowles." He looked out at the crowd of media. "The governor is not taking questions. We ask that you please respect his family's privacy during this difficult time. I can give you ten minutes."

The pretty brunette raised her hand and asked the same question again: "Was a body found?"

"The Coast Guard found a male body about a mile offshore of Freeport. We have identified the victim. He's an American citizen. We are not releasing his name pending notification of his next of kin. At this time we don't know if he had anything to do with Amber's disappearance."

"The governor mentioned foul play. Do you have any suspects?"

"We're still following leads. And that's all I can tell you. Once we have other news, we'll let you know. Thanks for your cooperation."

Drake stepped off the podium and headed inside, leaving the reporters shouting questions to his back.

Governor Knowles and his wife were waiting inside the conference room. He paced the floor while Sarah sat quietly at the table nursing a cup of coffee.

"So, what's next?" he asked, resting his hand on Sarah's shoulder.

"Governor, we'll keep following all our leads to find Amber, but the cruise ship departs tomorrow. Unfortunately, we can't hold them up any longer without evidence that a crime was committed," Drake answered.

"How can you say no crime has been committed? Amber isn't on that ship. Of *course* a crime was committed. She didn't fall overboard like the captain is suggesting. I just know it." Sarah gripped the table, her knuckles turning white.

"Not to mention the fact the Coast Guard recovered a body. This just doesn't add up." Governor Knowles scrubbed his face with his hands.

Rachel had seen that hopeless look before on parents' faces when they were told their child hadn't been found. She felt their pain. And she knew Drake was in a difficult position. They were all doing everything in their power to find Amber.

"We'll continue to put up flyers around town and keep Amber's face in front of the media. We'll keep the private boats searching," Rachel replied. "I have a forensics team that will be here later tonight with specialized equipment to facilitate a land search tomorrow. We'll search along the coastline close to the cruise ship docks."

Governor Knowles let out a long sigh. "Is there anything that we can do to hold the ship?" He directed his question at Drake.

"I'm afraid not. They have every right to leave. And your wife is right, Governor. Amber isn't there. Somehow she got off the ship. We need to concentrate our efforts on searching the water and the island. We're monitoring all private air and water traffic. And we have more people to interview," Drake said.

Governor Knowles helped Sarah up. "Please keep me updated. We're going back to the villa if you need us."

"Thank you both," Sarah said, with tears in her eyes.

Rachel waited until the door was closed. "That went well."

"I wish we had more to go on," Drake said. "I'm heading back to the *SeaStar* to see what Phipps and Cyndy have on those security tapes."

"Sounds good. Let me know what you find out. I'm going to check in with my office to make sure that everything is in place for the search tomorrow," Rachel said to Drake as he headed out the door. "I'll meet you back in the conference room later?"

"Sure. I'll call you if anything comes up before then."

Rachel realized she was famished, so she stopped by the front desk to ask for restaurant recommendations. The front desk clerk directed her to the hotel restaurant, The Blue Palm, and recommended she try the fish tacos.

As she headed toward the Blue Palm, she heard her name called.

"Hi. Ms. Scott?"

Rachel turned and saw a petite blonde approaching her. "Yes?"

"I'm Stacy Case. Investigative reporter with the *Miami Sun*." She reached out her hand to Rachel.

"Sorry, I can't comment on the governor's press conference," Rachel said as she shook her hand. "You'll have to contact his office for an interview."

"No, that's not why I'm here. I have some important information about the case," Stacy said.

Rachel studied the girl standing in front of her. She was young, in her late twenties. Short honey-blonde hair, with a smattering of freckles across her nose and cheeks. She wore a pretty blue skirt and matching blouse, but somehow looked like she would be more comfortable in a pair of jeans and sweatshirt. Rachel thought she recognized her from the press conference earlier.

"And what would that be?" Rachel asked cautiously. Reporters had burned her before when her daughter had disappeared, promising information to lure her into an interview.

Stacy looked her straight in the eye. "I think I know what happened to Amber."

CHAPTER 15

"I was just heading to the restaurant to get a quick bite to eat." Rachel motioned to the hotel's restaurant. "Come join me."

The hostess stand was empty and a sign read, *Seat yourself.*

Stacy followed her to a table in the corner. Only a couple of tables were occupied in the late evening lull.

"I hear the fish tacos are good," Rachel said, picking up a menu from the table. "Hotel clerk recommended them."

"Sounds fine." Stacy didn't bother picking up her menu. "Thanks for taking the time to talk to me."

A waiter came by and Rachel ordered the fish taco special and iced tea for both of them.

As soon as the waiter left, Stacy took a large folder out of her briefcase. Rachel watched as she dumped the bulging file onto the table.

"So you said you could help with the case?" Rachel began. "What do you want in return?"

Stacy feigned surprise. "What do you mean?"

59

"I've been doing this for a while. I know how it works." Rachel tapped the file with her finger. "You'll give me information if I give you an interview. Right?"

Stacy smiled at Rachel. "I know about your company, Florida Omni Search. I researched it when I found out that you were helping with this case." Stacy paused as she collected her thoughts. "I'm sorry about your daughter. I know that you went through a hard time with her disappearance."

"I'm still going through a hard time. It takes everything I have just to get out of bed in the morning. Looking for other missing people—like Amber—gives me hope. Hope that Mallory is still out there waiting to be found."

"Sorry. I didn't mean to offend you. I just wanted you to know that I did my homework. I take my work seriously. I'm not just some reporter out to land a big story."

"Again, I can't comment on an ongoing investigation. You said you may know what happened to Amber." Rachel waited until the waiter set down their drinks. When he left, she motioned for Stacy to continue. "Go ahead."

"I know a lot about the cruise industry. I've been researching it for some time now as part of my crime beat, and I think this information will help with your search." She paused and took a sip of her tea. "But you're right. I would like to get an exclusive interview with you and the governor."

"I can't speak for the governor, but I'll be happy to give you an interview once this is over." Rachel took a sip of her tea.

Stacy smiled, but she put her hand on the folder. "Not good enough," she said. "It has to be exclusive. And it has to be first. If it's just you and not the governor…Let's say I get two days' lead time with my story before you talk to any other outlets."

Rachel mulled this over. The reporter must think she really had something. And maybe she did. At this point, the investigators couldn't afford to turn down any kind of lead. And she didn't really mind giving this ambitious young woman an exclusive. Stacy reminded Rachel of herself.

"Fine," she said. "Exclusive. Two days."

Stacy slapped her hand on the large manila file folder and pushed it over to Rachel's side of the table. "This is everything I've got on the cruise industry. I've been writing a series about crimes and mysteries on board ships, and I've developed sources—very good sources—up and down the food chain."

The waiter came back and set down a huge bowl of chips and guacamole. Rachel was starving and immediately dug in. She picked up a warm chip, scooped a generous chuck of fresh guacamole on it, and popped it into her mouth.

"What kind of crimes are we talking about?"

"Let me start at the beginning. About nine months ago I got a call at the *Sun* from a woman named Brenda Sayers, whose daughter Melodie had disappeared on a family vacation cruise aboard the—wait for it—*SeaStar*."

"I think I remember reading about that. What happened?"

"Mrs. Sayers had read an article that I'd written about crimes committed against American travelers overseas." She stopped and scooped up a chip. "The mother said Melodie had been hanging around and drinking with some of the ship's employees. After a family dinner on the last night of the voyage, Melodie left to meet up with some people, and that was the last her mom saw of her. When she woke up around five in the morning, she realized that Melodie had never come back to the cabin."

"What did they do?" Rachel asked. She helped herself to another chip.

"They alerted the crew, who conducted a search. The police and cruise ship officials reviewed the security tapes, and the last image of Melodie was of her walking down the promenade deck. Cruise officials insisted that she'd been drinking, and they had witnesses who confirmed it."

"Did they say that she accidentally fell overboard?"

"You guessed it. The Coast Guard searched, but her body was never found. Mrs. Sayers believes that the cruise line covered up something. She made noise, got a lawyer. The cruise line offered her a million-dollar settlement. I got to wondering about how many other young women might have disappeared on cruise ships, so I started looking into it. And I've uncovered some pretty dirty secrets about the cruise industry."

CHAPTER 16

Stephanie sat up on the couch and turned on the TV. The warm electronic glow illuminated the dark room. She rooted around on the coffee table for her pills. Her head felt heavy, her thoughts fuzzy, and her mouth dry. She was hung over. She shook a yellow pill from the prescription bottle and swallowed it dry. She picked up the remote just as a breaking news story came on. The headline at the top of screen said, *Florida Governor John Knowles Press Conference*. Stephanie turned up the sound. The news anchor reported that they were waiting on the governor and his wife to issue a statement about their missing daughter. Stephanie stayed rooted to the spot. Beads of sweat popped on her forehead. Her hands shook as she lit a cigarette.

A few seconds later, Governor John Knowles and his wife, Sarah, appeared on the screen. Stephanie's eyes stayed glued to the television as she watched the governor step up to the podium, while Sarah stood deferentially by his side. They pleaded for the safe return of Amber. Even though Sarah appeared composed, Stephanie could tell she was panicked inside. It was killing her to stand there, helpless and fearful, in front of the camera.

Serves her right, Stephanie thought as she picked up the phone. Her hands shook so badly that she needed three tries to dial the number she knew by heart.

Stephanie remembered when her little girl was born. She'd named her Hope. She was so tiny, just a preemie, with tufts of blonde hair and dark-blue eyes.

"Hey, it's me." Her voice was still thick from smoking and drinking all night. "I need to go to the Bahamas. Can you get me a plane ticket?"

She held the phone away from her ear as the voice on the other end yelled at her.

"Listen here. You've got to help me. I think my daughter is missing."

CHAPTER 17

The conference room table was littered with files, paper, empty coffee cups, and takeout food boxes. Rachel pulled up a trash can and raked off some soda cans and napkins into it.

"Have a seat." Rachel motioned to Stacy. "Agent Reynolds should be here soon."

She watched Stacy glance around the room. A whiteboard with colored lines drawn on it—the timeline for Amber's disappearance—stood next to another board with photos of Amber and a diagram of the *SeaStar* cruise ship layout.

"So this is the war room?" Stacy asked, taking in all the details. "Impressive."

Rachel nodded. "The police and FBI are still interviewing crew and passengers over at the ship."

The door swung open and Drake walked in. "I got here as fast as I could." He looked over at Stacy. "This is the reporter you called me about?"

Rachel could see the distrust on his face. She wasn't sure about bringing Stacy into the mix of things, either—but something just felt right about her. Rachel made the introductions.

"Rachel says that you have information on the case?" Drake got right down to business.

"I do."

"You understand that everything we talk about is off the record?" Drake instructed.

"Of course."

"Let's hear what you've got."

Stacy recounted the story she'd told Rachel at lunch.

"Who are your sources?" Drake asked as he leaned against the wall and crossed his arms.

"Ex-employees of the *SeaStar* and some former passengers. Obviously, I can't give you names, but I think you'll find that they're reliable."

"Stacy took a cruise on the *SeaStar* twice—the same itinerary as Melodie and Amber. Seven-day cruise through the Bahamas. Stop at Cabana Cay, the private resort owned by SeaScape," Rachel explained to Drake.

"When I looked into cruise ship disappearances, I found out that fourteen people have vanished from various cruise lines in the last two years. Of those fourteen, five went missing from SeaScape cruises. The *SeaStar* is owned by the SeaScape corporation. All five of the disappeared were young women. I went to my boss with the story and he suggested that I take a cruise and see what I could find out."

"When was this?" Drake asked.

"My first cruise was six months ago. While on the cruise, I befriended a couple of the employees. One was a bartender who had worked on the *SeaStar* for two years. I told him that I was a travel writer and working on an article about cruise ships. I didn't think people would be open with me if they knew I was investigating missing passengers," Stacy said.

"You're right. They wouldn't," Drake said.

"The bartender and I became friends, and we exchanged phone numbers. He's from the Miami area, too, and we have a lot in common. I didn't get much information from him at the time, but a few weeks ago, he called me. He told me that he'd quit the *SeaStar* and he had information that I might be interested in." Stacy paused and tucked a piece of her blonde hair behind her ear.

"What kind of information?" Drake asked.

Stacy opened her file and pulled out a sheaf of papers that were stapled together. "I hit the mother lode. He wants to remain off the record for obvious reasons, but he claims that the *SeaStar* was smuggling drugs. He thinks that the Cabana Cay resort is a meeting place for transporting the drugs. While all the passengers are off the ship enjoying the island, some of the employees are loading or unloading cocaine and marijuana." She tapped the stack of paper. "Here's a copy of the transcript of the interview I did with him."

They waited while Drake read the transcript. Then he looked at Rachel. "Cabana Cay. That's where the ship is headed next."

"That's not all. The island has an interesting story. Care to hear?" Stacy asked.

"Sure," Drake agreed.

"Cabana Cay is a tiny portion of land that is connected to a larger island called Asylum Harbor. Asylum Harbor is sixty nautical miles south of Freeport. It encompasses hundreds of acres. When the cruise line bought the island, they built the resort Cabana Cay on the southern side of the island. That's where the cruise ships dock and let the passengers play for the day."

"I suppose a naturally occurring deep water port would be valuable to them," Drake said. "Makes good business sense."

"I think so," Stacy went on. "Asylum Harbor is a nautical term meaning to provide safe shelter from a storm. Legend has it that in the mid–sixteen hundreds the pirate ship *Royal Fortune* encountered a storm while sailing to the Bahamas, which was an international hub for pirates at the time. The *Royal Fortune* hit a coral reef and was smashed to pieces. The ship's captain, Jack McCormac, and most of his crew made it ashore at Asylum Harbor."

"Where they lived happily ever after?" Rachel asked.

"Not even. After several days of waiting to be rescued, Kinder Bonham, one of the pirates who survived the wreck, went crazy. He killed Captain Jack and most of the crew members in their sleep. The *Royal Fortune* was said to have been carrying millions in gold and jewels from a heist in Jamaica. They say Kinder buried some of the treasure that had washed ashore before another ship picked him up. He died from gangrene before he could get back to claim the treasure."

"And supposedly modern-day ships are still dealing in contraband fortunes there," Rachel said. "How did SeaScape come to own Asylum Harbor?"

"An eccentric billionaire, Bert Lindem, sold it to the company for a dollar to spite his grandchildren. Rumor has it that, as part of the sale, Lindem wouldn't allow SeaScape to change the name of the island. Something about bad luck. Anyway, who wants to vacation at an island called Asylum Harbor?"

"Certainly not me," Rachel agreed.

"So to get around the deal with Lindem, SeaScape renamed just that southern extension of the island Cabana Cay. The company built the resort there and uses that part of the island as a destination for its cruise ships in the Bahamas. They offer a day of water sports, diving, and snorkeling tours for the passengers. Disney Cruise Lines and other ships also have their own private islands for cruise destinations," Stacy explained.

"You visited Cabana Cay on your cruise?" Drake asked.

Stacy nodded.

"What did you find out?" Drake asked.

"When SeaScape bought the island, Asylum Harbor already had three small bungalows and a main residence. The cruise line spent over twenty million dollars in renovations, mostly on the other side, the Cabana Cay side. It now has a restaurant, bar, dive shop, gift shop, first-aid station, and private cabanas. The small bungalows are residences for the SeaScape employees who run the island. The Asylum Harbor area is off limits to the passengers and even most of the staff, and not many people have seen that part of the island. At least that's what my bartender said."

"Did you see the anything suspicious while you were there?" Drake asked.

Stacy shook her head. "I didn't, but my source told me that, one time, his boss asked him to help out when they were short-staffed. While he was unloading liquor and other supplies, he overheard a conversation that freaked him out."

"What was that?"

"One of the guys who lived on the island said that they were waiting for a shipment of cocaine to come in. This guy implied that the *SeaStar* was using the island as a cover to transport drugs into the States."

CHAPTER 18

"So what do you think about Stacy's story?" Rachel asked Drake. The reporter had gone back to her hotel to work on her story of Amber's disappearance.

"She gave us more information in two hours than we've gotten since we've been here," Drake said.

"That story about the drug smuggling is huge, but we still don't know what happened to Amber. Do you think the *SeaStar* could be engaging in human trafficking as well as drug trading?" Rachel asked.

"At this point, I think anything is possible. The next thing you know, somebody will call and tell me the sky is falling."

As if on cue, Drake's cell phone rang. He listened for a minute and then clicked off.

"We got a report back on Josh McCain." Drake leaned back into his chair.

Rachel waited expectantly.

"Josh McCain is a fictitious name. His real name is Shawn Gibson, and he's a DEA agent. He was working undercover aboard the *SeaStar*," Drake said.

"Wow. I guess that's why he was red-flagged in your system."

"Yep. According to the DEA, Shawn, aka Josh, had been with the *SeaStar* for about six months and was working on busting a drug ring."

"Stacy's informant was right, then. *SeaStar* is working the drug trade." Rachel chewed her thumbnail while thinking that over. "Does the DEA know where Josh…er…Shawn is now?"

"No. Mike Mancini is Shawn's commanding officer. I've known Mike for several years—we worked on a big case when I first started out with the FBI," Drake said. "We busted a biker gang in South Florida that was dealing meth and coke as well as running a prostitution ring. Mike had been undercover with the gang for two years. He's cool, but he'll want to protect his case and his agent. He's heading down to the Bahamas now and should be here by tomorrow morning."

"We find Shawn, we find Amber, is that what you're thinking?"

Drake paced the room. "Quite possibly. He had evidence that the *SeaStar* was being used for drug smuggling. Mostly cocaine and marijuana. This DEA undercover operation has been in the works for over two years and involves multiple cruise ships. Now that we know, we'll have to tread lightly so we don't botch up their investigation."

"Amber was with Shawn when she disappeared. So maybe she did see something she wasn't supposed to," Rachel said. "Wait a minute. The ring!"

Drake stopped pacing and turned to look at her. "What?"

"The ring we found. The initials were SMG. That could have been Shawn Gibson's ring."

Drake was already picking up the phone. "I'm calling the lab to see if they got anywhere with that symbol. We'll ask Mike Mancini, too. Let's see what information he can give us about Josh…er… Shawn."

CHAPTER 19

The diner had a 1950s decor, with red vinyl booths, Formica tabletops, and black-and-white checkered floors. The requisite jukebox sat in the corner, from which Elvis crooned something about blue suede shoes. This was something that you'd see in the States, thought Rachel, not the Bahamas.

Rachel and Drake ordered coffee while they waited for Mike Mancini to show up.

"You sure you don't want to try the island burger or a slice of coconut pie?" the waitress offered.

"You twisted my arm. I'll try the pie," Drake answered.

"Same here," Rachel agreed. "Sounds delicious."

They were working on their third cup of coffee, the coconut pie long gone, before Mike strolled in.

Rachel watched as Mike took off his leather jacket before sliding into the booth next to her. His muscles bulged under his white T-shirt and his arms were heavily tattooed. A scar ran across the left side of his eyebrow. He didn't look like a drug enforcement agent, she thought. More like the biker persona he used to be when he worked undercover. Mike exuded a toughness that Rachel found sexy.

Drake introduced the two.

"I used to work undercover," Mike said, as though he were reading Rachel's mind. "Biker gangs and drugs. It's nice to be on the other side now."

For once, Rachel found herself speechless. She didn't believe in love at first sight, more like instant attraction. And there was something about Mike she found very appealing.

"Heard you're interested in Shawn?" Mike asked.

"We think Shawn is one of the last people to have seen Amber. We have him on surveillance tape walking with her outside the ship's nightclub. Later, a cabin steward saw them walking down the corridor toward her room. We obviously need to locate him," Drake said.

Mike turned his coffee cup over and leaned back in the booth. "I'd like to talk to him, too. He hasn't been in touch with us in over two weeks."

"Can you tell us what he was involved in?" Drake asked.

Mike waited until the waitress had refilled their coffee cups before he spoke.

"We'd been trying to infiltrate cruise ships for some time—specifically the SeaScape Cruise Line. We think that the *SeaStar* is running cocaine and marijuana between ports. We got Shawn in place about six months ago. The last time we spoke, he confirmed that a big shipment was going down this week and that he had information about other things going on." Mike blew into his cup before taking a sip of coffee.

"Like what?" Drake asked.

"Shawn said he had information about passenger disappearances. Specifically, Mary Ellen Caughlin."

"I remember hearing about that," Rachel said, her eyes still on Mike. "A newlywed on her honeymoon cruise fell overboard. They found blood on the balcony and her husband passed out in one of the hallways. The cruise line said she was drunk and fell overboard."

"Yes, that was on the *SeaMist*. Also owned by the SeaScape conglomerate. Then another girl in her early twenties was on a family vacation and she was reported missing. Her family claimed she was depressed and possibly committed suicide," Mike said.

Drake and Rachel exchanged looks. This was fitting in with what Stacy had told them about suspicious disappearances.

"Was the cruise line somehow involved in those disappearances?" Drake asked.

"That's what Shawn thinks," Mike said. He drained the last of his coffee and pushed the cup away. "He also said one of the bartenders was dealing drugs to other crew members and passengers. We were supposed to meet up after the ship got back to Miami."

"How do you think that fits into Amber's disappearance? Not to mention what happened to Shawn?" Rachel asked.

"I wish to hell I knew the answer to that. Shawn must have run into some kind of trouble. He would have found a way to check in with us by now," Mike replied. "He's one of our best agents. He wouldn't have put Amber or any other passenger in harm's way if he could help it."

Drake looked down at his ringing phone. "Excuse me," he said as he got up from the table, "I need to take this."

Rachel pushed her hair back out of her face. "It's been a long day."

"Yes, it has." Mike turned to look at her. They were sitting so close she could smell the fresh, clean scent of his cologne. She wished she had dressed a little nicer than the faded jeans, flip-flops, and white linen shirt she had on. "I've heard a lot about you and the wonderful things you are doing with Florida Omni Search."

Rachel laughed nervously. "All good things, I hope." She hated feeling like she had a schoolgirl crush.

"Drake speaks very highly of you. He told me last night when we spoke about the work you did on the missing Alabama businessman. And of course I heard all about the Boy Scout you rescued from the Everglades." Mike smiled at her. "I saw you on *The Today Show*."

"What can I say? I found my passion. After years of selling cars and houses, I was burnt out."

Mike nodded his head. "I'm sorry about your daughter. I know that must be hard."

Rachel nodded. "After Mallory went missing, I couldn't work, didn't want to go out, and didn't want to live anymore. I spent all my nights cruising the streets, thinking I could find her. Spent my days in bed trying to sleep away the pain. It's better now, but you never forget. Do you have kids?"

"Yep. A ten-year-old daughter named Addison. I'd go crazy if I lost her."

"That's why I founded Florida Omni Search. I'd been so miserable. Then one day I was watching the news and saw that another boy in Miami had disappeared. Then a week later, a toddler from Orlando disappears. It was like one after another. All these kids were just disappearing without a trace. No one knowing what happened. Something in me just snapped. Here I was with all this money socked away in the bank and I knew that I had to find some way to help. I reached out to Janine, the missing boy's mom from Miami, and we joined forces to find these missing kids."

"You're doing a great thing," Mike said, reaching out and patting her shoulder. When he touched her, it felt like a current of electricity passed through her body.

Drake walked back into the diner and threw a twenty-dollar bill on the table.

"We gotta roll. A lifeboat was found in Freeport. The police traced the registration number back to SeaScape Enterprises," Drake said.

Mike got up from the table. "Mind if I tag along?"

CHAPTER 20

"Some boys playing on the beach this morning found the boat and dragged it up to their house," the policeman said as he pointed toward a bungalow. The faded-pink cottage looked in desperate need of repair. The shutters were barely hanging on and the paint was peeling in several places.

Mike had followed Rachel and Drake to the area of the beach that the police had cordoned off with crime scene tape. A small crowd had gathered around the yard just outside the tape's perimeter.

"The boy's mother found them playing in the boat and asked them where it had come from. They told her that it had washed ashore sometime last night. She had seen the news conference about Amber Knowles and called the police, thinking it might have something to do with her disappearance," the policeman explained to them.

They walked down to the lifeboat. The black dinghy had *SeaStar* written in white script with the number *21* and a smaller set of identifying numbers painted on the stern.

"Why didn't the crew tell us a lifeboat was missing when we interviewed them?" Rachel asked.

"Good question. They may not have known that it was missing right away," Drake said.

"More important, how did it get off the ship without anyone noticing?" Mike asked.

Rachel thought about that for a few seconds. "*SeaStar* docked at Freeport in the early hours—before sunrise. It's possible that whoever took it could have hidden somewhere on the ship, then used the lifeboat to get ashore."

"Pretty hard to do and not have someone see you." Mike walked around the boat.

"Aren't most lifeboats equipped with some sort of emergency box? Like flares, water, first-aid kit?" Rachel asked.

"The ones on the cruise ship all have that. Plus ownership paperwork," Drake answered.

Rachel peered into the boat. "Apparently this one doesn't."

"Anyone else have access to this boat?" Drake asked the policeman.

"Just the little boys, I think. We called you guys as soon as we found it." He shrugged his shoulders.

"Maybe Shawn and Amber used this lifeboat to escape?" she asked.

Mike kicked the sand around with his shoe. "Shawn's a smart guy. If he thought Amber was in danger, he would have done any and everything he could to protect her. Especially if he knew her father was the governor of Florida."

"If she and Shawn got off the boat and made it to the island, where are they now?" Drake wondered aloud.

CHAPTER 21

Drake had driven Rachel back to the hotel so they could change and gather the search team together. Janine had arranged for a rental car company to deliver a SUV to her hotel so she would have transportation around the island. She didn't want to rely on Drake to drive her everywhere.

Within a couple of hours, they were back at the site where the lifeboat was discovered. The east side of Freeport, where they'd found the *SeaStar*'s lifeboat, was a sleepy fishing village that was home to people who mostly made their money from selling their daily catch to restaurants. It consisted of tiny shotgun cottages with small sandy yards and rundown vehicles in the driveways.

Pulling a tube of sun cream out of her tote, Rachel slathered it on her arms and legs. She pulled her long auburn hair in a ponytail and put a Florida Omni Search cap on her head. This was what she lived for. It was what she did best. Finding missing loved ones.

Drake walked up to her. "Ready to go?"

"Yes." Rachel walked up to the front of her group that had gathered for the search.

"We are going to work in the usual teams." Rachel passed out the copies of the map to everyone.

Rankin Smartz led the search and rescue with his dog, Max, an adorable black Lab that Rankin had rescued when he was a pup. Phil, one of her tech guys, was in charge of all the specialized equipment. Scott, Georgia, and Steven were regular volunteers who donated their time and equipment when needed.

"Rankin and Max will start the search. Max can get Amber's scent from the dress she wore the night she disappeared. Phil will work closely behind with the equipment. Georgia and Steven will help canvass the area with flyers. The rest of us will follow the search grid. Remember to call in if you find anything." Rachel held up her walkie-talkie. "Let's get started."

Rankin gave Max a sniff of Amber's dress, and the dog took off toward the street. "I think we got a hit," Rankin said to Rachel as they quickly followed behind Max. Empty trash cans littered the street, and the smells confused the dog. He would take a few steps, sniff the ground, and then start moving again. Start, stop, and sniff.

"Good dog," Rankin kept reassuring Max as they went down a couple of blocks.

Max hesitated at the end of the street. Rankin bent down and gave him another sniff of the dress. "Come on, boy. Let's find Amber." Max started off again but stopped after a few feet and sat down.

Rankin rubbed Max's head and gave him more words of encouragement, but the dog just whined softly.

"Nothing now," Rankin said.

"Guess they found a vehicle or someone picked them up," Drake said.

Rachel sighed. "Dead end." They headed back to the pink cottage where the boat had been found.

"What now?" Mike asked.

"The police are canvassing the neighborhood. Maybe we'll get lucky," Drake said.

"I'm going to check in with the guys to see if the sonar equipment picked up something," Rachel said as she started packing up her gear. She turned to see a girl of sixteen or seventeen watching her. She was dressed in long cargo pants and a white tank top, and she carried a black backpack.

"Can I talk to you for a minute?" the girl asked in a Bahamian accent.

"Sure." Rachel smiled at her.

"I think I have some information about the girl you are looking for." She looked around nervously.

CHAPTER 22

Rachel took off her ball cap and wiped the sweat off her forehead with her arm. "Okay. Why don't we go sit down over there and you can tell me about it." Rachel pointed to a large palm tree that provided some shade from the heat—and some privacy from the other members of the team. Rachel thought the frightened girl might bolt if anyone else came over. Mike and Drake could be very intimidating.

The team had brought a large cooler filled with drinks, and Rachel grabbed some Gatorade for herself and the girl.

"I'm Rachel. What's your name?"

"Shondra Myers. I live down the street." She pointed toward the east end of the street—the spot where the dog lost the scent.

"Nice to meet you, Shondra. You said you know something about the missing girl?"

The girl nodded. She dropped her backpack on the ground beside her. Her eyes darted back and forth between Rachel and Drake.

"You can't tell my parents or anyone else, because I'll get into trouble."

Rachel wanted to reassure the girl, but she didn't want to make promises she couldn't keep. "Shondra, I'll do my best to keep this private, but you may have to make a statement to the authorities. Why don't you tell me what you know and we'll go from there. Okay?"

Shondra contemplated Rachel's words for a moment before beginning. "I'm supposed to be grounded, but the other night I snuck out to meet some friends. While I was walking down this way, I heard an argument." Shondra hesitated. She twirled her hair around her fingers. Her gaze shifted away.

Rachel followed her glance and saw Drake staring their way. She waved him off.

"It's okay. Go on," Rachel prompted her.

"I heard a girl yelling about something, so I hid around the corner to take a look. I saw a girl with blonde hair walking with some guy. I'm pretty sure the girl was the same one that's on the flyers you guys are handing out. The one you're looking for." Shondra reached down and pulled out a flyer from her backpack. "This is her."

"What did the guy look like?"

"It was dark and I couldn't see that great, but he sounded kinda young. He had a white shirt on. It looked like a uniform shirt like my daddy wears. He's a security guard at the Riveria Hotel."

"But you're sure it was Amber? How do you know, if it was dark?"

"Because she walked right under the streetlight and was closer to me. She had long blonde hair like the girl in the picture."

"Which way did they come from?"

"From the back of that house." She pointed behind her toward the pink house where the lifeboat had been found.

"Did you see anybody else with them?" Rachel asked.

"Not at first. They were walking and he was saying to hurry up. She was limping and telling him to slow down, that she hurt her foot."

"What happened next?"

"I heard the guy say something about finding a car and calling somebody. That's when the other guy showed up."

"What other guy?" Rachel asked.

"I didn't see where he came from. It's like he appeared out of nowhere. Everything happened so fast. At first I thought they were all together. Then he pulled out a gun. A dark SUV pulled up and he made them get in."

"Did you get a license number or the make and model of the SUV?" Rachel asked.

"Sorry. I got scared and didn't get a good look. It was maybe an Escalade or something big like that."

"What did the second guy look like?"

"He was big. He had a funny accent, but I couldn't tell what he looked like."

"If I showed you some pictures, do you think you could identify the man Amber was with?"

"Maybe."

"Would you mind telling that guy over there the story you just told me? He's helping me try to find Amber."

The girl hesitated. "Could we do this later? I'm late for work, and I'm already in trouble."

"Sure. Why don't we come see you after work? My friend Drake and I can meet you somewhere. Somewhere private and quiet."

"I guess that would be okay. I work at the Riveria Hotel. Cleaning rooms. My shift is over at four p.m. There's a small café called Julia's next to the hotel. We can meet there."

"Sounds good. Thank you, Shondra." Rachel watched the young girl walk away. What luck! A witness that saw Amber and Josh/Shawn the night they disappeared.

Rachel motioned Drake over after Shondra was out of sight. "We have a witness."

"That girl I saw you talking to?"

"Yeah. She said she saw Amber and two guys get into a dark SUV the night she disappeared."

"Why didn't you call me over?" He sounded pissed off.

"She had to go to work. Plus, she was nervous. She was worried we would tell her parents. I arranged for us to meet after her shift at a local diner."

"What time?"

"Four o'clock at Julia's Café. It's next to the Riveria Hotel, where she works. We need some photos of Shawn to see if she can identify him. Think Mike can get those for us?"

Drake had seemed to calm down some.

"I'll go talk to him now. I'll meet you back at the hotel around three and we can drive there together." He grabbed some water from the cooler. "Next time, you come get me when we have a potential witness."

CHAPTER 23

Julia's Café was a small, cheerful restaurant that served local fare. Colorful paintings by local artists adorned walls painted a rich yellow, and chili pepper lights hung from the ceiling. There were ten small tables and a meticulously clean lunch counter. The air held a delicious aroma of spiced chicken, crispy fried onion rings, and fresh Cuban bread.

Rachel and Drake got to the restaurant a little early to get a bite to eat and catch up. Rachel was famished after working most of the day without a break. After looking over the menu, they decided to order conch fritters for an appetizer, fire-roasted shrimp with Cuban bread for Rachel, and Drake got the pecan-crusted grouper over spiced rice. Mike had left the search site to check in with his office.

Rachel was disappointed that they hadn't turned up anything, but she hoped the lead Shondra had given them would amount to something. Rachel told Drake a little about what she knew of their witness. "Shondra's dad is a nighttime security guard and she cleans rooms during the day at the hotel next door."

"With her information and finding the lifeboat, it's looking like the captain was wrong with his theory that Amber fell overboard. At least—as of last night—we know that she was still alive. Assuming your witness really saw her," Drake said as they started on their dinner.

Rachel sopped up the sauce in her bowl with a piece of bread. She didn't want to waste a single drop of it. "She was very reluctant to give me much information about herself. Said she was grounded the night it happened and wasn't supposed to be outside."

"How do we know that Shondra is telling the truth and not trying to get attention like some teenage girls tend to do?"

Rachel leaned over the table and stared into Drake's eyes. "Because I believe her. She doesn't strike me as the type of person who would make up something like this."

"And you got that impression after only speaking with her for...what...ten minutes?"

"I think I have proven myself to you, or I wouldn't be sitting here. If I didn't think she was a reliable witness, I wouldn't have arranged this meeting."

"It's not up to you to judge whether a witness is reliable or not. That is for me to decide. And let's get one thing clear: You're here because the governor requested you."

"I see. This is about earlier." Rachel paused while the waitress cleared their table. "She was scared and I was afraid she would bolt if you came over. I wanted to get as much information as I could while she was sitting there. We have never had this problem before." Rachel wiped her hands with a napkin. "What's going on?"

"Nothing. Just getting heat from the boss." Drake anxiously glanced at his watch. "Speaking of which, it's almost four thirty. I think she's a no-show. How much longer do you want to wait?"

"Let's give it a few more minutes. She'll be here."

While the waitress wiped down their table, the door opened and a young girl walked into the restaurant.

"There she is." Rachel waved Shondra over.

"Hi. Sorry I'm late. Someone didn't show up for work today, and I had to do their work, plus mine." Shondra was still wearing her work uniform—a light-blue dress with buttons down the front. The word *Riveria Hotel* was stitched above the right breast pocket. On the left side, she wore a shiny bronze name badge that said, *Shondra Myers, Housekeeper.*

Rachel made the introductions and Shondra sat down next to her.

"Please tell Drake what you told me this morning."

Drake sensed her reluctance. "It's okay," he reassured her. "I'll try to keep what you say confidential. Rachel explained your parents would be upset."

Shondra nodded her head.

"Are you hungry? Would you like something cold to drink?"

"Just some ice water would be nice."

Rachel called over the waitress and ordered for Shondra while Drake listened as she told her story.

After she was finished, Drake pulled out his cell phone and handed it to her. "I have some photos for you to look at. Can you tell me if any one of these guys is the one that you saw?" Two of the photos were of Shawn. One was his department photo and the other was taken before he left for his cruise ship assignment. Mike was able to e-mail them to Drake. The other photos were random agents from the force. He placed them on the table in front of her. "Take your time."

"I'm really not sure," Shondra said. "It was dark and he wasn't near the streetlight. But he looks familiar. He turned around and looked in my direction when he got in the car. I saw part of his face."

"How sure?"

"I dunno. Probably seventy-five percent."

"And Amber? How do you know that was her?"

"I got a good look at her when she was coming up by the house. There was a small porch light and she walked right under it. Then I saw her face again when she was forced in the truck. She looked just the picture on the flyers you were handing out this morning. Long blonde hair and pretty."

"What was she wearing?"

"Shorts and a T-shirt. She walked with a limp."

"Okay. Let's go back to when you first saw Amber and the guy she was with. Did it look like he was forcing her?" Drake asked.

"No. I don't think so. Like I said, she looked like she'd hurt her foot and he was helping her. I heard bits and pieces of their conversation," Shondra told them. She closed her eyes tight like she was remembering.

"The girl was telling him to slow down, that her foot hurt. He was saying to hurry up, that he didn't know how much time they had and they needed to get away somewhere safe. Check in or call somebody." Shondra was quiet for a moment.

"They starting coming up to the street and I hid behind a corner. I looked up, and that's when I saw the second man approach them. And then the dark SUV appeared out of nowhere. It didn't have the headlights on, that's why they didn't see it at first. That second man had a gun. He forced them into the truck. Then they drove off."

Drake and Rachel sat quietly, digesting the information.

"Did you get a look at who was driving?" Drake finally asked.

"No. Sorry."

"Did you see anyone else?"

"No." Shondra finished her water. "I need to get going. I have to fix my dad's dinner before he leaves for work."

"Here's my card, Shondra. If you remember anything else, please call us. You've been a big help." Drake said.

Rachel said, "Thanks for coming, Shondra. We really appreciate it."

"I just don't want my dad to find out. He'd be so mad that I was out that night," Shondra said. "It was nice to meet you. I hope that you find the girl." She got up quickly and left the café.

Drake sat with his back against the booth. He ran his hands through his hair and then rested his hand on his forehead. Rachel had a fleeting memory of her ex-husband, Rick, doing the same when he was deep in thought about something.

"What are you thinking?" she asked him.

"It fits what our theory has been all along. Amber and Shawn walked back to her room. Something happened while they were in her suite."

"Like what?"

"Shawn's cover was blown or he got into some kind of altercation. Why leave the ship otherwise?" Drake thought for a minute. "Amber was there. She saw something. Or heard something. So now she's in danger, too. Shawn must have found a way off the ship with her. They were close enough to port. Someone either followed them or alerted someone else to be on the lookout for them."

"How does Danny Pezzini fit in? The body the Coast Guard recovered. Any word on that?"

"Until we get the autopsy report, I don't know. Cyndy is working on that angle."

"Thanks for the food. I was starving." Rachel grabbed her bag and followed Drake out into the Caribbean sunshine. They walked past Lucaya Harbor, where expensive yachts bobbed in the crystal-clear waters, toward the parking lot.

"First, we'll head over to the conference room and let Phipps and Cyndy know what we got."

CHAPTER 24

Shawn slowly came to consciousness, his whole body screaming with pain. He assessed his injuries. Gingerly touching his face with his fingertips, he felt blood trickling from his broken nose, his right cheekbone was puffy—probably broken—and his left eye was swollen shut. Just moving to a sitting position caused him to groan in pain. He probably had a few cracked ribs, too.

He peered around the room with his good eye. He wasn't sure how long he'd been out, but he guessed around eight hours, because now a thin strip of light filtered through a small window. The room was about a hundred square feet with a small cot, toilet, and sink. The door looked to be solid steel, and the window had bars. *Just like a prison*, he thought.

He wondered if Amber was being held someplace nearby. When they'd arrived at the island, he was afraid they'd get separated. As an undercover agent, he expected this kind of treatment if he was exposed. But dragging an innocent bystander into this mess was another thing. He hoped like hell she hadn't suffered the same kind of beating that he had.

Shawn couldn't believe how everything had gone from bad to worse so quickly. His shift had started just like any other. When

Amber and her friends approached him at the club, he recognized her from the staff briefing they'd had earlier that day. All VIPs on the ship were given preferential treatment. He was just taken aback to see how beautiful she was in real life. When she fell ill later that night, he offered to walk her back to her suite. She never mentioned to him that she was the governor's daughter, and he never let on that he knew.

He'd left Amber on the balcony, comfortably resting, while he visited the ship's infirmary to get her medicine. On the way back, he was attacked from behind while he opened the door to Amber's suite. He'd cursed himself—then and since—for letting his guard down.

A noise at the steel door brought him back to the present. The door swung open and a stocky man dressed in army fatigues and heavy, black boots walked in. Shawn didn't think this was the same man who'd beat him to unconsciousness.

"Who are you?" the stocky man demanded in a British accent.

"Josh McCain," he answered.

The man huffed and looked at him suspiciously. "Who do you work for?"

"*SeaStar.*"

The man's steely gray eyes bored into him. "You. Are. Lying."

Shawn elected not to say anything and, instead, just stared back at his tormentor.

"Maybe you need some persuasion?"

"I told you the truth. My name is Josh McCain."

The man shrugged his shoulders. "Your death wish." He turned and left the room.

A few minutes later, Shawn heard the door open again. This time the man brought a friend to the party.

"Last chance to talk to us. You have something to say?"

Shawn sat quietly, staring back at them.

The other man lunged toward him with lightning speed. A steel rod connected with a sickening thud to the side of his head. Before Shawn blacked out, his last thought was of Amber. And that, somewhere along the way, he'd made a big mistake.

CHAPTER 25

Phipps and Cyndy were in deep conversation when Rachel and Drake walked into the conference room.

"What's up?" Drake asked as they joined them at the table.

"We were just discussing Danny Pezzini," Phipps answered. "Some new information has come to light. Cyndy just got back from meeting with the coroner. The preliminary autopsy report shows blunt-force trauma to the head, but that's not what killed him. Cause of death was drowning."

"How did he get the injury to his head?" Rachel asked.

"The coroner believes that Pezzini could have fallen overboard and hit his head on the way down. The initial tox report found alcohol in his system. No drugs detected, but a full tox screen will take a few weeks," Cyndy said. "But that's not all. Luckily, his wallet was on him when the Coast Guard plucked him out the water. We found a receipt from room service in it. On the back was Josh's name and cabin number."

"We now have something to link Pezzini and Josh?" Drake took off his glasses and rubbed the bridge of his nose.

"Seems so," Phipps answered.

"Josh was on Pezzini's radar, apparently. We were just discussing a theory before you came in. Pezzini could've been working for Morrotti. They may have suspected Josh was undercover and Morrotti sent him to take care of the situation." Cyndy tapped her pen on the table. "Obviously they didn't know that Josh McCain was an alias for Shawn Gibson."

"The pieces of the puzzle are falling into place now." Drake grabbed a cup of coffee from the urn the hotel staff kept full for them.

"How did the meeting go with the witness?" Phipps asked.

Drake went over the details with Phipps. "She made a positive ID on Amber. She's less sure about Shawn. But we're assuming it's him."

"Back to Pezzini. He may have been following Shawn, waiting for the right time to get him alone, which is awfully hard to do on a cruise," Phipps said.

"But a very convenient way to dispose of a body," Rachel said. "He was able to get into Amber's suite. They fought. Either Pezzini fell or Shawn tossed him overboard."

"No one reported hearing a fight," Phipps said.

"True. But doesn't mean there wasn't one. Somehow Pezzini ended up in the water," Rachel said.

"If that's true, once Pezzini was out of the way, why did Shawn take Amber with him?" Cyndy asked.

"Shawn thought Amber was in danger and that leaving her on the ship was a bigger risk than taking her with him?" Rachel asked.

"Maybe. Or Amber was the target and not Shawn?" Drake added.

"The family hasn't received a ransom demand. And Pezzini had Josh's name on the receipt. I still think Amber got in the way, and for some reason, they had to bail," Phipps said.

"If Shondra's account of what happened that night is correct, Shawn and Amber were captured after finding a way to shore," Rachel said. "What happened to them?"

"Enzo Morrotti could be the key to all this," Phipps said. "If he suspected Shawn was undercover and threatening his drug operation, he could've arranged for him to be taken care of."

"I don't think they'd still be around Freeport," Rachel said. "If he went to such great lengths to capture them, he wouldn't risk keeping them around."

"Let's get together with Mike Mancini." Drake drew a big, red circle around Morrotti's name on the whiteboard. "See what he knows about Morrotti."

CHAPTER 26

Rachel walked into her hotel room after a long day. This was the hard part for her—spending all day searching and chasing leads with nothing to show for it. Even though Shondra provided them with an ID that Amber had made it off the ship, they were back to square one. Where were Amber and Shawn now? Was Amber still alive?

She tried not to let it get her down. Every successful rescue gave her hope that she would one day find her little girl. Mallory would be eight years old this year. Rachel often fantasized about finding Mallory and wondered if her daughter would still remember her. That was her biggest fear—that Mallory wouldn't know her.

She threw her bag on the bed and slumped down next to it. She was exhausted, and she needed food and a long, hot shower, not necessarily in that order. She grabbed the phone and called the Blue Palm restaurant and ordered a grilled mahimahi sandwich and french fries from room service. Then she saw that she had a message, and when she called in for it, the front desk told her that she had a package and someone would bring it up to her soon. It was probably from the office. Janine occasionally sent her mail when she was traveling. After her shower, she'd check in with her.

Rachel stripped out of her clothes and stepped into the shower. She was proud of her crew even if they didn't have any solid leads to Amber yet. In three years, she'd been involved in over twenty-five missing persons cases. Sometimes the outcome wasn't good. She didn't always find the missing person alive. But those she did find alive gave her hope. Somehow Amber and Shawn had made it off the ship and got to the island. The big question now—where were they?

It was time to think about the next steps.

She stepped out of the shower and wrapped a thick white towel around her body. Running her hand across the steamed mirror, she looked at her reflection. Her nose and cheeks were slightly sunburned despite the sunscreen she'd used, and her normally bright-green eyes looked dull—a sure sign that she was tired.

As she attacked her tangled, long auburn hair with a comb, she wondered if Mike Mancini was attached. She hadn't felt an attraction to anyone since her divorce from Rick. Not that her hectic schedule left her any time for dating. Mike was also the total opposite of what she was normally attracted to. Rick was always impeccably groomed, down to his thousand-dollar suits and weekly manicured fingernails. Mike had that dark, handsome, rugged look—his muscles bulged under snug T-shirts and tight jeans—and he was a good listener and seemed genuinely caring about her situation. He and Rick had only two things in common: They were both ambitious, and they usually got what they wanted.

What Rachel didn't know was if she was ready for a relationship yet.

After Mallory disappeared, her marriage to Rick fell apart. While he spent hours at the office working, she spent hours on the street following up on leads the police neglected. When several months passed and they still hadn't found Mallory, Rick thought it was time to start living their lives again. Rachel resented him for giving up so soon, and he resented her for not moving on. In addition, she always felt that he blamed her for Mallory's disappearance. If she had taken Mallory inside with her when the phone rang or didn't answer the damn phone to begin with…*No*, she thought, *I'm not going down that dark road again.*

When she walked out of the bathroom, she noticed the package the front desk had delivered while she was in the shower. She picked up the plain manila envelope and sat down on the bed to open it. It hadn't come from her office, because Florida Omni Search used white envelopes with the company logo. This envelope had only her name handwritten in thick black letters. She was opening the envelope when someone knocked at the door. She let in room service and put a generous tip on the ticket.

The smell of the herbed mahimahi and mango salsa was unbelievably appetizing. She took a bite of the sandwich as she sat back down on the bed. Rachel poured the contents of the package onto the coverlet. A plain sheet of white paper and a photograph fluttered out…

She picked up the photograph and turned it over. A little girl, about seven or eight years old with red hair and green eyes, gazed back at her. The image took a few seconds to register. Then Rachel gasped. The child was Mallory. Rachel's hand shook as she picked up the piece of paper. She slowly turned it over. Three words made her heart stop:

MALLORY IS ALIVE.

CHAPTER 27

Mike sat down beside Rachel and gently removed the picture she had firmly grasped in her hand.

"Rachel, we don't know for sure that this is Mallory. The photo could be a fake," he said cautiously.

She had called Mike when she couldn't reach Drake on his phone. Rachel felt like her whole world was coming apart when she saw that picture. Her heart raced and her mouth went dry.

Rachel flipped open her laptop and brought up the Florida Omni Search website, which showcased information about missing children, each with age-progression photos. She found the page that featured Mallory. One picture showed Mallory when she was three, and another photo, using age-progression software, showed her at eight years old. Both pictures showed her with big, round green eyes, vibrant red hair, a button nose, and full lips. In the photograph Rachel had just received, Mallory had short hair. In the Florida Omni Search age-progression photo, she had longer hair. Despite the difference in hair lengths, the two pictures were eerily similar.

"What kind of sicko would do this?" Rachel asked, glancing between the photo in her hand and the one on the Internet. Whether it was real or not, someone was telling her that Mallory was alive.

"I don't know. You've been in the media a lot the last few days. And Mallory's disappearance was a high-profile case," Mike said. "People do stupid stuff to get a rise out of someone."

"But what if this is something?"

"First things first, I'll call the front desk and see if I can find out who dropped this off," Mike said. "Then we'll go from there."

While he picked up the phone to call the manager, Rachel stared at the age-progression photographs of Mallory. About a year after Mallory had vanished, Rachel sent family photos of herself, Rick, and Mallory to the forensic imaging specialists at the National Center for Missing and Exploited Children. The image specialist merged all the photos in a complex program to create a photo of Mallory at age four.

Rachel updated the website every year with a new photo in hope that one day Mallory would be found. But now Rachel had an in-house specialist, Gregg Isbitt, who performed all the age-progression photos for Florida Omni Search. Gregg was an IT specialist formerly with the Atlanta Police Department and a friend of Red Cooper. She trusted him like every other member of her valuable team.

Mike hung up the phone. "No luck. The security camera isn't working, and the front desk clerk who took the package was busy checking in a guest and doesn't remember much about the boy who dropped off the package. He described him as a teenager wearing a baseball cap and shorts. That's it. The boy was probably paid by someone to drop it off."

"I still don't get what this means. Could it be the start of some kind of ransom? Four years later?"

"If it is, then they'll contact you again. I'd give this to Drake and have him take a look. See if he can run this through his lab."

Rachel nodded. "I left him a message."

Mike leaned over, gave her a hug. "I know you miss her terribly. We'll figure this out together."

CHAPTER 28

"Good morning. I ordered us some breakfast," Rachel said as she opened the door to a tired-looking Drake.

"Smells wonderful." Drake lifted the silver dome from one of the plates, which was covered with a large scoop of steaming scrambled eggs, crisp bacon, and chunks of hashed brown potatoes with onions and peppers. "Feeling better this morning?"

"Not really. Didn't sleep much last night. I tossed and turned." Rachel picked up her coffee mug. "Right now I need massive amounts of caffeine."

"I sent the envelope to the lab this morning. We should hear something soon," Drake said.

"Great. Thanks again for coming over last night. After Mike left, I didn't know what to do. I called the office, and Gregg said he'd take a look at the photo we scanned and e-mailed him. It's a long shot, but he might be able to tell if it's authentic or if someone used age-progression software. Either way, I'd like to keep this quiet for now."

"Sure. I think it's a diversion, but we'll see what the lab says." Drake poured a cup of coffee and pointed to her newspaper. "What are you reading?"

"Our friend Stacy Case did an article about Amber," Rachel said, handing him the front page of the *Miami Sun*. "I got a copy from the newsstand downstairs."

GOVERNOR'S DAUGHTER DISAPPEARS FROM CRUISE SHIP
By Staff Reporter Stacy Case

Former Miami socialite Rachel Scott is in the Bahamas today with her search-and-rescue company, Florida Omni Search, assisting the local police force and FBI to locate Amber Knowles, daughter of Florida governor John Knowles. She was reported missing early Sunday morning from the SeaStar *cruise ship when her friends and the school chaperone couldn't find her.*

Authorities believe that Ms. Knowles accidentally fell overboard. The SeaStar *informed the Coast Guard after an extensive search of the ship failed to locate the teenager.*

The FBI, which investigates the disappearance of American citizens abroad, is not authorized to hold a ship without evidence of a crime.

Governor Knowles and his wife, Sarah Knowles, have flown to Freeport and made a statement to the media. A reward of one million dollars has been offered to anyone who has information that leads to Amber's safe return. A tip line has been set up in coordination with Florida Omni Search.

The FBI has worked with Florida Omni Search on several missing persons cases. Florida Omni Search recently made headlines when they found a missing Boy Scout alive in the Florida Everglades.

"She left our investigation out of the article as we asked," Drake said.

"Her story is a little dated now. We know that Amber didn't fall overboard," Rachel commented.

"That's best left under wraps until we know for sure. Any leads from the tip line?"

"I checked in with Janine this morning. Nothing. Not even the crackpots and psychics have called in, which is unusual. "

"Give it some time."

"What's planned for today?" Rachel asked.

"The cruise ship has left port. Amber's two friends are staying with the governor and his wife for the rest of the week. Their parents have been notified and are on the way down. We're heading over there this morning to talk to the girls again. I want to see if they remember anything else about the night Amber disappeared—if they saw anyone else talking with her or Josh."

"You mean Shawn?"

"Yeah, they still know him as Josh." Drake stood up and brushed toast crumbs from his shirt.

"Okay. Let's get going, then." Rachel put down her coffee cup, grabbed her bag, and headed for the door.

CHAPTER 29

The governor's rented villa was situated on a high bluff that overlooked a beautiful private stretch of beach. Drake and Rachel drove up the long circular driveway and parked the car.

"Impressive digs for the governor," she commented as they walked up to the massive front door.

"The house belongs to a friend of the governor. It's more private than staying at a hotel. Especially since he decided to run for president, security is a little tighter."

Too bad they didn't think about that before letting Amber take a cruise. Rachel's thought was interrupted by the front door opening.

A uniformed maid led them inside. "The governor and his wife are waiting for you in the sunroom."

Drake and Rachel followed her through the house. The villa was surprisingly simple inside. Its terra-cotta tile floors were complemented by soft-blue and pale-yellow walls. Knickknacks, a vase of pale flowers, and a clear glass bowl of seashells and sand dollars decorated the villa. It was very calming and relaxing, and Rachel soon felt at ease.

Governor Knowles stood up as they entered the sunroom. Even though he was impeccably dressed in pressed navy slacks and a pinstriped button-down shirt with the sleeves neatly rolled up his forearms, he looked more stressed than he had the day before.

He smiled as he held out his hand to Rachel. "Nice to see you again, Rachel. Please come in and have a seat. Hello, Agent Reynolds."

Rachel regarded Sarah as she stood up to greet them. Her long blonde hair was pulled back in a neat ponytail, and she was dressed casually in khaki Bermuda shorts and a billowy white peasant blouse. Her flip-flops revealed freshly painted bright-pink toenails.

"Rachel, Drake, is there any news?" Sarah asked hopefully.

Governor Knowles put his arm around his wife and said with a strained smile, "We're hoping there's been some movement since yesterday…" He nodded to the maid who let them in. "Bring us something cold and a pot of coffee, please, Nadia."

Rachel and Drake sat down on the sofa opposite the Knowleses. The sunroom was minimally decorated with a sofa and loveseat covered in creamy-white denim, two casual wicker chairs, and a sea grass jute rug beneath a heavy glass coffee table. A ceramic bowl held tiny seashells and colorful sea glass. A sliding glass door led to a patio that overlooked the pinkish-colored sandy beach and emerald-green waters.

"Thanks again for coming. As you can imagine, this has been a very difficult time." He patted Sarah's hand. "Have you gotten any leads from the hotline?"

Rachel shook her head no and reiterated what Drake had already related to the governor. "But our witness saw Amber and Josh get into an SUV. We know somehow she got off the ship."

"But she must not be in a safe place, or she would have called us." Sarah twisted and rubbed her hands together nervously.

Nadia came in and set down a tray of lemonade and small sandwiches. A second maid, carrying a pot of coffee and cups, followed.

"Thanks," Rachel said as she accepted a glass of the cool, tangy drink.

"We're working closely with the DEA and the local police. Rachel has every available volunteer combing the area where the lifeboat was found," Drake said as soon as the maids had left the room.

"What about this Josh guy? Or whatever his name is. You said he's undercover DEA? What else do we know about him? How is he involved in this?" Governor Knowles stood and started pacing behind the small loveseat.

"Josh McCain is an alias. His name is Shawn Gibson. Mike Mancini, his boss at the DEA, says he's a respected agent and a stand-up guy. He's young, but has been with the DEA for some time now. Something happened on that ship that involved Amber. We think Shawn tried to get her to safety."

"The DEA is investigating the *SeaStar* for drug smuggling?" Governor Knowles asked.

Drake nodded. "We think Shawn's cover was compromised. Once they got off the ship, we're not sure what happened. We're working on it."

"So where are they now?" he asked.

Drake went over what he'd already told the governor over the phone. "The witness who saw them forced into a dark SUV unfortunately did not get the tag information."

"Is this a reliable witness? You said she was a teenager?"

"She identified Amber from our flyers. She wasn't one hundred percent positive identifying Shawn," Drake answered.

Sarah gasped. "Who the hell has my daughter?"

Drake and Rachel exchanged glances. "We don't know. That's a theory we're working on," Drake said. "We'd like to talk to the girls again to see if they can remember anything else about the night Amber disappeared. Something about Josh, maybe."

Sarah got up. "They're upstairs getting dressed. I'll get them."

They only had to wait a couple minutes until Nicole and Rowan joined them. Rachel thought they didn't look much better than the last time she'd seen them. They both looked tired and upset. She couldn't blame them. Their best friend was missing. And they were just about the last people to have seen Amber before she disappeared.

"I wanted to see if you remembered anything else about the last night you saw Amber," Drake started once the girls got settled.

"No. We've both thought about that night constantly," Nicole said while Rowan nodded in agreement. "All we can think about is what happened to her."

"Tell me again about Josh. The first time you saw him," Drake said.

"I don't remember seeing him until we went to the club that night, but Amber mentioned him the first day of the cruise," Rowan said.

"When was this?" Rachel asked.

"When we were walking up to the club, Amber said, 'There's the cute guy from the pool,' and pointed at Josh. But she never talked to him until we got to the club," Rowan said.

"Okay. So Amber saw him at the pool the first day on the ship, but never had a conversation with him until the night she disappeared?" Rachel clarified.

"Right," Nicole and Rowan said in agreement.

"We walked up to the Aqua entrance. Josh introduced himself and walked us to a VIP room. I remember that he said he was from

California and this was his first job on a cruise ship. He and Amber talked while Nicole and I went and got drinks," Rowan added.

"When we came back, Amber mentioned that she wasn't feeling well. Josh had left and we asked Amber if she wanted to go back to the cabin. She didn't want to ruin our evening, she said. After a few minutes, Josh came back to check on us, and Amber said she was leaving. I offered to walk her back, but Josh said he'd do it. That's about it," Nicole said.

She'd basically summed up what they already knew. "Did you take any pictures that night?" Rachel asked.

"Sure. I have a couple pictures of us at the club that night. Would you like to see?" Nicole asked.

Rachel exchanged glances with Drake. "Of course."

"Let me get my laptop. I downloaded them from my camera last night." Nicole left to get her laptop and was back within a minute. She booted up her Dell, found the file, and handed the computer over to Drake.

Rachel and Drake looked through the pictures of the girls. One showed Amber posing with Josh. She had her arm draped around his neck.

Drake started to flip to another photo.

"Wait! Go back." Rachel leaned closer to the screen. "Can you enlarge this?"

"Sure." Drake pushed the zoom button and the picture magnified.

"Is that who I think it is?" Rachel pointed to a man in the background.

Drake pushed his glasses up and peered at the screen. "Danny Pezzini?"

"Isn't that the guy the Coast Guard found?" the governor asked.

"Yes," Drake answered. "He was a passenger on the cruise."

"Do you think he is somehow involved? What do I need to do to get some answers?" Governor Knowles directed his question at Drake.

"We are looking into Pezzini and any possible connection to SeaScape Cruise Lines." Drake softened his voice. "With all due respect, Governor, let us handle the investigation. The last thing we want is Morrotti to know that we're looking into his business. The DEA has had this undercover operation in motion for over two years now. I don't want to compromise their involvement."

"That's what got my daughter into trouble in the first place! This DEA agent, Josh, or Shawn…whatever his name is! I want some answers and I want them now!" The governor clenched the sofa pillow.

Rachel could feel the tension in the room ratchet up a few notches. "John, I understand how frustrating this is. But you trusted me enough to bring me into this investigation. Please let us do our jobs."

Governor Knowles sat down next to Sarah. Rachel could see some of the tension leave his face. The girls sat motionless, looking frightened. She felt so bad for all of them.

"I want to meet with Mike Mancini and hear for myself what he thinks happened on the *SeaStar* that night."

"I'll let him know," Drake assured him.

"Thank you."

Drake cleared his throat. "Do you mind if I e-mail these photos to myself?"

"Sure, whatever will help," Nicole answered.

"Thanks," Drake said. "I want to send these to Mike as well. He's tracking down possible members of Morrotti's team. He might see something out of place."

Rachel's phone buzzed. She looked down at the number and let out a sigh.

"I need to take this. Be right back." She pulled open the sliding glass door and stepped out onto the patio. A strong breeze had picked up and the palm trees swayed. A fragrant plumeria scented the air. "Rachel Scott," she answered, even though she knew who was calling.

"Hi, Rachel. It's Rick. You have a sec?"

"What's up?"

"We need to talk."

"Okay, then. Talk."

"I'd like to see you in person."

"Not going to happen anytime soon. I'm in the Bahamas working on a case."

"I know that. I'm here, too."

"Here where? In Freeport?"

"Yes. I wouldn't call if it wasn't urgent."

Rachel sucked in a deep breath. "What's wrong?"

"I can meet you at your hotel tonight for dinner," Rick said, ignoring her question.

"How do you know where I'm staying?" Rachel asked, realizing that he'd probably called Janine at the office.

"Your office told me. Seven o'clock, okay?"

"Sure. Meet me at the hotel bar," Rachel said before disconnecting.

She wondered why Rick was calling her now. She intended to find out, but she wasn't too keen about meeting with him. She reentered the room. Everyone except John and Drake had left.

"Sarah took the girls out for shopping and lunch. I think they're going stir crazy just sitting here." Governor Knowles stood up from the couch.

"I'm sure it'll be good for them to get out for a bit." Rachel shook his hand. "We'll keep in touch."

Drake followed Rachel outside. "Everything okay?" he asked.

She nodded her head. "Just the office checking in."

"Let's head back to the hotel and call Mike. See what he came up with on Pezzini." Drake started the car. "We need to step this investigation up a notch."

CHAPTER 30

Rachel got to the hotel bar early and sat at a table near the entrance. She ordered the house white wine and waited for Rick. She wondered what he wanted and, more importantly, what the hell he was doing in the Bahamas.

She remembered the first time she met Rick. She was just out of college and needed to buy a car. She walked into the local dealership in Miami and found a car…and a husband. She was looking in the window of a used SUV and someone behind her said, "This one has low miles and is a one-owner trade-in. Just got her yesterday."

Rachel turned and saw a cute salesman smiling at her. He thumped the SUV's roof.

She drove away with a new car and he walked away with her number. He waited a couple days before calling her under the pretense of checking in with her to see how the car was doing. They ended up making plans to meet for lunch the following day. After a six-month courtship, Rick asked her to marry him. The first night of their honeymoon, Rachel realized she was pregnant.

Rachel kept her job selling real estate while she was pregnant. When Mallory was born, Rachel hired a nanny. Rick had opened several new luxury dealerships with a new partner and was gone most of the time. Rachel tried to reduce her hours and spend more time with Mallory. She didn't want her daughter raised by strangers.

The day Mallory disappeared the nanny had called in sick. Rachel was putting together a huge commercial deal and was up to her neck in negotiations. Rick was on his way out of town to open up a new dealership in Orlando. It was a beautiful day. She let Mallory play outside on the front lawn while she sat on the shaded porch and crunched numbers, trying to make the deal work. Rachel heard her phone ring inside. She called to Mallory, "Be right back, honey." She was inside for only a minute—two minutes tops. But that was all it took. Mallory was gone when she went back outside.

Mallory's disappearance took a toll on their marriage. Rick left. Rachel quit her job in real estate and put all her money in Florida Omni Search. Now she spent her days looking for Mallory—and all the other missing persons.

Rachel took a sip of the chilled wine and played nervously with the cocktail napkin, folding it into tiny squares and then shredding it to pieces. She checked her watch and realized Rick was late. She decided to wait five more minutes before leaving. It was unusual for Rick to be late. He was usually very punctual.

She'd last seen Rick two years ago, when they'd finally sold their last joint piece of real estate, a large residential lot in Pembroke Pines, which they'd bought as an investment when they were first married.

She remembered that day like it was yesterday. They were to meet at the title company and sign the closing papers. She got there early to avoid him. But just as she was signing the documents, Rick walked into the room. Rachel could tell that he'd started drinking again. His body looked swollen, not hard and lean like it had been before the divorce. His skin was pale and he had a faint sheen across his forehead. When he leaned in to give her a hug, his breath smelled so sour that she wanted to throw up.

The scene was awkward, and she just wanted to sign the papers and get out of there. Other than a couple of phone calls a year to update him on leads about Mallory, she never saw him or spoke to him. That was one perk of leading a busy life and traveling the country.

"Hello, Rachel." A voice from behind her jarred her out of the unpleasant memory.

She looked up to see Rick standing at her table. He looked good. The beer belly, paleness, and sour breath had disappeared. He was tan and fit, wearing pressed khaki pants and a white polo shirt that hugged his biceps and chest. As he sat down, she could smell a mix of spearmint and clean aftershave.

"You look lovely." Rick reached over and gave her a peck on the cheek. "Sorry I'm late."

"Hi, Rick. Want something to drink?" Rachel asked as she waved over the cocktail waitress. He ordered a soft drink and waited for the waitress to leave.

"I've been following the story on the Knowles girl. How's it going?"

"We're following up on some leads," Rachel answered.

"What about the friends who were on the trip with her? Someone had to have seen something. A girl just doesn't disappear on a cruise without someone knowing something," Rick said.

Rachel winced like he had hit a nerve. "Did you come all the way here just to talk about my case, or do you have something else in mind? Because I'm really busy," Rachel said, sounding testier than she'd wanted to. She didn't think she could deal with his small talk.

"I wanted to tell you something, and I thought it was better to speak with you in person," Rick said, picking up his drink and taking a sip.

"Mallory?" Rachel asked. She held her breath, thinking about the picture she'd received.

"Oh, no. Is that what you thought?" Rick said. "No, not Mallory. I wanted to tell you that I got married. We're here on our honeymoon."

Rachel let out a long breath. Relieved and irritated at the same time. "I think I would've liked it better if you'd called." She downed the rest of her wine.

"It was a coincidence that we're here when all this happened with the governor's daughter. I heard you were in town and thought I would tell you in person."

Rachel looked around the restaurant. "Where's your new wife?"

Rick smiled nervously. "She's at the spa getting a massage. I didn't want this to be awkward between us."

"Well, congratulations, I guess." Rachel thought back to the picture of Mallory in her hotel room. Should she share that with Rick? After all, he was Mallory's father. No matter that he deserted Rachel after Mallory had been kidnapped. Since she didn't have anything concrete to go on, she decided she'd keep the photo quiet until she learned more. No sense in getting his hopes up. She reached into her purse and threw a twenty-dollar bill on the table. "Thanks for letting me know. I need to get back to work."

"Rach, wait." Rick grabbed her arm. A look of pain quickly passed on his face. "I just wanted to let you know that I haven't given up on her. I'm still hurting, too."

She nodded, pulled back her arm, and strode out of the bar, not looking back.

CHAPTER 31

"Don't let the name Asylum Harbor fool you," said Matt Danbury, Stacy Case's informant. She had gotten him to agree to speak to Rachel and Drake about his employment with *SeaStar* and the experiences he'd had while working at Cabana Cay.

"Asylum Harbor has pink sand beaches," Matt said. "The color of the water is so bright blue it hurts your eyes if you stare at it too long. Plumeria is everywhere. It's very tropical and lush, and they work to keep it that way. Cabana Cay, on the south end of the island, is more like a resort. Passengers can use the lounge chairs and umbrellas on the beach and get something to drink from the tiki hut. And next to that is a small restaurant that cooks up jerk chicken, conch fritters, and Johnny cake—all the island favorites. People can rent cabanas if they want…you know…*privacy*"—here Matt waggled his eyebrows—or they can rent Jet Skis, kayaks, or paddleboats."

Matt shook his head. "It looks nice and inviting, but looks can be deceiving." He leaned back in his chair and took a sip of his soda.

Drake, Mike, Rachel, and Stacy were all crammed in the conference room with Matt. They were enthralled with his description of the legendary island.

Rachel studied Matt. He was tall and skinny, and his dark hair was sprinkled with bits of gray along the temple and around his ears. He talked with a lisp.

"Matt, can you give us some background on your employment with the cruise line?" Drake asked.

Matt looked nervous. "Stacy said this was all confidential, right?" He looked back and forth between Stacy and Drake.

Drake looked at Mike for confirmation. "We'll try to keep your name out of the investigation. Can't make any promises, though," Mike answered.

"I hope so. These guys are not people you want to mess with," Matt said.

"Go ahead," Stacy prodded him. "Tell them what you told me when we first met."

"I started with SeaScape a couple of years ago. I was first put on the *SeaMist*, which ran the West Caribbean route—Tampa to Cozumel and Grand Cayman—doing baggage handling. Like when passengers check in, we made sure their luggage was delivered to their cabins. It's routine stuff, but I learned my way around, and I found out that all ships have secret passageways that go from one end of the ship to the other. We called it the 'rat maze.' Anyways, after a year on the *SeaMist*, I put in a request to work on the newer ship, *SeaStar*. They didn't have any openings in baggage, so I opted for bartending. I had a part-time job at a nightclub in college, so I knew my way around a bar. So I was promoted and moved to the new ship."

"This is where you worked when you met Josh?"

Matt nodded. "Josh was hired on about six months after I started. He was a VIP host at the clubs, and it was his job to know everyone. He'd order bottles of champagne and top-shelf liquors for the VIP guests. Make them comfy, be at their beck and call, and make sure everyone had a good time. Josh and I become good buds. We were roommates for a while. I also worked with three other bartenders, and we rotated shifts. But I'm getting ahead of myself. Prior to Josh coming aboard, I started noticing something unusual."

"What was that?" Drake asked him.

"Diego, one of the other bartenders, always got friendly with some of the customers. Mostly the younger women." Matt paused and caught Stacy's eye.

She nodded for him to go on.

"One night, a girl came into the club by herself. Her name was Melodie. Melodie Sayers. Maybe you heard of her from the news. She disappeared from the *SeaStar*, and the crew said she fell overboard. I worked the night she disappeared. Diego had been talking and flirting with her all night. While I was restocking the bar, I saw him hand a white tablet to Thomas Reese, the other VIP host on duty that night. Thomas served Melodie her drink. I think that Thomas and Diego gave Melodie some type of drug—like a roofie, maybe—to have sex with her. And I bet it wasn't the first time. Diego flirted with lots of female passengers."

Matt had everyone's attention around the table.

"Thomas left his shift early that night, and I saw him leave the club with Melodie. That was the last anyone saw of her."

"According to the police report, Melodie was last seen walking by herself along the promenade deck," Stacy interjected.

"Maybe that's what the report said, but that's not what happened. I know what I saw. Thomas and Melodie left the club together. Do you want to hear what I think happened?" Matt asked the group.

"Go ahead." Drake motioned for him to continue.

"We all know the video cameras are installed only around public areas. I think Thomas told Melodie he'd meet up with her later so there wouldn't be any footage of them together. Remember those secret passageways? The ship has a lot of storage areas, too. I think he went to her cabin and took her somewhere else on the ship. My first thought was that he drugged her and raped her, and she accidentally died. With the amount of alcohol she drank that night coupled with the drugs, she may have had a seizure or stopped breathing. I think Thomas panicked and called Diego. I was with Diego when he got a phone call. He didn't say who it was from, but I could tell something was wrong. Diego asked me to cover for him, and I didn't see him again until later that night. When I asked where he went, he told me that the less I knew, the better. The next thing I knew, the captain called for a search of the ship for a missing passenger, Melodie Sayers. It didn't take much to put two and two together. So I originally thought she was dumped overboard."

"But you changed your mind?" Stacy prompted him.

Matt shrugged. "Yeah."

"Why's that?"

"Later that day, the supervisors and security staff questioned all the staff. I kept my mouth shut." Matt looked sheepishly at Stacy. "I should have said something, but…not my business, you know? Plus, I was afraid I'd lose my job. Anyway, the next day we docked in Cabana Cay, and my boss asked me to stay behind and help restock the ship—something that Diego normally did. But for some reason he asked me to do this. It was my first time behind the scenes at Cabana Cay."

"Cabana Cay looks like a gorgeous place," Rachel commented.

"It is, but Asylum Harbor, the north side of the island, is downright spooky. As soon as we docked, most of the passengers went ashore. Thomas and I took a golf cart over the sandy trails that run through the back of the island. It is like a big maze. Trails shoot off to different sections of the island. When you get to Asylum

Harbor, where most of the island employees live and work, there is an electronic gate. You have to have a remote to open up. I guess it's to keep nosy passengers away."

"How far is that from Cabana Cay? I mean, would passengers wander that far off?" Rachel asked.

"About a seven- to ten-minute drive on the cart. On foot, it would probably take twenty minutes or so. Security is pretty good at keeping the passengers in designated areas," Matt answered. "Anyway, Thomas drove. He and Diego usually went together on these missions while I stayed behind and worked the bar, because some passengers like to stay on the ship. So the bar is always open. While we were on the golf cart, I asked Thomas what happened with Melodie." Matt reached for another can of soda. He popped the top and took a long swallow.

"Thomas acted like it was no big deal. He said, 'That bitch was drunk and she fell off the ship.' I asked him what had happened, but he got pissed and told me to mind my own business. So then I asked him where we were going and what we were supposed to do. He said that I asked too many questions."

"What did you do while you were at Asylum Harbor?" Drake asked. Rachel could sense he was getting a little impatient.

"Thomas said we were supposed to be stocking the ship with items that were running low. I found this to be a bit unusual because we always restocked before the ship left Freeport. When I questioned it, Andy said we'd run out of certain liquors and had to restock from supplies at Asylum Harbor. This was not true because I know what we had on hand. Diego and I do inventory, and I'd know if we were out of something."

"Where did you go to restock?" Drake asked.

"We rode along this trail for about three miles before we came across a large plantation house. Thomas told me the house was used for visiting executives. Then we passed a row of bungalows—more staff accommodations, apparently—then a big warehouse. We pulled up to a side door, where a guy was waiting for us. We loaded a trailer with about twenty cardboard boxes. After that, we hitched it to the cart. The whole process took about fifteen minutes. I asked Thomas if the cart could pull a heavy load, and he just laughed. Said the golf cart was retrofitted for speed and towing capacity."

"Did the guy waiting for you say anything to Thomas?"

Matt thought back. "No, not anything specific that I remember. I'm not even sure if he spoke English."

"Then where did you go?" Mike got a lot more interested in the conversation.

"We took the same path back. As we passed the main plantation house, I saw something weird."

"What was that?" Mike asked.

"Two people walking along a pathway that led from the house. It was just a quick glance in between the palm trees, but I saw a girl that looked a lot like Melodie Sayers. I told Thomas to stop and back up. I told him that I saw the girl who was missing, but he just laughed and said I was losing my mind."

"What was she doing when you saw her?" Mike asked.

"Like I said, it was just a quick glance, but she was walking and the man was holding on to her elbow." Matt stood up and motioned for Stacy to stand beside him. He grabbed her elbow. "Like this. He was kind of guiding her down the pathway. She looked a little unsteady on her feet."

"What was she was wearing?"

Matt closed his eyes like he was remembering that day. "A pair of shorts and a T-shirt, I think. It all happened so quick."

"What happened after that?" Mike prompted.

"We pulled up to the dock and loaded the boxes onto the tender. I suppose they were taken onto the ship. I went back to my cabin after that and slept until my next shift."

"How long after that did you quit the cruise line?" Drake asked.

"When we got back to port the next day, I was told I was being moved back to baggage. No explanation about why. I had a really uneasy feeling since we left Asylum Harbor. I had a few days off before the next cruise, but I never went back. I didn't want to work baggage again, and I just didn't like the vibe. I think Johansen suspected something was wrong, too. When I told him what I'd seen, he said that I was better off not talking about it."

"I met the other bartender, Johansen, when I took my cruise. He told me to talk to Matt and gave me his number," Stacy explained.

"Where's Johansen now?" Rachel asked.

Stacy and Matt looked at one another.

"Don't know," Matt said, shrugging his shoulders. "It's like he fell off the face of the earth. After Stacy got in touch with me the first time about an interview, I tried to call him. His number was disconnected, and another friend from the ship said he'd just up and quit. No one knew how to reach him."

Rachel looked to Stacy for confirmation. "Have you been able to find him?"

"No. We tracked him down to his apartment in Miami, but his roommate said he came home one day, packed up his stuff, and moved back to Mexico."

"Is there enough evidence for us to look around Asylum Harbor?" Rachel asked Drake.

Drake rubbed his chin and looked at Mike. "No. We don't know what to look for. It would just be a fishing expedition. We could never get a warrant."

Rachel got up from her chair and looked Drake straight in the eye. "Can I speak to you outside?"

They exited the conference room. Drake leaned against the wall with his arms crossed.

"We have to get on that island. Amber could be there."

"I agree that something strange is going on there, but let's leave the drug investigation to the DEA. Our witness saw Amber forced into an SUV with Shawn. What makes you think she's on Asylum Harbor?"

"Matt saw Melodie Sayers. It's worth taking a look."

"Matt thought he saw a girl that looked like Melodie. That's not enough for us to storm the island and search for Amber. Now, Mike—he may have enough to go on with the DEA."

"Were you not just with me at the governor's house when he reamed us out? His daughter is missing, and while this might be a dead end, that's a chance we can't afford to lose." Rachel threw her hands up in the air. "You wanted my help on this case. I'm telling you that Asylum Harbor is where we need to search next."

"First of all, the governor requested you for this case. We didn't." Drake held his hand up when Rachel tried to interrupt. "Phipps and I have a meeting with the police department, and we'll see what they have so far. While we're at it, I'll see about getting us on Asylum Harbor." Drake walked back over to the conference room door. "But just remember, we have to do things by the book. I can't go guns blazing onto the island without proper authority. We have to work together with the local police and DEA. I have to make the case in court."

"I understand that, Drake. You have to do things by the book." Rachel lowered her voice. "But I don't, and time is ticking."

CHAPTER 32

"What was so important that couldn't wait?" Rachel wondered aloud.

She was waiting with Drake to see the governor. He'd wanted to see them immediately.

"I don't know. All his aide would tell me is that something came up and he needed to discuss it with us right away."

Governor Knowles walked into the room at the same time the doorbell rang.

"Sorry for the wait," he said as he sat down. "Sarah will be down in a minute. She's very upset."

"What happened?" Drake asked.

"I think it's better that Sarah—" he started to say when a commotion broke out in the foyer. They heard shouting, and Governor Knowles excused himself to see what was going on.

Rachel and Drake exchanged puzzled glances. "This just gets better and better," Rachel said.

"Calm down, Stephanie," they heard him say. "Let's sit down and talk. Nadia, please tell Sarah her sister is here."

Rachel leaned over toward Drake and whispered, "Sister?"

The governor walked in with his guest. Rachel couldn't help but let out a small gasp. Looking at the visitor was like seeing an older version of Amber.

The woman had long, messy blonde hair, beautiful blue eyes, and the same full lips as Amber. She was wearing a hot-pink tank top, faded blue jeans, and a pair of worn flip-flops.

Governor Knowles cleared his throat. "Rachel, Drake, I'd like you to meet Stephanie Sloane, Sarah's twin sister." He paused for a second. "And Amber's biological mother."

CHAPTER 33

"Hello, Stephanie." Sarah walked into the room, clearly not excited to see her sister. "I take it you've met Rachel and Drake."

"I was just getting around to that," Governor Knowles said. "Drake is an agent with the FBI and Rachel is with Florida Omni Search. They're assisting us with the search for Amber."

Rachel was at a loss for words. *Stephanie is Amber's mother? What the hell is going on here?*

"Where's Amber? What happened to her?" Stephanie asked, slurring her words.

"Let's get something to drink and talk." Sarah tried to grab Stephanie's arm.

"No!" Stephanie jerked her arm away and almost fell. The governor grabbed her around the waist to steady her.

"Stephanie, why don't you go upstairs and freshen up. Then we'll talk." Governor Knowles tried to calm her down.

Tears flowed down her cheeks. "You may have stolen Amber from me once, but you won't do it again. She's *my* daughter! I want to know what happened to her!" Stephanie turned her gaze to Sarah. "You did this—to keep her away from me."

"That's enough, Stephanie. Come on. Let's go." Governor Knowles took her firmly by the hand and tried to lead her out of the room.

"I came here to find my daughter." Stephanie turned her attention to Rachel. "Do you know where she is?" The fight seemed to drain her and she fell limp against the governor.

"Not yet," Rachel said. "We're still looking for her and following up on leads."

"As soon as you get settled, we'll all sit down and talk. Rachel and Drake can give us an update on the search. Okay?" Governor Knowles said calmly, like he was speaking to a child instead of an adult woman.

"Okay." Stephanie looked resigned as she walked with the governor out of the room.

"Sorry about that," Sarah sat down and ran her hands through her hair. "This is what we wanted to see you about. Before it got into the media. You see, we adopted Amber when she was a few months old."

"The resemblance is uncanny," Rachel said.

Sarah nodded. "Stephanie and I are fraternal twins. Amber favors her mother more than me."

"How did you come to raise Amber?" Drake asked.

Sarah sighed. "I guess I should start at the beginning. Even though we're twins, we couldn't be more unalike. Stephanie has always been more troubled. In high school, I was the studious one and Stephanie was the rebellious one. While I won academic awards and dancing trophies, Stephanie did drugs and ran away from home several times. She was diagnosed with a learning disability, but instead of getting her the help she needed, my mother babied Stephanie. She made excuses for her, which made the situation worse instead of better."

"Undiagnosed learning disabilities—or even if they're diagnosed but left untreated—do tend to disrupt kids' lives," Rachel observed.

"I suppose. Dad traveled so much that he left all the decisions about Stephanie up to our mom. Anyway, I went away to college and Stephanie stayed home and bounced from job to job. I met John at school and we got married right after graduation. Then Stephanie got pregnant. She wanted to keep the baby, but she couldn't support herself, let alone a child. John and I wanted kids and we'd started trying right away. But after my second miscarriage, we had some tests and found out that we'd never have children."

"I'm sorry," Rachel said.

Sarah's voice trembled as she told her story. "That news was hard for me to take. So when we found out that Stephanie was pregnant, we offered to help her. At first, she refused, but after the baby was born, reality hit. Stephanie realized she couldn't raise a baby and still go out and party every night. Our mom had just passed away with cancer, and Stephanie had nobody else to turn to."

Rachel could tell this was difficult for her to explain. As the governor's wife, always in the public eye, Sarah put on a good face. She was a very popular public figure, spending her time doing charity work. Not only was Sarah beautiful and married to a handsome, powerful politician, she was very lovable and the public couldn't get enough of her. But now, Rachel knew she was seeing a rare side of Sarah Knowles.

"When Amber was three months old, Stephanie took us up on our offer. She had no income, no job, and no real desire to get one. So we took Amber. About three months later, Stephanie disappeared. She was gone for a week. I was worried out my mind. We hired a private investigator who eventually found Stephanie."

"Where was she?" Rachel asked.

"A seedy motel outside of Panama City Beach with some guy she barely knew. When the PI found her, she was drugged out of her mind." Sarah grabbed a tissue and dabbed at the corner of her eyes. "We put her in rehab and she agreed to let us adopt Amber. She promised to clean herself up and go to a local community college. We offered to support her if she stayed in school."

"How did that work out?" Rachel asked.

"I wanted so badly for her to straighten up, but deep down, I knew from past experience she wouldn't do it. I'd seen our mother bribe Stephanie before, and it never worked. She'd try, and then give up. The drugs had a stranglehold on her. Stephanie lasted at community college about one month. One afternoon she never came home after class, and I knew she was gone. That time she stayed away for over a year. The adoption had already gone through, so we just moved on with our lives."

"Not many people know about the adoption?" Rachel asked.

"Only family members. The general public doesn't know that Amber is adopted. We'd appreciate if you kept this private."

Governor Knowles came back in the room. "Stephanie's resting upstairs. Apparently, she saw the news about Amber and caught a flight down here. She came straight here from the airport."

"Does Amber know she's adopted?" asked Drake.

"No, she doesn't. Stephanie's kept her word on that. And we'd like to keep it that way," Sarah answered.

"We all agreed it was best that Amber didn't know. She thinks Stephanie is her aunt," Governor Knowles said. "That's the reason I asked you to come here. I wanted to tell you about the situation with Stephanie. We tried to call her yesterday before the press conference to let her know about Amber before she heard it on the news. We couldn't reach her." He scrubbed his face with his hands.

"We don't want this situation with Stephanie to distract attention from Amber's disappearance."

"Yes, of course," Rachel and Drake both agreed.

"Does Stephanie have any relationship with Amber?" Rachel asked. She was confused about why Stephanie would just show up after not showing any interest in her daughter before.

"Not much. Stephanie doesn't attend family functions. She didn't even show up at Amber's high school graduation a few weeks ago," Sarah said. "She stays pretty much to herself, and we prefer it that way."

"I guess that sounds harsh to you," Governor Knowles added.

"We're not here to judge you. We appreciate your letting us know," Rachel said. "Besides, it may be a good thing that Stephanie is here. She could be helpful."

Governor Knowles and Sarah looked at her like she was crazy. "The only thing Stephanie would do is get in the way," he commented.

CHAPTER 34

The Royal Bahamas Police Force was located near the center of Freeport. The one-level pink stucco building had white columns and was adorned by a red crest that spelled out *Courage, Integrity, and Loyalty*. Drake and Phipps had set up a meeting with Assistant Commissioner Johnson, who was in charge of the Knowles investigation. They met with him in a small, cramped office filled with file boxes and discarded magazines. Johnson was a large man all the way around. He stood at six and a half feet, and weighed well over two hundred and fifty pounds.

"Welcome, Agents Reynolds and Phipps," Johnson said as he greeted them.

"Thanks for seeing us on short notice," Drake said as they sat in tiny, worn chairs in front of Johnson's desk.

"What can I do for you?"

"We have some information that we believe may led us to Amber Knowles."

"Okay. Let's hear it."

"We interviewed a witness that told us SeaScape Enterprises was involved in illegal activities on their private island, Cabana Cay. We'd like to check it out."

Johnson leaned back in his chair and contemplated what Drake was telling him.

"Who's this witness, and what type of illegal activity are we talking about?"

"A former employee of SeaScape. He mentioned that he saw a woman who looked like she was in distress. A woman who..." Drake paused, not quite sure how to continue. Phipps and Drake had assured Mike that they wouldn't compromise the DEA's investigation and bring up the possibilities of drug smuggling. But they needed the cooperation of the Royal Bahamas Police Force if they were to investigate the island.

"Who resembled Melodie Sayers," Phipps finished for him. "A former passenger on the *SeaStar* who was believed to have fallen overboard."

Johnson looked skeptical. "Where did you find this former employee?"

Phipps watched as Drake consulted his notepad, even though he knew it wasn't needed.

"His name is Matt Danbury," Drake answered. "Stacy Case, an investigative reporter with the *Miami Sun*, has been working on a series of stories about cruise ship crimes. She came to us with information from a couple of former employees of the *SeaStar*. They claimed to have witnessed a girl on Cabana Cay who may have been held on the island against her wishes. She looked like Melodie Sayers."

"I see," Johnson said as he shuffled some papers across his desk. "And you think Amber is being held against her will on the island?"

"Exactly." Drake looked over at Phipps. "We'd like to go to the island and check things out."

Johnson seemed to think about it. "Be right back." He abruptly got up and left the room.

"Wonder what that was about," Phipps asked as soon as Johnson left.

Drake just shrugged his shoulders. "Don't know."

Drake took the time to look around the bare-bones office. Besides the beat-up desk, leather chair, and two guest chairs, the decor was nil. File boxes were stacked haphazardly against the walls. There was one picture frame on the desk. Drake leaned over and turned the frame around. Staring back at him was a beautiful woman and little girl beaming at the camera.

"My wife and daughter," said a voice behind him.

"Oh, sorry. Curiosity always gets the best of me," Drake said, as he flipped the frame around. "How old is your daughter?"

"She would have been fifteen years old this year."

Drake was taken aback by his answer.

"My wife and daughter died in an accident a few years ago."

"Oh, I'm sorry. I didn't know."

"Of course you didn't." Johnson waved his hand, brushing away the sympathy. "Thank you. It's okay." He settled back in his chair. "Now, about this business of Cabana Cay. I spoke to the lead investigator on the case, and we can arrange to have one of our men go with you to take a look around the island. We'll set up a time and get back to you later today."

Phipps looked over at Drake. He looked unhappy, but he didn't complain. Instead, he slid his business card over to Johnson. "Here's my number. I look forward to hearing from you."

They got up and followed Johnson to the front of the building. Officers passed them in the hallway, but the activity seemed almost languid compared to cop shops in the U.S. *It's the heat*, Drake thought. *Or maybe less crime.*

The assistant commissioner held the door open for them, ushering them out. "I'll be in touch."

Drake was silent as he pulled the car out of the parking lot. He reached over and cranked up the AC.

"I wonder what that was all about," Phipps broke the silence.

"I don't know, but I don't like it. He should have questioned us more about the disappearance." Drake jerked his thumb toward the police station.

"I agree," Phipps nodded.

Drake turned the car toward the hotel. "Let's hope this is the lead that'll break the case."

CHAPTER 35

Amber didn't know how long she'd been sedated. The window in her room was heavily curtained and she couldn't tell if it was day or night. The last thing she remembered was the nurse who gave her some water before pumping something into her IV.

It took a minute for her eyes to adjust to the dark. Then she struggled to sit up and get a better look around the room. To her shock, she realized she wasn't alone. A dark figure sat in the chair across from her bed.

"I see you're up." A man's voice.

Amber was too scared to speak at first.

"Who are you?" she said, finally finding her voice. She was still hoarse.

She heard a click, a soft light came on, and she got her first look at her visitor.

An older gentleman—maybe her dad's age—dressed in an expensive charcoal-gray suit, his dark hair slicked back, stared at her. At first Amber thought that he was a good-looking man, but his smile, like that of a Cheshire cat, gave her the shivers. He looked familiar somehow.

"Hello, Amber. My name is Enzo Morrotti. I own the *SeaStar* cruise ship."

Suddenly, Amber realized where she'd seen him before. His picture was in her cabin. Amber processed this information through her fog-hazed brain. For some reason, the thought of having him in her room should be a comfort to her, but it wasn't. Instead, a mix of anger and confusion raced through her body. She felt blazingly hot from a mix of the drugs and her emotions. She wanted to kick off the sheets covering her body.

"Why are you here?"

The corners of his mouth upturned and he smiled as though the question amused him.

"I'm checking to see how you're doing. I heard you had quite an experience on the ship." Morrotti stood up and walked over to the side of the bed. He was taller than she'd thought—over six feet—and lean with muscle. He reached over and poured her a glass of ice water.

She paused for a few seconds before eagerly taking the cup of water. The ice water tasted delicious and soothed her raw throat.

"Take it easy. You don't want to get sick. Slow sips," he said in a fatherly way.

"Why am I here?" she asked again.

"You're hurt. We brought you to a private clinic to recuperate."

"I understand that. But where are my friends?" Amber asked. When he didn't answer right away, a feeling of dread settled into the pit of her stomach. "I'm sure everyone is worried about me."

"We'll talk about that in a minute." Morrotti hesitated before he spoke again. "I need to discuss something with you first."

"What?" Amber sat up straighter and tried to relax. She didn't want him to know that she was scared.

"I want you to tell me what happened while you were aboard the *SeaStar*." His crystal-blue eyes locked into hers.

Amber thought about his question for a moment. Of course she remembered most of what happened on the cruise, but some parts were still a little fuzzy. Like how she got here. Her last thought was of her and Josh on the lifeboat.

What she couldn't figure out is why the owner of the cruise ship was here asking these questions. Why not the police or the FBI? And where the hell were her friends? Her parents?

"I don't remember that much," she finally said. She leaned over to take another sip of water and then winced from the pain in her ribs. "Just that I felt sick. One of the crew members walked me back to my cabin. After that is when things start to get a little hazy."

"Do you remember the name of the crew member that helped you?"

She wasn't sure how much to tell him. Something didn't feel right about his questions. He was trying too hard to make her feel comfortable. Her heartbeat kicked into overdrive and she wanted to bolt from the room.

"Josh." Amber forced herself to meet his gaze. To show him that she wasn't afraid despite her heart jumping out of her chest. "Josh was his name," she repeated.

"How much more do you remember?"

"He helped me to the cabin. When I told him that I didn't feel well, he offered to go to the infirmary to get me some medicine." She debated about telling him more until she understood what he wanted from her. "The last thing that I remember is waiting for him to come back."

Morrotti looked at her suspiciously. He cleared his throat. "So you have no idea how you got off the ship?"

"No." She rubbed her hand along the right side of her head. "I have a bump on my head. I must have fainted or passed out and hit it when I fell. That must be how I hurt my ribs, too." She looked over at Morrotti to gauge his reaction. He eased away from her bedside and sat in the chair again. He looked at her, stone-faced, with no emotion.

"Yes, you were in bad shape when we found you."

"You asked me how I got off the ship," Amber said confused. "I don't know. Where did you find me?"

"On the Freeport shoreline. My security crew found you."

She knew he was lying. Why was he here? Why was he so eager to find out what she remembered? Something didn't add up. She had to get out of this creepy place.

"Where are my parents?" she asked again. "They should be here by now. I want to call them."

Morrotti settled back and smiled. "I think we both know your parents aren't coming. Now tell me what you know about Josh McCain."

CHAPTER 36

Rachel woke up a few minutes before the alarm went off. The time was almost 5:00 a.m., her usual time to get up. A creature of habit whether she was on the road or at home, she always started the morning with a cup of coffee, strong with a splash of cream. Then no matter where she was, if the weather was good and water was available, Rachel took her stand-up paddleboard out for a spin. Her YOLO board was too hard to travel with, but the hotel concierge had hooked her up with a rental place on the island. She had missed the last couple of days due to *The Today Show* appearance and flying down to the Bahamas, so she was eager to get out on the board today. Paddling always helped to clear her head and reenergize her.

While waiting for her coffee to brew, Rachel put a rash guard over her red bikini and grabbed a towel and sunscreen. Today was going to be a good day. She could just feel it.

She filled her to-go cup with coffee, threw her cell phone and keys into her bag, and left the room. The concierge had arranged for a board to be delivered to the hotel for her, and she picked it up at the desk and headed toward the beach. The paddleboard was a standard twelve-footer, similar to the one she had at home. She'd be comfortable on it.

The sun was just peeking over the horizon, adding an orange hue to the brilliant-purple skies. As soon as Rachel's feet hit the sand, she felt her tension melt away. Making sure her waterproof backpack was secured, she slung it over her shoulder and then gently pushed the board into the water. With one hand holding a paddle and the other gripping her board, she expertly straddled the board and then stood up. Dipping her paddle into the water, she stroked evenly through the small waves, determined to explore.

Rachel loved having the Caribbean waters all to herself. She glanced down just as a huge stingray swam under her board. Colorful fish darted in and out around the coral reef. She let her mind wander as she paddled.

The thought of visiting Asylum Harbor was exciting. She was anxious to find something that would lead to Amber's safe return. After studying her maps last night, she realized that they had a large task at hand. The island was huge and there was a lot of ground to cover. Cabana Cay took up only a small southern portion of the island, but Asylum Harbor was vast, with a lot of inhabitable-looking areas. She figured that they'd probably be there all day, and she'd need every available volunteer on hand to accomplish an effective search. By the time they finished, she'd have left nothing unturned. If Amber was there, they'd find her.

She wondered if Mike was planning on attending the search. Drake hadn't mentioned it the last time they'd talked. She knew Mike was worried about finding Shawn—and salvaging his own investigation as well. From the little time that she'd spent with Mike, she could tell he had the same passion and fire about his job that she did about hers.

He wasn't a guy she'd typically be attracted to, but something about him just felt right. She tried to think of the things that made him so different from her ex-husband and all the other men she'd dated. *For one*, she thought, *he's a good listener*, which moved him quickly up to the top of her list. Plus, he was a good-looking man, and beneath that tough exterior, she was sure he was a teddy bear. And she couldn't deny that the attraction was mutual. When he touched her, she felt the sizzle that romance novels always described but she'd so easily dismissed.

Like a schoolgirl, she fantasized about what it would be like to kiss him. She wondered if his kiss would be tender and soft, or hungry and passionate. *Probably passionate*, she thought, as she made her way back to the shore. She could feel the burn in her arms and legs as she jumped off the board and let the cool waters wash over her. She lugged her board onto the sand and prepared to head back to the hotel. She was just minutes away from—

"Hey, Rach." A voice interrupted her thoughts.

She was surprised to see Mike standing on the sidewalk. He was dressed in running shorts and a tank top. His muscles glistened with sweat.

"Hi. What are you up to?" Rachel felt herself blushing.

"Just finishing my run. What about you?" He looked over at her board.

"Paddleboarding," Rachel said. "My Rx for stress relief."

"I bet. I've seen those around the beach. I need to try that sometime."

"I've got a board at home. The concierge set me up with this one to use. You'll have to go with me next time." Rachel dipped her head to the side and took a handful of hair, twisting it around in her hand, wringing out the excess water.

Mike seemed to consider her offer. "Maybe I will. Do you go every morning?"

"I try. It's been a little hectic lately."

"Right." Mike swiped his forehead with a hand towel. "Any news on the photo?"

Rachel still couldn't shake that someone was messing with her, but a part of her wanted to believe that it was real. Mallory was alive and someone had her. The photo looked like the real deal.

"Nothing yet. Drake sent it into his lab, but we haven't heard anything."

"Let me know if I can help in any way." Mike smiled at her. "I need to get back to the room and shower. Get ready for our meeting this morning."

"Me too." Rachel picked up her board.

"Need help with that?"

She expertly hoisted the board on top of her head to distribute the weight. "Thanks, I got it. See ya in a few."

Rachel could feel Mike's eyes on her as she walked across the street to the hotel.

She left the board with the front desk and headed up to take a shower. She was eager to see what Drake had in store for them at the meeting.

CHAPTER 37

"We're leaving in a few minutes to head over to Cabana Cay." Rachel held her cell phone in one hand while searching for her purse with the other. "If you could ask Red to call his friend Vance Pearson who runs a charter here in the Bahamas…We may need to use his boat if something turns up."

Rachel gave her final instructions to Janine before she left to meet up with Drake and Phipps. She'd been crushed at this morning's meeting to find out that they'd be escorted by the Royal Bahamas Police Force and that a cruise line representative would give them a guided tour. So much for a full, unencumbered search of the island. She wasn't even allowed to bring her search team. With Drake and his team running the show, she didn't have much choice in the matter.

She ended her conversation with Janine and gathered the rest of her stuff. According to Drake, this would just be a look-see operation, although she knew that he had agents ready to go if they found something of interest. So she had a backup plan of her own as well. Her team would be on standby, waiting for further instructions.

Rachel met Drake and Phipps in the lobby and they drove to the boat dock, where a representative of the Royal Bahamas Police

Force would meet them for the trip to Cabana Cay. This was supposed to be a surprise visit, but somehow Rachel thought it would be anything but that.

The marina was busy with boats coming and going. Charter fishermen hauled tourists out for a day of deep-sea fishing, private yachts headed out for leisurely cruises, and colorful sailboats ready for a fun day skimmed the coastline. Drake spotted the slip where a thirty-two-foot cabin cruiser waited for them.

"Hi, I'm Quinn Miller with Special Ops. Assistant Commissioner Johnson asked me to give you folks a lift to Cabana Cay." He waved them onto the boat. "Welcome aboard."

Drake stepped on board first and helped Rachel. After everyone was settled on the deck, the captain moved them out into rather calm waters.

"Did you contact the folks at Cabana Cay to let them know we were coming?" Drake asked Quinn.

He nodded. "Assistant Commissioner Johnson arranged for us to take a tour of the island and meet with the manager."

"How long will the trip take?" Rachel asked.

"About thirty-five minutes or so." Quinn leaned back into his chair as he answered. He was slim and dressed in uniform blues. His dark skin contrasted with the white boat.

Everyone was quiet with his or her thoughts as they approached Cabana Cay. It was just as Matt had described. From afar, the island looked very tranquil. Beautiful sugary beaches with shallow turquoise waters. Hammocks strung up between palm trees, gently swaying with the breeze. A lone man in the distance raked the sand to smooth away the footprints the previous cruise passengers had left. *Amber's footprints should have littered that beach*, Rachel thought. She should have been having fun with her friends, playing volleyball and dancing under the palm trees.

The captain radioed the island manager to let them know of their arrival. Rachel would have preferred to come unannounced, but nothing could be done about that now.

As they disembarked, they were met by a gentleman dressed in a SeaScape uniform—white pressed shorts and a navy-blue shirt with the company logo on the right breast pocket. His accent confirmed that he was a native of the Bahamian islands.

"Welcome to Cabana Cay," he greeted them warmly. "I'm Joe Vermillion, the island manager."

Quinn stepped forward and shook his hand. "Sorry for any inconvenience. As Assistant Commissioner Johnson told you, we're still searching for the missing teenager from the *SeaStar* cruise liner. Miss Amber Knowles."

The man nodded his head but didn't speak.

Quinn continued, "In light of some new witness statements, we thought it was prudent to search the island."

"I spoke to Mr. Morrotti, owner of the *SeaStar*, and he instructed me to tell you that you have our full cooperation," Joe replied.

"Very well, then," Quinn said. "These are Special Agents Drake Reynolds and Lee Phipps with the FBI. And Ms. Rachel Scott with Florida Omni Search."

"Nice to meet all of you." Joe pointed toward the golf cart. "I'll take you on a quick tour of the island first? Then you can ask any questions you feel necessary. Cabana Cay is a large island, so we'll take the golf cart."

The golf cart had two seats up front and three rows of seats behind it, seating up to eight adults. Rachel sat up front with Joe and the guys sat behind her. He gave them a quick history of the island. Most of what he said they already knew from Stacy.

"Mr. Morrotti bought this island in August of two thousand two from an eccentric billionaire. Morrotti wanted a private island excursion for his cruise line passengers to enjoy."

"How long have you been with the cruise line company?" Rachel asked him.

"Since two thousand three. I came on board in the middle of the island renovations. Mr. Morrotti invested a lot of money to get the island ready. There wasn't much here at the time. Just a couple of bungalows and a main residence. He fixed those up for employees, and then built the restaurant, bar, and dive shop for the guests."

"Does the staff live here full time?" Drake asked.

"We have eight people who live on the island."

"What do they do?"

"I oversee the whole island. We also have a cook and maintenance and security personnel who stay here full time as well. The rest of the employees arrive on the island with the ship. The dive shop manager, bar staff, waitresses, and activity coordinator all come from the ship. Several employees pull double duty," Joe explained. "Work on the ship and on the island."

The golf cart came to a rolling stop at a line of small bungalows.

"These are the private cabanas that we rent out to passengers for five hundred dollars a day." Joe got out of the cart and led them up the stairs to the cabana on the end. He unlocked the door and led the way inside. "As you can see, they have air-conditioning. Living area with sofa and small kitchenette. Compact fridge holds cold drinks. Private bath with shower—indoors and outdoors."

Rachel walked around the cabana. It was about three hundred square feet, with an ample outside deck. She could see it would be a nice refuge from the heat of the day.

"These cabanas are kept locked during off days from the cruise lines?" Phipps asked.

"Yes. We clean after guest departures and then do a quick run through before the next guests arrive. The only occupants are cruise passengers. Our staff accommodations are located on the other end of the island."

"Can we see those?" Drake asked.

"Sure," Joe answered without hesitation.

They all climbed back on the golf cart and headed down the trail. Within a few minutes, they'd left behind the fun part of the island, and the trail became smaller, more overgrown, and less inhabited.

"Not many people get to see the behind-the-scenes stuff," Joe commented. They pulled up to a gate and he pressed a button on a remote-control device. "This area is off-limits to our guests. For safety and security reasons."

And to hide dead bodies, Rachel thought, but didn't say aloud.

The gate swung outward and Joe eased the cart through. Immediately, Rachel spotted a large warehouse off to the right.

Joe followed her gaze. "That's where maintenance keeps all their equipment, plus the other resort golf carts. The laundry facility and storage are there as well. We'll see that on the way out."

After a few hundred feet, they rolled to a stop. "These are our employee quarters. Five bungalows, each with two bedrooms, a kitchenette, bathroom, and living area. My wife and I live in that one." Joe pointed to one of the middle bungalows.

"Your wife works on the island as well?" Rachel asked.

"Yeah. She's a former nurse and runs the first-aid station while the passengers are onshore. She also helps out at the gift shop. Everyone pitches in during arrival days."

Joe unlocked the door to his bungalow and let everyone in.

Structurally, the bungalows were similar to the private cabanas, but larger to accommodate the needs of full-time employees. Joe's place was well kept. His wife had added personal touches, including family photos and monogrammed pillows.

"It's not much. We have a house in Freeport as well. Of course, most of our time is spent here on the island."

Rachel felt that she was intruding in his personal space. She took a quick look around and walked back outside with Drake and Mike. Everything seemed normal. But there was that nagging feeling Rachel always got when something was off. She couldn't put her finger on it. It was very quiet and eerie. Rachel felt a chill go down her spine.

"Who lives in the main residence?" Rachel asked.

"Mr. Morrotti uses it when he comes to visit."

"Which is how often?"

Joe paused for a second. "Um...about twice a year. Sometimes other people from the corporate office stay there as well."

"Is it occupied now?"

"Yes, it is. One of the regional directors is here."

"Can we take a look around?" Quinn asked.

"Sure. I believe they're out inspecting the island."

They followed him up the steps to the plantation-style house. Rachel admired the old home. It was a white two-story frame house with a wide front porch. Tropical foliage surrounded the yard. Joe pushed the screen door open and they followed him inside. Delicious smells came from the back of the home.

"Judy is cooking lunch." Joe sniffed the air. "Smells like her famous conch soup and corn muffins."

At the mention of her name, a lady wearing a red apron walked around the corner. She was petite with short, wavy salt-and-pepper hair. "Hello."

Joe made the introductions. "They're looking for the missing American girl."

"Oh, I see." Judy wore a puzzled expression. "Excuse me for asking, but I thought I saw on the news that she fell overboard. Why in the world are you looking for her here?"

Rachel thought she caught an irritated look that Joe shot Judy. Quinn answered for them. "It hasn't been determined what happened to her. We have to follow up on every lead."

"Certainly," Judy answered, and then changed the subject. "Would you like some conch soup? There is plenty for everyone."

"Thank you, but we still have some ground to cover," Quinn graciously declined.

"It sure smells good, though." Rachel's stomach growled. She wouldn't mind a taste of the island delicacy.

Joe showed them around the rest of the downstairs and then headed out to the back of the house. He pointed out a small shed that he explained held more equipment—mostly lawn care.

"Would you care to see anything else?"

"I think we're good here," Quinn said. "We don't want to disturb your guests."

"Very well. We'll take the cart back to the warehouse. Then finish up at the restaurant. I'll be happy to have the chef prepare you a sandwich and a cold drink for the ride back."

"That would be nice," Rachel answered for all of them.

A quick tour of the warehouse revealed what they expected. Laundrymen folded towels and the maintenance staff repaired equipment. The storage area contained items the staff needed to run this private island. Quinn seemed satisfied that everything was in order.

"Do you have any questions Joe could answer?" Quinn asked.

Drake looked around. "You mentioned you have several employees who stay here on the island. Other than Judy, do you have any young women who live here?"

"Judy is the only woman who stays on the island full time. Our security and maintenance staff are all men." If Joe thought the question was peculiar, he didn't show it.

"Do you run security cameras on the island?" Rachel asked.

Joe nodded. "Only on Cabana Cay around the restaurant and bar area. You'll have to talk to the head of security at SeaScape if you need more information."

"I think that does it. We appreciate your time," Drake told him.

Rachel felt differently. She thought that they'd only scratched the surface of the island. Remembering back to last night, when she'd looked at her maps, she knew the island was very large. It covered close to a thousand acres, and they still hadn't explored most of the terrain—or truly searched most of the buildings. She itched to get her people out here with equipment and take a look around without Joe to "guide" them. That probably wasn't going to happen, though.

Their last stop was the island's restaurant, Coco's Two BBQ. The restaurant featured pulled-pork sandwiches, hot dogs, hamburgers, rotisserie chicken, and salads. It was served buffet style, just like on the ship. The chef also prepared light meals for the staff who lived there year-round.

"This is Chef Tyree," Joe said, introducing them. "He'll fix a box lunch to take with you."

They all elected to try the pulled-pork BBQ sandwiches with chips and iced tea. Chef Tyree boxed the lunches up and put them in a large bag with plastic silverware.

"Have a safe trip back." Chef Tyree handed them the lunch.

"Can I answer any other questions for you?" Joe asked as he guided them back to the waiting boat.

Drake shook his head. "We appreciate your time, Joe."

"I hope you all come back again. Next time as cruise guests?" Joe laughed.

"Sure. Thanks again." Drake led the group back onto the boat.

Quinn took his lunch inside to eat with the captain. Drake, Phipps, and Rachel sat on the deck and ate in silence.

Phipps was the first to speak. "I don't know about you two, but something was a little off back there."

"I thought the same thing," Rachel said, relieved that she wasn't the only one who felt that way.

"I didn't see anything out of the ordinary," Drake commented.

"That's right—nothing out of the ordinary. Everything was just too…" Rachel trailed off in thought.

"Too normal?" Phipps finished for her.

"Yeah. Too normal," Rachel answered. "I don't know if it's because they knew we were coming or the island is just plain creepy. I would love to go back with some of my guys and equipment. Take a look around without the guided tour."

"Not possible. We were lucky that Assistant Commissioner Johnson set this up so quickly," Drake answered. "We'll just have to start from square one."

The boat slowed down, making its way to the dock.

Rachel pointed toward shore. "Wonder what's going on there." A few police cars and an ambulance were parked in the lot.

CHAPTER 38

Amber was never sure what time it was. Her room was kept dark most of the time. The nurse came in about every hour to check on her. She took her vital signs, although she seemed to know that Amber was feeling better and wasn't sick anymore.

She didn't know what was going on. She couldn't leave her room because the door was locked from the outside. But she wasn't tied up or threatened, and nobody seemed worried that she might scream. After Mr. Morrotti's visit, Amber thought that this was some kind of kidnapping plot. He wanted to get information about her involvement with Josh, but she'd repeatedly told him that she didn't know him that well. She was just a passenger on his cruise line. None of his questions made sense to her. Maybe he just wanted to get money out of her family because her dad was governor.

Whether these people wanted money or some kind of political connection, Amber knew now that she hadn't been "rescued." She wondered if Josh had been in on the scheme. He was insistent that she was in danger and needed to leave the ship with him. What she couldn't figure out was who'd tried to kill them on the cruise ship and how Josh fit into all this.

Nothing made sense to her anymore. She didn't know why she was here or what these people wanted. *Nothing good can come of this.* What she needed was a plan to escape.

She thought she was being held on an island—maybe she was still in the Bahamas. She could still taste the salt air, feel the ocean breezes, and hear the sounds of the tropics when the nurse occasionally left a window open for a bit of fresh air. Too bad there were security bars on the windows. That was her first clue this wasn't some kind of private clinic.

Amber knew she needed to get stronger, so she exercised. When the nurse left, she got up and stretched, did stomach crunches, push-ups, and jumping jacks. Her ribs and ankle still ached, but she pushed the pain out of her mind. She also did the visual imaging that her father had taught her. When she wanted something, she pictured the events in her mind exactly how she wanted them to happen.

And after her exercise routine every day, she planned her escape from Hell Island.

CHAPTER 39

Quinn asked them to stay on deck while he checked out the activity on the dock. After speaking to another officer for a few minutes, he made his way back to the boat.

"An accident. A deckhand got injured on the docks," Quinn explained. "You guys are good to go."

Drake thanked him for his time and said they would be in touch.

"Well, that was a disappointment," Rachel said.

"What did you expect? To find Amber hiding in one of the cabanas?" Drake asked.

"Of course not. It wouldn't be that easy. I just hoped we would see some of the weird goings-on that Matt suggested. It was basically a deserted, creepy island, just like he described."

"It's probably a different vibe when the passengers are there," Drake commented, walking back to the car.

Rachel agreed. "Probably. But I still can't shake that feeling. That feeling that something was off."

"We've got no proof that Amber was smuggled to that island. Everything looked on the up and up. I think we need to focus on where she was seen last. In Freeport, by the beach."

"That's a dead end. We've got no other witnesses other than Shondra, and she wasn't that much help."

"At least we know Amber's alive. Or she was at that point, anyway," Drake said.

"Still doesn't shake my bad feelings."

They got back to hotel and headed straight for the conference room. It had been cleaned of all the trash and clutter. The whiteboard still held Amber's last location and the timeline of her disappearance. Manila file folders had been stacked neatly in the center of the table.

Drake shook his head. "Cyndy and her OCD. She can't stand clutter. Her desk at headquarters is meticulous."

Cyndy walked back into the room. She was carrying a takeout bag from the Blue Palm restaurant. "Did I hear someone say my name?"

"Yeah. I was just telling Rachel about your OCD problems."

"Hey, I was raised to clean up after my messes." Cyndy plopped down on one of the leather conference room chairs. "What did you guys find out? Anything good?"

She pulled out her sandwich and wolfed it down in four bites. Then she rolled the aluminum wrap into a ball and tossed it across the room, where it landed in the trash.

"Nope. Nothing at all." Drake sat down across from Rachel. "That's the problem."

"We didn't see anything out of the ordinary," Rachel agreed.

"So let's take a look at what we do have." Cyndy wiped her mouth with a napkin and walked to the whiteboard. "Governor Knowles will want a report from us tonight. We need to give him something."

The whiteboard looked pretty bleak. Witness names were on the left side. Amber's friends, Nichole and Rowan, were at the top of the list because they'd been among the last to see Amber, and they knew the most about her movements that night. Consuela, the *SeaStar* staff person who'd seen Josh and Amber walking down the hall on the way to her suite, was on the list. Shondra, the witness who'd seen Amber and Shawn get into a SUV, was the only other person on the list. A timeline ran through the middle of the board.

"Here's what we know." Cyndy ran through the timeline again for what felt like the millionth time. "Amber disappeared from the *SeaStar* sometime between twelve thirty a.m. and two thirty a.m. Consuela was the last to see them when she delivered room service to the cabin next door. There's no video footage of them getting off the ship, nor did Josh/Shawn use his key card. A full search of the ship was conducted around four a.m., after which the captain informed the Coast Guard of a possible person overboard."

She grabbed an erasable marker from the whiteboard's tray. On a smaller board under *Notes*, she wrote, *What we don't know is HOW they got off the ship*. She then added, *Lifeboat found*.

"I talked to the cruise ship authorities about the lifeboat that was discovered along the Freeport shoreline. They said it came from a storage area in the engineering compartment of the ship. This lifeboat was part of a small inventory of damaged boats. So it looks like Josh/Shawn had an exit strategy in case something happened." Cyndy looked at Drake for approval.

"That's feasible. Mike told us that Shawn was well trained to get out of a sticky situation if it was warranted," Drake agreed.

"We're assuming that Shawn's undercover investigation was compromised and somehow Amber got in the way. Shawn and Amber escaped in the lifeboat. That wouldn't have been easy, so Shawn may have had help." Cyndy put the marker down and stood against the wall. "Maybe another crew member on the ship?"

"That's a distinct possibility," Drake added. "Given that his security card wasn't used and he wasn't caught on videotape. Amber, either."

"Shondra confirms that she saw Amber and Shawn get into a dark SUV. Possibly at gunpoint or under dire circumstances," Rachel added.

"Someone on the ship, someone who knew Josh was undercover, was notified that he was missing and set up a search for him." Cyndy picked up the marker and wrote, *Who?*

"Captain Martin or—who's the head of security on the *SeaStar* again?" Drake asked.

"Edward Schultz," Phipps said.

"Right, Edward Schultz," Drake said, and Cyndy scribbled the names down on the whiteboard.

"If Captain Martin or Edward Schultz set up a manhunt for Shawn and Amber and they were captured, where would they have taken them?" Rachel asked.

"Where's Mike Mancini when we need him? He'd be a big help now," Drake said, sounding frustrated. "What we suspect based on our initial investigation into Stacy's interviews with former employees is that the *SeaStar* is connected somehow to drug smuggling—and maybe more, if those reports about employees giving female passengers roofies are true. Unfortunately, we have no proof. Yet."

"And our little jaunt to Cabana Cay didn't come up with anything," Rachel confirmed.

"We should check out any company real estate holdings in Freeport and surrounding areas that the *SeaStar* or SeaScape Cruise Lines may own," Drake suggested.

"Already being done. I should have a report coming through sometime today," Cyndy answered.

"I'd love to get another crack at Cabana Cay. We didn't begin to cover the island." Rachel reached into her messenger bag and pulled out her maps. She smoothed out a large map of the island. "Asylum Harbor covers over half of the whole island. Cabana Cay is just a small portion of the south end. We didn't even go all the way around the island." Rachel tapped her pen on the map.

"What do you suggest? I don't think we'll be able to go back without a warrant or the support of the Royal Police, or both," Drake said.

"What if I go back as a passenger, like Stacy did?" Rachel asked. "Another cruise leaves in two days. Three nights with one day at Cabana Cay."

"We may not have two days," Cyndy said as, whiteboard duties finished, she sat back down in her chair.

"An unofficial night excursion, then? We can go by private boat and take a look around without Joe looking over our shoulder."

"We have to cooperate with local police. And they clearly don't want us poking around Asylum Harbor alone," Drake said.

"Well, *you* have to cooperate with them. *We*, Florida Omni Search, were requested by the family." Rachel couldn't resist a little dig. "I don't have to maintain any kind of diplomatic relations. A teenager is missing and at risk, and I'll do whatever it takes to find her."

"*You*, Florida Omni Search, have no authority at all," Phipps said, sounding annoyed. "You have no legal standing. No law enforcement credentials. You're here only because the FBI and the Bahamas Police allow it. You do something dumb and the cops here arrest you, you're just one more U.S. civilian who needs to get bailed out."

Rachel stared at him in shock. "Then I guess while you're off making nice with the local cops, I'll be careful not to get arrested when I cruise Asylum Harbor looking for our victim," she said.

"You don't believe she's here in Freeport?" Drake asked, already knowing her answer but trying to smooth over the roughened tempers.

"No." She looked at their skeptical faces. "I just have a feeling."

"Well, while you're wasting valuable time searching around Asylum Harbor, we'll see what we can find out around Freeport." Phipps got up and walked out of the room in a huff.

"What's his problem?" Rachel asked Drake.

He shrugged. "He got an ass-chewing from the boss. There's a lot of heat coming down right now. Director McIntosh wants us to find Amber Knowles yesterday."

"Well, that's understandable. Governor Knowles is pressuring everyone. He wants his daughter back." Rachel sighed. "I know the feeling."

CHAPTER 40

Amber was ready. Tonight was the night she'd escape. She had Nurse Judy's schedule down cold. The plan was elementary at best, but she'd tried it before, and it had pretty much worked—although that had been back when she was in high school and she'd wanted to sneak out of her house. As a plan, it wasn't much, but it was all she had.

She put the pillows under the sheets and propped them up so it looked like she was sleeping. Then she hid behind the door and waited for the nurse to check on her. Amber's plan was to attack her from behind, then make a run for it. The scary part was, she didn't know what was waiting for her on the other side. But she had to take the chance.

She hunched down behind the door and waited. Amber visually prepared herself for the attack. Weird, but she felt guilty because the nurse had been so nice to her. But the nurse must know that Amber was being held against her will. *Nothing personal, Nurse Judy, but I have to get out of here and find my way home*, Amber thought.

After what felt like an hour, Amber thought something was wrong. The nurse should have checked on her by now. As Amber started to worry, she heard faint footsteps coming down the hall toward her room. She took a deep breath and let it out slowly. *Here goes nothing.*

CHAPTER 41

Red Cooper had secured a boat from his friend Vance Pearson. They were waiting for Rachel and Stacy at the Freeport docks. Stacy had pleaded with Rachel to let her tag along, and Rachel agreed after realizing that Stacy knew the island pretty well and could be an asset to their search. Stacy had taken two cruises on the *SeaStar* and had provided Florida Omni Search and the FBI with valuable information, so Rachel gave her the thumbs-up. This would be a small, informal search. Rachel didn't want the rest of her crew tagging along. She figured they'd have less of chance being spotted with only the four of them.

"Hi ya, Red." Rachel gave him a quick hug.

Red Cooper was an original member of Rachel's team. Stocky, short, and bald, Red had gotten his nickname when he was younger and had a full head of red hair. Rachel had met Red while he was investigating Mallory's disappearance. At the time, he'd been a detective with the Miami PD. Rachel was impressed that he'd put his heart and soul into looking for her daughter. She'd felt that he was the only one who'd truly believed her story and that he'd done everything he could, within his limits, to help her.

Afterward, when Rachel set up Florida Omni Search, she approached Red about signing on. He hadn't needed much convincing. Red had been ready to retire from the Miami PD, but he hadn't been ready to pick up the golf clubs on a permanent basis yet, either. Now he was one of her most trusted and loyal team members.

After studying the maps of Asylum Harbor, they had decided to come around the north end of the island. Rachel wasn't sure how good security was on the remote part of the island, but she was prepared to find out.

"You girls ready to go?" Red asked.

"Ready as we can be," Stacy answered for them.

Rachel followed Red aboard, and he introduced them to his friend, the owner of the boat, Vance Pearson.

"Vance, nice to meet you. And thanks for helping us out." Rachel shook his hand. "Are you familiar with Asylum Harbor or Cabana Cay?"

He nodded. "As Red probably told you, I run a fishing charter. I retired down here from Miami a few years ago. I pretty much know my way around the islands. I've seen Asylum Harbor from afar, but I don't get too close." Vance looked over at Red. "They have patrols around the island."

"Patrols? What kind?" Rachel asked.

"A couple of times I've seen small speedboats cruising just offshore. I've heard talk around the docks about tight security there. You know, because of piracy, I guess."

"I don't think they're worried about piracy," Stacy said, rolling her eyes.

"We're going to find out real soon." Rachel grabbed the maps out of her messenger bag. "Let's sit down and go over the plan before we leave."

For a fishing charter boat, the accommodations were nice. *Vance must live on the boat full time*, Rachel thought. The cabin below had a small living area, with a kitchen, sleeping alcove, and bathroom.

She spread the map out on the table. It was a chart of all the islands surrounding Freeport.

"Nice. Where did you get that?" Vance asked.

"One of our techie guys at the office got it for me," Rachel said proudly.

"That's more updated than mine."

"We went to the island earlier today," Rachel explained. She told Vance and Red about their visit and what they saw. And more importantly, what they didn't see. "I know something is going on there and I want to get a closer look at the Asylum Harbor side."

Vance looked at Red.

"When she gets one of her hunches, she's usually right," Red said, shrugging his shoulders.

"I tend to agree with Rachel. Based on what my informant told us about possible drug smuggling on the island, I think we need to take a closer look," Stacy said.

"Let's get going, then. Sun is setting, perfect time for a little cruise," Vance said as he started to get up from his chair.

A loud noise startled the group. Rachel turned around in her seat. "What was that?"

"Stay here. I'll check it out." Red started for the deck as a figure appeared in the doorway.

Everyone sat in stunned silence. Rachel finally found her voice. "What are you doing here?"

CHAPTER 42

Amber tried to steady her breathing as she watched from behind the door. Nurse Judy walked over to her bedside and leaned over Amber's bed. Any second now she would realize that Amber wasn't in it. *Here goes nothing.* Amber sprang into action and ran full force into her. *Nurse Judy's made of steel*, Amber thought, almost staggering under the impact. She'd underestimated the nurse. Amber felt like she'd hit a brick wall. Where Amber had expected the nurse to feel soft and frail, Judy was built more like a truck. They tumbled over the bed and landed on the other side.

Amber then realized her mistake. This was not Nurse Judy. She froze in terror. If this wasn't the nurse, then who was in her room?

"What the hell..." a man's voice flowed up to her ear.

Amber started punching his face. She thought that Judy must have somehow known of her plan and sent someone else to her room instead. Amber's adrenaline kicked into overdrive. She had to escape.

"Amber. Stop," the voice said. "It's me, Josh. I'm here to help you."

She rolled off of him and made a run for the door. She didn't trust him. Didn't know *who* she could trust.

Josh jumped up and went after her, grabbing her arm. "Amber, wait. It's not safe to go by yourself."

Amber turned around and faced him in the darkness. "How do I know I can trust you? Where have you been?"

"I don't have time to explain. But believe me, we have to leave now while we can. We only have a small window of opportunity."

"You said that last time, and we were caught." Amber stood defiantly.

"Look, I was working on the ship as an undercover DEA agent. My cover's been blown, and now we're both in danger. These are very nasty people we're dealing with, and we have to get out of here. Follow close behind me. We have to move quickly."

Seeing no other options, she followed quietly behind Josh. Once they got into the hallway, Amber could see that she was being held in a house, not a hospital or clinic like she'd been told. In the small living area, a TV blared the news. Judy sat slumped over in a recliner.

"Is she dead?" Amber whispered.

Josh shook his head. "Just knocked out."

To the left was a kitchen with a small countertop and bar stools. The ice maker dropped a load of ice and they both froze at the sudden noise.

Josh opened the door and they moved quietly out into the night. Amber's feet sank into soft sand, which confirmed that she was still on an island. They quickly made their way around the house to where an ATV was parked.

Amber jumped into the front seat and Josh took the wheel. The moon was full and gave them plenty of light, which was both a good and bad thing. They could see where they were going, but anyone who might be looking for them could see them easily as well. From the corner of her eye, Amber noticed movement behind some vegetation. She gasped when a man jumped out and held a gun at them.

Oh no, not again, she thought as she closed her eyes tightly.

CHAPTER 43

Stephanie Sloan tentatively stepped inside the cabin doorway. "I want to help." Her eyes pleaded with Rachel.

"Who is this?" Red asked Rachel.

Rachel took a deep breath. "Everyone, this is Stephanie Sloan. Stephanie is Amber's aunt."

Rachel had told Red and Stacy about the meeting with the governor but kept to herself the part about Stephanie's true identity as Amber's biological mother. She didn't think it was crucial for anyone else to know that information, plus she made a promise to the governor not to reveal their family secret.

"Stephanie, how did you get here?" Rachel asked.

Stephanie gave her a sly smile. "I followed you from the hotel."

"I don't think it's a good idea for you to be here."

"You're going to look for Amber and I want to help you. I promise I won't get in the way."

Rachel looked at the rest of the group. "Give us a minute, please." She motioned for Stephanie to follow her outside onto the deck.

Stephanie had pulled back her long blonde hair into a French braid and she looked comfortable in white capri pants and a turquoise

T-shirt. It amazed Rachel how much Amber looked like her. She wondered if Amber had ever given any thought as to how she favored her "aunt."

"Do John and Sarah know you're here?"

Stephanie shook her head. "I told Sarah I was going shopping and borrowed their rental car."

"If you really want to help, then I can arrange for you to pass out flyers or work the tip lines. But you can't come with us."

Stephanie stood with her arms folded across her chest. "Don't patronize me. I don't want to pass out flyers. I want to go with you to find Amber, and I won't take no for answer."

Rachel started to say something and Stephanie held out her hand. "Please, Rachel. All my life I've been the irresponsible one. I wanted to be a good mom to that little girl, but I tried and I failed. When I saw Amber was missing, something inside of me just snapped." Tears slid down her cheeks and she wiped them with the sleeve of her T-shirt. "I haven't used since I've been here, and for once in my life, I'm thinking with a clear head. This is my chance to make things right. Please let me help you. I promise I won't get in the way."

Rachel stared at her for a minute. Knowing Stephanie's past history, Rachel didn't think involving her in the search for Amber was a good idea, but Rachel also knew the pain of losing your only child. Plus, if they did find Amber, having someone with them that Amber knew, would make a rescue run smoother. At least that is what Rachel hoped. "Okay, you can come. But you have to do what I ask and follow our plan."

"Thank you." Stephanie smiled as she followed Rachel back inside the cabin.

Rachel hoped she wouldn't regret this.

CHAPTER 44

Vance cut the engine and lights once they got close to the island. Even though it was one big island, there was a distinct difference between Asylum Harbor and Cabana Cay. Earlier in the day, with its colorful flowers, cabanas, and water toys, Cabana Cay had looked like a welcome retreat for tourists. Asylum Harbor, in contrast, now lay before them as dark and still as a tomb.

"If I remember correctly, there should be a path that leads to the heart of the island. It's only visible from the shoreline, though." Vance turned to the group. "We'll anchor here and take the dinghy to shore. It'll be quieter and easier to maneuver."

"Sounds good." Rachel got up and stretched. Her body vibrated with excitement.

"You got the flashlights?" Red asked.

"Right here." Rachel threw her bag over her shoulder. She was nervous but felt safe with Red. She knew that he'd be carrying his weapon, and Vance was probably carrying as well.

Vance lowered the small craft into the water. Rachel went first, carefully climbing down the ladder, followed by Stephanie and Stacy. They scooted over to make room for Red and Vance.

Rachel went over the plan with everyone again as they quietly made their way to the island. Red, Stacy, and Rachel would investigate around the island, and Vance and Stephanie would stay with the boat and serve as lookout. Rachel had expected Stephanie to put up a fight with that decision, but she complied. Rachel's group would communicate with Vance via walkie-talkie. She didn't want to rely on poor cell phone coverage.

She gave final instructions to Vance and Stephanie. "If security approaches you, tell them you're having mechanical problems with the boat and have called for help."

Red added, "If we aren't back or haven't checked in within the hour, call the Coast Guard."

Vance nodded. "Good luck."

The three of them headed toward the sandy path, with Rachel silently praying that they'd finally find Amber.

CHAPTER 45

Mike called Rachel's room for the fifth time. No answer. He tried her cell phone again. No answer. Straight to voice mail. This silence was highly unusual for someone who had a reputation for being available whenever she was needed. Mike took the stairs down to the lobby level of the hotel and knocked twice on the conference room door before opening it.

Drake, Phipps, and Cyndy were sitting around the table, drinking coffee and eating takeout while perusing their laptops.

"Hey, have any of you heard from Rachel tonight?"

Phipps and Cyndy shook their heads, while Drake scooted back from the table.

"No. She said she was going to her room to eat and do some research on her computer. I haven't heard from her since four or five o'clock." Drake saw the concern on Mike's face. "Why, what's up?"

"Probably nothing, but I've been trying to call her for the last hour, and her cell phone is turned off. No answer on her room phone or at her door, either."

"What about Red? Maybe she went to his room," Drake suggested.

Mike shook his head. "Tried that, too. Do you have his cell number?"

Drake picked up his phone and scrolled through the numbers until he found it. He pressed the dial button and speakerphone. The phone rang twice and went to voice mail. He left a message for Red to return his call.

"I don't like it that neither of them is answering and can't be located."

"Knowing Rachel, they're probably..." Drake paused for a second. "Oh shit."

"What?" Mike asked.

"She better not have." He stood up and grabbed his jacket.

"What is it?" Mike asked again, getting irritated.

"We had a disagreement earlier in the day about Asylum Harbor. She wanted to go again on her own, and I told her that wasn't a good idea. I bet she went anyway."

"That's what I wanted to talk to everyone about. The DEA and Coast Guard are going in at three o'clock this morning with a warrant to search the place. The *SeaStar* is supposed to be docking there, and we're doing a raid."

Drake looked at the clock on the wall. It was almost 9:00. She had a three- or four-hour jump-start on them. "She's probably already there. Do you have a boat we can use?"

Mike waved his hand. "Let's go."

CHAPTER 46

Rachel led the way down a sandy path through the island. Luck, for once, was with them—they didn't need their flashlights because the moon lit the way through the maze of trails.

"I feel like we're going in circles," Stacy said. "Everything looks familiar."

Red stopped to check his compass. "Nope. We're good. Still heading south toward Cabana Cay."

"We should be getting close to the main area of Asylum Harbor, where the residences are located," Rachel whispered. "I'm surprised that we haven't been detected by any of their security team."

"Maybe they don't really have any security." Stacy swatted a mosquito on her arm.

"They have security. We just haven't seen them yet," Red said.

"Did you hear that?" Rachel asked.

They stopped and listened. "What?" Stacy whispered.

"Music. Coming from over there." Rachel pointed toward a path that branched off to the right. "We must be close to the main house."

"Let's check it out." Red headed toward the music.

They stopped when they got closer and hid behind a grove of trees. A group of men sat around a fire pit, drinking and listening to music. Rachel counted six of them. The men seemed to be having a good time.

Red tapped her on the shoulder and pointed to the ground. They'd stacked their rifles next to them.

"Some security," Stacy muttered under her breath.

A tiny voice spoke up from behind them. "They always do this the night before the ship comes in."

Rachel almost jumped out of her skin. They whirled around to find a young boy standing in front them holding a gun.

Rachel looked him over. He appeared to be about eleven or twelve years old. He wore baggy camo shorts and a torn, dirty white T-shirt. His feet were bare. She held out her hands to show she wasn't carrying a weapon. The boy looked warily back and forth between her and Red.

"Who are you?" Rachel kept her voice low. She looked back toward the men, but they hadn't heard them—yet.

"The question is, who are you guys?" The young boy spoke in a heavy Bahamian accent.

Rachel tried to remain calm. She'd come too far to find Amber to get in trouble now.

"My name is Rachel." She thought about lying to the boy and sticking to the story about their boat being stranded. But she decided to go with the truth. "We're looking for a missing girl. Have you seen her?"

The young boy studied her for a few seconds. "There is no girl on the island. You need to go back to your boat."

Rachel looked at Red and he nodded for her to continue. "What is your name?"

He hesitated for a minute before replying, "Benji."

"Okay, Benji. This girl is in trouble. She has a family that misses her. If you know anything, anything at all—"

Her words were interrupted by gunfire.

CHAPTER 47

"It's okay," Shawn said when he felt Amber tense up beside him. "It's just my buddy, Andy. We worked together on the *SeaStar*. He's going to help us escape."

Andy jumped in the back of the ATV and they took off. The ride was bumpy and Amber held on for dear life. She could see the moonlight glistening off the water in front of them.

"Please explain to me what's going on," Amber demanded.

"My real name is Shawn. I work for the DEA. I've been undercover on the *SeaStar* for the last few months." Shawn gauged her expression as he came clean. "The guy who attacked us works for the owner of the cruise line. Somehow my cover was blown."

Shawn stopped the ATV a few hundred yards from the shoreline and let them out. Then he rolled the vehicle into the heavy foliage, hiding it behind some dense undergrowth. "We'll walk from here. Be careful, and stay close to me. This is our only shot to get away."

"Where were you all this time? How did you escape?" Amber was still curious as to how all this came to happen.

Shawn put his finger up to his mouth. "Shhh. We need to be quiet. I'll fill you in on the details later." Just then, a roar of vehicles split the night sky. "They found us! Hurry! We've got to run!"

They sprinted toward the beach. Amber was glad for the time she'd spent working out in her room.

"That's our boat!" Andy pointed to a dark shape lying on the shoreline.

Amber pumped her legs as fast as she could, but running on sand was exhausting. Her ankle throbbed and she was already breathless.

Shots rang out. Amber felt a bullet whiz by her head. Panic clenched in her throat.

"Go! Go! Go!" Andy yelled as Amber took a flying leap into the boat.

"Get down and stay down!" Shawn pushed her head down with one hand and started pushing the boat into the water with the other. Andy shoved from the other side and the boat headed away from shore. More bullets whizzed over their heads.

They jumped in the boat at the same time and Andy cranked the motor. The engine caught and Andy threw open the throttle. The small boat wasn't built for speed, but it churned into the waves, jolting Amber against the hull.

Amber couldn't catch her breath. She was in full panic mode. She realized that she and Josh/Shawn were now making their second escape in another boat. First, the cruise ship. Now this. She felt like she was having déjà vu.

"Where are we going?" She tilted her head to the side, still afraid to sit up.

"There's a private island just a few miles west of here. We could make that." Andy peered behind him to gauge how much of a head start they had gotten.

Shawn looked behind them, squinting in the darkness to see what kind of distance they'd put between themselves and the shooters. "Why not Freeport?"

"Too far. We'll never make it. Those guys have bigger boats and more firepower. If we make it to the private island, maybe we can find help," Andy said as he steered the bouncing boat through the dark waters. "It's our only option at this point."

"*If* we make it?" Amber couldn't believe this was happening. One moment she was planning her escape from Nurse Judy, and the next she was being rescued—again—by Josh McCain. Or Shawn. *Whatever his name is.*

"They're gaining!" Shawn yelled. "Let's go!"

"We're at full power! I told you this was a crapshoot," Andy said. The boat was one that Cabana Cay let the passengers use to cruise around the island. It was an eighteen-footer, much smaller compared to the larger cabin cruisers that the island security crew was chasing them with.

Their pursuers had stopped shooting, and Amber took a chance of looking up. She could see a couple of larger boats coming up fast behind them. One had a spotlight trained on their wake. *We'll never lose these guys*, she thought. Her anxiety was hitting at an all-time high.

"How much farther?" she shouted.

"Another five minutes, maybe," Andy yelled.

Looking at the boats closing in on them, she shouted back, "We don't have five minutes!"

"She's right," Shawn agreed with her. "In about two minutes, we're toast."

Amber looked at Shawn, hoping and praying he had an answer. The situation looked very bleak. She wondered if she would ever see her parents again.

"Andy, we have to go to Plan B." Shawn kept his eye on her.

"Plan B?" she asked.

"Yeah. When I say *go*, Andy will start shooting at them. When they're distracted, you and I'll jump from the boat. They can't chase down all of us." He looked toward the shore. It was still a few hundred feet away. "Think you can swim that far?"

"Yeah, I think so," Amber said.

"See those faint lights on the coastline?"

She nodded. "Yes."

"Swim fast and furious toward there. Don't look back and don't wait for us. When you get to shore, don't rest. Hightail it to the nearest house. Find a phone and call for help. Then hide."

She took a deep breath and mentally prepared herself.

"Jump out to the left and swim hard. Out of the way of the boats. You can do it. I'll be right behind you."

Andy yelled, "You gotta go. Ready?" He took aim for the boat right behind them.

"Ready."

Andy fired, and their pursuers fired back. But this time, Amber went overboard.

CHAPTER 48

Stephanie did not like being told what to do. And she did not like sitting around, especially while Rachel and the others went off to search. So when Vance went to relieve himself in the bushes, she took off at a sprint. She didn't know where she was going or what she'd find out. All she cared about was for once doing something—anything—to help her daughter.

She decided to go in a different direction than Rachel's group had taken and ran down another path that led away from the beach. Before long, she reached a row of houses that she assumed was the employee housing that Rachel had talked about earlier. If Amber was being held anywhere, Stephanie bet it would be in one of those residences. She didn't have a plan, but she was always a fly-by-the-seat-of-her-pants kind of gal. Her only goal was to get Amber away from this place in one piece.

All the houses looked dark and vacant, and she didn't hear any noises. She tentatively approached the first house. Either everyone went to sleep early, or Rachel was wrong, and no one stayed here overnight while the ship was at sea.

The first house was locked. She walked quietly across the deck and peeked in the window. A curtain was open and the inside was pitch black. She didn't hear anything.

She moved on to the next house. That house was also locked. The curtains were closed and she didn't hear any noise. *It was too quiet,* she thought as a chill ran down her spine. She turned around to make her way across the deck and back down the stairs and stared straight into the barrel of a gun.

"Don't move." The man holding the weapon was dressed in long, dark pants and T-shirt. "Island security."

Stephanie froze. She'd been in tough situations before, and this wasn't the first time someone had pointed a gun at her. So far she'd been lucky and hadn't been hurt. She just hoped her time hadn't run out.

"Who are you?" the security guard asked.

She had to think fast. Her life and maybe Amber's depended on it. She decided to go with what Rachel told her to say if they ran across security.

"I'm looking for help. Our boat broke down and I need to use your phone, please."

"There are others?" he inquired.

"My boyfriend stayed with the boat. Can you help us?" Shit, she didn't know what else to say.

He looked at her suspiciously and then lowered his gun. "This is a private island. You're trespassing."

"Sorry. Our radio is busted and we need help." Her eyes pleaded with him.

"Come with me." He motioned her off the deck. "I'll need to escort you to the security office."

Stephanie ran her sweaty palms down her capri pants. She had no choice but to go with him. God, she hoped she hadn't screwed up. Again.

CHAPTER 49

Shining a flashlight that lit their way down the path and through the dense vegetation, the security officer followed Stephanie down the trail. He mumbled something unintelligible into a headset, probably about her. She had an uneasy feeling in the pit of her stomach. She didn't think he and his buddies planned to help her. She had to do something before they got to wherever he was taking her.

She'd sized up the man before they started walking. She had a good two to three inches in height on him. She stood at five foot ten and was pretty strong. Good athletic genes ran through her family, and she figured she could outrun him. His only advantage, she thought, was the gun. How could she get that away from him?

After walking about three to four minutes, she heard faint music and laughter. They must have been getting close to the "security office." She slowed her pace and tried to gauge how close the guard was to her. If these men had, in fact, kidnapped Amber, her guard wouldn't have any qualms about shooting her and dumping her body in the water. She had to try to get away. Her odds were better one-on-one than being surrounded by many men. It was now or never.

She worked up her courage and swirled around quickly, running head-on into her escort. The element of surprise was on her side as she smashed into him. He lost his balance and they tumbled to the ground, Stephanie on top. The man grunted and tried to roll her off of him. Stephanie desperately felt around for the gun, her hand running through the silky sand. *Damn, where is the gun?* It had to have been jarred loose in the fall.

The man was stronger than he looked. For a shrimp, he had a lot of power. He tried to pin her arms down and call for help on the radio, but she reached up and ripped the earpiece off.

"Come on, you bitch. Get off of me," he said as he thrust his body to the side and rolled her. Suddenly, he was on top. She tried to get her knee up and into his groin, but he had her pinned down. He punched her in the face and she tried not to cry out. She didn't want to alert his crew. She felt blood trickle out of her mouth.

Her hand finally grazed cool metal. She tried to get a grasp on the gun, but he knocked her hand out of the way. He grabbed her hair and pulled her face up to his.

"We are going to get back up, and you're going to cooperate," he told her. "If you don't, I will not hesitate to shoot you."

She nodded as he helped her up. She brushed the sand off her shirt and pants. He picked up the gun and pointed it at her.

"Let's go," he started to say before a girl's scream pierced the night. "What the…"

It was the opportunity Stephanie needed. With all the fight she had left in her, she tried to grab the gun again with one hand and kick him in the balls with her feet.

This time, he was ready for her. As he'd promised, he didn't hesitate to shoot.

CHAPTER 50

The shot grazed her calf, but the force from the gunshot was powerful enough to knock her down. Stephanie yelped in pain while grabbing her leg. Her hand came away bloody.

"Get up!" The man yanked her off the sand. "I warned you. Now let's go."

She heard voices heading their way and realized she was trapped. She couldn't escape now. Within a couple of minutes, five other men had caught up to them.

"David, what happened?" an older gentleman asked her captor.

David explained the events leading up to her getting shot. "What do you want me to do, George?" he asked.

"Let's get her to first aid." George turned to Stephanie. "Judy, our nurse, can wrap that for you. It doesn't look too bad." George radioed Judy but didn't get an answer. "That's strange." As he started to call her again, another voice came through his radio.

"George, this is Joe. We have a situation."

"What now?" George asked no one in particular. "What is it, Joe? I have my own situation here."

"Judy has been knocked unconscious and our visitors are missing."

"Wait for my instructions." George signed off and then turned to David. "Take them with you," George said as he motioned to the other crew, "and see if you can find the missing visitors. I'll follow with her and wait at first aid for Joe."

Stephanie watched as David and the other men ran toward the beach. She could vaguely make out the shoreline through the palm trees. *Now what?* she wondered. The searing pain in her leg was making her woozy.

George radioed back to Joe and explained what was going on.

"I don't feel so good," Stephanie said.

"Come on," George said, gripping her shoulders tightly. "Let's get you fixed up and then you can tell me why you're really here."

Stephanie hobbled along with him and tried to formulate another plan to get out of this mess. Before she could take another step, shots rang out again.

"Jesus, now what?" George said.

"We found our missing visitors," David's staccato voice came through loud and clear on the radio. "They launched one of the boats. They got a head start on us."

George cursed. "Follow them. Take Manny and Simon with you. I'll catch up."

A feeling of dread ran through Stephanie. She'd bet anything that Amber was the "visitor" that David was talking about. Rachel must have found her before she could. Stephanie hoped and prayed that her daughter and her rescuers would get far away before these guys caught up to her.

When they finally got to the beach, Stephanie could just faintly see two boats in the distance. Maybe Rachel had Amber safe on one of them.

George radioed Joe and gave him an update. "I sent David, Manny, and Simon after our visitors. They took the cabin cruiser."

"Go after them," Joe instructed. "We don't want any more mistakes."

"What about the girl?" George responded.

There was a moment of silence before he got an answer. "Take her with you. Make sure she doesn't come back."

Stephanie's eyes opened wide with horror. She knew what that meant.

CHAPTER 51

Rachel spun around just in time to see the men jump up and grab their guns. She froze. Red grabbed her by the sleeve and pulled her down with him. The men ran off in the other direction and didn't even see their unexpected guests hiding behind the bushes. Rachel looked at Benji expectantly. He shrugged his shoulders and then took off after the other men.

"Damn, that was close." Rachel breathed a sigh of relief.

"Don't count your blessings just yet. I'm sure the boy will tell them we're here." Red leaned against the tree.

"Forget that! Where did those shots come from?" Stacy's hands were shaking.

"Good question. I think we need to get out of here," Red said.

"No! We just got a big break with those guys leaving. We need to follow them—and fast. The shots could have something to do with Amber." Rachel looked at Red.

Red nodded. "Okay, but let's check in with Vance first. I'm sure he heard the shots, too. We need to let him know what's going on."

Rachel waited while Red called Vance on the walkie-talkie. Nothing. Red tried several times to contact either Vance or Stephanie, but nobody answered.

"This can't be good." Red tried one more time to call them up on the radio. No answer.

"Could we be out of range?" Stacy inquired.

"No. These are state-of-the-art radios. They work when cell phone signals are unreliable. We have a fifty-mile range on these babies," Red explained.

Rachel grew impatient. "Red, we need to go. Vance can take care of himself."

"You're the boss. We don't know what we're getting into. Everybody needs to keep on their toes." Red grabbed his gear and headed in the direction the armed men had taken.

More gunshots.

"What the hell is going on?" Stacy said.

"Sounds like the Fourth of July down at the beach. Do you want to go back to the boat?" Rachel asked. She was worried that this was getting to be too much for Stacy. Even though the reporter had insisted on coming along, the gunfire was more than anyone had expected.

"Hell no. You're stuck with me," Stacy said.

Rachel calculated that it would take about ten to fifteen minutes on foot to reach the Cabana Cay side. That's where the shots sounded like they were coming from—and the direction the men had been headed.

"We should stick close to the trail but not walk directly on it. I don't want to chance running into security on the way down there." Rachel took over the lead. "It'll take us a few minutes to get down to the beach area."

"I'm really hoping that—" Red's words were cut off by the radio.

"It's Vance," he answered.

"Hey, buddy, we were getting worried. Did you hear those shots?" Red asked him.

"Yeah, man. What the hell is happening? And where the hell is Stephanie? She's disappeared! When I went to the bushes to take a leak, she took off."

"Did he just say that Stephanie is gone?" Rachel asked.

Red nodded. "Where did she go?"

"I don't know. One minute she was here, the next she was gone. I think she went looking for Amber. She was just telling me how helpless she felt and guilty for sitting around doing nothing. I went to take a piss, turned around, and she was gone."

Red shook his head. "I just tried you on the radio a couple of minutes ago. Nobody answered."

"Sorry, man. I left it with Stephanie, and she had turned the volume all the way down. I just now noticed when I picked it up to call you."

"How long ago did she take off?"

"No more than five minutes."

Red told him that they were following the armed men toward where they thought the gunshots had come from.

"Do you want me to stand by?"

Red affirmed, then asked Rachel, "Is it time to call the Coast Guard?"

"Let's check this out first. Have him call the Coast Guard if he doesn't hear from us within twenty minutes."

Red relayed the message to Vance before signing off.

"What are we going to do about Stephanie?" he asked Rachel.

"I don't know," Rachel said. "I don't know how we can find her. I hope she either heads back to the boat after hearing those gunshots—" She suddenly stopped. "Did you hear that?"

Everyone listened. "Sounds like a boat motor," Stacy said.

"We're close to the beach," Red said. "But is the boat coming or going? And who the hell is on it?" They picked up the pace, and in a few hundred feet they came to the electronic gate that separated Asylum Harbor from Cabana Cay.

"Now what?" Red said.

Rachel had forgotten about the electronic gate. The gate was too high to climb and too long to go around. "I'm sure there are sensors. When I was here earlier, we were in the golf cart, and the manager had to use a remote control to open it up."

"This is so weird to see a gate on an island. Why is it there?" Stacy asked.

"Joe, the island manager, said it's for the safety of the cruise passengers. I guess so they don't get lost and wander into the Asylum Harbor side," Rachel answered.

"More like they don't want passengers to see the behind-the-scenes stuff going on," Stacy commented.

The gate opened with a creak, catching them off guard.

"What the heck?" Stacy said as Rachel grabbed her arm and pulled her behind the trees.

"Someone's coming," Red whispered as he crouched down behind Rachel.

They watched silently as a golf cart barreled down the pathway. As it got closer, Rachel recognized Joe Vermillion at the wheel. He was yelling something into his radio.

"That's the island manager," she whispered.

"Let's wait till he goes through, and then we can sneak past the gate," Red said. He watched the manager open the gate and drive through. Red waited a few seconds until Joe's cart picked up speed. Red counted down, watching the gate starting to shut. Then he said, "Go!"

They raced through the gate before it closed. Rachel looked back and saw the cart careen around the curve. "I think we're good."

Just past the gate, the trail intersected with several other pathways.

"Which way?" Red asked.

Rachel pointed. "That way leads to the private cabanas, I know. If we keep going straight, we should hit the beach area in a few hundred feet." She rubbed the sweat from her forehead and led the group to the beach area. Even at night, the temperature was warm, and the exercise and anxiety combined to make her feel sticky. Still, the island on the Cabana Cay side of the island looked inviting. Freshly planted flowers flourished along the neatly trimmed pathway. "They're getting ready for the next set of passengers."

"Boat comes in tomorrow morning," Stacy confirmed.

"Now we're exposed. No place to hide." Rachel commented as the heavy vegetation and palm trees cleared.

"I don't think that's a problem." Red pointed when the beach came in view. The sand was raked clean, with nice long rows. The moonlight afforded a view of two boats in the distance and a third was getting ready to launch.

Stacy stopped in her tracks. She looked over at the last boat. Two men were dragging a blonde woman with them. She was wearing white pants and a blue-green T-shirt. "What are they doing?"

Rachel looked closer. "I think we found Stephanie."

CHAPTER 52

"How long will it take us to get there?" Mike had loaded his service pistol, a Glock 22, and shoved it in his holster before they left. Now their boat was streaking to Asylum Harbor under full power, but it wasn't going fast enough for him. He'd called into headquarters and put a hold on the raid until he checked out the situation at the island.

"About thirty minutes or so." Drake was silently cursing Rachel for going to the island without him. Red was probably with her, and that at least was something. But Red should have known better, too.

Mike watched the boat slice through two-foot waves and wondered for the hundredth time what had possessed Rachel to go to the island without him. She had to have had some kind of lead to take a chance like that. The mission was just too dangerous. He wished that she would have trusted him enough to confide in him.

He both admired and cursed her persistence and hardheadedness.

"What's the plan?" Drake asked.

"I've tried to call her cell phone again. And Red's. Still no answer. So who knows what they're doing. The *SeaStar* is supposed to be docking at the island tomorrow around seven a.m. I imagine the staff is preparing for its arrival. I'm not sure what kind of resistance we'll get coming in without notice."

Drake agreed. "The staff seemed relaxed when we were out there, but what worries me is what we didn't see. Security might be tight."

"Where do we dock? Asylum Harbor or Cabana Cay?" Mike asked him.

"We'll cruise around the island and check it out first."

CHAPTER 53

The first thing that surprised Amber was the coolness of the water and the sting she felt when she dove in. She kicked her legs hard and pushed through the water with her arms. Her first goal was not to get run over by the boat of bad guys behind them. Her second goal was not to drown or get eaten by sharks while making her way to the island. If she could do those two things, she might live.

She stayed underwater as long as she could. She wanted to break the surface and see if Shawn was behind her, but she was too scared. So she stayed down as long as her breath would allow—until her lungs were on fire. After what felt like hours instead of minutes, she came up for air. Amber couldn't see the boats, but she could hear them in the distance. She also couldn't see Shawn or Andy or anyone else, just the moonlight shining on dark waves. She pushed away thoughts of what might be under the water, swimming around her, and struck out toward the shoreline.

Amber could faintly see lights, and it gave her an extra push to make it to shore. *I can do it*, she said to herself over and over. Focusing on the shoreline, she did the breaststroke through the inky-black water, watching the lights get closer. At some point, she realized that the water was shallow and that she could stand up. But she didn't dare in case someone was looking for her. She couldn't see or hear the boats anymore, and she didn't know what had happened to Andy or Shawn.

She was alone and scared.

CHAPTER 54

"Get Vance on the radio! Call the Coast Guard!" Rachel broke into a sprint toward the beach.

"*Wait!*" Red called after her. "Be careful! We don't know if anybody else is down there."

Rachel paused. "I don't see anybody."

"Still, it doesn't hurt to be cautious," Stacy agreed with Red.

By the time they got to the beach, the boats were almost out of view. Red radioed Vance and told him to bring the boat around.

"It will take at least ten minutes for Vance to get here." Rachel threw her hands up. "Meanwhile, they're getting farther away." She cursed herself for letting Stephanie come along. Now, instead of looking for clues to Amber's whereabouts, she was using her resources to rescue Stephanie.

Red spotted the tiki hut where the water sports equipment was rented. "Hang on. I've got an idea."

He ran to the hut and found it unlocked. A row of keys hung on a peg board. Whoever ran the water sports place was well organized. The keys were numbered to correlate to the numbers on the rental Jet Skis. He selected two keys and headed back to the girls.

Red pointed to the last two Jet Skis in a row of bright-green-and-purple Jet Skis that garnished the shoreline. "This is our ride." He tossed a key to Rachel. "You and Stacy can ride together."

"What about Vance?" Stacy asked. She put on the life vest that Red handed her.

"I'll call him and tell him where we're headed. He'll use the GPS from our radios to find us."

Red helped them push off before getting on his own Jet Ski. He felt an uncomfortable twinge in his chest as they set off.

CHAPTER 55

Amber paused just a few feet from the sandy shoreline. Her wet T-shirt and shorts clung to her skin and she shivered despite the warm temperature. An outside porch light flickered from the deck of a vacation home. She didn't see any movement from either side of the house. *Now or never,* she thought. She walked carefully through the shells and coral and was thankful she'd still been wearing her tennis shoes when she jumped overboard. She crept up to the beach house. She wondered if anyone was staying there. The deck was devoid of any sign of inhabitants. No beach towels, swimsuits, or beach chairs littered the deck. She crept quietly around the house, down a pathway that led to an outdoor shower. Amber jumped as a security light came on and bathed the area around her with light.

Instinctively, she crouched down and waited for the light to go off. After a few seconds, she cautiously stood up and rounded the corner of the shower where she saw a side door. She turned the knob. To her amazement, the door was unlocked. Amber started to push the door open, but someone grabbed her from behind. She tried to scream, but whoever it was put his hand over her mouth and pushed her into a dark room. When she stumbled over something hard, her attacker lost his grip, and they sprawled together onto a concrete floor. She felt the wind get knocked out of her.

"Amber, it's me."

She was relieved and irritated at the same time.

"Dammit, Josh! Quit sneaking up on me!"

"Shawn," he reminded her. "My name is Shawn."

"Whatever. Just get off of me." Amber stood up, rubbing her scraped skin. "What happened to everybody?"

"Security is probably scouring this place looking for us. We need to find a phone."

"What happened to Andy?"

"I don't know. I jumped right after you. He kept going. I'm sure those guys have figured out by now that we abandoned ship."

"Do you think Andy's hurt? Where could he go?"

"I don't know. I hope he's all right, but right now we have to figure out a way to get help. So let's look for that phone."

Amber went to turn on the light switch and Shawn caught her hand.

"No way. We don't want to draw attention to ourselves."

"Sorry. Reflex." Amber stood still until her eyes adjusted to the dark.

Shawn started moving through what seemed to be a storage and laundry room. "Stay behind me. We want to find a phone, computer, any kind of communication device."

"I'm right behind you."

The air was stale and musty, and Amber had to fight an impulse to sneeze. "I don't think anyone has been here in a long time." She could faintly make out white sheets covering some of the furniture.

Shawn walked around the kitchen and found a phone hanging next to the refrigerator.

He picked it up and cussed. "Just my luck. Dead."

CHAPTER 56

Stephanie waited for the right time to make her move. George had one eye on her and the other on the boats ahead of him.

"We're getting really close," she heard David yell through the radio.

George picked up his radio to respond. "You should be hitting Big Dog Cay any minute now. That's probably where they're headed."

"In about one minute, we'll be right on top of them!" David responded.

"You know what to do!" George answered.

Stephanie was ready. The moonlight shone on a shoreline less than a few hundred feet away. Gunshots erupted from the other security boat, grabbing George's full attention. She thought she could make it to shore if she was judging the distance correctly. Silently counting to three, she held her breath and hoped for the best. Then she jumped.

✦ ✦ ✦

Hitting the water hard, Stephanie struggled to find the surface. She gulped what felt like gallons of salty ocean, but the coolness of the water took away some of the pain in her leg. She expected George to circle around and come back to run her over, but he kept going. He probably figured she would drown. But she was stronger than she looked.

She got her bearings in the dark water and slowly started to swim toward the shoreline, doing the breaststroke and conserving the use of her bad leg. She estimated she'd reach land within ten to fifteen minutes at this pace. She just hoped she wouldn't be too late to help Amber.

As she was close to shore, Stephanie felt something bump against her leg, and then she felt a white-hot blast of pain that nearly blinded her. She shrieked. The water was now up to her chest as she struggled to make it to shore. Another bump. *Oh my God*, she thought as a sharp pain went up her right leg, *it's a shark.*

She reached down with a fist and punched the shark as hard as she could. Her mind was numb to the fear. Just a few more feet and she'd reach shore. She reached down to feel the damage to her leg. There was a gaping hole where her calf should have been.

Feeling lightheaded, she started swimming slowly toward shore again. The waves helped by pushing her forward. She was gulping more and more salt water and she was sure she was trailing blood behind. Her good foot touched down on sand, and she dragged herself up onto the beach. She saw a cottage directly in front of her but didn't know if she could make it any further. The clouds parted and a stream of moonlight shone brightly on the beach as she inspected her leg. She was right. A good chunk of her calf was gone. Blood poured out of the wound, and Stephanie felt her hope drain away as well. She shivered from shock and cold.

She'd never be able to tell her daughter how sorry she was for everything. For all the years she'd missed. She'd never be able to tell Amber how much she loved her.

As Stephanie laid her head down in the sand, the moonlight and stars faded from her vision.

CHAPTER 57

"Look around and see if you can find anything we can use to call for help. A laptop, cell phone, anything," Shawn instructed Amber as he hung up the worthless phone. "I'll check the bedrooms. Maybe I can find us some dry clothes and towels."

Amber fumbled around in the dark, looking for anything that would help them. Her eyes were adjusting to the darkness. A bit of moonlight cast weak but broad lines throughout the vacation home, helping her find her way through each room.

She searched the living room and kitchen, her wet shoes squishing on the plush carpet. A small desk in the corner looked promising, and she pulled open the drawers. But all she found were bits of papers and a couple of pens. The kitchen didn't turn up anything, either. She tried the phone again, just in case. Nothing. In a junk drawer, Amber found a small pocketknife. She hung on to that, slipping it into the waistband of her shorts.

"Nothing," she heard Shawn say as he came back into the living room. "The cheap bastards must have turned off the phone and Internet service while they were gone."

"I didn't find anything, either," Amber said.

"I did find a change of clothes." He handed her a sundress and a pair of flip-flops. "Not sure if this will fit you, but it's all I could find."

She held up the dress. It was longer than something she'd normally wear, but she could make do.

"It'll work," she said, heading for the doorway. "I'll change in the kitchen." She went back to the junk drawer for the scissors she'd seen and cut off the bottom of the dress so the skirt fell just above her knees. She decided to leave her tennis shoes on, even though they were soaked. When she walked back into the living room, Shawn was standing at the window, looking out.

"Do you know where we are? Or how many other homes are out here? Maybe we can check those out," Amber said. She noticed that he had changed as well and now wore baggy jean shorts and a golf shirt. Despite the seriousness of their situation, she couldn't help but stifle a giggle. He looked like a little boy wearing his father's clothes.

"We're on Big Dog Cay. Andy said it's got five houses in all. This island is owned by one person, and the family uses it as a compound. We can try the other houses and see if we have any luck." Shawn eased over to the sliding glass door that led to the back deck, which faced the shoreline. He gently pulled back the blinds and peered outside.

"See anything?" Amber asked quietly.

"No," he said, continuing to peer out the window. "The clouds keep rolling in and out, covering the moonlight. I think we should go ahead…" He hesitated for a moment.

"What?" She urgently whispered.

"I do see something. I think…Someone is crawling along the sand. I think it's a woman. She looks hurt."

Shawn ran back to the kitchen. Amber followed.

"What are you looking for?"

"Some kind of a weapon. I lost mine when I bailed from the boat." He grabbed a knife from the butcher block and tucked it inside a potholder, which went into the front pocket of his shorts. "This will have to do."

Amber remembered the small knife that she'd found in the kitchen. She'd tucked it in her shoe when she'd changed into the sundress. She hoped she wouldn't have to use it.

Shawn went back to the sliding glass door, checking the surroundings again. Amber looked out from the window. She saw nothing.

"You need to stay here where it's safe while I go check this out," Shawn said. "I'll be back in a few minutes."

"Okay. Be careful." Amber sat down on the couch and put her face in her hands. She could feel a migraine coming on. This happened when she was stressed or tired. She concentrated on taking deep breaths, inhaling through her nose and blowing out slowly through her mouth. *When will all of this finally be over?*

CHAPTER 58

Shawn edged cautiously around the back of the home. He studied the area, watching for any signs of movement. Seeing nothing, he continued toward the beach. Whoever swam ashore was now lying motionless on the sand. He heard a boat motor and some shouting just a short distance away. Fingering the knife in his pocket, he made his way to the figure. As he got closer, he realized it was woman, with blonde hair. Something was familiar about her.

He looked around again before moving closer. The woman moaned softly, and he could see that she was seriously injured. Shawn glanced back to the house but didn't see any movement. What had happened to Andy and their pursuers? How did this woman figure into the equation? He didn't remember seeing a woman in the boat with the shooters, but then again, he hadn't gotten a good look as he ran for his life. She didn't seem to be part of the island's security crew, though. Her dress was more casual—definitely not a uniform.

"Hey, are you okay?" Shawn stepped closer. Her leg was bleeding and her head was turned to the side, so he couldn't see her face. Shawn walked around and knelt down beside her.

The woman continued to moan. It sounded like she was trying to say something. "Ammmer. Ammmer."

He pushed a piece of blonde hair off her face. "What did you say?" Her blue eyes stared directly at him as a sense of confusion came over him. She looked just like—

"Aunt Stephanie!" Amber cried out as she crashed down beside Shawn.

Shawn fell back in surprise. "What? What's going on here?" He looked from Amber to the woman lying in the sand and back again. "I told you to stay inside!"

"It's my aunt. Oh my gosh, she's hurt."

Shawn's mind was reeling. So many questions went through his mind. Most importantly, what was her aunt doing here?

"Aunt Stephanie, how did you get here?"

"Boat. Looking…for…you." Her breath was ragged.

Shawn ripped off his shirt and used it to make a tourniquet to wrap it around her leg. He was stunned to see that her calf was almost shredded to bits. Muscle and cartilage were ripped away, and only stark-white bone was left. It looked like she'd been attacked by a small shark or barracuda. Her skin was pasty, and she'd obviously lost a lot of blood. He wasn't sure if she had any other injuries.

"Who's looking for me? Mom? Dad?" Amber held her hand.

"I…love you. So sorry…I left you…all…alone." Stephanie's eyes rolled back into her head.

"What? What do you mean?" Amber couldn't make sense of what her aunt was trying to tell her. "I love you, too. Please stay with me."

Shawn felt for a pulse, but it was faint. He shook his head at Amber as tears fell down her cheeks. This felt like a bad dream to her. Nothing made sense.

"She's lost some blood and has a faint pulse. Do you think you can help me carry her up to the house? I saw a first-aid kit in the bathroom."

Amber nodded her head.

Shawn looped his arms under Stephanie's and gently lifted her up. "Grab her legs. Gently. Watch out for her injury."

They carried Stephanie up to the house and laid her on the sofa. Shawn grabbed the first-aid kit and properly attended to her wound while Amber put a cool cloth on her aunt's head.

"I just don't understand what is going on here. I haven't seen my aunt in over a year."

"She looks just like you," Shawn commented.

"My mother and aunt are twins. That's why I ran out to the beach. I stepped out onto the balcony to get a closer look and I thought it was my mother." Amber started to cry again. "This is just all so surreal."

Shawn lifted Amber's chin up. "Listen, you have to hold it together if we're going to make it out of here. We've done all we can for your aunt right now. She needs medical attention." He tucked a blanket around Stephanie. "We need to leave her here and go find help. Ready?"

Amber wiped away her tears and nodded. She leaned over and gave Stephanie a kiss on the forehead, then followed Shawn out the door.

CHAPTER 59

"Mike, it's a call from the Coast Guard." Drake handed the ship's radio to him. "They just got a distress call from a boat near Asylum Harbor."

Mike had coordinated with the Coast Guard when they headed to Asylum Harbor. He was upset with Rachel for putting herself and her team in a precarious position. He took the call as Drake listened in.

The voice on the radio said, "A man identifying himself as Vance Pearson called in about five minutes ago. He said he's on a search-and-rescue mission with Rachel Scott. He reported shots fired at Cabana Cay." The Coast Guard gave him Vance's last coordinates.

"We're headed that way," Mike said. "What's your ETA?"

"Seventeen minutes" came the reply.

"We're less than a half hour out. Please update us when you arrive."

Mike handed the radio back to Drake.

"Great. Just what I feared—Rachel's on the island and she's in trouble."

✦ ✦ ✦

Andy opened the throttle as far as it would go. He didn't have to look behind him to know the cruiser was about to overtake him. He secured the gun in his pocket and dove off the boat. The water was shallow, as he had expected, and he swam as close to the bottom as possible. He didn't dare come out of the water until he was a few feet away from the beach. Andy heard the other boat come around looking for him. He confirmed his Glock was still there and then quickly ran toward shore.

Not knowing which way Shawn and Amber had gone, he looked for footprints. He'd given Shawn pieces of neon-green ribbon to leave as markers when he got to shore—something he'd learned during armed forces special teams training. The trick would be finding small ribbons in the dark on a huge island, even if it was only half the size of Asylum Harbor. Keeping an eye out for the security guards, Andy stealthily made his way in the direction he thought Shawn must have gone.

From studying the map of the island, he knew that a main house faced the beach about a hundred yards from where he now stood. A few hundred feet down the beach were four smaller cottages. Andy had heard that a well-known millionaire owned this island and used it exclusively for his friends and family. What he didn't know was if any of the island homes were now occupied.

He had to work fast. The security guards would be all over him soon. He approached the house from the side and looked for signs that Shawn had been there. A multitude of palm trees and other tropical vegetation surrounded the house—good cover while he checked out the home. It looked vacant—no lights, no noise. So far, so good. Except, where was Shawn?

He saw a side gate that he assumed led to the back of the home. Hanging from the gate latch was a neon-green ribbon. Bingo. Now the question was, were they still here? Two sets of footprints led up to the side door. Amber and Shawn were probably together. He felt better knowing they'd both made it safely to shore.

He decided to check the perimeter of the home before going in. Andy walked around toward the deck and spotted two people running down the beach. He crouched under the deck to give him cover as he assessed the situation. It was Shawn and Amber. Just as he was about to go help, a silent shot whizzed right past his ear.

Andy looked around but couldn't figure out where the shooter was. He watched as Shawn and Amber ran off in the distance oblivious to the fact someone was trying to shoot them. He didn't want to give his position away and alert the shooter, so he waited. There—in the cover of darkness—one of the security guards reloaded his gun. Andy couldn't see if anyone else was with him and he didn't know how many guards had been in the boat. He didn't think he could get off a good shot at this distance, so he decided to wait for them to come closer.

The guard hesitated and then looked toward the beach. Andy held his breath as the guard walked within five feet of him and made his way down to the beach. Andy pulled his gun out and debated whether he should take the guard down now or wait till he got closer. He didn't know if anyone else was with the guard. Just as Andy decided to follow, another guard burst through the palm trees and ran toward the beach. He watched as the guards conversed before taking off after Shawn and Amber.

Satisfied that no one else was coming, he took off after the guards.

CHAPTER 60

"What are we going to do?" Amber asked. A cramp had developed in her side and she felt like she couldn't breathe. She didn't know how much longer she could hold up.

"I don't know yet." Shawn noticed she had slowed down some. "Come on, we need to put some distance between us and the guard."

Amber tried to pick up her pace. Instead, she stumbled and fell flat on her butt, hurting her ankle again.

Shawn turned around and helped her up. "What happened?"

Amber winced as she tried to put weight on her ankle. "I don't think I can walk on it anymore."

"Amber, we have to go." Shawn looked around. He was sure the guard was right behind them. It worried him that he couldn't see him anymore. He didn't want to walk straight into an ambush.

"Just go without me. I can't do this anymore, Shawn." Amber started crying. "Just go."

Shawn grabbed her at the elbow. "I'm not leaving you. It's not an option. The house is just a few feet away." He softened his tone. "Come on, Amber. You do can this. We're really close."

Amber took a deep breath and leaned on Shawn. They slowly made their way to the back of the beach house. With every step she took, a sharp pain shot up her leg. The pain reminded her of the time she'd gotten a hairline fracture doing a cheerleading stunt. If she could cheer an entire game with a broken ankle, she could walk a few hundred feet with a sprained one.

The beach house looked to be at least twenty-five years old. It was made of concrete block and painted a bright yellow. Next to the house was a gazebo with a bench. It was covered in plumeria vines but afforded a view of the water and the trail to the main beach house. Shawn made Amber sit on the bench while he checked out her ankle. It was starting to swell. As he removed her shoe, a pocketknife fell out.

"Where did you get this?"

"At the other beach house. I found it in the kitchen."

Shawn studied the pocketknife before handing it back to Amber. He didn't know how many of the security guards were on the island and if Andy had reached shore or not. It was hard to come up with a plan without knowing those specifics. And since the island seemed to be without phone service, hiding until they could find help was probably their best option. A pocketknife and kitchen knife weren't the best protection until then.

"Let's see if we can find better weapons," he said, helping Amber to her feet. "This way. We'll try the side door and see if it's unlocked like the other house."

Amber leaned on Shawn as they made their way around to the side. As soon as they rounded the corner, they came face-to-face with one of the security guards.

"Stop. Not another step."

Shawn put his hands out. He recognized the guard as one of the guys who'd witnessed his beating back on Asylum Harbor. Shawn studied him closely. The guard looked nervous and unsure of himself. He hoped that worked in his favor.

"She's got a hurt ankle," Shawn said to the guard as he pointed to Amber's leg.

The guard glanced down to her leg and shrugged. "Don't care."

Shawn looked around but didn't see anyone else. Where were the other guards?

"Let's take a walk down to the water." The guard held his gun steady at Amber. "No funny stuff. You try anything, she dies."

Shawn pulled Amber close to him and she put her arm around his shoulder. "Lean on me," he whispered in ear.

The guard took tentative steps toward them. "I should have killed you when I had—"

Before he finished his sentence, they heard a pop. The guard fell face down on the sand, dropping his gun. Amber screamed as another dark figure stood in the shadows.

"It's Andy." Shawn held Amber close to him. "It's okay."

Andy walked out of the shadows where Amber could see him clearer.

"That's the second time you saved me." Shawn walked over to the dead guard and picked up his gun. His heart was pounding a mile a minute. "Thanks, bro."

"Not a problem." Andy stepped over the guard's body. "Are you guys okay?" he asked Amber.

She nodded her head. "Think so."

"How many more guards? Do you know?" Shawn asked.

"I don't know. I already took out another one. He was waiting in the shadows behind this one. Snuck up on him and put 'em in a sleeper," Andy said. "I saw you guys at the other house and was about to meet you down at the beach when I heard him sneak up on you and take some shots. I hid near the deck and he never saw me. I followed him and his partner down to the beach and they led me to you."

"Good job. I owe you one." Shawn pointed over to the cottage. "If we can hide Amber in the house someone, then we can go after help. Instead of waiting for them to find us."

Andy thought this over while Amber shook her head.

"No, please don't leave me alone."

"I think Shawn's right. It's much safer for you to hide while we take out the rest of these guys."

Amber looked up at the house and considered her options. She noticed movement on the deck. "Shawn!" she screamed, pointing at the deck, but she was too late.

Several things happened at once. It was all so fast Amber wasn't sure what happened until it was all over.

The gunman shot off a round, and Andy hit the ground, a red spot blossoming on his chest. Shawn pushed Amber aside before a second shot rang off. He fell over into the sand, blood pouring from his shoulder.

Amber stood frozen to the ground with terror. She closed her eyes and waited for certain death.

CHAPTER 61

Rachel hadn't driven a Jet Ski in a while, but it was easy to get the hang of. She'd checked the gas gauge, and the tank was full. At least she wouldn't be stranded out in the ocean. The sea had a two-foot chop, which made the ride a little bumpy, but she had no problem keeping up with Red. Stacy rode on the seat behind Rachel and had her arms wrapped around Rachel's waist.

The only problem was the boat they were following was getting away. In daylight, it would have been easier to follow. But even with a fairly nice night with some visibility, following a fast boat on dark water was hard to do.

Within fifteen minutes, using the built-in GPS tracker in the radios, Vance had caught up with them. They abandoned the Jet Skis and hopped back on the boat.

"Do you have any idea where those guys were headed?" Red asked. "We lost sight of them about a mile back."

"There's only one island that I know of that's close to here—Big Dog Cay. It's privately owned. As far as I know, it's got a main residence and a few guesthouses. Rarely occupied. That's it."

"Let's go, then." Red settled back, his face grim.

Vance adjusted the boat's course. "Should take us just a few minutes to get there."

"Call the Coast Guard and let them know our change in direction," Red instructed.

Stacy and Rachel anxiously waited in the cabin. "I knew this was a bad idea," Rachel admitted to Stacy. "I never should have let Stephanie come on this trip. Now I'm responsible for losing a member of Governor Knowles's family while trying to rescue another."

"Don't beat yourself up about it." Stacy rubbed her on the arm. "You're not responsible for her actions."

"Something had to have happened between the time she left Vance and when she got captured."

"You think she found Amber?"

Rachel shrugged. "They were chasing someone in that first boat."

"The Coast Guard is meeting us at Big Dog Cay." Red looked at Rachel with concern in his eyes.

"What?" Rachel knew that look. It wasn't good news.

"Mike Mancini is also on his way, with Drake and his crew. They coordinated a search for us with the Coast Guard."

"Good. We'll need the help."

"I don't think Drake will be too happy that we didn't notify him," Stacy reminded Rachel.

"I tried to convince him to come along. He wanted to wait."

"Guys, we're here. And guess what?" Vance slowed the boat, taking note of two smaller boats perched on the beach. "We've found the other boats."

CHAPTER 62

A quick search of the boats didn't yield any clues as to where anyone was. Rachel studied the footprints embedded in the sand. "Looks like they split up."

"I believe the main house and another guest cottage are that way." Vance pointed to his right. "Not sure where that leads." He pointed to the other set of prints.

"Let's head toward the main house and stay together this time," Rachel instructed.

They walked along the sandy path that led up to the beach house.

They heard gunshots. Then a scream pierced the night.

Rachel spun around. "Where did that come from?"

Another scream.

"That way." Vance took off running while the rest followed.

✦ ✦ ✦

Stephanie threw her arms around the guard's neck. His shot went wild as they both tumbled down the deck stairs. Stephanie landed on top of the guard and they both struggled for the gun. She was losing strength fast. Her leg had started bleeding again and she started trembling.

Amber screamed for her aunt when she finally realized what was going on.

The gun went off and Stephanie rolled off the guard. He stood up and stumbled toward Amber.

Vance got to the beach house first. He motioned for the others to stay put. Drawing his gun, he took aim. He knew he had only one good shot. Taking a deep breath, he steadied his hand and fired.

The guard fell forward and landed at Amber's feet. She ran toward her aunt and collapsed on the ground.

Rachel rushed toward Amber. The terrified look on her face stopped her. Rachel realized Amber didn't know who she was. She had no idea what the poor child had been through.

"Amber, I'm Rachel Scott. Your parents sent us here to look for you." Rachel glanced down at Stephanie. "Your aunt Stephanie came with us, but we got separated. Are you injured?" Rachel asked in a soothing tone.

Amber shook her head no. "My aunt is hurt badly, though."

Rachel quickly looked the teenager over and didn't see any wounds, although her right ankle was swollen.

"What about my aunt?" Amber's voice quivered. "She saved my life."

Rachel looked at Stephanie's injuries. Her leg was already bandaged and soaked with blood. She also had been shot in the abdomen. Rachel felt for a pulse but couldn't find one and Stephanie wasn't breathing. She started doing CPR while Vance came over to help.

Stacy was squatting beside Shawn's body. "I think this is Josh McCain." She recognized him from the photos Rachel had shown her. "He has a pulse." She took off her belt and used it as a tourniquet for his shoulder. "I think he's coming around," she said as Shawn's eyes fluttered open.

Red came back from his reconnaissance. "There's another dead guard on the deck." He bent down next to Andy who was close to Shawn. "No pulse. I think he's gone. Does anyone know who this is?" Red noticed Andy wasn't wearing a uniform like the rest of the guards.

"Andy. He helped Shawn rescue me." Amber answered.

"We can get the full story once Shawn and Amber are patched up," Rachel suggested.

Red nodded. "I'll head back to the boat and alert the Coast Guard that we need a medic helicopter. Stacy can come with me and grab our first-aid kit. We'll do what we can until the Coast Guard can get here."

"Think you can make it back to our boat?" he asked Amber.

Rachel continued to perform CPR. She looked up at Red and shook her head. Stephanie wasn't responding.

"I don't want to leave my aunt. She saved my life."

"Go ahead," Rachel told Red. "I'll stay with Amber." He sprinted down the beach toward the boat.

Within minutes, the Coast Guard arrived. They loaded Stephanie and Shawn in the medic copter. Amber wanted to go, but Rachel insisted she stay with her and wait for her parents. Rachel watched as another boat pulled up to the shoreline. Mike jumped off and ran toward her. She sighed with relief, knowing everything was going to be okay.

EPILOGUE

"How can we ever thank you?" Governor Knowles shook Rachel's hand and then gave her a hearty embrace.

"Just seeing Amber back with her family is thanks enough." Rachel looked over at Shawn, who was propped up in his hospital bed. "He's the real hero."

Shawn shrugged. "I felt responsible for getting Amber into that mess."

Mike and Rachel were with the governor, Sarah, and Amber in Shawn's hospital room to give them an update and say their goodbyes. Drake and his crew had already briefed the governor and were on their way back to Quantico.

A few minutes earlier, Shawn had explained to everyone what had happened the last few days:

"I had a feeling that something was off before we set sail for Tampa," he'd said. "My suspicions were confirmed when Andy came by our room the night before we left. He'd overheard a conversation between the head of security, Edward Schultz, and another security guy. Schultz said they planned to get rid of me. At first Andy thought they meant fire me, until Schultz said that someone was being sent to 'shut me up permanently.' So I prepared as much as I could. I told Andy that I was undercover and asked him if he trusted me enough to help. We'd both served in the armed forces—although at different times and places—and he couldn't resist helping a former brother out.

"What I didn't count on was meeting Amber and getting her involved. When I walked her back to the suite that night, I was as surprised by the attacker as Amber was. Looking back, I should've been more alert. Pezzini must have followed me back from the commissary. When I unlocked Amber's door, he pushed me inside. He immediately saw Amber on the balcony and forced me out there with her. Pleading with him didn't get anywhere and I ran out of options. Pezzini had a gun pointed at Amber and she was ready to jump overboard.

"Just remembering her straddling the rail, leaning over the edge precariously, is terrifying. Pezzini was distracted for a moment when Amber leaned over the edge. I rushed him and knocked the gun out of his hands. It went off, but no one got hit. We struggled, and Pezzini fell overboard. He almost took Amber with him, but I grabbed her in time. She fell off the railing and hit her head. I didn't know how badly she was injured or how many other Morrotti's men were after me.

"I was afraid that with Pezzini falling from Amber's balcony, Morrotti might think she had something to do with his death, or had something to do with our drug sting. I thought neither of us was safe. At this point, the only person I trusted on the ship was Andy. So I decided we had to make a run for it. I would contact Mike once we were safe on land. At least that was the plan.

"Convincing Amber to leave with me was tricky. I wasn't ready to reveal to Amber who I really was. In case we were caught, I figured the less she knew the better. I stuck close to the truth and told her that I was a government agent working for her father and was on the boat to protect her. Little did I know that Amber had had an argument with her parents refusing security on the cruise. I guess that worked in my favor.

"Getting off the boat was a little difficult, but with Andy's help, we did it. Like I said, on my rare days off, I explored the ship. One day I found a storage room where rubber dinghies that needed repair were stashed. I knew where I could launch a boat in an emergency. So I got a dinghy ready.

"Amber and I hid on the ship until it was close to shore. Andy helped us launch the dinghy without being seen, and we made it to Freeport. Then we looked for a safe place to go. Captain Martin or Edward Schultz must have put out a call to their crew when we were reported missing, because a black sport utility vehicle found us really soon and almost ran us over. Before we could react, two large men overpowered us and threw us in the back of the truck.

"They taped our mouths and bound our feet and hands. After a short drive, they loaded us onto a boat and took us below. I'll never forget the frightened look in Amber's eyes. Within an hour, we arrived at our destination.

"We were led off the boat onto a sandy beach. It was then that I realized we were at Cabana Cay. After being loaded onto a golf cart, we traveled down a narrow path until we came to a large plantation house. 'This is weird,' I remember thinking. The house looked out of place on a seemingly deserted island. It reminded me of a large sugarcane plantation home. Then Amber and I were separated. I was ushered into a small, dark room and bound to a chair. I braced myself for an interrogation and a possible beating, which is exactly what happened.

"What I didn't understand is why they didn't throw us overboard or kill us while they had a chance. Why keep us alive? Morrotti must have suspected that I was an undercover agent and knew

I would put some major heat on SeaScape Cruise Lines. Or put them out of business for good. Maybe having Amber with me confused them just enough that they weren't sure what my deal was. I mean, why would an undercover agent be traveling with a high school student, right?

"For two days, I was beaten and interrogated. I was given small amounts of water and bread. But I never revealed my true identity. Then a miracle happened. When Andy realized I was missing, he had found out from a friend of his on the security team that I was being hidden on Asylum Harbor. When the ship docked at Cabana Cay, Andy hid in one of the empty cabanas after the ship left that night. He knew it would be a few hours before someone noticed he was missing. Andy put his special forces training to good use and spent the next thirty-six hours finding his way around the island looking for me. He was able to sneak into the security office and swipe a gun. He followed another guard and found where I was being held. He overpowered the guard, knocked him unconscious, and hid his body in the bushes. Boy, was I happy to see Andy.

"Getting Amber was a different story. I wasn't really sure if she was even still on the island. I figured if she was then she was probably being held in one of the cottages. But Andy hadn't found her when he was searching for me.

"Just as we were about to check out the cottages, we saw Judy getting off an ATV and head into the main house with a large bag. We heard her say something on the radio about Amber before she went inside. Andy left to go secure a boat while I went inside the house. I surprised Judy in the kitchen and subdued her. It took me a while to find Amber's room. When I did, I was the one in for a surprise. She had been planning to escape that night and was waiting for Judy to come in. Amber attacked me before I could tell her who I was. Once she realized it was me—and it took some convincing for her to trust me again—we left the house. We used Judy's keys and took the ATV down toward the beach. We met back up with Andy, who had acquired one of the rental boats. What we didn't know was that Rachel and her team were on the island at the same time looking for us."

Amber got up and gave Shawn a hug. "Thank you for rescuing me, and for trying your best to save my aunt. I'll never forget that."

Rachel had been told earlier that morning that Stephanie Sloan had succumbed to her injuries on the way to the hospital. She was pronounced dead upon arrival along with Andy White.

Governor Knowles shook Shawn's hand. "Thank you for looking after my daughter. I'm sorry about your friend Andy. He was very brave to do what he did and I'll never forget it."

Mike Mancini then gave Governor Knowles an update on the DEA's investigation into SeaScape Cruise Lines.

"The DEA found over twenty million dollars of cocaine in a hidden compartment on the *SeaStar*. They had been secretly using Cabana Cay as a meeting place to transport cocaine and marijuana into the United States. We're looking into some ties between Morrotti and one of the largest Cuban drug lords.

"Morrotti suspected Shawn was undercover and sent one of his henchmen, Charles Jacobsen, who had a suite next to Amber's, to take care of Shawn. Danny Pezzini worked for Jacobsen and was sent to do the dirty work. Like Shawn said, Amber just happened to be in the wrong place at the wrong time.

"One of the employees, a security guard who worked with Schultz, admitted to drugging female passengers and sexually assaulting them. Melodie Sayers was one of those passengers, and she was taken off the ship and kept at Asylum Harbor, where she was passed around by the security guards. Unfortunately, we believe she was killed and her body was dumped.

"The good news is that Morrotti, Captain Martin, Schultz, and some of their crew are being held without bond on multiple charges."

The governor and his wife thanked Rachel and Mike again. After promising to keep in touch, Rachel left the hospital and headed to the hotel to pack.

✦ ✦ ✦

Waiting by the hotel lobby elevator, Rachel heard her name being called. She turned around to see Mike waving at her.

"Hey there. Glad I caught up with you," Mike said, almost out of breath.

"Hi. I thought you had already left."

The elevator opened and Mike stepped in with her.

"I'm heading back to Jacksonville this evening. Tying up some loose ends here first."

"Are you still upset with me?" Rachel asked. After the rescue on Big Dog Cay, Mike let her know that he wasn't happy with her decision to go to Asylum Harbor without telling him or Drake.

He shook his head. "No, but if I didn't care about you, I wouldn't have been so upset. You could've been hurt."

"But I'm not." Rachel smiled at him.

"No, you're not. But let's not rehash this. I wanted to discuss a couple things with you. You left the hospital in such a hurry, I didn't get a chance to tell you something important."

Rachel's heart did a little flip-flop. "Okay."

"When we raided Morrotti's office in Miami, our computer geeks found some photos of Mallory on his computer that were copied from your organization's website. There was also a background report on you from a private investigator that Morrotti was known to hire. We think he sent that photo of Mallory to your hotel room as a diversion."

Rachel felt relief and frustration at the same time.

"Why would he do that?"

Mike shrugged his shoulders. "To divert your attention away from the *SeaStar* case."

"Are you sure it was him?"

Mike nodded. "Sorry. I don't think it really had anything to do with Mallory's disappearance. It was just a sick prank on his part."

Rachel nodded.

"Also, I just wanted to let you know I made a big decision this morning."

"What's that?"

"I've been thinking about this for a while. It's time for me to move on. I'm retiring from the DEA as soon as this case is done."

The elevator door opened and they stepped out.

"Wow, that is a major decision."

"Yeah, I guess so. But for the better. I need to spend more time with my daughter and less with the bad guys."

Rachel stopped at her hotel room door. "So what will you do?"

"Private consulting work. That's after I take some much-needed time off."

She fished her room key card out of her pocket. "Well, I guess this is good-bye, then."

Mike leaned over and gave her a soft kiss on the lips. "Not good-bye. See ya later."

Rachel watched as Mike turned around and got back on the elevator. She smiled and gave him a small wave.

Burn Out

BURN OUT

TRACI HOHENSTEIN

f THOMAS & MERCER

Acknowledgments

I would like to thank the following people who helped make this book possible. To all my first readers for their invaluable insight and critiques of this novel: Carl Hohenstein, Shirley Satterfield, Michelle Couch, Stephanie Roessler, Lisa Abrams-Morris, Leann Thompson, and Sheila Pennington. Thanks to Suzette Breland for your expert legal advice and for graciously letting me use your name. Jeroen Ten Berge for the brilliant cover art and my new editor, Kay Keppler, who has an amazing way with words.

Author's note: Santa Rosa Beach is a real town. It's a place where I proudly live and play. We're home to the world's most beautiful beaches. The police and fire department are fictionally named in this novel, but their courage and honor is real. My husband and the firefighters he works with at South Walton Fire District are the best of the best! The Donut Hole, La Paz, and The Red Bar are some of my favorite restaurants in the area, and YOLO Board is headquartered in Santa Rosa Beach.

*To my husband, Carl Hohenstein,
and all the firefighters at South Walton Fire District*

Chapter One
Samantha Collins's story
Santa Rosa Beach, FL, Thursday 6:36 p.m.

Just breathe. Stay focused. I repeated the mantra to calm myself. This fire wasn't my first, but my heart still raced a thousand beats a minute as I made my way through flames so vivid I thought I was in hell.

I crawled along the hallway, gripping the fire hose. The smoke was thick and I couldn't see past my gloves. Angry, orange flames danced up the walls. The heat was intense, even through my protective gear.

Leading my crew through the maze of Campbell's Farmers' Market, I pictured the layout in my head. Now, with flames roaring all around us, it looked completely different. I had to get to the rear of the building where the owner's son had last been seen in his office.

My knees throbbed, and my wrists and hands stung, but I knew every second counted when a person's life was in jeopardy. I dismissed my pains and focused on moving forward.

Creeping through the dense smoke, I found what I thought was the door to the office. I stopped and felt the door before cautiously pushing it open. The smoke was not as heavy as it had been in the hallway. I slowly made my way around the office and motioned to Kevin and Mack, the guys on my crew, to look around the desk.

I felt around the floor and my hand hit on something hard near the back of the door. I called out to Mack and showed him the body.

"Command. Occupant located. We're heading out. Conditions are worsening," I spoke calmly into the radio, though on the inside my adrenaline was pumping overtime.

Mack and Kevin carried him out while I followed closely behind holding the line. I heard a crash and turned around to look. Seeing anything through all the heavy smoke was nearly impossible, but in the distance a sliver of light gleamed. *What the hell was that?*

When we got within a few feet of the front door, I felt a shiver go down my spine. Turning around, I saw a figure heading toward the rear of the building. *Where did that person come from?* I turned my attention to the front door to ensure my crew was safely outside. Knowing full well it was against protocol, I made a split-second decision to follow. As I was making my way back through dense smoke, my air tank suddenly beeped, sending out a signal I was running low.

The person had firefighter gear on, but as I got closer, I could just barely make out who it was. *What the hell is he doing here?* I quickened my pace, bumping into furniture and equipment, trying to catch up. Tripping over something, I landed hard on my side. Within a couple of minutes I heard the frantic call through my radio.

"Mayday!" Command called in a desperate tone. "One firefighter unaccounted for. Mayday!"

My last thought was of Bella and Gracie, my sweet little girls, before the roof collapsed into a fiery crash all around me.

Chapter Two

Miami, FL, Monday 8:30 a.m.

Florida Omni Search was located a block off the beach in Miami. Rachel Scott, the founder of the company, had converted an old souvenir shop into their office.

She walked through the door juggling a briefcase in one hand and three coffees and a bag of bagels in the other. "Good morning, everyone," Rachel said with a smile. She dropped everything onto the reception desk.

"Coffee. You're my savior," said Janine.

"Good morning, Ms. Scott." Red Cooper reached into the white bakery bag and pulled out a bagel.

"I forgot to pick up a new coffeemaker this weekend. I was too busy doing nothing," Rachel said.

"I don't blame you. After the hellish month we've had, you deserved a break," Janine said.

Janine Jensen was the cofounder of Florida Omni Search and Rachel's closest friend. She was a few years older than Rachel and wore her wavy hair shoulder length. She had a hippie look and favored long skirts with flip-flops year-round.

Rachel had been traveling the last month on two back-to-back difficult searches for missing people. It kept her mind busy and her karma bank account full.

"Anything come in over the weekend?" Rachel took a sip of her caramel-flavored latte, savoring the sweet taste and the hit of caffeine.

Florida Omni Search was a nonprofit organization that specialized in the search and rescue of missing people. It ran twenty-four hours a day, seven days a week, and the volunteers answered the toll-free hotline, fielding calls from law enforcement agencies and family members requesting assistance.

"We only had a couple of calls," Red said while looking at the call log. "One was for a runaway teen from Orlando, but she was found safe and sound with her boyfriend at a rest stop about an hour away from home. The other call you may want to look at. A firefighter was reported missing from Santa Rosa Beach."

Red Cooper was Florida Omni Search's top investigator. His real name was Winston, but he earned the nickname "Red" during his childhood because of his thick, curly red hair. These days Red was short, beefy, and bald. He was also a former detective from the Miami Police Department, divorced three times, no kids, and an avid collector of Harley Davidson motorcycles. He ran Cooper Investigations out of the Florida Omni Search offices and, in exchange for free rent, worked on Rachel's cases when she needed assistance. He was a jack-of-all-trades—background checks, surveillance, and sometimes, personal security. Rachel had known Red for a long time and trusted him with her life.

"Santa Rosa Beach is up in the North Florida Panhandle, right? Near Panama City Beach?"

"Yes. It's about a twelve-hour drive from here."

"Who called it in?" Rachel flipped through the call log. Most calls were routine. Runaway teenagers usually topped the list, followed by adults who were thought to be missing, but turned up a couple days later. Sometimes the FBI or other law enforcement agencies called to request assistance. She'd worked some pretty high-profile cases and had sophisticated equipment most agencies didn't have the budget for.

"This came in from the missing firefighter's mother. According to her, the daughter was on duty when a call came in for a warehouse fire. She went into the building with her crew to search for a victim, and during the rescue, she disappeared. The roof collapsed and she was presumed dead." Red took a bite out of his bagel. A blob of cream cheese fell on his chin. "But here's the kicker. Her body was never found."

"When did this happen?" Rachel grabbed a napkin and handed it to him.

"The fire was Thursday evening. The firefighter's mom, Nora, called us on Sunday. There's a little more to the story and I think you should hear it from her." Red handed her the number.

"Here's to a busy morning!" Janine said, raising her coffee cup.

"Enjoy breakfast. I'll be in my office," Rachel said.

Rachel's office was covered with artwork and letters from children of family members she'd helped find. Artwork motivated her more than all the degrees and awards that used to hang in her former real estate office.

She'd come a long way from the days when she'd been a Miami socialite and real estate mogul. Back then, her time was filled with multimillion-dollar business deals, shopping, nightly parties, and events. She'd always been dressed to the nines in Dolce & Gabbana, Tori Burch, and Gucci. She'd had weekly manicures, facials, and visits to the hair salon. Maintaining her lifestyle had cost thousands of dollars a month.

The disappearance of her three-year-old daughter, Mallory, had changed all that. The day Mallory vanished was the day Rachel's old life vanished forever, too.

Chapter Three

Rachel replayed the morning Mallory disappeared, just like she did every day. That day had been hectic. The nanny who normally cared for Mallory had called in sick. Rachel had been trying to close a big real estate deal that involved a piece of commercial property. If it closed successfully, she'd net a ninety-thousand-dollar commission. Her husband, Rick, owned several luxury car dealerships throughout Florida and had been on his way out of town.

After breakfast, she'd quickly gotten Mallory dressed. Mallory had insisted on wearing her princess costume, complete with tiara and little high-heeled shoes. Everyone had always told Rachel that Mallory looked like a miniature Little Mermaid with her long, curly red hair and bigger-than-life emerald-green eyes. It had been a beautiful day so she'd taken Mallory outside to play. While Mallory played with her dolls on the front lawn, Rachel sat on the porch crunching numbers, trying to find a way to save the deal.

Mallory had asked over and over, "Mommy, will you please come play with me?"

"Baby, Mommy is busy working. In a little while, okay?"

"Please, Mommy. I'll let you be the princess if you want," Mallory had pleaded.

"In a few minutes, honey. Let me finish this. Okay?"

Mallory had poked her lower lip out. "Please?"

She heard the phone ringing inside. "Mallory, I'll be right back." She'd run inside to answer it. It was probably Rick calling to say he'd made it to the airport. She'd been inside only a couple of minutes. When she came back outside, Mallory was gone.

Frantically, she'd looked everywhere for Mallory. Front yard, inside the house, backyard, garage, and up and down the street. Everywhere. No Mallory. Her world had come crashing down all around her.

That's all it took. Two minutes and her daughter vanished. No leads, no witnesses, nothing. It was like she'd fallen off the face of the earth.

Weeks later, when the story got hot and received national attention, all the wacky leads had come in. The police had followed up on as many as they deemed reasonable. It wasn't enough for Rachel. Mallory was never found.

She felt the guilt of not spending enough time with Mallory. She cursed herself for not paying attention the morning she was taken. Rachel's obsession with finding Mallory took a toll on her marriage. Rick eventually moved out and their divorce soon followed.

Rachel took all her anger and grief and turned it into a positive thing. She would never stop looking for Mallory, but she realized that she had the money and resources to help find other missing people.

After a year of putting together her team—forensic experts, experienced search and rescue volunteers, and top investigators—she started Florida Omni Search. Now, three years later, she had located over a hundred missing children and adults. She rarely turned down a case and would help just about anyone who needed her. With over 2,300 Americans, including children, reported missing every day, how could she not?

Rachel sat down at her desk and picked up a picture of her and Mallory that she kept in a silver frame. The picture had been taken at Disney World the year Mallory disappeared. She was standing in front of Cinderella's castle, holding Mallory in her arms. Mallory was wearing her pink tutu and eating an ice cream cone. She had chocolate sauce dripping down her little arm and a huge smile on her face.

Rachel had tears in her eyes as she put down the photo. She hardly recognized the woman in the picture. The woman she used to be. The beautiful, well-put-together woman with long auburn hair and makeup that was always perfect. Staring at the picture, she longed to hold Mallory again in her arms. "I will always, always look for you. I will never give up," she said. She repeated those words every day as she looked at her daughter's smiling face. She missed her little girl so much it physically hurt.

She wiped away her tears and took a deep breath as she refocused her energy on helping the missing firefighter. She dialed the number on the paper Red gave her, and after several rings, a child answered the phone.

"Hello. This is Rachel. May I speak to Nora?" The phone clunked down with a clatter. After a few seconds, Nora picked up.

"Hello?"

"Nora, this is Rachel Scott from Florida Omni Search. I'm returning your call about Samantha."

"Oh, Ms. Scott," Nora cried on the phone. "Thank you so much for calling me back. I've seen you on that TV show about missing people. I hope you can help me find my daughter, Samantha. I just know something bad happened to her."

"I'll help you in any way I can, Nora. Why don't you tell me what happened?" Rachel leaned back into her chair and listened to Nora's bizarre story.

Chapter Four

After speaking with Nora about her daughter's strange disappearance, Rachel committed herself to finding Sam. Before she headed up to Santa Rosa Beach, she wanted to find out everything she could on the case. She ran a Google search, which came up with an article that was posted under "Breaking Local News" in the *Walton Sun*, the local newspaper, that morning:

FIRE DESTROYS CAMPBELL'S FARMERS' MARKET
ONE FIREFIGHTER DECLARED MISSING

The Santa Rosa Beach Fire Department responded to a fire at Campbell's Farmers' Market Thursday night.

Fire Chief Glen Toomey said the twenty-five-thousand-square-foot warehouse that housed the farmers' market caught fire around 6:30 p.m. The owner's son was reported to have been trapped inside. Lt. Samantha Collins and her crew were the first to respond and went inside to locate the victim. After the firefighters pulled him from the building, they noticed Lt. Collins was missing. A mayday call was quickly sent out with no response from Lt. Collins. A few moments later, the roof collapsed.

Firefighters and investigators have searched the rubble and the surrounding area, but Lt. Collins has not been found. Her firefighter helmet, however, was discovered in the rear parking lot. A source close to the investigation said the police department is stumped. They do not know what happened to Lt. Collins.

In an interesting twist, her husband, Ken Collins, former captain of the Santa Rosa Beach Police Department, was arrested two months ago for running a marijuana grow operation from his property. Samantha was scheduled to testify at his trial later this week.

Charges had been filed against Samantha Collins in the case, but were later dropped when no evidence could be found that she knew about the grow operation. Samantha's mom, Nora Prince, does not believe Collins would intentionally leave her children, ages four and six. Prince was watching her grandchildren while Collins worked her regular shift at the fire department.

"Something happened to my daughter," Prince said. "She wouldn't leave her kids. She was worried about what was going to happen if Ken was convicted and sent to prison. But she is a strong person and was planning on going to his trial to show support."

Collins's best friend, Tammie Boyles, repeated the same sentiment.

"Sam would never run from her problems. She was concerned about money and wondered how she would support her and the kids without Ken, but she was working it out. She would never leave them at a time like this."

Santa Rosa Beach authorities are considering Lt. Samantha Collins a "missing and endangered adult." Anyone with information is asked to call the Santa Rosa Beach Police Department.

The news article confirmed everything Nora had told her. Rachel emerged from her office to find Janine at the front desk. She was training a new volunteer to answer the phone.

"Janine, I'm going to drive up to Santa Rosa Beach after lunch. Will you find out what volunteers we have there and put them on standby? Also, I'll need the number for the fire marshal's office. I want to call them on the way and set up a meeting for when I get there."

"Okay, I'm on it. Red just left to run some errands, but he can help out when he gets back." Janine grabbed her notepad to take notes. "What about Peter and Rankin? You want them to go with you?"

Peter Moore and Rankin Smartz were part of her search team and usually went on all search and rescue cases with Rachel.

"Just let them know what's going on. I'll call as soon as I meet with the investigators and get a better handle on the case. This isn't going to be your run-of-the-mill disappearance case. I can feel it." Rachel gave her the details of the conversation she'd had with Nora and what information she'd gleaned from the news article.

"Are you taking Maggie with you?" Janine asked. Maggie was a black Lab Rachel had had since she was a puppy. She bought Maggie for her daughter on her second birthday. Maggie was her only companion since Mallory's disappearance. She rarely went anywhere without her.

"Not this time. I was hoping she could stay with you and Jack," Rachel said, smiling hopefully. Jack was Janine's seven-year-old and he absolutely adored Maggie.

"Of course," Janine said, smiling. "Jack has been missing her lately." When he was two years old, Jack had been abducted by Janine's husband after a nasty custody battle. Rachel was still dealing with the loss of her own daughter and had seen the news about Jack's disappearance. She'd reached out to Janine, and together, they'd helped track down Jack and his father. They'd formed a tight bond and opened up Florida Omni Search together. Janine had a drive and determination equal to Rachel's.

"I'm going home to pack, so call me on the cell with the information when you get it. Pretty please," Rachel said.

"Bossy," Janine replied back.

"You know you love it."

"Do you need me to make hotel arrangements for you?"

"No, I already took care of that. I'm going to stay at a rental house my friend Michelle Couch owns. You remember Michelle?"

"Sure. You guys went to Florida State together."

"That's right. She's a psychologist and lives near Santa Rosa Beach. Thankfully she owns a few rental properties in the area and graciously offered to let me stay at one. I'll call you with the address and number when I get there." Rachel gave Janine a hug good-bye.

They had a great working relationship. Janine had full custody of Jack now, so she rarely traveled with Rachel. She had years of administrative experience and was better equipped to run the office. On the other hand, Rachel liked to get out and meet people. She also had an amazing sixth sense and a knack for knowing what made people tick. The arrangement worked well for them.

Rachel walked back to the parking lot and unlocked her SUV, stashing her briefcase. It was another change in her life. She had traded in her black 7 Series BMW for a black four-wheel-drive Tahoe. She climbed in and headed home.

Rachel actually had two homes. When Mallory went missing she couldn't bear to sell her house. In the back of her mind, she felt that one day Mallory would come back home. And she didn't want strangers living there if that happened. So she kept it empty except for a live-in maid and her ex-husband, who was the maintenance man. It was crazy to spend what she did to keep the empty house, but she couldn't help it.

Her second home was a cute three-bedroom Florida bungalow near the beach. It had a small pool, hot tub, and a yard for Maggie. She was rarely home, so it suited her nicely. And it was a quick drive from the office.

It didn't take Rachel long to get everything she needed for the trip. She always kept a suitcase packed since she traveled on the road quite a bit. Ever since Mallory disappeared, her longing to help others had gotten stronger.

Rachel heard her phone beep, letting her know she had a text message. She checked her BlackBerry. Janine had sent the phone numbers she needed to get started with the case.

She called the fire marshal's office to make an appointment with the lead investigator, Jeff Stanton. Jeff said he was familiar with her work. Rachel Scott and Florida Omni Search had made national headlines when they'd recently been involved in a high-profile case involving the only daughter of Florida governor John Knowles. They agreed to meet at Jeff's office the next morning at 8:00 a.m.

She threw everything in the back of her Tahoe and went inside to get Maggie and her things. When she took Maggie to Janine's, she always packed extra food and toys in case she was gone longer than she'd expected. She grabbed the bag of Science Diet dog food and reached into the wicker basket for Maggie's favorite squeaky toys. The purple dinosaur, a yellow duck, and a red plastic ball all went into a baggie.

Maggie sat watching Rachel with great interest, her thick black tail wagging. Her tail was so long and heavy that it would probably be illegal in some states. One unintentional whip of her tail would leave a bruise on someone's leg.

The loyal black Lab jumped eagerly into the Tahoe. Rachel rubbed Maggie on top of her head. "Good girl. You're going to Jack's house for a few days. Aren't you lucky?"

Maggie gave a cheerful bark.

Chapter Five
Santa Rosa Beach, FL, Monday 10:30 a.m.

Ken Collins was wearing a standard-issue gray prison uniform. His hair was brown with silver streaked throughout—kept clean and short, military style. His face was graced with wrinkles and his eyes were the color of iced tea. Pacing in his eight-by-ten jail cell, he thought how screwed up his life had become in such a short amount of time. He reflected back to just a few days ago when he'd received the worst news of his life.

"Get up, Ken. You got a visitor." *The prison guard rapped on his cell.*

Ken threw his legs over the top bunk and jumped down. He wasn't expecting anyone. His lawyer came by every Tuesday like clockwork to discuss his case. But today was Friday. He wondered what was up. Ken walked with the guard down the long hallway toward the visitors' room. However, the guard kept walking.

"Where are we going?" *Ken asked, puzzled, after they passed the visitors' room.*

The guard kept walking in silence.

"I thought I had a visitor," *Ken mumbled as they passed through two security doors. They stopped in front of the warden's office.*

What the hell? *Ken thought.* This could be really good or really bad. The warden wasn't known for having social visits.

The guard rapped on the door. "Ken Collins," *the guard announced as he opened the door.*

"Thank you. You can leave," the warden instructed the guard.

"Ken, please, have a seat." The warden gestured to a chair across from his desk.

The nameplate sitting atop a putty-colored metal desk read Buster Radcliffe.

"Ken, I know you're wondering what you're doing here," Buster began.

Ken nodded his head.

"Well, you do have visitors, but before you see them, I wanted to talk to you first." Buster straightened up in his chair. He was six foot five, and even though he was on the skinny side, he was solid muscle. With thick red hair and a smattering of freckles across his face, he looked a lot younger than his fifty-four years. Ken thought he looked like Howdy Doody.

Buster and Ken had a long friendship that had started when Ken was promoted to captain at the police department. Ken had sent many men to this same jail. Buster and Ken had appeared in court together. They were both members of the local Kiwanis and Rotary Clubs. They ran in the same social circles. Yet Buster treated Ken like any other prisoner. He acted like he'd never existed outside the prison walls.

"Okay," Ken said, a man of few words.

"There's no easy way to say it. Your wife has disappeared."

Ken came out of his chair. "What?"

"There was a fire last night over at the farmers' market and Sam and her crew responded. They were inside the warehouse trying to find the owner's son. After they pulled him out, Sam went back in." Buster paused. "There was an explosion."

Ken's face drained of color. "But I thought you said she disappeared?" He had trouble getting the words out. "Is she hurt?"

"I don't know. They found her helmet outside the back door of the warehouse. The state fire marshal's office is still investigating. They searched the warehouse, but they didn't find her. Police Chief Gladstone is here to see you and he can tell you more about what happened. Your lawyer's here, too. I wanted to let you know what was going on before you met with them."

Ken slowly sat down in his chair again. "Thank you." He didn't know why he said that. His beautiful wife was missing, and he was in jail and couldn't do a damn thing about it.

A million thoughts went through his head. His first thought was that Sam left him. She couldn't take the strain of his trial, all the mounting bills and the pressure of an investigation. So she just got up and left. That was the best-case scenario because it meant she was alive. But he couldn't believe that Sam would ever leave the kids behind. Something bad must have happened and Samantha was hurt, or worse.

"Sorry to be the bearer of bad news." Buster got up from his chair and walked over to the door. He gave Ken a hearty pat on the back as he stood up. "Good luck, son."

Ken followed the guard back down the same hallway they had just walked ten minutes ago. This time the guard stopped at the visitors' room. It was a large, surprisingly clean, and bright room with many tables and chairs. A large box of toys sat in the corner, along with a small bookcase that held children's books and magazines. Ken had never wanted his children to see him in a place like this. He'd asked Sam and her mother not to bring them here. He would rather they remembered him as a good dad. Not a common criminal.

He recognized his former boss sitting next to his attorney.

"Ken, I'm sorry about Samantha," Chief Gladstone said.

Suzette Breland, his attorney, nodded in agreement. "We're all shocked by the news. Did the warden give you the story?"

"Yes, he just did. Some of it. What happened?" Ken felt numb as he sat down.

Chief Gladstone went through the events on the night of the fire. "No one knows why Samantha went back into the fire. We did a search of the area last night and again at daybreak. Nothing was found, except Sam's helmet. But we're still investigating. Your mother-in-law came to the scene this morning. She's obviously very upset. She said she was going to call in a special search team."

Ken felt his mouth go dry.

"When was the last time you spoke to Sam?" Chief Gladstone asked.

"Tuesday." He cleared his throat. "She and Suzette came to visit."

"We went over her testimony for the trial," Suzette said, picking at her nails. She had painted them a bright pink, which matched the bright-pink highlighted section of her hair. She dressed a little promiscuously, but she had the reputation of being a bulldog in the courtroom. She didn't take no for an answer and fought like hell for all her clients.

"How did she seem to you?" Chief Gladstone asked.

"Like always," Ken said. "She was a little stressed about the trial and about money. But she seemed to be holding up pretty good." He sighed.

"She didn't mention wanting to leave the area or get away from it all?"

"No, absolutely not. I thought about that, but she'd never purposely leave the kids. What are you getting at? That she was planning on leaving us?"

"I'm just trying to cover all the bases, Ken. You know how this works."

"Well, I'm telling you she wouldn't leave. Sam doesn't run away from her problems."

"How about threats? Anyone been threatening her?"

Ken shook his head. "You mean the local drug cartel?"

"Anyone at all."

"No. I don't know that she'd tell me if she felt threatened by anyone. Sam tries to be the tough one. And she wouldn't want me to worry about anything while I'm in here, anyway."

"How about you? Have you gotten any threats lately?"

"I haven't exactly been making friends," Ken said smugly. "But nothing specific."

"Okay. If you think of anything else, let me know." Chief Gladstone looked Ken over for a few seconds. "I'm really sorry about this, Ken. I know how much you care for your family."

Ken nodded. "Thanks."

"I'm going to talk to the judge today to see if we can get a postponement," Suzette said. She pushed her chair back and stood up. Today she was wearing a tight blouse with a short, dark skirt that showed off all her assets. Ken wondered how she got away with dressing like that in the courtroom. It just suited her perfectly, though. "In light of everything that has happened, I don't think it will be a problem."

"Okay. If we're done here…" Ken said.

"I'll be in touch, son." Chief Gladstone got up to leave.

Chapter Six

Santa Rosa Beach, FL, Tuesday 6:00 a.m.

After a twelve-hour drive from Miami to Santa Rosa Beach, Rachel had a hard time getting up and ready for her meeting the next morning. Michelle had set her up with a nice beach house overlooking the beautiful sugar sand beaches and crystal-clear waters of the Gulf of Mexico. She wanted to stay in bed listening to the waves crashing and the calls of the seagulls.

Santa Rosa Beach was a small coastal town that was home to about ten thousand people year-round. During the summer tourist season, the population soared to about fifty thousand, give or take a few. Most people who lived here were either retired or worked in the tourist industry—as fishermen, hotel workers, restaurant employees, real estate agents, and kitschy clothing and gift boutique shop owners.

Rachel drove over to a popular local diner called the Donut Hole to grab a cup of coffee before her meeting with the fire investigator. The waitress took her order of stuffed french toast with bacon, and she settled in to read the paper. The *Walton Sun* had run a full-length feature about Samantha and the warehouse fire. Rachel read the highlights of the article again.

"Hi. Excuse me, but are you Rachel Scott?"

Rachel looked up from the newspaper and studied the man standing before her. He was tall and good looking, with thick, dark hair and kind eyes. She put him to be around mid to late thirties.

"Yes. And you are?"

"I thought I recognized you from the news shows about missing people. Samantha's mom said you might be coming up here to help us." He held out his hand. "Mack Dixon."

She instantly recognized his name from the article she'd just read.

"Ah, Samantha's partner from the fire department." Rachel shook his hand. "Please have a seat." She motioned to the chair across from her.

"Sorry to disturb your breakfast, but I wanted to say hello and see if there was anything I could do to help." Mack sat down. "Sam's a good friend of mine."

"Sorry to hear what happened." Rachel paused while the waitress set down her food and offered Mack some coffee. "I'm meeting with Jeff Stanton this morning to go over the case. Anything you can tell me about Sam would help."

"Sam and I are close. We've known each other since grade school. Her husband and I are also good friends. I was best man at their wedding." Mack let out a deep breath. "I keep going through my head what happened that night and nothing makes sense."

"What did happen that night?" Rachel asked. "The paper doesn't say much."

"Well, all day long Sam had seemed a little distracted. She'd gotten a phone call around dinnertime that upset her. She didn't want to talk about it when I asked if she was okay. I just figured it was Ken. His trial is scheduled to start this week and she was going to testify."

Rachel chewed absently on her thumbnail. It was a bad habit she'd picked up recently when she was deep in thought. "Do you think Ken's involvement with marijuana had anything to do with her disappearance?"

"I've thought about it, but I hope not. It does seem a coincidence that Sam disappeared right around the time his trial is supposed to start."

"Did you get a chance to talk with her again?"

Mack shook his head. "We got called to the warehouse fire just a few minutes later."

"How many were on your shift?"

"Five, including me and Sam."

"Would you walk me through what happened? Give me a better understanding on how she disappeared?"

"Sure. We got the dispatch call around dinnertime. The owner had called it in. Apparently, his son was late for a family dinner and the dad went back to the market when he didn't answer his calls. The son is diabetic and the dad got worried something was wrong. But when he got there, the place was on fire. Our crew went in to get the guy while the other firefighters started pulling hoses." Mack paused to take a few sips of his coffee.

While Mack was drinking, Rachel took the time to admire his athletic build. He was a good-looking guy. She could easily imagine him posing for one of those firefighter calendars that featured barechested men with nothing on but bunker gear pants and suspenders.

Mack continued. "Sam went in first and Kevin and I were right behind her. We got to the office, found the son, and pulled him out. But then I turned around to talk to Sam, and she wasn't there. I tried calling on the radio, but she didn't answer. I alerted the chief, but by the time we put out a mayday, the roof had started to collapse. I didn't think she'd made it." Mack rubbed his face with his hands.

Rachel could tell he was devastated. Tears welled up in his eyes.

"It was like losing my best friend."

She thought about it for a minute and took a sip of her coffee. Her breakfast went untouched. Mack's story was mesmerizing. She couldn't take her eyes off of him. "Do you know how the fire started?"

"No. I'm sure Jeff Stanton can tell you more. I *can* tell you the fire burned fast and hot, which is typical of arson. Some kind of accelerant was probably used." Mack hesitated for a second. "We've had our share of arson over the last couple of months, so it wouldn't surprise me if it was ruled as arson."

"Do they know who started the other fires?"

"They're still under investigation. Jeff can probably tell you more."

Rachel looked down at her watch. "I have a meeting with him in about fifteen minutes, so I should get going. Do you mind if I call you later?"

Mack wrote down his number on a napkin. "Anything I can do, just let me know. Good luck with your meeting." He handed her the napkin. "I hope you find out what happened to Sam. She's special to a lot of people, including me."

Chapter Seven

Rachel walked into the Santa Rosa Beach Fire Marshal's office at 8:00 sharp. She told the receptionist that Jeff Stanton was expecting her.

The receptionist replied warmly, "Of course. Just take this hallway down to the end. He's in the last office on the left."

As Rachel walked down the hallway, she couldn't help but notice how nice the offices were. She'd expected the cold, drab decor of other government offices she'd visited. Gunmetal-gray desks with beat-up file cabinets crossed her mind. Instead, she saw solid oak desks with pictures of families in nice frames. The walls were adorned with certificates of achievements and degrees.

When she got to Investigator Jeff Stanton's office, the door was ajar. She knocked twice and poked her head around the door. The first thing that struck her about Jeff was that he looked like Will Ferrell—curly dark hair with blue eyes a little too close to his nose.

"Hi. You must be Rachel Scott," Jeff said as he stood up from his desk and shook her hand. "Please have a seat."

"You have a very nice office."

"Thank you. I inherited most of this from the last investigator. I've only been here about six months. Transferred from the Tallahassee office." Jeff got down to the business at hand. "So you want to help with the Samantha Collins case?"

"Yes. I was contacted by the family to see if I could help find her," Rachel said. "Can you tell me where you are on the investigation?"

"Instead of telling you, why don't I show you? We can take a ride over to the site and then I'll tell you what we've got so far."

✦ ✦ ✦

As they drove up to the warehouse, Rachel saw a large wooden sign with *Campbell's Farmers' Market* in big red letters. Underneath, it read, *Family Owned and Operated For Over Fifty Years.* Jagged pieces of the roof were charred, and the smell of smoke still hung in the air. Two yellow forklifts and a bulldozer were parked along the edge of the parking lot.

"We've got a lot of rural farms within a hundred miles of the beach. Most of them contract with Campbell's to sell their produce and goods. It's really busy during tourist season and weekends. Been around for a long time," Jeff said. "The front of the market has stalls that people can lease. The back of the warehouse has two offices and a large storage area."

"It's so sad to see it burned down."

As they got out and looked around, Jeff said, "The fire was huge. Four stations responded to the call. We needed twenty fire-fighters and five hours to put it out."

"How big is the warehouse?"

"It's about twenty-five thousand square feet, including the offices and storage space."

"This is the main entrance?"

"Yeah, Sam was last seen here when they pulled out the owner's son. She must have gone to the rear entrance, because that's where we found her helmet. Then she disappeared." Jeff shook his head. "Strange. We have no idea what happened to her."

"Was any of her other gear found?" Rachel asked.

"Just her helmet in the rear parking lot. It's like she vanished into thin air."

That was how most people responded to her questions about missing loved ones. "They just vanished into thin air" was a common response.

Rachel followed Jeff around to the back of the warehouse. "Have you searched the woods around here?" Rachel pointed to the large empty lot, thick with trees and underbrush, behind the warehouse.

"The police department came out Sunday with a couple of their search and rescue dogs, but they didn't turn up anything."

"Have you talked with any of the neighbors?" Rachel noted the warehouse had a residence to the west, an empty lot to the east, and a convenience store across the street.

"We interviewed the neighbors next door and the clerk who was on duty at the convenience store the night of the fire. No one remembers seeing anything unusual."

"Take me through what happened that night," Rachel said. Even though she had heard the story first from Nora and then from Mack, she wanted to make sure she didn't miss anything. Every detail was critical.

"The call went out around six thirty p.m. Because the owner said he thought his son, Mike, was in the building, Sam's crew went in first. Sam found Mike on the floor behind the door of his office. Mack and Kevin dragged him out to the front door, which is about a thousand feet from the office. When they got out, they started CPR. It was Mack who noticed Sam was gone. He took a quick look inside the front door and didn't see her, so he put in a mayday call. Then the first explosion hit and the roof collapsed."

Mack's story matched with the investigator's. "How long was it until someone searched the rear of the building?"

"The district chief was first on scene with Station Three. He drove around the building when they first arrived. He didn't see anything out of the ordinary. When Sam and her crew went in to locate the victim, the chief stayed with the pump operator in front of the warehouse. There were two other trucks that came to assist with the fire. They arrived after the first explosion."

"I met Mack Dixon this morning. He mentioned you had some fires lately that were ruled as arson."

"We've been investigating a possible arsonist for the last couple months," Jeff confirmed.

"You think the same person started the warehouse fire?"

"It's too early to tell. We're still waiting on the lab to come back with test results and it takes a while."

"What does your gut tell you?"

"Off the record…This could be the work of the same person who set fire to a couple of properties last month. The first fire was a beach house—it was vacant, so nobody was hurt, thank goodness, but it was totaled. It was fully involved by the time firefighters got there. The arsonist pried a door open and then used gasoline as an accelerant."

"And the second one?"

"That was at Nick's Seafood Restaurant out on the beach highway. Same MO. The restaurant was closed for the night. The back door was pried opened and gasoline was used."

"Did Sam work those other fires?"

"Well, that's the interesting thing. All the fires were on Sam's shift. Coincidence? I don't know. But whoever set those fires was an amateur. Gas is an easily traceable accelerant," Jeff explained. "Lots of people set their property on fire to collect insurance or get out from under the debt. Pros would use something that would be harder to detect."

"Did the owners of the properties check out okay?"

"Yep. The vacant house was paid for and the owner didn't have any debt or any motive to have started the fire. The owners of the restaurant were mortgaged to the hilt, but we didn't find any evidence to point to their involvement, either."

"Tell me again how the arsonist gained access."

"They broke in through a back door in both cases. We're waiting to see if the tool marks match in each of the cases. After the warehouse fire, I put a rush on it. I should hear something soon."

"No fingerprints or any other evidence left at the crime scene?"

"Nope, not so far. I'm meeting with Police Chief Gladstone tomorrow to go over the case file. I'll let you know what we come up with."

They walked to the front of the warehouse and stood in front Stanton's truck. Rachel took a camera out of her pocket. "Do you mind if I take some pictures?"

"Go right ahead."

While she took some shots around the front of the warehouse, she said, "I read the article about Sam's husband, Ken Collins, and his involvement in the marijuana operation. It seems like Sam was under a lot of pressure with the trial and everything else that was going on. Do you think she saw an opportunity to run?"

"We thought about that scenario, too."

"She could've waited for an opportunity and took off. A risky one, but it could have happened. I've seen all kinds." Rachel took a few more pictures of the charred building.

"Have you talked with Sam's family yet?" Jeff asked.

"That's my next stop."

Chapter Eight
Santa Rosa Beach, FL, County Jail, Tuesday 9:30 a.m.

Ken lay on his bunk and stared at the ceiling in his jail cell. He couldn't believe Sam was missing. It was his fault and there was nothing he could do about it. He'd never felt so helpless in his life.

He thought back to the day when his life began to unravel. It had started as a routine traffic stop. He'd been training a rookie and it was midnight, almost the end of their shift. They'd pulled over a guy driving a late-model Camaro with a broken taillight.

His trainee had approached the car and, after speaking with the driver, thought he'd smelled marijuana. The driver was a nineteen-year-old male named Jason Blum. Jason had admitted he'd smoked a joint before being pulled over.

After a search of the car revealed several bags of marijuana in the trunk, they'd arrested Jason. Deals had been struck, and Jason was given immunity from prosecution in exchange for disclosing his source.

The sting operation, which had included the police, sheriff's office, and DEA, was the largest in the county. It had ultimately ended with the arrest of Pedro Gonzalez, who was a part of the local Mexican drug cartel. They had been growing a strain of marijuana called "Cush," which was popular with teenagers and college students. Cush was known to give a quick and long-lasting high. It was expensive to grow and expensive to buy, but the high it gave the user was worth the cost.

One night, not long after the bust, Ken and his buddies had been sitting around a fire in his backyard drinking beer and talking about the case. Patrick Hart, a firefighter who worked with Sam, said he'd watched a show on the Discovery Channel about how to grow marijuana. Ken mentioned to Patrick how much money had been confiscated during Pedro's arrest.

"That's a lot of moola. I wonder who'll take over the local marijuana market now that Pedro's out?" Patrick had asked as he popped open another beer.

"Maybe you should look into it. You could finance your little real estate endeavors," Brent, one of Ken's buddies, had said.

Patrick was trying to save his money to put a down payment on a fixer-upper he'd planned to flip. "No way. I don't know anything about that stuff," he'd said.

"Thirty K a month profit sure would help me out," Ken had said. "I could learn pretty fast how to manufacture it if I knew I could make that much money."

Ken made a decent salary at the police department and Sam was doing well at the fire department, but with the high cost of living in a beach community, they were just making ends meet. With two kids to raise and now a second mortgage on the land, the idea had been tempting.

After his buddies had left, Ken couldn't get the idea out of his head. He'd gotten on the computer and researched the equipment needed to get started growing marijuana. He'd been amazed at all the websites that were dedicated to growing and manufacturing marijuana for profit.

He'd been very tempted to try it out. At first he'd thought of it as an experiment to see if he could get the plants to grow and produce a viable product. He hadn't believed how easy it was to get started. Once he'd rented a private post office box, he ordered the seeds and special lights for indoor growing through one of the websites.

He hadn't wanted his wife or anyone else to find out what he was doing. Finding the perfect place to grow the marijuana had been easy, too—he had a nice, large pole barn on his fifteen acres of land. His wife never went out there and it was practically hidden from view with all the trees.

Within a few months, he'd produced a viable plant to harvest. Then he'd just needed to figure out how to market the product. That was the tricky part. One wrong move could land him in jail.

One night he'd called Patrick and invited him over. He hadn't been sure how Patrick would react, because they hadn't talked much about the marijuana bust since that first night. He'd known Patrick since they were teenagers and sometimes Patrick could be a little unpredictable. But Ken hadn't known anyone else who had the money to invest in such a big operation. After a few beers, Ken had brought up the subject again.

"Hey, I have something to show you. Want to take a walk?" Ken had asked.

"Sure, buddy. As long as it involves keeping your clothes on."

"Come on, smart-ass. It's in the pole barn."

As they walked along the trail that led to the barn, Ken had asked, "Remember the drug bust I did, back a few months ago?"

"The local Mexican Mafia. Sure, I remember. You got some of those guys hog-tied back in the barn?"

"Nope, something better." Ken had unlocked the door and they'd walked into the barn.

"Don't tell me you're starting your own little grow operation back here."

Ken had switched on a light. The florescent lighting had given off an eerie, green glow. Three large rectangular pots filled with blooming, sweet-smelling plants sat in the middle of a long table. He'd heard Patrick swear under his breath.

"What…the…hell?" Patrick had asked.

"It's just a little experiment. These plants are maturing and I've already harvested one. Look over here." Ken had motioned excitedly to another smaller table. There were three small baggies of what looked like dried herb inside them.

"I sure hope that's oregano you have in there."

Ken had laughed. "I bought some seeds online and started my own little experiment. This stuff is so easy to grow. You wouldn't believe what they sell online. There's just one small problem."

"What would that be?"

"I can't test it. You know…I'd never pass a random drug test at the department. It wouldn't look good if I was tested and came up positive."

"Don't look at me, buddy. I'm in the same situation. Are you really thinking of doing what I think you're doing?"

"Maybe. I dunno." Ken had shrugged his shoulders. "It seems like a good way to make some serious dough. And think about it. I'm a trusted officer at the police department. I know firsthand when a raid is going down. This is almost idiot proof."

"How much money are we talking about?"

"To get started, I need a few thousand dollars for more seeds and equipment. I figure we could produce enough plants to net about fifty grand every couple of months."

"I don't know, Ken. Have you really thought this out? Who're you gonna sell to?"

Ken had thought about this for a while, and he'd worked out a plan. After arresting Jason and the rest of the drug cartel, he'd found out how the system worked and thought he could replicate it, but with better results. And less chance of getting caught.

"I'm going to sell to Jason Blum. He was the middleman who worked with Pedro. He was let off with probation as part of the sting."

Patrick had looked at Ken with disbelief. "You really think that's a smart thing to do?"

"Sure. We cut him in. He's got contacts with all the small-time distributors. What else is the kid going to do? He knows no other trade than selling dope," Ken had said, like it was all easy street.

"Sounds like you really researched this. How do I fit in? And it better not be what I'm thinking."

"I need seed money. Literally. About ten thousand dollars to get us started. We split profit fifty-fifty. You put up the money, and I'll take care of everything else. Your hands stay clean."

"Ten thousand?" Patrick had looked at him hesitantly. Ken had known that he'd be a hard sell, but he'd also known that Patrick loved money. Firefighters didn't make a lot of money and most of them had second and third jobs. This would be an easy, almost fail-proof way to make a buck. And Patrick was all about the easy buck.

Patrick had a small inheritance from his dad, and he'd once confided to Ken that he was going to use part of it as a down payment for a fixer-upper he'd found that was a good deal. He was going to try and make extra money flipping houses, just like all those mega-rich real estate investors did.

"You'll get it back after the first crop. We're talking six months or less."

Patrick hadn't said anything. He'd just stared at the plants.

"Come on, man. I have two kids, a wife, and a good job. I know the risk. You're a single guy—no one depends on you."

Patrick had looked hurt at this last comment.

Ken hadn't wanted to beg, but he knew of no one else he could trust. "This is a great opportunity. All you have to do is put up the money."

Patrick had taken a look around at the barn. "What about Sam?"

"What about her?"

"Does she know?"

"No. I don't plan on telling her. She never comes out here. For all she knows, I'm working on building some furniture for the girls' room." Ken picked up one of the plants and held it up to the light.

"Let's say we do it for one year. When we make a little money, you can quit. You'll get your ten K back with one hundred percent interest. You can buy that house you want and sock the rest away for a rainy day."

"Let me think about it. I'll get back to you. Let's go back and finish off that six-pack."

Patrick had eventually come around, and a few months later, they'd been in business. And now his wife was missing and he just might be the cause of it.

Ken hit his fist against the cinder block wall and cursed. All because of him, his family was suffering. He would find a way to make it right. He had to.

Chapter Nine
Santa Rosa Beach, FL, Tuesday 11:00 a.m.

Rachel entered Nora's address into the GPS. After taking several dirt roads off the main highway, she found the place. Nora lived in a double-wide trailer on the outskirts of town. Rachel pulled up to the trailer, anxious to get started. She'd talked with Janine on the way and had given her the go-ahead to call the police chief to get permission to put together a search around the warehouse. She would need Peter and the rest of the team to head up here. The quicker they got started, the better the chance of a good outcome.

Two women were sitting on a deck in worn lawn chairs sipping drinks. Rachel got out of the truck and walked toward them.

"Be careful of that first step. It's a little wobbly," the older lady called out. "You must be Rachel. Thanks much for coming here. I'm Nora and this here's Tammie."

Rachel cautiously walked up the stairs onto the deck. It looked like the whole thing could cave in at any second. "Hi. Thanks for meeting me."

"Have a seat. I'll get you some iced tea. It's hot today," Nora said in her slow, Southern drawl.

Nora looked older than her fifty-five years. She had perfectly coiffed, bleached-blonde hair, and despite the heat and humidity, her face was caked with heavy makeup. She wore capri stretch leggings with a long, sleeveless purple tunic top covered with rhinestones that spelled out *Beauty Queen*.

Rachel sat down on one of the saggy lawn chairs, its plastic fibers frayed around the edges, as Nora went inside to get her drink.

"So you're here to help find Sam?" Tammie studied Rachel, looking her up and down. "Nora told me all about you."

"Yes, I'm here to help. You're a friend of Sam's?"

Tammie nodded her head. "Sam and I go way back. We've been friends since the fourth grade. Anything you need to know about her, I can pretty much tell you."

"That's good to know. The more I know about her, the better chance of finding her quickly."

Nora came back out and handed Rachel the tea, the glass already sweating with tiny beads of water rolling down the side.

"Wasn't sure if you liked lemon or not. It also has a little mint in it."

"This is fine, thanks." She took a sip of the tea. It was delicious, nice and sweet the way her mom made it. There was nothing like sweet iced tea on a hot summer day.

"Tell me more about Sam," Rachel said to Nora. "When we spoke on the phone, you said you didn't think Sam would leave on her own accord. Why do you think that?"

Nora adjusted her heavy frame in the chair and patted the sweat from her brow with a damp paper towel. "Sam was over here the morning before she went to work. I watch Bella and Gracie while she works at the fire department. That morning, she came a little earlier than usual because she said she wanted to borrow my newspaper and look through the classifieds to see about getting another job."

"Why was she looking for another job?"

"The fire department put her on probation when she got arrested as an accessory. Even though the charges were dropped, I think the department was waiting on the outcome of Ken's trial to see what they should do with her. She wanted to find something part time to help pay the bills and as security just in case. The lawyer was costing them a lot of money, and they were tapped out. They'd already taken out a couple of loans on the land and the house."

"What else did she do while she was here?"

"I heard her on the phone talking about selling the house. When I asked her about it, she said she had called a real estate agent because she wanted to get an idea of what it would sell for. We got in an argument about it."

"Why is that?"

"Her daddy and I gave her the land when she married Ken. It's been in the family for a long time. I didn't want her to sell it." Nora wiped the sweat from her brow again, smearing some of her makeup in the process. "Why would she do that if she was planning on leaving? And the most important thing, she loves her kids more than life itself. She would never leave them. She would never leave me." Nora started to tear up. "Sorry. I'm just so worried about her."

Rachel leaned over and patted her on the knee. "It's understandable. I know what you're going through." She sat her tea glass down on the deck. "Would Sam make any money from selling her house?"

"Not with the market the way it is. Besides, the IRS froze their bank accounts because of the dope mess Ken got them into. I doubt she would make anything at all." Nora finished her tea in one long gulp. "Sam was never a person to run from her problems, if that's what you're thinking. She always took care of her responsibilities."

Nora started to tremble, her words coming out more slowly and unsteadily. "I've already lost so much," she cried. "Excuse me, I'll be right back." Tammie helped her up and watched as she walked into the trailer.

Tammie sat back down in her chair. "She's been through a lot these past few years." She told her that Nora had lost Breck, her oldest son, in an accident and then her husband shortly after that to a heart attack.

"How awful," Rachel said. "I wasn't aware of that."

"Samantha and her grandchildren are all she has." Tammie stood up. "It's getting hot out here. Let's go inside and check on her."

Rachel followed her into the trailer. The living room had a large bookcase that was crowded with trophies and ribbons. There were pictures of Sam dressed in pageant gowns and bathing suits. She was a beautiful girl with long blonde hair and brilliant blue eyes. Her smile was huge and bright. Rachel got a closer look.

"Samantha won more pageants than any other little girl in Florida," Nora said quietly.

Rachel swirled around to find Nora sitting on the couch, wiping her tears away with a handkerchief.

"Before the accident, she was a happy little girl. We traveled all over the South going to beauty pageants. Samantha won every one of those pageants, hands down."

Rachel looked over at Tammie, who was propped up against the kitchen bar. She nodded her head at Rachel.

"The accident changed everything. It took my beautiful girl away from me. But it didn't take her spirit."

"What accident?" Rachel asked, confused.

"Sam was in a boating accident when she was twelve. She got cut up pretty bad by a boat propeller blade. She almost died," Tammie told her.

"Wow, I'm sorry. I had no idea," Rachel said. "So, Samantha has scars from her accident?" The more she knew about scars, tattoos, and any other body markings, the better.

"She'd had plastic surgery, but you can still see the scars if you look closely."

"Do you have any recent photos of Sam?" Rachel would put the photos on the Florida Omni Search website. The site featured a page that showcased all the missing people and their information: vital statistics, date missing, and under what type of situation. The photo would also be helpful for her staff to produce flyers and develop a media packet.

Nora got off the couch and walked into another room. She came back a few moments later with a couple of pictures. "Sam didn't like having her picture taken much after the accident. I only have these to give you."

Rachel took the photos from her. Sam was still very pretty. Her blonde hair was now cut short, in a stylish bob, and framed her face. However, her eyes seemed a little dull and her smile not as big. Rachel could see the faint scars that made a trail down her face. "Thank you, Nora. I'll make copies and give these back to you."

"Anything I can do to help find my baby."

Rachel swung the conversation back around to Sam's disappearance. "I heard that all charges had been dropped against Sam for the marijuana operation. Was she worried about any repercussions from local drug dealers?"

"She was worried about the safety of her and the kids," Tammie answered. "When Ken started dealing dope, he pissed off a lot people, especially the drug dealers he put behind bars."

"Did she receive any threats?" Rachel asked.

"Not that she told me. People said that Ken had stashed some of the money he got from the drug dealing. Sam was scared people would come after her for it, thinking she'd know where it was. But she didn't have a clue what Ken did with the money—if there was any truth to it," Tammie said.

"Was there anyone else, besides yourself, Sam was close to that she might have confided in?" Rachel asked Tammie.

"She and Mack are pretty tight. But they always have been. She leaned on him after Ken was arrested. I came by her house a few times to help watch the kids, and Mack was always there. Of course, they work the same shift at the fire station, and you know those people are like a second family to her."

"Okay, thanks for all the information." Rachel looked at her watch. "I need to get things started. We're going to do another search around the warehouse. The police department may have missed something the first time. Nora, you might want to think about having a press conference to get Samantha's face out there. Someone somewhere might have seen something, and we need all the help we can get. I can coordinate that for you through the police department."

"Sure. Whatever you think will help find Samantha. Thank you again for coming down here to help us." Nora walked her to the door. "Believe me when I tell you something happened to Sam. She wouldn't leave without saying good-bye."

"I'll do everything I can to find her." Rachel gave Nora a hug. "I'll check in with you tomorrow."

Rachel treaded lightly down the steps and walked back to her truck.

Tammie yelled at her. "Hey, Rachel. Wait up for a sec."

"Yes?"

"I didn't want to say anything in front of Nora. Is there any way we can talk in private later?"

"Sure. What's on your mind?"

Tammie looked back at the trailer. Nora was sitting on her chair with another glass of tea, watching them.

"Something about my last conversation with Sam is bugging me. Here's my number. Call me later?"

Rachel took her number and promised to call her. As she drove down the long driveway, she picked up her cell phone and put it on speaker while she checked her voice mail. There was only one and it was from Janine.

"You're good for tomorrow's search. Peter and the rest of the team are on their way up. And I talked with Chief Gladstone and he wants to coordinate with you. Call me back for more info."

Rachel pressed the End button and put her phone away.

This would be the most intense search she'd ever done. She didn't have much to go on. Questions about what happened to Sam went through her mind. Did Samantha plan this fire as an escape from her life? Or was this the work of the town's arsonist and Sam got in the way? Had the drug cartel wanted revenge and retaliation for the business Ken stole from them and gone after Sam instead? Or did Ken—now in jail—have something to do with his wife's disappearance?

All she knew was that the answers would come in time. They always did.

Chapter Ten
Santa Rosa Beach, FL, Wednesday 7:00 a.m.

It was 7:00 in the morning and the heat was already intense. The Florida sun was bearing down and sweat trickled down Rachel's back. It was early August and still the dog days of summer.

Rachel was always amazed at the number of volunteers that turned out for searches. All she had to do was put the word out to the local media, which is what she did after meeting with Nora yesterday. She also contacted Chief Gladstone and got the ball rolling on a coordinated search of the warehouse grounds where Sam was last seen.

The volunteers included members of the police department, firefighters from Sam's station, plus members of the public. Rachel was happy to see that even Mack Dixon and Jeff Stanton had made it out for the search.

Red and Janine had sent up their main search team, which was specifically trained in forensics, to round out the volunteer list. Florida Omni Search used specialized equipment in their searches. In Sam's case they were using search planes, ATVs, and sonar equipment.

"Okay. Just to highlight what the chief said, stay in your group of four and within your search grid. If you see anything at all that looks suspicious, use your marker and call it in immediately," Rachel said, wiping the sweat from her brow with a handkerchief. She never went on any search without her purple hankie. It was a good luck charm of sorts that one of her first clients—an elderly lady who had Alzheimer's—had given to her. The woman had gotten lost while walking home from the grocery store and was found twelve miles away in a neighboring town.

Rachel glanced at her map of the area. The terrain was pretty easy—flat, sandy ground with dense ground cover and pine trees. The volunteers would have to pay extra attention to the tropical undergrowth to see anything out of the ordinary. Unfortunately, they'd have to watch out for snakes and other vermin as well. A first aid station had been set up for minor emergencies.

The police department had searched the area on the night Sam disappeared and again the morning after, but did not find anything other than Sam's helmet discarded by the back door. One theory, Rachel thought, was that Sam might have been knocked unconscious by the blast from the propane tanks and her helmet had come off. She could have suffered head trauma and wandered off. Point Washington State Forest, which encompassed over fifteen thousand acres and ten miles of hiking and biking trails, was within walking distance of the farmers' market. They had a lot of ground to cover and precious time was wasting.

Chief Gladstone came over and asked if she was ready to go. Rachel thought he seemed a little anxious to get started. He'd been reluctant when she'd called him to coordinate the search, but he seemed to be warming up to her. When she came at the family's request on some of the cases, she never knew how the authorities would treat her. Some thought she was some kind of quack, like a psychic or clairvoyant, and didn't like her butting in on their territory. Others were grateful for the help. She figured Chief Gladstone was somewhere in between the two.

Chief Gladstone's demeanor fit his physical profile. He was a stocky man with thinning gray hair—complete with a Donald Trump comb-over—and a round, doughy face that was always red, which gave him an appearance that he was always mad about something.

Getting a large search team together in a short amount of time required a well-balanced plan. Fortunately for Rachel, she had a lot of practice. She grouped the people into separate categories. The experienced searchers and equipment handlers would be involved in the ground search. The volunteers, who had not received the training that Florida Omni Search mandated, staffed a relief station with water and snacks. Another group was also set up to administer first aid. The last group handled communications and they were responsible for marking the map as groups called in their locations and anything that was found. The area would be noted and the police department would tape it off and process the scene.

Rachel would be teaming up with Peter Moore, who was her specialist in ground searching. He had an impressive military search and rescue background. Peter had been with Florida Omni Search since the beginning. He'd moved to Miami when he retired from the military and had been one of Rachel's real estate clients. He knew this area well, because he'd been stationed at Eglin Air Force Base, which was about forty-five miles west of Santa Rosa Beach. He was one of the first people Rachel contacted when her daughter disappeared. Also in her group were Chris Cumbie and Darcy Black, another forensic specialist team. They would start their search at the rear of the warehouse, where Sam's helmet was found, while the other teams set out to search the state forest area. Rachel gave flyers to some of the volunteers and sent them across the street to canvass the neighborhood.

Nora had given Rachel some clothing Sam had recently worn. She handed it off to Rankin Smartz, who was the dog handler. His dog, Max, was an adorable and capable black Lab that reminded her of her Maggie. Rankin and Max would start at Sam's LKP, search and rescue lingo for *last known position*, which was the rear of the warehouse.

Searching in a grid system was tedious work, but it was also the most effective. After an hour had passed, Rachel heard the crackle of a call on the radio. One of the search group members reported finding an object and gave their exact location over the radio.

"Group five. Stay where you are. We're on the way," Rachel instructed. "Grab the thermal equipment, Chris."

They headed out with Chief Gladstone and his crew. It was a quick walk to where the group was waiting. She was thankful she'd dressed appropriately and worn plenty of sunscreen. The weather was humid, and her T-shirt was clinging to her chest. She wore her typical search and rescue outfit. The long khaki pants protected her legs in the dense undergrowth. Most of the low-lying bushes had prickly vines and weeds. Her boots and socks always picked up sandspurs. Even though today's temp would probably reach ninety degrees, she wore a light, long-sleeved T-shirt with the Florida Omni Search logo on it, to prevent sunburn and scratches on her arms. Her baseball cap protected her from ticks and other icky bugs.

They got to the site where one of the search groups waited for them. The head of the group, Casey Simmons, was one of her best volunteers. He had been with the Florida Omni Search for about three years. He was always available for searches and he never missed a thing.

"Whaddaya got?" Chief Gladstone barked out at the group. He was red-faced and breathing hard by the time they got there. Rachel didn't think the police department got exciting action like this. The most crime he saw was probably drunken teenagers on spring break and an occasional Peeping Tom.

"We first saw some red fabric in the bushes, right here. When we got a closer look, we found this." Casey pointed to the bush. He had put down a marker when he saw it—just like he was trained to do. He also had taken a few photos with the digital camera he always carried.

One of the officers on Chief Gladstone's crew put on a pair of gloves and reached down. He pulled out a pocketknife and turned it over in his hand. Rachel noticed it had a Maltese cross on the side.

"That's a firefighter emblem, right?" Rachel asked him.

The officer bagged it along with the red fabric. "Yep. Looks like it."

"Get this back to base. Let Mack Dixon take a look at it and see if it belongs to Sam," Chief Gladstone said as the other officer handed him the bag.

Rachel got her radio out. "Rankin, can you get Max over here? Let's see if he can pick up a scent." She gave him their position again.

A few minutes later, Rankin and Max came to the site. He gave Max another sniff of the scent and they took off with the black Lab leading the way.

Rachel and her team followed Rankin and Max for about a half mile along a worn path through the woods. She could hear the chief behind her, gasping for breath and struggling to keep up. Every few minutes Rankin would give Max encouragement. The path suddenly ended at a dirt road.

Max wandered around the dirt road a bit and finally settled down on his hind legs. He let out a whine as Rankin soothed him and gave him a treat.

"Where does the road lead?" Rachel asked.

"It dead-ends at a fishing camp this way." Chief Gladstone pointed east. "And if you go the other way, it hooks back up to the highway by the farmers' market. We got some people living out here in maybe six or seven trailers, too."

"So, it's probable someone picked her up?" Rachel asked.

"Probable, yes. But we don't know if she had help, someone took her, or she went on her own. Anything is possible." Chief Gladstone wiped his forehead with the sleeve of his shirt. "Let's head back." His drab, olive-green uniform was soaked with sweat.

Back at the warehouse, Mack Dixon and Jeff Stanton were waiting anxiously for them. The officer handed Mack the baggie with the knife in it.

Mack took a look at the pocket knife. He turned it over slowly in his hand. "Sure looks like Sam's knife. Her kids gave it to her for Mother's Day last year."

"Sentimental value. Something she always kept on her?" Rachel asked.

"She never went anywhere without it."

"What about the red fabric?"

"Have no idea. That could be anything."

"What was she wearing when you last saw her?" Rachel asked.

"When we came on shift, she had on civilian clothes. I think she was wearing jeans and a dark T-shirt. We wear our standard firefighter uniform while on duty, which is dark-navy slacks and a work shirt with the fire department logo," Mack explained. "The clothes she wore when she came in that morning are still in her locker."

"We'll run these for fingerprints," Chief Gladstone said, shaking the evidence bag. "I'll let you know what we come up with." He nodded toward Rachel and Jeff.

Rachel thanked all the volunteers and went to her truck to grab some water and call Nora to give her an update. After talking with Nora, she'd call in reinforcements. She scrolled through the directory on her cell phone and hit the Dial button.

Chapter Eleven

Santa Rosa Beach, FL, Wednesday 12:00 Noon

Stacy Case was a reporter for the *Miami Sun* who'd befriended Rachel on her last case in the Bahamas. It didn't take long for the two to form a friendship. Stacy was good at her job as a reporter and proved to be a great source of information. Rachel would describe their relationship as a give and take. Stacy used her investigative skills to help Rachel with her cases, and Rachel returned the favor by giving Stacy exclusive interviews on juicy stories.

Rachel had planned on leaving a message, thinking Stacy wouldn't answer her phone while she was on vacation. She was surprised when Stacy picked up on the first ring.

"Hey, girl, how's your vacation going?" Rachel asked her.

Stacy was in Arizona at the Canyon Ranch Spa. *Probably soaking up the sun, eating fresh, healthy food, and taking yoga classes*, Rachel thought dreamily. She wished she were there, too, getting massages and facials. Canyon Ranch was one of her favorite spots for R&R.

"Just reading a book and then, later today, taking a hike with Guido."

"Guido? Are you serious?" Rachel laughed.

"Yeah. He's one of the fitness instructors. Funny name, but he has a nice ass. What's up with you?"

"I'm working on a new case. Something big." Rachel switched the phone to her other ear.

"That's nothing new," Stacy said. "Let me guess. You need some help."

"Yes, I do. And you know I hate to bother you, especially while you're away on vacation. Going on hikes with Guido and stuff."

"You know me better than that. I'm itching to get back into things. I've been here three days, and to be honest with you, I'm going stir-crazy. Whatcha got?"

Stacy was just as much a workaholic as Rachel was. Rachel was surprised Stacy even took the time to get away. She assumed her boss at the *Miami Sun* had something to do with it. Stacy had written a huge story about the last case they'd worked on together. The missing daughter of Governor John Knowles cracked Stacy's career wide open.

"I'm in Santa Rosa Beach, which is up in North Florida. A firefighter went missing. Her name is Samantha Collins. It's been a few days since she disappeared and so far we have squat."

Rachel heard some rustling on the other end of the line. "Hang on, I'm getting a pen," Stacy paused. "Okay, go ahead. Give me something to go on."

Rachel gave her all the details she knew so far. "I'm really looking for some information on her husband, Ken Collins. He was a former captain of the Santa Rosa Beach Police Department. He got busted this past February for marijuana possession, but there's more to it. He was growing and selling pot out of their backyard, apparently without Sam's knowledge."

"Yeah, I remember hearing about it," Stacy said, writing everything down. "He was partner with another firefighter and they got busted. It was a big story. Some guy in my office did the feature on it. I'll look it up."

"His partner was Patrick Hart. They got bonded out, but then Ken did something to violate his bond. Not sure what, but he's back in jail awaiting trial."

"Okay. Got it. What about the wife?"

"Samantha Collins. She's now officially missing," Rachel replied. "It was first assumed that she perished in the fire, but they didn't find a body. Her helmet was the only thing found when they did a search of the warehouse. Today, we did a search around the wooded area and found a pocketknife that belonged to her."

"That's strange. Are you thinking her husband's grow operation had something to do with her disappearance?"

"Could be. It's very suspicious that she disappeared the week before she was supposed to testify at his trial."

"You think she ran?"

"Not sure. From everything I've heard so far from Sam's mom and her friends and coworkers, the trial was a big problem, financially and emotionally. But I think she was on her husband's side. They have two kids together. I'm going to the jail this afternoon to talk to Ken and see what he has to say."

"Okay. Let me get on the computer and do some digging around. I can get on the next flight back to Florida."

"I know this goes without saying..." Rachel started to say.

"Yeah, I know. Keep your name out of it and keep it quiet." Stacy sighed.

"Thanks, Stace. Travel safe. Call me when you get in."

Stacy was a hound dog when it came to tracking down information on someone. If anyone could help her figure out what happened to Sam, it was Stacy.

Chapter Twelve
Santa Rosa Beach, FL, Wednesday 3:35 p.m.

This is déjà vu, Ken thought as he made his way back to the visitors' room. He was anxious of any news—good or bad—that involved Sam. As he walked into the room, he saw a beautiful woman with long auburn hair sitting next to his lawyer. He guessed that was who Chief Gladstone had talked about. The woman who ran the search and rescue company. Now that he took a good look at her, he recognized her from several cable network shows like *Nancy Grace* and *America's Most Wanted*. She wore a white skirt and turquoise top that showed off her tanned figure. Ken thought she resembled the girl from the movie *Pretty Woman*.

His attorney, Suzette, stood up from the table and made the introductions. Ken was shocked to see that his attorney was dressed a little more appropriately today in a black pantsuit. She still wore her blonde hair with the trademark hot-pink streak in it, though. "Rachel works with Florida Omni Search. Nora called her and asked if she could come down here and help us find out what happened to Samantha," Suzette said.

"I've seen you on TV before. You worked on the Amber Knowles case," Ken said, looking at his lawyer. "That was the governor's daughter who went missing a few months ago."

"Yes, that was me," Rachel confirmed. "I'm sorry we have to meet under these circumstances. I know you want to find your wife. Can you tell me why you think Sam would have disappeared?"

Ken ran his hand through his hair. "I just can't believe this. Sam wouldn't leave our kids, not with everything that's going on."

"Your mother-in-law said the same thing to me when I asked if Sam would have left on her own."

"I heard you guys were doing another search today. The police already did that once. Did you find anything different?"

"The police do the best they can, but we have equipment and resources most law enforcement agencies don't," Rachel explained. "We did find a couple items of interest. The police department is processing, so I only have some photographs." She put them on the desk in front of him.

Ken stared at the pictures. "What's this?"

"It's a piece of red fabric, probably from an article of clothing."

He pointed to the other picture. "This is Sam's knife. Where did you find it?"

"Our searchers spotted the red cloth first, about a half mile from the farmers' market. Then the knife was found under a bush near the cloth," Rachel said. "Are you sure the knife is Sam's?"

"Yes, I'm sure. I picked it out with the kids for her Mother's Day gift last year. She had lost her other one during a fishing trip. I was going to get it engraved for her, but never got the chance." Ken scrubbed his face with his hands.

"Did she always carry the knife with her?"

"She never went anywhere without it."

Click. It was like a lightbulb went off in her head. That was the same thing Mack had told her. She didn't say that to Ken, though. But she had an inkling: Mack and Sam had something going on.

"Where did she keep it?"

"She always kept it on her while she was on duty. She put it in the front pocket of her pants. "

"When was the last time you spoke to Sam?"

"Last Tuesday, a couple of days before she disappeared. She came with my lawyer to talk about the case."

Rachel looked at Suzette for confirmation. She nodded her head in agreement.

"Did you notice anything unusual about her demeanor?"

Ken shook his head. "The chief asked me the same questions. If there was something bothering Sam, she hid it well. She's a rock."

"Did you know she was putting the house up for sale?" Rachel asked.

"What?" Ken exclaimed. The question stunned him. "No, I didn't. I mean, we'd talked about it, but I didn't think she'd do it."

"The house is in her name only?" Rachel asked, already knowing the answer.

"Yes. It's part of her family's land. Her father deeded it to her right before we were married. We have about fourteen acres with a main house and then the guest house and barn." Ken sighed. "I told her not to sell it."

"Nora said she was talking to some real estate agents last week. She was trying to get a value on the place."

"Money's tight. I know. But I told her not to do anything drastic without talking to me first."

"Nora said that Sam was also looking for another job. She was watching the kids while Sam went on interviews. Sam said it was almost impossible for her to find anything. No one wanted to hire her, it seems."

"It's because of what I did. It's all because of me she wants to sell the house. Because of me, she can't get a job. And because of me, she's missing." Ken pounded his fist so hard on the table Rachel jumped in her seat.

"Calm down, Ken. We are just trying to find out what happened," Suzette said.

"Someone who's putting their house up for sale, looking for a job, and has two beautiful children to look after…That doesn't sound like someone who would just up and disappear," Rachel said.

"I don't think so, either. Something bad happened," Ken agreed.

"Suzette said you were getting death threats?"

"That's typical. I'm an ex-cop who helped put away most of these bastards in here." He waved his hand around the room. "They keep me in a separate cell away from the others. I eat, exercise, and shower by myself."

"Why would any of these people want to hurt Sam?" Rachel asked.

"To get back at me, I'm sure. I told her to be careful and not go anywhere alone."

"Did anyone know her routine? Work schedule? Where you live?"

"Sure, lots of people. It's a small resort town. Everybody knows everyone. It wouldn't be hard to find out when Sam worked."

"Are Mack and Sam close?"

Ken looked at her for an uncomfortable moment before answering. Rachel could see the tension in his face. "They've been friends for a long time."

"Mack seemed to think the fire was intentional."

"Mack was with her that night. He should've never let Sam out of his sight and *never* let her go back into the building. If anything has happened to her, I blame him," Ken said.

"In his defense, I don't think he knew. Their focus was on getting the victim out of the building and getting him medical attention. He said he thought Sam was behind him the whole time."

"Well, she wasn't, was she?"

"Look, Ken, I'll do whatever I can to find Sam. We'll be in touch." Rachel stood to leave, smoothing the wrinkles in her white linen skirt. Ken's last words stopped her in her tracks.

"I'd talk to Mack again if I were you. Since he and Sam were having an affair." Ken got up from his chair, scraping the legs across the linoleum tile. "Guard, I'm ready to go."

Chapter Thirteen
Santa Rosa Beach, FL, Thursday 10:00 a.m.

Rachel went to the airport to pick up Stacy. It was the least she could do after she'd asked her friend to cut her vacation short.

Stacy was waiting outside the baggage terminal for her. She threw her one bag into the backseat and climbed into Rachel's truck.

"Traveling light, huh?" Rachel asked.

"No need for a lot of clothes at a health spa. Bathing suit and a couple pairs of workout clothes."

"Did you throw Guido in your bag, too?"

Stacy laughed. "No. Guido has lots of women to keep him company at the ranch. I am but one in his long line of conquests."

"Are you sure you went to Canyon Ranch and not some nudist colony? I don't remember anybody named Guido when I went there. Only Helga. Large Swedish woman with hands the size of ham hocks."

"Helga's still there. Best massage ever," Stacy said while rolling her shoulders.

"Thanks again for coming back. You look well rested." Rachel admired Stacy's healthy glow. Stacy wore her honey-blonde hair pulled back in a ponytail, and she looked ten years younger than her thirty-five years. She was petite, only five foot one and about 115 pounds, with inquisitive green eyes and deep dimples in both cheeks. Stacy could light up a room just with her presence.

"Oh, there will be payback."

Rachel laughed. "I thought there might be."

"I started looking into Ken Collins last night," Stacy said, adjusting her seat.

Rachel had expected nothing less. Once Stacy got a sniff of a good story, she was like a bulldog. Persistence and determination were her middle names. She might be small, but she was feisty.

"What did you find out about the marijuana operation?"

"Well, as you know, Ken got started after the arrest of Jason Blum and Pedro Gonzalez. He and Patrick Hart ran the grow operation out of Ken's barn. What you probably don't know is that they produced a particular brand of marijuana called Cush."

"Wait. There are different types of marijuana?" Rachel interrupted.

"You novice, you." Stacy laughed. "Remember when you could buy a huge dime bag for ten dollars?"

"I never did that kind of stuff growing up."

"Yeah, right. I forgot—you were a goody-goody cheerleader." Stacy rolled her eyes. "Anyway, there's been all kinds of progress—in technology, plant breeding, you name it. Now you can get all kinds of marijuana, and it's more expensive than it was back in our day. It gives different kinds of effects when you smoke it. Some highs are longer than others, depending on what type of marijuana you smoke," Stacy explained.

"I see you did your homework. What kind of high does Cush have?"

"Well, Gary, the guy I work with at the *Miami Sun*, originally did the story on Ken. He was a big help," Stacy continued. "Cush is very popular with the younger crowd, but also with people who smoke it for medicinal reasons. It gives a quicker and longer-lasting high, but it's expensive."

"So how much money were they making?"

"Gary said they were clearing about fifty grand every couple of months. And here's the interesting part. The guy Ken first arrested—Jason Blum? He cut a deal with the DA's office to catch the bigger fish, Pedro Gonzalez. Jason just got a slap on the wrist and probation. So, when Ken gets ready to start his little business, who does he turn to handle distribution?"

"Jason Blum?"

"You got it. Smart, huh? Jason already had the contacts. So Ken and Patrick sold to Jason, who in turn distributed to other small-time dealers. We're talking a street value of about a couple million dollars' worth of marijuana a year, with plans to produce more."

"Wow. Not too bad for a couple of newbies."

"Of course, Ken thought they were invincible. With his being a captain at the police department, he had the perfect setup. He kept his hands clean by selling to Jason, the middleman, and kept his name out of where the dope was coming from. Working at the department, he could keep an eye on Jason and also an ear to the ground about any drug busts going down before they happened."

"If he had it so good, how did he get caught?" Rachel asked.

"Good question." Stacy paused. "Ready for this? An anonymous tip. Somebody blew the whistle on his operation."

"An anonymous tip brought it all down?" Rachel asked.

"Yep. A couple of undercover officers went sniffing around the Collins's property without a warrant. They couldn't see much from the property line, but apparently they smelled marijuana, so they went back to the judge to get a warrant. They raided the property while Ken was on duty. Sam was home with the kids and let them in. They confiscated about a million dollars' worth of plants and several thousand dollars' worth of equipment. They also searched the home and got a couple of computers and other stuff," Stacy said.

"And Sam was implicated as well?"

"Yes, she was. Even though she denied knowing what Ken had done. The DA's office decided there wasn't enough evidence that she'd been involved, so they dropped the charges against her."

"And Patrick?"

"He got off easier than Ken. Since the grow operation was on Ken's property, Patrick was charged only with accessory and money laundering. They both got bail. Then Ken violated his bail a couple of months later when he left the county without permission to visit family. Ken said it was a misunderstanding, but the judge threw him back in jail without any fanfare. Now Ken's trial is postponed due to Samantha's disappearance. Patrick is being tried separately."

"So, hubby is in jail, the bad guys are after you, you've got money troubles piling up, and no job prospects. Sounds like an incentive to run far, far away," Rachel said.

"But she has two kids who she adores, right?"

"Yeah, there is that." Rachel pulled into the driveway of the beach house and they sat with the truck idling.

"But you could've read all that in the papers and on the Internet," Stacy said. She had that trademark look on her face, like the cat that ate the canary. "Want to know something that wasn't in the papers?"

"Of course."

"Gary told me that some people think Mack was the anonymous tip."

"Really? Why Mack?"

"Because Mack is in love with Sam. Always has been, according to my source."

"Your sources at the paper sure have a lot of inside information. Are you going to tell me who it is?" Rachel asked, half-jokingly. She knew Stacy would protect her sources to the bitter end.

"Yes, they do, and no, I won't."

"Ken did mention to me that Mack and Sam were having an affair." Rachel gave Stacy the details about her meeting with Ken at the jail.

"Sometimes the husband is the last to know. Did he think that had something to do with Sam's disappearance?"

"If he did, he didn't say. We didn't exactly leave things on a good note." Rachel thought Ken held some bitter feelings toward Mack.

"Have you wondered if Mack might have had a hand in Sam's disappearance?"

Rachel shook her head. "He's not on the top of my suspect list. I think he's truly stumped about what happened to her. The drug cartel—or what the locals call the Mexican Mafia—they're at the top of my list."

"I would suppose so." Stacy patted her on the leg. "Be careful. These so-called Mexican Mafia are dangerous people."

"I heard all about Pedro."

"Pedro Gonzalez is just a little fish in a big pond. It's Richard Flores, the head of the gang, you need to worry about. He's famous for cutting people's appendages off for messing around in his business. They're well known in the South Florida drug trade."

"So you think these guys have something to do with Sam?"

"I don't know. I'm just saying, be careful who you talk to and what you do."

"Thanks. When are you heading back?"

"I thought I'd stick around here for a while. I have some vacation time left, and besides, this could be another big story for me." Stacy smiled and rubbed her hands together.

"Then let's get you settled in. Wait till you see this place. The views of the beach from your room are stunning. Then we can get some lunch and plot our next move."

"Sounds good to me," Stacy said, reaching for her bag. "Here's the first article written about Ken's arrest. You can read it while I freshen up."

They walked inside the beach house and put their things down. While Stacy went upstairs, Rachel took the article outside on the deck to read. The beach was dotted with brightly colored umbrellas and people taking advantage of the lovely day. Teenagers played volleyball and sunned themselves, kids built sandcastles, and surfers rode the small waves rolling in.

The article was dated several months ago, when Ken was first arrested:

Police Officer Charged with Running Marijuana Grow Operation

A captain with the Santa Rosa Beach Police Department has been charged with running what officials describe as a multimillion-dollar marijuana operation.

Kenneth Jay Collins, 35, has been charged with trafficking marijuana, possession with intent to sell, plus manufacturing a hallucinogen, according to arrest records. He is being held in the Walton County Jail.

His attorney, Suzette Breland, said, "I haven't had a chance to get into the allegations with my client."

He is scheduled to be in court next Tuesday.

Collins owns a home on fourteen acres in the rural part of Santa Rosa Beach, where undercover officers found over 600 marijuana plants, 40 pounds of marijuana, and several grow rooms with high-tech watering and lighting systems, operated by a $30,000 generator, police spokesman John Paulsen said.

Paulsen also said that an accomplice would be charged in the next couple of days.

Rachel thought it was time to meet with Patrick Hart. If Ken was getting threats, maybe Patrick was, too. She picked up the phone book to see if he was listed. There was only one Patrick Hart in the directory. *Here goes nothing*, she thought as she dialed the number.

Chapter Fourteen
Santa Rosa Beach, FL, Thursday 1:20 p.m.

When Rachel first talked to Patrick, he was reluctant to meet with her. She was used to it. Most people didn't want to get involved in an investigation that involved a missing person. So she played the guilt card: *Don't you want to help your best friend find his wife?* She hated to do that, but it worked. She got lucky and was able to get him to agree to meet with her. After having a quick lunch with Stacy at the beach house, she drove over to the Donut Hole to meet with him.

Rachel walked into the popular diner and immediately inhaled the delicious smells of donuts, cakes, and pastries that were made fresh daily. The bakery items were displayed in a glass case by the cash register where the hostess greeted Rachel. The lunch crowd had thinned out and she looked around for Patrick. She spotted a lone man sipping a drink, and she recognized him as the man pictured in the article she'd read that morning. Plus, he was the only redhead in the diner with a thick, bushy mustache. She walked up to his table and introduced herself.

"So, you want to talk to me about Sam?"

"Yes," Rachel said, sitting down at his table. "Thanks for meeting with me."

"You realize I'm not supposed to talk about this. My attorney didn't think it was a good idea with the trial coming up and everything."

Rachel smiled and took a deep breath to relax. She knew, after speaking with Patrick on the phone, he wasn't going to make this easy for her. However, she'd had years of experience in dealing with difficult people and had a reputation around Miami for being a tough negotiator.

The waitress came over and took Rachel's drink order of sweet tea with lemon. She was tempted to add a key lime donut to her order, but decided to grab a bag to go when she left.

"You should try the lunch special. Meatloaf is always a good choice," Patrick suggested.

"Thank you, but I already ate," Rachel politely declined. "I don't want to do anything to compromise the investigation. I'm only interested in any information you may have about Sam's disappearance."

"I could get in a shitload of trouble…on top of everything else that's going on." Patrick nervously picked at his nails. "But Sam's in trouble and I figure I'm part of the reason."

"Why is that?" Rachel asked.

Patrick looked at her like she was an idiot or something. "Because." He said his words slowly and quietly. "Of what Ken and I did. The marijuana operation."

"Sam is missing because you and her husband were allegedly involved in something illegal?" Rachel asked, choosing her words carefully.

Patrick looked around the restaurant and leaned over to whisper, "We put those Mexicans out of business. They didn't take lightly to that. They're out for blood. Don't matter if it's mine or Ken's. They start with our families and work their way in."

"You think Pedro Gonzalez may have done something with Sam?"

Patrick nodded his head.

"Pedro would know Sam's work schedule? Her routine?"

"It wouldn't be hard to figure out, especially if he was following her. She works every three days, twenty-four-hour shifts. Like I said, he was out for revenge."

"What kind of relationship do you have with Sam?"

Patrick thought about it for a minute before he answered. "I grew up with Sam. We've known each other since grade school. I was best friends with her older brother, Breck. We all went to firefighter school down in Ocala together. Sam and I joined the department within a couple of months of each other."

"I heard Breck died in a fire a couple of years ago?"

"Yep. About killed Sam and her mom. They were really close. He wasn't even supposed to be working that day. He came in to cover for a buddy who had a family emergency."

"What happened?" Rachel asked.

"There was a fire in a furniture store. He was on the roof when it caved in. He broke his neck when he fell. Sam and her family were devastated. Now with Sam missing, Nora is beside herself."

"Is Sam having an affair with Mack?" Rachel asked, looking closely at his reaction.

The question caught him off guard. Patrick stared at Rachel for a few seconds before answering. He waved his hand away, dismissing the question. "Just rumors. Mack and Sam were always close."

Patrick's food arrived and he dug into his meatloaf and mashed potatoes. The meatloaf was covered in tomato gravy and the potatoes were smothered with melted butter and topped with parsley. It smelled delicious and Rachel wished she'd gotten a plate, even though she had just eaten lunch with Stacy.

"How was Sam getting along with Ken in jail? I heard she was planning on putting the house up for sale."

"I know she was having a hard time making ends meet. They had a second mortgage on their place. With the way the real estate market is, I doubt she could have sold it for what it's worth."

"If Sam had wanted to have run away, do you have any idea of where she would have gone?"

Patrick thought about it for a minute, slowly chewing his food. "I've wondered the same thing myself. I don't know. She didn't have any friends or close family that I know of, outside of here. And apparently she didn't have any money." Patrick picked up a napkin and wiped his mouth. "I don't think she ran. I think Pedro got her."

Chapter Fifteen
Santa Rosa Beach, FL, Thursday 2:40 p.m.

Patrick Hart had a cabin he used for fishing and hunting. It was about an hour north of Santa Rosa Beach. The cabin had been in his family for years. When his father died a couple years ago, he willed the place to Patrick, his only son. Since his suspension from the fire department, he'd spent more and more time at the cabin. He liked to go there to relax and get away from it all. The stress of the impending trial was beginning to wear him down. He checked in with his attorney to let him know that he was going back there for a few days.

After lunch with Rachel, he went to his house and started packing. His supplies at the cabin were running low and he'd have to make a pit stop at Walmart. He was loading up the truck when he heard the crunch of gravel. He turned to see Mack's black truck easing around the curve to his house.

"Hey, Pat. I've been trying to call you," Mack said as he got out of the truck.

"Yeah, sorry. I got your messages. I've been trying to get some things done around here."

"You didn't show up for the search for Sam," Mack said with a bit of an accusing tone.

Patrick shuffled his feet in the gravel. "I didn't hear about it till the last minute. I was already up to my eyeballs in painting. Want to see what I got done?"

Mack followed him inside. Patrick had bought the brick, ranch-style house in a foreclosure sale a few months before. The fixer-upper required many repairs and Patrick spent most of his free time working on it. Rumors had swirled around town that Patrick used the money from the marijuana operation to buy and renovate his new home.

All the windows were open to air out the intoxicating smell of paint. The dining room, which had once been covered with dark wood paneling, was now covered with new Sheetrock and was freshly painted a bright yellow.

"Looks good," Mack said as he walked around, paper crinkling under his feet.

"I know you didn't come all the way out here to look at the house. What's up?" Patrick asked, getting a beer out of the refrigerator. He tossed one to Mack.

"I just wanted to talk to you about Ken."

"What about him?"

"You met Rachel? The lady from Florida Omni Search?" Mack asked.

"We met for lunch today. How did you know?"

"Cleve called me and said he saw you two at the Donut Hole. Anyway, Rachel is working on a theory that the drug cartel had something to do with Sam's disappearance. But I'm starting to doubt it."

Patrick wasn't surprised Mack knew about his lunch meeting with Rachel. Cleve worked at the fire department and the Donut Hole was a local hangout for firefighters and police officers. Santa Rosa Beach was a small town and everyone knew everyone else's business.

"She mentioned the same thing to me. I happen to agree with her."

"I don't doubt they'd be out for revenge. But why kidnap Sam? If they did have something to do with the fire, why not just leave her there to burn? Or put a bullet in her head?" Mack took a swig of his beer. "It just doesn't make sense to go through all the trouble to snatch her and hide her somewhere. Swift, painful deaths are their specialty, so I hear."

"What does this have to do with Ken?"

"I'm thinking Ken might know where Sam is. You and Ken are pretty tight. What do you think?"

Patrick took a long pull from his beer before answering.

"I haven't seen or talked to Ken since he was arrested, so I don't know what's going on with him. But I do know he would never do anything to hurt Sam. Besides, what could he do while he's in jail?"

"No, you got me wrong. I don't think he's hurt her. He may have helped her get away. She was supposed to testify at his trial this week. Maybe he arranged for her to 'go away' for a while."

Patrick finished his beer in one long gulp, belched, and threw the can in the trash. He reached in the fridge for another. He shrugged his shoulders. "I guess anything is possible."

Mack continued to stare at him.

"What? You think I helped her? Is that what you're implying?" Patrick asked.

"Just covering all the bases."

"I'm in enough trouble as it is, Mack. Like I said, I haven't talked to Ken in a few months."

"What about Sam?"

"I went by her house a couple nights before the warehouse fire. She called and asked me to come by and pick up some stuff I had in her storage shed. When I moved out of Mary Ann's house, I stored some furniture there. Sam said she was getting ready to put the house on the market and was trying to clean everything up."

Mary Ann Lipscomb was Patrick's latest girlfriend. They'd lived together for about a year before Mary Ann got bored with him and kicked him out. Having a felon for a boyfriend didn't appeal to her, either.

"That was the last time you spoke?" Mack asked.

"Yes. I already told the chief that." Patrick was beginning to feel like this was an interrogation.

"How did she seem to you?"

"She was in good spirits, I guess. She said she was ready to move on. Fresh start and all."

Mack noticed some small boxes lined up in the foyer.

Patrick said, "I'm going out to the cabin for some fishing this weekend." He was getting tired of all the questions and was ready for Mack to go.

"It should be a good weekend for it. Nice, cool weather, no rain," Mack said, walking back to the front door. A glint of silver caught his attention. "Is that a new Halligan?"

Patrick hesitated. "Yeah."

Mack picked up the tool and examined it. The Halligan bar was a common tool firefighters used to break into locked doors. "What happened to your old one?"

"Stolen. My whole toolbox in the truck was lifted. Probably by some neighborhood kids."

"Did you file a police report?"

"Yeah."

Mack put the tool down and walked out the front door. "How long are you going to be gone?"

"Just a few days. Wanna go?" Patrick asked, even though he knew Mack wouldn't take him up on the offer.

"I wish, man. I got to work tomorrow. Besides, I'd like to hang around and help Rachel out."

Another jab, Patrick guessed, at his unwillingness to help search for Sam. He decided not to respond.

Mack got into his truck. "Have a good time." He waved as he backed down the driveway.

Patrick was glad to see him go. Mack could be a pain in the ass sometimes. All his insinuating questions were bugging him. He cleaned up all the paint mess and locked up the house. Throwing a suitcase in his truck, he decided it was time to get to the cabin and check on things there. He didn't want to keep his lady waiting any longer than necessary.

Chapter Sixteen
Lake Juniper, FL, Thursday 4:15 p.m.

Patrick made a hard right off the highway onto a dirt road that seemed to go nowhere. The more he drove the truck down the endless dirt road, the darker it became. Not many people knew about this area. It was a rural area, consisting mostly of hunting land and farms. He made another turn, and after driving about a mile, the forest opened up. His little log cabin came into view. It had been built by his grandfather many, many years ago.

Patrick had been about five years old when his grandfather bought the land. It was over fifty acres of hunting and fishing property and came with an older cabin his grandfather had deemed uninhabitable. So they made it into a storage place for all their hunting gear. It was decided the new cabin would be built closer to the lake. Patrick, his dad, and his grandfather built this new log cabin by hand, log by log. It was a small two-bedroom cabin with a living room, fireplace, tiny kitchen, and one bathroom. The wrap-around porch had views of the lake where fish, such as rainbow trout and bream, were in abundance. This had been an escape for the men in the family. Now his dad and grandfather were deceased and Patrick was the sole owner of the cabin. He brought some of his buddies here occasionally, but most of the time he came by himself. He relished the quiet.

Patrick had plans to eventually add on to the cabin and build an additional bedroom and bath. If everything went according to plan, he would need the extra room.

Driving to the cabin gave him time to think. He was ready to get away from the mess that was going on with the upcoming trial. He had already accepted the fact he would probably lose his job at the fire department—a job he'd held for many years with an exemplary record until now. No one else would hire him. He'd be lucky to get a job flipping burgers at McDonald's.

It was ironic he'd got caught in a drug-dealing scheme. He'd never been one to do drugs. He'd smoked a little in high school, but he was mostly a beer drinker. Never in his wildest dreams had he thought he'd be caught manufacturing and selling an illegal substance. Marijuana. Never. But here he was. Arrested and awaiting trial.

He blamed himself, but he also blamed Ken. He'd let Ken talk him into the whole thing. The promise of big money and never getting caught is how Ken sold the idea to him. He'd made big money, all right. That part of the promise came through. But he also got caught. Ken had ruined his life and now he was going to lose his job. And he had no serious prospects of ever having another job. And who'd want to date an ex-con? No one he would be interested in, that's for sure. So he had to come up with a plan. To get the girl of his dreams back and have a life that should have been his to begin with.

As he parked his truck in front of the cabin, he felt himself starting to relax a little. He hopped out and started unloading his supplies. The front door squeaked when he opened it. He'd have to remember to get the WD-40 and oil the hinges.

"Honey, I'm home!" he yelled out and then chuckled to himself. No one answered back, as usual. He unloaded some of the boxes and headed back to the truck to get the cooler.

Whistling while he worked, he opened the refrigerator door and stashed the eggs, milk, cheese, salad mix, and beer he'd bought at Walmart. Tonight the menu would be simple, but luxurious. A single man's go-to dinner. Steak on the grill, buttered baked potato, and a salad.

He marinated the steak with some brown sugar, soy sauce, and spices and placed it in the fridge. He washed the potatoes in the sink, scrubbing the skins with a vegetable brush. Grabbing a dish towel, he dried them, poked a few holes in the skin with a fork, and wrapped them in aluminum foil to put on the grill with the steaks. Then he took some time to tidy up the place. His date was waiting for him and he wanted the cabin to look good.

He lit some candles, which smelled like apples and cinnamon, and placed them throughout the small living area. He started a fire in the fireplace, taking pleasure in hearing the crackle of the fire, and he fluffed the pillows on the couch and straightened the afghan his mom had made.

Glancing at the kitchen clock—a black cat with a swinging tail, which was another gift from his mother—he realized it was almost time for his date. He brought his suitcase in from the truck and took a shower, relishing the fact that in just a couple of hours he was going to be reunited with the love of his life.

Chapter Seventeen
Lake Juniper, FL, Thursday 5:30 p.m.

She was being held in some dark room that had a damp and earthy smell. She was pretty sure today was Thursday, but it was hard to tell because there was no light to keep track of the days and nights. And "The Asshole," as she liked to call him, had taken away her watch and other jewelry when he kidnapped her.

She looked at her surroundings. She had a couple of small Coleman battery-operated lanterns—The Asshole had warned her that she shouldn't keep them on all the time because once the batteries were gone, they were gone. She had an army surplus cot with a moldy-smelling blanket and pillow as well as a makeshift toilet—basically a bucket for her to take a piss in. She also had a cupboard with a couple loaves of bread, some peanut butter, a jug of water, and some Skittles. How considerate. The Asshole remembered she liked Skittles. Some diet.

But there must be some reason why he wanted her to live, or he wouldn't have left the food and water. One thing she knew, she'd never eat peanut butter and Skittles again if she ever got out of here. *Correction*, she thought, *when I get out of here*.

She'd had a lot of time to think, and she kept her mind active so she wouldn't go crazy. The events of her kidnapping that night of the warehouse fire played over and over in her mind like a broken record.

It was her turn to cook for the crew. Every shift, someone was responsible for making dinner. Everyone raved about her homemade chili, so that's what she made. Her cell phone rang as she was putting the cornbread and salad together. She didn't recognize the number, but she answered the call anyway.

"Hello."

"Hey, little lady. How are you doing?"

It took her a second to recognize the voice. And only one person she knew called her "little lady." She hated that. And hated him.

"What do you want? I'm a little busy." She popped the cornbread in the oven and then stirred the chili on the stove top. The smell of spicy tomatoes and onions filled the room.

"I need to talk to you. Can we meet when you get off shift?"

She put the spoon down, motioning to Mack to take over dinner. She walked outside where she could talk in private.

"I don't think it's wise to be seen together, let alone talk. I said all I needed to say to you last weekend."

"It's really important we talk. There are some things you need to know before you go to court next week. Please."

Leaning against one of the fire trucks in the bay, she let out a deep sigh. "Whatever you need to tell me, you can say over the phone." The last thing she wanted to do was see him in person again.

"It's not safe for us to talk about this over the phone. I need to see you in person."

This was starting to get old. She needed to end it, for good this time. "I'm hanging up the phone now. I have nothing to say to you. I don't want to see you. I'm done. Please don't call me again." She disconnected and turned off her phone.

As she went back inside, Mack was setting the table. She knew her face was hot with anger and she took a couple of deep breaths to settle her nerves.

"Everything okay?" He knew she was stressing out due to her husband's trial.

"Yeah, sure." She nodded toward the other guys sitting at the table listening.

Mack got her meaning. Can't talk. He was the one person she could count on right now, and it killed her that she couldn't tell him everything.

"Okay, then let's eat."

Just then the alarms went off, indicating they had a call.

Everyone froze and listened to the voice of the dispatch operator coming over the speaker. After getting the information on the fire, they quickly dressed in their bunker gear and took off.

She could smell the smoke before they rounded the corner to Campbell's Farmers' Market. She directed her crew once they got there, knowing that her first priority was to locate the victim and get him and her crew out safely.

Once inside the burning building, she couldn't help but think how easy it would be to run from her problems. Here was the perfect opportunity. She'd already stashed a little money away in case she had to leave. It wasn't enough to get far, but she could start over somewhere else. She knew Ken was in over his head with the trial and now the Mexican Mafia wanted to hurt him. She'd received threats, too, but she thought the kids would be safe with her mom. The thing was…Could she leave her kids? She didn't think so. They'd already lost their dad…at least until after the trial or jail time. No, her kids needed her. She chastised herself for even thinking that way. She put the thought out of her mind and focused on the task at hand.

A few minutes later, they found the victim and she led her crew toward the front of the warehouse. She was bringing up the rear and saw that Mack and Kevin already had the victim out the door.

Then she saw something. A quick flash off to the side. She turned to see better. It looked like the figure had on firefighting gear. Did someone else come in without her knowing? She made the split-second decision to go investigate. As she was making her way toward the back of the building, her air tank warning went off. She only had a few seconds. When she got close, she realized who it was. She heard Mack's frantic mayday call over the radio. She went to answer the call when suddenly she tripped over something. The roof caved in and then everything went black.

The next thing she knew, she was riding in the back of a van. She thought she was in an ambulance at first. Then she realized she was alone and her arms and legs were bound. Her mouth was so parched she could barely whisper and her head hurt. She felt nauseated and dizzy. After what seemed like a long time, the van came to a stop. She held her breath when the van door opened. She couldn't believe what she was seeing.

"What the hell are you doing?" she said, croaking out each word painfully.

"Shhh. Don't talk. We'll have plenty of time for that later." He lifted her gently out of the van and brought her inside. "I'm getting you away from all this. Where you'll be safe from everyone."

Sam tried to sit up, but he pushed her back down. "Just relax. If you play nice, you can stay here. I have to go back in a couple of days, but I'll make you comfortable before I go."

He took out a syringe and leaned over her.

She started to protest. "What is that?"

"Just a little something to help you sleep. Tonight has been traumatic enough." She could barely feel the needle prick her skin. Before she could say anything else, her eyelids closed and she went into a deep sleep.

The next time she woke up, she was here in this dank, dark place. The Asshole had left a note that said he had to get back to town, but would be back soon. His explanation of why she was here—to keep her safe—made no sense whatsoever.

Her thoughts were interrupted by the sound of a gunshot. She had heard a few shots off in the distance when she first got to this hellhole, so she figured she was close to a hunting lodge. But the sound of this one was a lot closer. Like right outside the door.

She listened for a few more minutes and thought she heard footsteps, then a creaking noise. Sure enough, the door was opening.

Instinctively, she crouched in the far corner and waited for whatever hell she was going to face next.

Chapter Eighteen
Santa Rosa Beach, FL, Thursday 5:35 p.m.

Jeff Stanton had been staring at the open file on his desk for the past thirty minutes. The fire at Campbell's Farmers' Market had him baffled.

Jeff had worked as the Santa Rosa Beach Fire Marshal for six months since transferring from the Tallahassee office. He had a wife and a stepson whom he adored. His other love was fire. He had been fascinated with fire since he was a child. Not in a pyromaniac kind of way, but a scientific way. How it started, what made it burn, how to put it out. What fuels the fire? So it was natural he became a firefighter. For the first two years of his career, he fought fires. But he realized he was more interested in how and why it burns.

He trained to become a fire marshal. He worked in the Tallahassee region, and when an opening came up in Santa Rosa Beach, he applied. His wife was from the area and wanted to move closer to her parents. His stepson, Zane, was autistic—his wife's former husband left her because he couldn't handle the situation—and she wanted her parents' help. Jeff was in the process of adopting Zane and looking forward to expanding his new family.

This was the seventh fire his office had investigated since his arrival. It was also his most challenging. There had been two other suspected arson fires in the last two months, but this was the first one involving a missing person.

They'd proved that the fire had been set intentionally, and whoever did it either wasn't skilled or didn't care that it was sloppy. Gas was used as an accelerant—which was the most traceable source. The perp who'd set the fire splashed gas throughout the warehouse and then lit it on the way out. The warehouse wasn't equipped with smoke alarms, so the victim never knew what happened. The smoke had become so thick he had no chance of escaping. Sam and her crew had come at the right time. Another minute and a rescue would not have been possible. Plus, the propane tanks the owner had stored in back for weekend BBQs were full. They'd exploded a few minutes after the victim was pulled out.

An interview with the victim didn't glean much information. He'd closed up shop at 5:00 and gone to his office to do paperwork. He was turning off his computer and gathering his things to go home when he smelled smoke. He opened his office door and saw the warehouse in flames. That was the last thing he remembered. Whether he'd been overcome by smoke or his blood sugar was low—he was diabetic—was unclear. He'd passed out and didn't remember the firefighters bringing him out. His next memory was waking up in the ambulance on the way to the hospital.

What happened to Lt. Samantha Collins was the most puzzling thing. There was no reason for her to go back into the warehouse. Not only was it against protocol, it was stupid. Even if she saw something or someone in the warehouse, she would have notified her crew. And then to leave her fire helmet at the back door was even more puzzling.

He remembered some advice his former boss had given him when he was training as a fire investigator: "If you hear hooves, it's probably horses, not zebras." In other words, usually the most logical answer is the correct one. Her helmet could have come off during the explosion. Maybe she'd become disoriented and wandered off. It was quite perplexing and he'd thought of the different scenarios so many times his head hurt.

As a fire marshal, the easy part of the job was done. He'd found the cause of fire. But who started it and why? And more importantly, what had happened to Samantha Collins? He was still waiting for fingerprint analysis to come in, but he held out little hope for it. The farmers' market was a public place and it would be hard to exclude everyone. The gas cans hadn't been found.

The police department was helping with the investigation, and so far they hadn't turned up anything, either. There was talk about the Mexican Mafia, but he hadn't heard of any concrete leads.

Sam's husband was in jail, so he was ruled out…unless he'd had help. But according to the warden, Ken was surprised to hear about Sam and was upset when told the news.

Of course, the family of Campbell's Farmers' Market was investigated thoroughly, but nothing had come up. Their finances were solid and they had a nice insurance policy—nothing outrageous or suspicious. As the owner pointed out, his son was in the building during the fire. Why put your life on the line? So they were ruled out. That left other unknown suspects. Now he was back to square one. Who and why?

Jeff shuffled the paperwork around on his desk and thought about what to do next. He always worked better at the scene of the crime. He opened his desk drawer and pulled out his camera. On his way out of the office, he stopped by to tell his assistant, Valerie, he was leaving. Valerie Crumpton reminded him of his grandmother. She was in her late fifties, had an ample bosom, and always wore themed sweaters around holidays. It didn't matter if it was eighty degrees on Halloween; she had on her orange sweater decorated with witches and pumpkins, and wore it with matching orange-and-black polka-dot socks. His staff adored her, mainly because she brought in fresh muffins and sweet rolls once a week and never forgot a birthday or anniversary.

"Valerie, I'm leaving for the rest of the day. I'm going back out to the farmers' market."

"Okay, Mr. Stanton. See ya tomorrow morning." He'd asked her to call him Jeff, but old habits never die.

He didn't know what he hoped to find out at the warehouse, because he'd been out there several times since the fire. He just had a feeling that he was overlooking something obvious.

The drive to the farmers' market only took a few minutes. He parked around back and got out of his state vehicle. He looked around the perimeter, focusing on the woods behind the warehouse, and took photos. Putting on his work boots, he entered the shell of the warehouse. Days before, his investigative team had sifted through all the debris and sent samples to the forensics lab.

He looked again at the back door where someone apparently had forced entry. There were tool marks on the side of the door frame. Forensics had taken a mold and sent it to the lab. They would determine what type of tool was used, and hopefully that information would help them find a suspect.

Jeff took another look around and something shiny caught his eye. He reached into his pockets and found his gloves. Reaching into a mound of debris, he pulled out a buckle. Some reflective fabric had melted onto the buckle. He was familiar with this type of buckle. It was normally found on bunker gear of firefighters. The reflective strips were on the jackets they wore. Intrigued, he went back to his truck and pulled out his toolbox, which he carried with him at all times. He went back to the debris pile and took some pictures. Then he went to work sorting through the rubble until he got to the bottom of the pile. What he found next stunned him.

Chapter Nineteen
Santa Rosa Beach, FL, Thursday 7:30 p.m.

"He was too weird for words." Rachel went to dinner with Stacy and filled her in on the details of her meeting with Patrick.

La Paz was a Mexican restaurant that Michelle, Rachel's friend, had suggested they try. It was packed with tourists on a perfect late-summer night.

"Weird how?" Stacy asked.

"Well, it was nothing he said. It was more what he didn't say. He had this nonchalant demeanor."

The waitress brought over steaming plates of enchiladas for both of them. "Man, this looks good," Stacy said, digging into her food. "Mmm, whoever thought to put lobster meat into an enchilada was genius. I think I've died and gone to heaven. Sorry, you were saying?"

"The fact that he's shown no interest whatsoever in helping look for Sam is strange. Ken is supposed to be one of his closest friends and Patrick grew up with Sam. If I was in that situation, I'd be doing everything I could to help find her."

"You're right. That is weird."

"He said he thought her disappearance had something to do with revenge from the drug cartel."

"You think he's hiding something?"

"I do. And I intend on finding out what it is."

"What can I do to help?"

"Do some more digging. He was living with someone recently. Mary Anne Lipscomb, I think. Maybe we should start there."

"I'm on it," Stacy said in between huge bites of food. "Man, this is so good."

Rachel laughed, pointing at Stacy's almost-empty plate. "I can tell. Are you going to lick the plate when you're done?"

"I'm a little more civilized. I plan on using my finger to get the leftover sauce up."

Rachel took a sip of her margarita and looked around the restaurant. It had a dazzling interior, which was decorated with typical Mexican flair. Colorful sombreros adorned lime-green walls, light fixtures were in the shape of red peppers, and a roaring fire crackled in the main dining room, even though it was still in the dog days of summer.

"Earth to Rachel. Come in, Rach." Stacy had a look of amusement on her face.

"Sorry. What were you saying?"

Stacy plucked the lime out of her margarita and downed the rest in one gulp. "I was asking you if you wanted to take the paddleboards out in the morning. I checked the surf report for tomorrow. The forecast calls for less than two-foot swells. Perfect day for it."

Stacy was a paddleboard enthusiast just like Rachel. She was more competitive and liked to race, while Rachel preferred to paddleboard for fun and relaxation. The type of board Rachel had, the YOLO, which stood for "you only live once," was manufactured in Santa Rosa Beach. While she was here, she planned on visiting the company's warehouse and picking out a new board.

"Sure. It'll have to be early. I want to go to the firehouse and talk to some of Sam's coworkers."

After dinner, they returned to the beach house. Stacy retreated to her room to work on submitting a story to the newspaper, while Rachel sat outside on the deck and watched the waves roll lazily in. She loved the smell of the beach, the feel of the smooth sand on her feet, and the soothing sounds of the crashing waves. She was momentarily distracted when her cell phone buzzed. She didn't recognize the number and picked it up. "Rachel Scott."

"Hi, Rachel. It's Jeff Stanton. Fire marshal's office."

"Hi, Jeff. What's up?"

"Sorry to call so late. I just got back from a meeting with the police chief and thought I'd give you the news before the media gets wind of it."

"Yes?" That didn't sound good. She was glad she was sitting down.

"We officially ruled the warehouse fire as arson."

"I guess that doesn't come as a big surprise. What happened?"

"Test results came back late this afternoon. An accelerant was used, just like we thought."

"What kind?"

"Gas. Just like the other arson fires."

"How is the owner's son doing?"

"He's good. He got out of the hospital today."

"He never saw anyone?"

"Nope. He walked his assistant to the door, said good night, and returned to his office around five to do some paperwork. The fire started a little after six, we believe."

"Any ideas on why Sam went back into the fire against protocol?"

"Well, I found something else in the rubble that we missed the first time we went through."

"What?"

"This information hasn't been released to the public. The chief wants to keep it under wraps," Jeff said. "Pieces of a mannequin were found."

"A mannequin?" Rachel asked incredulously.

"Firefighters sometimes use a mannequin in their training. Like for CPR classes or search and rescue drills. We think the mannequin was clothed in a firefighter bunker suit."

"A training mannequin. Why would that be at the warehouse?" Rachel asked.

"A good question. Chief Gladstone is talking to the fire chief now. We'll find out if any training equipment is missing from their department."

"Does Mack know?"

"No. I'm sure the police will be talking to everyone again at the fire department. That's all I got for now."

"Okay. Thanks for the heads up." Rachel disconnected. She hated that she couldn't share this bit of information with Stacy, but she didn't want to compromise the investigation. Stacy would run with a juicy tidbit. She went inside the house to get her notebook. Whenever she was working on a case, she kept a written journal of events that happened during the search. Finding a missing person was like putting together a jigsaw puzzle. She just had to make sure she had all the right pieces. She wrote in her journal:

Possibilities: X starts fire and plants a mannequin to distract Sam. X knew her routine and knew she would break from protocol to rescue someone. Who is X? Pedro Gonzalez? Would the Mafia go through the trouble of setting fires just to kidnap Sam? Ken Collins? He could have set it up to get Sam away from everything. Which means she had to be in on it? Sam had access to fire equipment. So did Mack, Patrick, and other firefighters.

Rachel looked over her notes and sighed. No matter which possibility was right, all she knew was she had to find Sam. She owed it to Nora and to Sam's little girls. She'd search every square mile of this beach town if she had to. She needed some help getting information about the Mexican drug cartel, too. She wasn't ready to rule them out yet. And she knew just whom to call.

Chapter Twenty
Santa Rosa Beach, FL, Friday 7:45 a.m.

Rachel was just having her second cup of coffee when she heard a knock on the door. She and Stacy had gotten up before daybreak to take the paddleboards out on the Gulf. Stacy had been right. The water had been perfect for paddling. A pod of dolphins had followed them for about a half mile down the beach, making her wish she had brought her waterproof camera with her.

When they got back, Stacy quickly showered, then left to meet a former colleague for breakfast. It was still early when the visitor arrived, and Rachel wasn't expecting anyone. Her heart skipped a beat when she glanced through the front door window. Then she opened the door.

"Hello, Mike." She stepped aside and let him in. Mike Mancini was a former DEA agent she'd met while working on another case. He'd recently retired from the DEA and was working as a private investigator in Jacksonville. Mike was the only person she knew who had experience in dealing with drug gangs.

Mike bent down and kissed Rachel on the cheek. She thought he smelled wonderful. Like a mix of mint and something woodsy. A tingly feeling went down her spine and all her unresolved feelings for him came back in full force.

"You look nice," Mike said, admiring her long, tanned legs.

"Thank you. I just got back from paddleboarding." Rachel wondered if she should go put on jeans. She felt naked in front of him with her tiny board shorts and bikini top.

"Nice place," Mike said, looking around the beach house.

"Isn't it? My friend Michelle was nice enough to let me use her vacation home while I worked on this case. I wasn't sure how long I would be here." Rachel opened the sliding glass door that led out to the deck. "Want to go outside and have some coffee?" She grabbed the coffee carafe and an extra mug.

He followed her out onto the deck and took a seat. He hadn't changed much since she'd last seen him, just a few months ago. He still had the "biker" look going on with a snug white T-shirt under a black leather jacket and distressed blue jeans. He looked good, she thought. Real good. She had a hard time keeping her feelings in check around him. It was hard to maintain a professional relationship with a handsome man who obviously liked you as well.

"This is a surprise. I didn't expect you until later this week," Rachel said. When she'd called him last night, he'd said he would be glad to help out, but he wouldn't be able to leave for another couple of days. The drive from Jacksonville took about four hours, so she figured he must have left before the crack of dawn.

"The case I was working on wrapped up sooner than I thought. So here I am."

"I'm glad you came."

"Tell me what you got so far."

Rachel sat down on the chair next to Mike, curling her legs up under her, and brought him up to speed on the case. She ended by telling him about the conversation with the fire marshal. She trusted Mike not to say anything to anyone about the mannequin. "I think Sam may have gotten mixed up in something that was bigger than she could handle."

"And the Mexican drug cartel may have been responsible for her disappearance?"

"Maybe. The head of the gang, Richard Flores, was pissed that Ken and Patrick zeroed in on his territory. Not to mention Ken was the person who initially busted one of his guys, Jason Blum, then turned around and used Jason to run his deals. I think Flores had something to do with it—whether he kidnapped Sam or she set up this whole thing to get away from him."

"Flores is a sadistic and unpredictable son of a bitch. The rumors that have circulated about him are gut-wrenching, to say the least. He's a legend among the Mexican Mafia. You need to be careful."

"I've already been warned. It's why I wanted to see if you could help me out. I figure if Flores had something to do with Samantha's disappearance, then the more I know about him, the better chance I have of finding her," Rachel said. "What can you tell me about Flores?"

"Where do I start?"

"How did he get involved in the drug trade?"

"Richard, or little Ricky as he was called when he was younger, grew up dirt poor in Mexico City. His mom was a prostitute. His dad was absent most of his life. Ricky learned to survive on the streets. When he was just six years old, he went to work for Richard Gomez, peddling weed and stealing from tourists. By the time he was sixteen, he was Richard Gomez's right-hand man. He'd proved his loyalty to Gomez by murdering rival gang members."

"When did Flores come north?"

"Right around then, Gomez relocated his Mafia family to San Diego and increased his family gang members. Flores's power grew, too. But Flores grew tired of being the little guy. He had loftier aspirations. One night, Gomez mysteriously disappeared. No one questioned it because they were scared of Flores. Flores was next in line and took over operations."

"That's one way to get a promotion."

"He decided to move the gang to Florida when California started cracking down hard on drug trafficking. Flores had connections in Miami and knew he could build his empire here. He wanted to establish himself as a prominent businessman, so he bought up real estate and businesses to launder his drug profits. He donated money to the appropriate politicians and charitable organizations. Attended the right parties and mingled with the 'in crowd,' all the while expanding his share of the drug trade."

"Why did he decide to come to Santa Rosa Beach?"

"He started expanding operations all through Florida and then into southern Georgia. Santa Rosa Beach was a good place for him because of the location—it's easily accessible by water, close to five major cities, especially Atlanta and Mobile, but also a low-key spot to distribute his wares."

"And then—"

"Everything was going smoothly until Blum and Gonzalez were arrested. Then the DEA turned the heat on Flores, and he was rumored to have disappeared back into Mexico City."

"Do you think he's out for revenge because Ken Collins arrested one of his guys?" Rachel asked.

"I think he's out for revenge because Ken Collins stole money from him by taking over his drug clientele."

"When did Flores find out about Ken's operation? He could have been the tipster if he knew."

"I don't know when Flores found out, but I'm sure it was pretty easy. He has sources," Mike said.

"If Flores did have something to do with Sam's disappearance, what would he have done? Hold her somewhere?"

"If Flores got Sam, it's not good. He's not the type to ask for ransom. He doesn't need money. Kidnapping would be strictly revenge."

Rachel shuddered. That was what she was afraid of. "Let's hope she ran away, then."

"What can I do to help?" Mike asked.

Rachel smiled. She knew she could count on Mike to jump right in and use any resource to get the job done.

"Check your sources and see if you can find out if Flores knows anything about Sam's disappearance." Rachel laughed.

"Right. Like it's that easy."

"Also, I'd like to know if Flores has property around here. It might be a good place to search."

"Okay. Let me make a call." Mike pulled his cell phone out of his pocket. Rachel had to wait only a couple of minutes before Mike had the info he needed.

"Flores owned several rental properties in the area, and he funneled a lot of money through them. I'm having a list sent to my e-mail. We can start there," Mike said. "But don't hold out too much hope. If Flores had anything to do with Sam's disappearance, he wouldn't have dumped her body at any of his properties."

"Flores is just one suspect I'm contemplating. Mack Dixon, who Ken says was having an affair with Sam, is another."

"Ken would be at the top of my list."

"Why is that?"

"Spouses are almost always the first suspect. His wife disappears the week she was supposed to testify at his trial? That's just not sitting right with me."

"It's kind of hard to set a fire and kidnap your wife while in jail," Rachel argued.

"Just because he's in jail doesn't mean he couldn't arrange for it to happen. He's an ex-cop. A drug dealer. I'm sure he has plenty of contacts."

"I don't know. When I talked to him, I didn't get that. He seemed genuinely concerned about his wife and his kids. He said over and over that Sam wouldn't leave the kids."

"Criminals lie. Look at his track record. He was a trusted member of the police department and he was selling dope right under their noses."

Mike had a lot of experience in busting dirty cops involved in drug dealings and other illegal activity. She knew that Ken would probably be at the top of his suspect list.

"Nora, Samantha's mom, is holding a press conference at the warehouse tomorrow at ten a.m."

"Sounds good. Something will shake loose soon," Mike assured her. "I'll make some more phone calls and meet you at the conference tomorrow."

"Do you have a place to stay? We have an extra room." Rachel hoped she sounded friendly and not too forthcoming.

"Thanks for the offer, but I already got a place down the road." Mike got up from his chair.

"At least come back over tonight for dinner. Stacy and I are going to the seafood market to get some fresh shrimp for pasta." *I hope I don't sound desperate*, she thought, regretting the invitation as soon as it came out of her mouth.

Mike paused at the sliding glass door. "Okay. Sounds great." He smiled. "You had me at pasta."

Immense relief flooded through her. Rachel felt like she was sixteen again and had a schoolgirl crush. "Great. See ya around seven-ish."

Rachel watched him leave. She had mixed emotions about Mike. When they'd worked together in the Bahamas, they'd had a definite chemistry. Today, he seemed a little detached. She didn't know what to expect from him, but she was glad he was here to help.

Before heading upstairs to take a shower, she glanced at her phone. She had a missed call and voice mail. She checked her messages and listened as Tammie asked if she would meet her tomorrow before the press conference. Rachel thought back to the day she'd met Nora. Tammie had said she had something important to tell her about Sam. She wondered if this had something to do with Sam's affair with Mack.

Chapter Twenty-One
Santa Rosa Beach, FL, Saturday 8:15 a.m.

The next morning Rachel woke up with a good feeling. The nasty weather didn't match her mood. She sat on the deck and watched thunderclouds roll in from the Gulf. A pod of dolphins was frolicking in the waves without a care in the world. When raindrops started to fall, she grabbed her coffee cup and headed inside. Stacy was finishing a bagel and looking over her e-mail.

"Good morning, sunshine," Stacy said as she shoved the last bite in her mouth.

"Won't be sunshiny here today. I feel great, though."

"Does Mike Mancini have something to do with that?" Stacy teased.

Rachel laughed. "I don't know what you're talking about."

"You can't play coy with me, missy. I saw the way he looked at you all through dinner."

Mike had shown up for dinner right at 7:00 and brought flowers. It hadn't taken much to tempt him with homemade shrimp scampi and a nice bottle of wine.

"Mike is just a friend. I don't have time for a relationship."

"Who said anything about a relationship?" Stacy said. "You just need a little companionship. Big difference."

"That's what Maggie is for," Rachel said with a twinge of regret. She missed her black Lab and hated leaving her for so long. However, she knew Jack was taking good care of her.

"That is not the kind of companionship I was talking about and you know it."

Rachel grabbed her brush off the counter and started attacking her long auburn hair. It was already getting frizzy from the humidity. She twisted it into a bun and secured it with a clip.

"What time are you leaving?" Rachel asked, eager to change the subject. She wasn't ready to discuss her feelings about Mike just yet. Stacy was intuitive—it's what made her a good reporter. And once she had taken hold of something, she wouldn't let it go. That was something they had in common.

"Tsk-tsk. Changing the subject. But I'll let it go for now." Stacy closed her laptop and put it in her briefcase. "I'm planning on leaving for the airport right after the press conference."

Stacy had to go back to Miami for a meeting with her boss, but would be coming back in a couple of days.

"I can take you to the airport after the conference," Rachel offered.

"Thanks, but Mack offered to give me a ride to the conference and then to the airport. It'll give me a chance to talk to him again so I can turn this story in when I get to Miami." Stacy was writing an update on the search for Sam for the *Miami Sun* and had spent the last day interviewing firefighters who'd worked with Sam.

"Any word on Patrick's ex-girlfriend?"

"I'm working on it," Stacy said as she gathered the rest of her things.

"Great. I'm going to get dressed. I have to meet Tammie in about an hour. She said she wanted to talk to me in private, and I'm anxious to hear what she has to say."

"Sounds good. I'll see you there."

Rachel headed upstairs to change. She was looking forward to getting this press conference done, and she hoped it would bring in the lead she needed to find Sam.

✦ ✦ ✦

Rachel pulled up to Tammie's house. The home was a brick two-story with black shutters and a small manicured front yard with a Tampa Bay Buccaneers flag stuck in the flower bed. She walked up to the door and rang the bell.

After a moment, she heard Tammie yell, "Be right there."

Tammie opened the front door with a baby on one hip and another small child wrapped around her legs. She wore sweatpants and a white T-shirt, which had baby food splattered across her chest. Her long dirty-blonde hair was pulled back in a loose ponytail.

"Hang on a second. Let me give the kids to my husband and I'll be right out to talk. It's quieter out here."

"Okay." Rachel took a seat on one of the rocking chairs and waited.

She heard some yelling inside and the baby crying. A few minutes later, a frazzled-looking Tammie walked back outside. She took the other chair and let out a sigh.

"Sorry about that. It's my husband's only day off and he thinks he can just sit around all day and watch TV."

"It's okay," Rachel said. "So you and Samantha have been good friends for a long time?"

Tammie nodded. "My family moved next door to Samantha's when I was six years old. We moved from Georgia when my dad got a better job here. Sam and I have been friends ever since."

"I was amazed at all the trophies at Nora's house. From talking to the guys at the fire department, Sam doesn't strike me as the beauty pageant type, even though she's a beautiful girl. How did she get involved in pageantry?"

"Sam is a rough-and-tumble tomboy at heart. But her mom was the one who pushed the beauty pageants on her. Until she was twelve, she was on the kiddie pageant circus. Her daddy worked two jobs like most firefighters do. So, he didn't have much say in it. Two to three days a week you could find him at the fire station and on his off days he mowed lawns—except for Sundays. He wasn't around a lot when Sam was growing up, but she loved her daddy."

"Why did her mom want her to be in pageants?"

"Nora is a former beauty queen herself. She started entering Sam into pageants when she was just a baby. She won the Little Miss Walton County, Little Miss Sunshine State, Miss Junior Florida, and dozens of other titles."

"Doesn't that cost a lot?"

"Yes. That's why her daddy had to work so hard. Pageants can be very expensive. And Nora knew how to spend it. Dresses, coaches, fake teeth—or flippers, like they're called in the kiddie pageantry—and travel. Sam said it cost thousands."

"She was successful, though, from the awards I saw."

"Sam was almost guaranteed to win any pageant. She had inherited her momma's good looks—beautiful curly blonde hair, cornflower-blue eyes, and a smile that lit up a room. She didn't like the makeup and fancy dresses and all the time spent with dance and pageant coaches, but that's what you had to do to win pageants. Sam would rather have been outside climbing trees and making mud pies."

"But she went along with it."

"She was good at pageants. She could win over the judges just by a wink and a smile. And boy, was she a natural. It was like she was born to be on stage. She won pageant after pageant. She even won some college scholarships," Tammie said.

"What happened to change all that?"

"Well, the unthinkable happened. The summer before Sam turned twelve, she had a horrible accident. Her dad had a rare day off and took Samantha fishing with him. She loved the pageants, but loved spending time with her daddy more. She would've followed him to the ends of the earth. Early one Sunday morning, she went off with her daddy and big brother to Millers Lake for a day of fishing. It was really a hot day, so her daddy let her go swimming after they had lunch. Sam didn't see the other boat until it was too late. The boat hit her, and the propellers ripped into the right side of her arm, shoulder, and part of her face."

"That must have been terrifying!"

Tammie nodded. "They rushed her to the local hospital and then Life-Flighted her to the Atlanta children's hospital, but she'd lost a lot of blood, and then she got an infection, so it was touch and go. She had five surgeries, including some plastic surgery to reduce the scarring."

"I guess it put an end to her days of pageantry," Rachel said.

"Yeah, it did. I don't think Nora ever truly forgave her husband. Sam missed a whole year of school and was held behind. The family had tons of medical bills and Nora had to get a job to help."

"She wasn't at school with her friends. That must have been hard. Was she lonely?"

"Sam grew closer to her older brother. They were at home a lot by themselves. Her brother always wanted to be a firefighter like his dad. She hung out with him and all his friends."

"When did she decide to become a firefighter?"

"When it came time to graduate high school and think about college plans, Sam decided to follow in her brother's footsteps and go to fire college. Her mother was devastated, to say the least. She wanted Sam to go to the junior college and get a business degree."

"I have the recent pictures of Sam that Nora gave me. She's still beautiful. You can barely see the scars on her face."

Tammie agreed. "She looks great. She doesn't think so, though."

"So, she went to fire college in Ocala." Rachel tried to move the story along. She could hear Tammie's baby starting to cry in the house. She figured it wouldn't be long until Tammie's husband started yelling for her to come back inside.

"Yep. She graduated with honors from fire college. She got the job at the fire department a few months after graduation."

"What happened to her brother?"

"Breck met a girl, got married, and moved to Miami. He was working for the Miami Fire Department when he was killed. They were at a fire, and Breck was on the roof when it caved in. He fell and broke his neck."

"That's horrible. And she lost her dad as well?"

"Yes, to a heart attack about a year after Breck's death."

"I see why Nora is so emotionally distraught." Rachel absently chewed on her thumbnail. "How did Sam and Ken meet?"

"Sam met Ken soon after joining the fire department here. They dated maybe six months. Then Sam got pregnant. They got married and moved into a trailer on her parents' land while they built a house. By the time the house was ready, she was pregnant again. Another girl. Born twenty-one months later. They settled down. Ken was working his way up at the police department and Sam juggled the girls and working at the fire station. They seemed to be doing fine."

"Then Ken gets arrested and the whole family is thrown into turmoil again," Rachel finished for her.

"Yep. Now with Samantha missing and Ken in jail, Nora's clinging to those girls. She feels like a curse has been put on her family, and Sam's little girls are all she has left. Finding Sam alive and well would be a godsend for Nora. She's already lost so much." Tammie shook her head.

"Did Sam know about Ken's marijuana operation?"

Tammie looked a little uncomfortable at the question.

"Tammie, you're not betraying Sam's confidence. This conversation is between us. I need to know everything I can about Sam if I'm going to find her."

Tammie took a big breath. "The police interviewed me. I don't want to get into trouble."

"I promise that what you say is between us," Rachel said again.

"She knew, but she wasn't involved that I know of. She kind of turned a blind eye to it."

"When did she find out?"

"Ken hid it from her at first. He told Sam he was working on a project for the department. She never went to the barn. She called it his 'man cave.' But he started spending more and more time back there, and one day, curiosity got the best of her. While Ken was at work, she walked back there and found the door locked. She thought it was strange. He'd never locked the barn door. When he got home, she asked him about it, and he made up some story that he'd bought some expensive tools for his project and wanted to keep them locked up."

"Did that explanation satisfy her?"

"At first. Then Ken started buying a lot of stuff. And he started taking her out for nice dinners, and he was always buying toys for the girls. Sam did most of the bill paying for the family, and she knew how much he made. When she asked him where the extra money was coming from, he said he'd earned a bonus check. But she didn't buy it. She went out to the barn with bolt cutters and broke in."

"I bet she was surprised."

"Yeah, to say the least. She was shocked. The whole barn had been transformed into a grow factory. There were rows and rows of plants, special lighting, and all kinds of chemicals and bottles. When she realized what he was up to, she was pissed off. She confronted him. He told her how much money he was making growing weed and said he was saving most of it for retirement. He promised he'd stop after he made a certain amount."

"Did she know Patrick was involved?"

"Oh yeah, and she wasn't happy about it, but Ken said he'd needed some start-up money, so he cut Patrick in on the deal."

"Why was she unhappy that Patrick was involved?"

"Ever since she broke up with Patrick, she's tried to keep her distance from him. She tolerated him because Ken liked him."

Rachel looked shocked. "Patrick and Sam dated? Before she married Ken?"

"Yeah, I thought you knew that. She and Patrick were high school sweethearts. Patrick was so possessive. I'll never forget this goofy heart charm he gave Sam. It was a heart in two pieces. She wore one half on a necklace and he had the other half." Tammie leaned back on the bench and stretched her legs out. "Patrick proposed after college, but Sam turned him down. They had a nasty breakup."

"I had no idea. And Ken and Patrick remained friends?" Rachel wondered why, when they'd met at the Donut Hole a couple of days ago, Patrick hadn't mentioned that he'd dated Sam.

"Things had already started going sour with Patrick—if you ask Sam, she says she and Patrick had already broken up by the time she met Ken. Patrick denies it. He begged her to take him back, but once she met Ken, things happened fast. Eventually, Patrick came back around. He was friends with her brother and his friends. It's a small town and all." Tammie shrugged her shoulders.

"Did Patrick ever get married?"

"No. But he had a serious live-in relationship with Mary Anne Lipscomb. She's an older lady who runs the local pharmacy. They broke up a few months ago—before Patrick was arrested. He moved out of her home and bought a new place just outside of town. I don't think he's seeing anyone now. In my opinion, he never really got over Sam. He thought they'd get married and have kids."

"Ken was okay with that?"

"I don't think Ken knew Patrick was still pining for Sam. Ken's the most laid-back, easygoing person I know. Even as cop, he rarely raises his voice. If he knew Patrick was still in love with Sam, he never mentioned it."

"What about Sam? Did she know Patrick's true feelings?"

"I think so. But she ignored it, or didn't have time to think about it between her job and raising those two little girls. She hoped Patrick would find someone else."

"Is Patrick a vindictive type of person?"

Tammie thought about it for a minute. "I'm not sure. He went a little psycho after the breakup, but he never did anything to hurt Sam. I know he's crazy about her little girls. Always buys them presents on their birthdays and stuff."

"He was pretty upset about getting arrested, though," Rachel said.

"It was his own stupid fault for going along with Ken's idea. He knew the risks when he got involved."

"What about Mack Dixon? I heard he and Sam were close."

"They've been friends for a long time. But I think they became even closer after Ken got arrested. Mack stepped in to help out. He was always around the house when they were off shift." Tammie closed her eyes like she was trying to remember something. "She was bothered about something a couple days before she disappeared, though."

"Did she say what it was?"

"That's what I wanted to talk to you about." Tammie hesitated.

"Go ahead," Rachel prompted when she sensed Tammie's reluctance. "This conversation is between us. I'm not going to repeat anything you tell me."

"She stopped by my house on the way home from her shift one morning. She was upset. I thought it was Ken or the trial. I asked her what was wrong. She said she'd gotten herself into a mess with Mack. When I asked her what she meant, she said to just forget it."

"Did you find out what it was?"

"No. It was the last time we spoke."

"Any idea as to what kind of mess she was in?"

"No, but I can guess," Tammie said. "She was fooling around with Mack and someone at the station found out. That's grounds for termination. I think it's also why she was looking for another job."

Rachel glanced at her watch. She had only a few minutes to get back to the beach house and get ready for the press conference with Samantha's family. She was glad it had stopped raining and the sun was making an appearance. "Okay. I'll keep this information to myself. Thanks for your time, Tammie. If you think of anything else, please call me."

Tammie nodded her head. "I appreciate it. I don't want anything coming back on me."

"Will you be at the conference?"

Tammie shrugged her shoulders. "I'll try. It depends on my husband's mood." As if on cue, Rachel could hear Tammie's husband yelling for her to hurry up. "He's a little grumpy. Working all those extra shifts since the baby was born."

"Okay. I hope to see you there."

Rachel drove back to the house thinking about her conversation with Tammie. She wondered what exactly Sam had meant by "getting in a mess with Mack." Sam was already on probation at the station and was looking for another job. Why would she care if someone found out about her and Mack? Something else was going on with Mack. Maybe Stacy would get it out of him when they met. Mack just might be the key to all this.

Chapter Twenty-Two
Santa Rosa Beach, FL,
Saturday 11:00 a.m.

A mob of people was standing outside Campbell's Farmers' Market when Rachel got there. Nora had insisted on holding the press conference there since it had been the last place Sam had been seen. It had been almost a week since Sam's disappearance and nothing new had turned up.

The local and national news people showed up in droves. Sam's unusual disappearance was turning out to be a big media sensation. The story had gotten the attention of *Nancy Grace* and other cable news networks. Stacy Case was covering the story for her paper, the *Miami Sun*.

Chief Gladstone took the podium. "Good afternoon. I'm Police Chief Gladstone with the Santa Rosa Beach Police Department. We're here today with Samantha Collins's family and Rachel Scott of Florida Omni Search. Each will make a short statement. First, I'll give you an update on the investigation.

"Let me first say that I know the public has a very keen interest in Samantha's disappearance, and we appreciate it. We are now classifying this as a criminal investigation, and because of that, there are still a number of details we cannot get into and we won't be taking any questions today regarding the investigation.

"We've found an item that's been identified as Samantha's about a half mile from here. We are initiating a second canvass of this area and will extend it an additional twenty miles.

"Our detectives and searchers are continuing to follow up on many leads, including Samantha's activities prior to her disappearance. We would like to encourage anyone to call in any tips you may have. It is oftentimes the smallest detail—something that may seem inconsequential to you—that is the piece of the puzzle we need to crack a case wide open. If you saw or heard something unusual or know anything about Samantha, no matter how insignificant it may seem to you, give our investigators a call or send us an e-mail.

"We want to remind all citizens that a reward of twenty-five thousand dollars has been established for information leading us to Samantha. Anyone with information regarding Samantha Collins's whereabouts is urged to call our tip line or to dial nine-one-one.

"Thank you. I will now turn over the podium to Rachel Scott of Florida Omni Search."

Rachel pushed down the nerves in her stomach as she stepped up. This part was always the hardest. She hated press conferences, but viewed them as a necessary evil.

"As of this afternoon, our search and rescue crews will have searched every location of interest. It encompasses an extremely wide area of land around the warehouse. In addition, we've used the best equipment available for searching this terrain. It's very important to us that family and friends of Samantha—as well as the public—know that our commitment and resources are unwavering. We won't give up until Samantha is found. Thank you."

Rachel stepped aside as Nora walked up. She wore a flowery sundress, and her blonde hair hung loosely around her face. She looked like she'd aged considerably since Rachel had first met her. The pain of losing a husband, a son, and now a daughter had taken its toll on her, but Rachel could still see a hint of the former beauty queen's looks. Samantha's two girls, Bella and Gracie, were standing beside Nora while she pleaded for the safe return of her daughter.

"If anyone out there knows anything about where Samantha is, I am asking you, as her mother, to please call the tip line. Her daughters miss her and need her. I miss her so much. Please call. Even if you think it's nothing, we need your help to find her. And, Samantha, if you can hear me, there is nothing we can't handle together. Please come home." Nora wiped the tears away from her eyes.

"We're so grateful for the support and work of the police department, as well as the hundreds of searchers, volunteers, and firefighters. Thank you to everyone for your support in trying to find Samantha."

The media shouted out to Nora and Rachel, despite the chief's request for no questions. One of the officers ushered them safely to a private area that was set up for the conference. Someone had thoughtfully put out some water and snacks for everyone.

Stacy made her way through the throngs of the media and found Rachel. She pulled her aside and whispered in her ear. "I heard that one of the investigators found something interesting at the site the other day."

Rachel's stomach dropped. "What?"

"Pieces of training mannequin dressed in firefighting gear."

Rachel tried to look indifferent, but Stacy didn't buy it.

"You knew?" Stacy's voice filled with hurt.

"It was supposed to be confidential. I was asked not to disclose it yet."

"Then why am I here helping you? I thought we were friends. That you *trusted* me."

"I do trust you. You know that, Stacy. I gave my word. It has nothing to do with us being friends."

"I think it does. You've given me stuff off the record. This is no different."

"Yes, it is. You aren't listening. I gave my word I wouldn't say anything. I would've told you as soon as I could."

"It would've been too late. Obviously. Someone beat me to the punch."

"I'm sorry, but I won't go back on my word."

Stacy checked her watch. "I have to go. My plane leaves in one hour."

"Okay. Please don't be upset with me."

"I'll see you when I get back." Stacy turned around and made her way through the dwindling media crowd. Rachel let out a long sigh. She knew there was a risk in being friends with a reporter, but she'd thought Stacy understood there were some things she couldn't discuss when there was an ongoing investigation. Rachel walked back to her truck where Mike was waiting for her. She tried to put it out of her head.

"Is everything okay?" he asked. "You look upset."

"No, I'm fine. It'll work itself out."

"Are you ready to drive by some of these rental properties?"

"Sure. I want to see for myself if Flores is hiding something."

Chapter Twenty-Three
Santa Rosa Beach, FL, Saturday 11:34 p.m.

Rachel was vaguely aware that she must be dreaming again. She was watching her little girl, Mallory, playing in the front yard. One minute Mallory was playing with her dolls, and the next minute she vanished in front of her eyes. Rachel ran around the yard yelling Mallory's name over and over. However, this dream was a little different than the one she usually had. In this dream, her throat burned every time she screamed Mallory's name. Her lungs felt like they were on fire. The coughing and choking sensations woke her up.

Rachel struggled to open her eyes. The room was filled with smoke. She was so stunned by this that she thought she was still dreaming. Then she noticed a flickering of bright-orange color all around her room and realized she was not dreaming, but living a nightmare. Panic seeped through her body, and for a moment, she was entranced by the fire.

I have to get out of here. She looked around, but could see no way out. The room was quickly engulfed in flames, and the smoke was making it hard for her to breathe. It felt like a knife was slicing through her throat and lungs.

Rachel kicked off the covers and thought about her dwindling options. It would be impossible to go through the bedroom door. The doorway was blocked by a wall of flames. She glanced at the window where the fire was starting to eat away at the curtains. Her bedroom was on the second floor and faced the beach. It would be a long drop down, but hopefully the sand would cushion her fall. Choking on the smothering smoke, Rachel started wrapping her hands around the sheets to protect them from the glass. At most, she thought she might get some burns and a broken bone by jumping. The only other option was to stay and be burned alive.

Just as she started to brace herself, the window shattered and fragments of glass rained down around her. At first, she thought the intensity of the heat blew out the window. Then a dark figure entered through the window and reached out for her.

Chapter Twenty-Four

She instinctively backed away. "Rachel. It's Mack." A hand reached out to hers. Relief flooded through her body. She quickly grabbed Mack's hand and he guided her to a ladder leaning against the house. As they were climbing down, a blast of fire came out from the downstairs and propelled the ladder away from the house. They hit the ground hard about twenty feet away, the sand barely cushioning their fall. Rachel was stunned for a few seconds.

"Are you okay?" Mack leaned over her, checking for injuries.

She nodded while gulping fresh air.

"Easy. Take it slow," he said, while rubbing her arm.

"What…happened?" Rachel asked, confused. She could hear sirens in the distance.

"I'm not sure. Something downstairs must have exploded. Stay here while I get the paramedics. I'll be right back."

Rachel tried to sit up but immediately regretted it when she started feeling dizzy. She lay back down and stared at the moonlit sky, bright with twinkling stars, thinking about what just happened. This was not an accident. Somebody meant her harm and wanted her out of the way.

An ambulance and a fire truck pulled up the drive just as Mack walked around front. He took the paramedics back to where Rachel was still lying on the beach. Mack stayed with her as they loaded her up on a gurney and strapped an oxygen mask across her face.

Mack sat down beside her inside the ambulance and brushed a piece of hair out of her face. "You'll be okay. I'm going to ride in the truck with you to the hospital." She smiled weakly at him and then everything went black.

✦ ✦ ✦

At the hospital, she awoke to whispered voices.

"Hello?" she croaked out. Her mouth was parched and her throat felt like it was on fire. She felt the pressure of an IV taped to her left arm. Her right hand was covered in bandages. Images of a fire flooded her memory.

Mack's face suddenly appeared in front of her.

"Hey. Look who's awake." He smiled at her.

"What happened?"

"There was a fire at the beach house."

The pain medication was making her thoughts fuzzy. She was struggling to remember the details of what happened. "I saw you in the window."

Mack nodded his head. "That's right. I was driving by and saw the flames. I tried the front door, but the fire was too intense. I found a ladder in the storage area underneath the house and climbed up to get you. You got a mouthful of smoke, but the doctor says you'll be okay." He pushed the button for the nurse and alerted her that Rachel was awake.

"My knight in shining armor." Rachel smiled, and pointed to a carafe on the nightstand next to her bed. "Water?"

"Ice chips." Mack took a spoonful and fed it to her.

"Thanks."

"Everyone is worried about you. Mike is down at the cafeteria getting some coffee," Mack said as the doctor walked in. "I'll go get him for you while the doctor talks to you."

"Thank you," Rachel said gratefully.

Dr. Schmitz told her she was a lucky girl. No lung damage that they could tell. She had second-degree burns on her right hand, lacerations on her face and hands, and a sprained ankle. He said she would stay overnight for observation, and if everything went well, she could leave in the morning. The nurse came in to give her a mild sedative and something for the pain.

Mike walked into the room as the doctor left. He kissed her on the forehead. "I was worried about you."

"Thanks for being here. The doctor said I can get out of here tomorrow."

"Do you want me to stay with you tonight?" Mike pointed to the couch in the room.

"No, I'm okay."

"I hope you don't mind—I called your office to let them know what happened. And Stacy. She'll be back up here tomorrow morning."

"Thanks." Rachel ate a few more ice chips. She thought her voice was coming back stronger. "Any idea of how the fire started?" she asked as Mack walked back into the room.

Mack cleared his throat. "No. I talked to Jeff Stanton and he was heading out to the scene. I'm sure we'll know something soon."

"This was the work of the arsonist, wasn't it?" Rachel asked.

Mack and Mike exchanged glances.

"It's a strong possibility," Mack said.

"Apparently you got the attention of someone who doesn't want you poking around," Mike said. "I'd feel comfortable if you stayed with me for a while."

"I guess that's not a bad idea." Rachel felt her eyelids getting heavy.

"The nurse must have given you some strong drugs for you to agree so quickly." Mike laughed.

"Okay. I'm going to get out of here. Let you get some rest." Mack said his good-byes and left the room.

Mike grabbed a blanket and pillow and settled down on the couch by Rachel's bed. He was going to stay whether Rachel liked it or not. Within a couple of minutes, he was asleep.

Chapter Twenty-Five
Santa Rosa Beach, FL, Monday 7:30 a.m.

When Rachel awoke the next morning, the first thing she saw was Mike stretched out on the uncomfortable couch. He looked so peaceful and sweet with a blanket tangled up around him, his left arm thrown over his chest and his long legs hanging over the end of the couch.

Rachel vaguely remembered the fire, but couldn't understand what Mike was doing on the couch. She hated to wake him, but she needed to understand what happened to her. Sitting up, she cleared her throat.

Mike shot straight up. "Hey. You're awake. How do you feel?"

"Ready to get out of here. What are you doing?"

"I wanted to stay and make sure you were okay."

Despite the pain and achiness, she smiled and felt herself melt on the inside. Oh God, did she have a huge crush on this man.

"What's the story on the fire last night?" she asked.

"Mack happened to be driving by and saw the smoke. He called it in and managed to get you out in one piece." Mike ran his hand through his thick, dark hair. "I guess I owe him one."

The nurse walked in and checked her vital signs. She told Rachel everything looked good and that the doctor would be in soon. She would probably be released this morning.

"I'm going to head down to the cafeteria and get some coffee. Need anything?"

Rachel looked down at her gown. "I guess I'm going to need some clothes. Most of my stuff must have been destroyed in the fire."

"Yeah, I talked with Stacy this morning. She caught an early flight and will be here soon. She said she was bringing you some things."

"Thanks for everything. I'll be okay if you need to go."

"I'll be back soon."

Rachel let the nurse do her thing while she thought about what her next move should be. Someone must think she was a threat. She wondered if Flores had gotten wind of her poking around in his business. The afternoon before the fire, she and Mike had driven by all his rentals, but they didn't find anything that was out of place. Three of the four units had tenants. The fourth was vacant with a For Rent sign in front.

Well, one thing is for sure, she thought, *I'm not going to let someone run me out of town.* First things first. She needed to replace her stuff, and she needed to find another place to stay.

The door opened, interrupting her thoughts, and Jeff Stanton poked his head around the corner.

"How are you?"

"Good. I think they'll let me leave today."

The nurse took off the blood pressure cuff and told her everything looked good. "I'm going to take the bandage off so you can take a shower. Just be careful with your arm. I'll be back soon to clean it and put a clean bandage on."

Rachel nodded.

"The doctor will be by shortly," the nurse said as she walked out the door.

Jeff pulled up a chair next to her bed. "I wanted to come by and see you. I went to the beach house earlier. Not a pretty sight."

"What do you think happened?"

"Another possible arson," Jeff said.

"Really?"

"I won't know for sure until the tests come back, but I would guess a gas accelerant was involved. Plus, the tool marks on the side door look familiar."

Rachel's face paled.

"You're lucky Mack drove by when he did. Another couple of minutes…" He let the thought trail off.

Stacy walked into the room carrying a cheerful balloon and flower bouquet. "Hey, girl." She looked tentatively at Rachel.

"Hey, thanks." Rachel sat up straighter in bed.

Stacy looked over at Jeff. "Sorry to interrupt."

"It's okay. Looks like she needs some cheering up."

"I brought a few things for you." Stacy held up a bag with her other hand. "Change of clothes, makeup bag, toothbrush…and voila! Trashy magazines for your guilty reading pleasure." She put the copies of *Life & Style*, *Star*, and *OK!* on her nightstand.

"You got a mirror in there?" Rachel asked.

Stacy hesitated. "Are you sure?"

"Is it that bad?"

"No, of course not. You've just got a few badges of heroism." Stacy reached in the bag and pulled out a makeup case. There was a small mirror on the flap. She handed it to Rachel.

The first thing Rachel noticed was that her eyebrows were singed. She ran her finger over what was left of her right eyebrow. She also had several small cuts around her mouth and forehead.

"I guess it could be worse." A tear slid down her cheek.

Stacy walked over and gave her a gentle hug. "Oh, honey, it could have been a lot worse. You're alive, and we'll get you back to normal in no time."

"Did anyone see anything?" Rachel started to get angry.

"No, unfortunately not. But trust me when I tell you this…We will get this guy," Jeff said.

"I know you will." Rachel was grateful for his support. Jeff seemed to be the kind of man who went above and beyond the call of duty. Working with someone who truly enjoyed his job and was willing to share information without prejudice was refreshing. "Thanks for stopping by."

"Call me when you get to feeling better. We'll get together with Chief Gladstone and come up with a new plan." Jeff got up and left the room.

Stacy took his place by Rachel's bed.

"Hey, I'm really sorry with the way we left things. I shouldn't have given you any heat about the tip."

"I'm sorry, too. I wish I could tell you everything, Stacy. You are one of my dearest friends. You know that."

"I promise not to get hotheaded again. I know we have to draw the line between business and friendship sometimes."

"If you would just know when to keep your big mouth shut," Rachel said.

"I know, sometimes it gets me in trouble." Stacy laughed. "Now let's get you showered and dressed. It's time to get out of here."

Chapter Twenty-Six
Lake Juniper, FL, Monday 4:40 p.m.

Sam sat at the table, staring at the meal The Asshole had fixed for her. The steak and potatoes had grown cold, which was just as well because she had no appetite.

"What's wrong? You need to keep up your strength."

"I told you, I'm not hungry. Being kept locked in a dark cell does that to you."

"I said I was sorry. I couldn't help it. I had things to do."

"Why are you doing this?"

"To keep you safe."

"I was doing fine without your help." Sam poked at her salad. The lettuce was drowning in the ranch dressing and the tomatoes were mushy.

"No, not really. You have no idea what was going on around you." He smiled at her. "Did you know Pedro Gonzalez had someone following you?"

"What?" Her fork hit the plate with a loud clang.

"Yeah. One of Gonzalez's goons was hanging out around the fire station watching you. Following you on calls. Biding his time."

"Is that what you called to talk to me about the night of the fire?"

"Yes. And to offer you a safe place until I could handle the matter."

Sam took a deep breath to control her anger.

"My welfare is none of your concern. I can take care of things myself. Now, if we can quit this whole charade, I need to get back to my girls. My life."

"I'm sorry. That is not an option right now. It's too dangerous for you to go back. Especially in your delicate condition."

Sam's face went pale. "What?"

"Don't play me. You know what I'm talking about."

Sam thought hard. *How in the world would he know about that? No one knew.* She laid her hand protectively over her stomach.

"Look, I'm tired of your games and I'm not playing along anymore." Sam abruptly pushed away from the table and stood up.

"Sit back down. Now." The Asshole had a crazy look on his face. She'd seen the look only one other time and it scared the crap out of her.

"No. I'm ready to go. Either you take me home or I'll walk back." She slammed her hand down hard on the table. "Enough!"

His eyes met hers as he slowly reached under the table and pulled out a gun. He pointed it at her stomach and said in a quiet voice, almost whispering, "I said, sit down. If you're good, I'll let you sleep in the cabin tonight. I need your cooperation if this is going to work. We're going to Millers Lake."

Sam sat slowly back in the chair. She'd listen to what he had to say. Pretend to cooperate. Then devise a plan to escape this craziness.

Chapter Twenty-Seven
Santa Rosa Beach, FL,
Tuesday 9:20 a.m.

Mike had Rachel moved into the same hotel where he was staying. It was one of those hotels with rooms designed as efficiency apartments. She had a kitchenette, separate bedroom and bath, and a small living area, which she set up as her office. Stacy insisted on staying with her again, although she joked that she might have to up her health insurance policy. Rachel replaced her wardrobe and laptop, which had been destroyed in the fire.

When Janine and Red found out what had happened, they both offered to come up and stay with her. But she insisted they stay in Miami. A few new cases had come in and it made more sense for them to stay there.

She put on a pot of strong coffee to brew and fired up her computer to update her website and blog. When Mallory had gone missing, Rachel spent her nights on the computer visiting various missing persons' websites. She would read through all the stories and wonder what had happened to each person. Of course, a lot of those cases were runaways, family abductions, people with drug and alcohol problems, and people with psychiatric problems.

But regardless of why a person was missing—family abduction, runaway, or kidnapped by an unknown person—the families went through the same range of emotions. The feelings that Rachel knew so well—the empty pit in your stomach, the sleepless nights, the hurt in your heart, the helplessness, the not knowing. Dedicating her life to helping find missing people—especially children—had been an easy decision to make.

One thing Rachel found true: Publicity is essential in the days just after a person goes missing. In addition to assisting people with finding their loved ones, she maintained the Florida Omni Search website so other people she couldn't help could download a tip sheet and list of helpful resources.

Rachel logged in to the Florida Omni Search website and was happy to see that Janine had put up Samantha Collins's picture and information on the home page of the site. Rachel wrote a short update on the case and then turned her attention to updating the blog. She was working on a three-part piece about how to travel safely in foreign countries, with a special emphasis on teenagers who travel during spring break. She'd had a lot of experience in that area when she took on the case of a missing teenager who had disappeared while on a spring break cruise. She reviewed her notes, opened up the word processing software…but the words wouldn't come to her. Her thoughts were jumbled and filled with Sam Collins. She couldn't focus and her hand still throbbed where she'd gotten burnt.

A knock at the door brought welcome relief. Mike walked in with a bag of donuts and a cup of coffee. "What are you working on?"

"I was trying to finish an article for my blog, but I just can't focus. All I can think about is Sam."

"Me too. It kept me up all night." He handed Rachel a chocolate donut. "Maybe some sugar will help."

She took a bite of the donut. "Yummy."

"Are you feeling better?"

"Yes. My hand still hurts a little, but the swelling on my ankle has gone down."

"Good. Just take it easy." Mike sat down and handed her a cup of coffee. "You know, I think we're looking at this all wrong."

"What do you mean?"

"We agree Sam was probably kidnapped. She wouldn't leave her kids. Right?"

"Yes."

"So the question is not who, but why would someone want to kidnap her?"

"Revenge. The Mafia wanted to send a message to Ken."

"Then why hasn't her body shown up? I've looked into Mafia executions—specifically Richard Flores's gang—and all of them left the bodies where they could be found immediately. He doesn't have a history of kidnapping. Just killing."

"Okay. So that leaves…?"

"Why are most people kidnapped?"

"Sexual abuse," Rachel said. She shuddered at the thought, but it was true. Ninety percent of abductors are men and they sexually assault their victims in over half of those cases. That was one thing that kept her up at night. *Who had Mallory, and what terrible things might they be doing to her?*

"And money."

"Sam isn't rich."

"No, but her husband was rumored to have stashed some money. Who would benefit from it?" Mike asked.

"I imagine the Mafia would want their take."

"Anybody else?"

"A lot of people may have known about the money. Her best friend, Tammie—but I don't picture her pulling off a kidnap plot. She has kids and a husband who demand a lot of her attention." Rachel thought for a minute, chewing her thumbnail. "And Mack, her other best friend and possibly her lover—but he was with her the night she was kidnapped."

"Keep going."

"Patrick. He was a little creepy when I met with him. He seemed to still harbor some resentment toward Ken."

"Now we're getting somewhere."

Rachel's cell phone buzzed on the table. "It's Stacy. I need to take this. She left this morning to meet with a source."

After a few minutes, she got off the phone.

"You're not going to believe this." Rachel smiled. "This case just took an interesting turn."

"What?" Mike asked.

"Sam is pregnant."

Chapter Twenty-Eight

"Huh?" Mike looked confused. "Pregnant?"

Rachel rolled her eyes. *Typical male response*, she thought.

"Stacy met with her source, who told her Sam had taken a pregnancy test the day she disappeared."

"Who was her source?"

"She didn't tell me. But if I had to take an educated guess, I'd say Mack or someone at the police station. Who else would have that intimate type of information? I already interviewed her best friend, Tammie, and she wasn't even sure what kind of relationship Sam and Mack had."

"So, I'm assuming it would be Mack's baby? If the rumors are true, that is."

Rachel shrugged her shoulders. "Your guess is as good as mine. This calls for another visit to Ken." She picked up her cell and starting dialing.

"Who are you calling?"

"Suzette Breland, Ken's attorney, to arrange another visit. And then I'm calling Red. I should have thought of this earlier. I want to run a background check on Patrick."

✦ ✦ ✦

While Rachel waited in the parking lot outside the county jail for Ken's attorney to show up, she thought about what Mike had said. Maybe he was right; they needed to follow the money trail.

Rachel saw Suzette's black Mercedes roll into the parking lot. She stepped out wearing a short, black skirt; lemony-yellow silk blouse that complemented her deep, dark tan; and stylish Jimmy Choo slingbacks. When the lawyer pushed her sunglasses to the top of her head, Rachel noticed Suzette's trademark—a thin, bright-pink highlight intertwined through her honey-blonde hair.

"Thanks for coming," Rachel said as she walked up to her.

"Not a problem." Suzette pulled her leather briefcase out of the back of her car. "How are you? I heard about the fire." She pointed to Rachel's bandaged hand.

"Word gets around fast, huh?"

Suzette shrugged her shoulders. "Small town, and all that."

"I'm fine, thanks for asking. Just a minor burn. Some cuts and bruises."

"What's going on with the case?"

"That's what I need to talk to Ken about." Rachel paused. "Samantha is pregnant."

Suzette showed no emotion. "And it's not Ken's."

"I don't know that for sure."

"May I ask you where you got this information?"

"A confidential source."

Suzette raised her eyebrows at her.

"Apparently, the night Sam went missing, the fire chief and crew, along with a police officer, went through Sam's things at the fire station. Her bunk room was clean, but one of the officers found a pregnancy test in the trash."

Suzette looked at her suspiciously. "I don't see Sam throwing something like that in the trash for all to see."

"No. It was wrapped in a paper towel and then put inside a CVS pharmacy bag."

"The deputies were rather thorough, then."

"Yes, they were."

"Anyone could have put it there."

Ah, here we go, Rachel thought.

"The fire station isn't locked when the guys go out on a call," Suzette continued. "One of the wives or girlfriends of the crew could have come by to surprise their guy and left it there."

"According to my source, the crew was questioned. No visitors came by that day. The trash is emptied after each shift," Rachel said. "Plus, Suzette, do you really believe that some random girl just came by the station to use the bathroom and leave a pregnancy test in the trash?"

Suzette threw her hands up. "I don't discount anything."

"Come on. Sam's pregnant and that, my friend, adds another element to this crazy case." They started walking toward the jail.

Suzette noticed Rachel was limping. "Are you sure you are up to this?"

Rachel looked down at her foot. "It's just a sprain. I'm good. Let's get this over with."

"Ken isn't going to take this very well."

"I figured that. He already thinks Mack and Sam were having an affair."

"So why tell him about this? He's already worried about her disappearance and the trial," Suzette said. "Why go there?"

"Because, despite everything, I believe that Ken still loves and cares about Sam. And because I need to find her. They have two little girls who need their mother."

"We both can agree on that," Suzette said.

They walked the rest of the way in silence. After going through all the proper procedures, they were led to the visitors' room.

"Do you mind if I talk to Ken alone first?" Rachel said quickly, before Suzette rejected her idea. "I think he would take the news better from me."

Suzette was about to protest when Rachel interrupted her.

"Please. Just give me five minutes."

"Okay. But if Ken refuses to answer any questions—" Suzette started to say.

"I'll come and get you."

Suzette walked to the couch. "I'll be right here."

Rachel was walking to the visitors' table when they brought Ken in. Even though it had only been a couple of days since her first visit to see him, he looked like he had aged another ten years. She didn't have much time, so she cut through all the pleasantries and jumped right in.

"Was Sam pregnant?" The question hit Ken like a ton of bricks.

"No. Why are you asking that?"

"Because we found a pregnancy test Sam took."

"No way. Where did you find this test?" Ken asked.

"It was discarded in the trash can at the fire station." Rachel watched the color drain from Ken's face. "The investigators found it when they searched her bunk room and the bathroom at the fire station."

Ken thought for a moment, scrubbing his face with his hands. "Oh boy. If Sam is pregnant, it's not mine. I had a vasectomy when Gracie, our youngest daughter, was born."

Rachel sat in silence.

"Plus..." He waved around the room. "I've been staying at these luxury accommodations for the last couple of months. No conjugal visits here."

That's what Rachel had expected to hear, but she was still a little surprised.

"It can't be confirmed the test was hers, but since she was the only female at the department that day, and the trash is taken out each shift..." Rachel let the words fall.

"So you think Sam got knocked up by someone else." Ken finished the sentence for her. "I guess it confirms my fear about her affair with Mack."

Again, she sat in silence. This was difficult for her. She didn't want to get involved in any obvious marital discord between Samantha and Ken Collins. Her first priority was to find Sam. And that meant figuring out what was going on prior to her disappearance. Sometimes uncomfortable situations like this one would come into play when she was trying to locate a missing person. But she had to get down to the nitty-gritty. Find out what Samantha was doing before she disappeared. What made her tick? Who was in her life and what were their roles? Who was with her the day of her disappearance? What was on her mind? These were difficult questions that had to be asked. She just hated to be the one who had to ask them.

"I don't know if it was Mack Dixon. I know you said the last time we met to ask Mack, since he was having an affair with Sam. Well, I did ask, and he's denied any affair. Tammie even said she knew nothing was going on between them."

"That doesn't mean it didn't happen."

"Why did you think there was an affair?"

Ken just gave her a hard look.

Rachel put her hands on the table and leaned over. "I'm sorry, Ken. I have to ask. I'm just doing my best here, trying hard to find your wife. Unfortunately, it means having to ask the tough questions."

"I found a birthday card Mack had given Sam. Let's just say it was romantic in nature. I never mentioned it to Sam."

"When did you find the card?"

"Sam's birthday was in January. I found the card hidden in her closet. That's all I have to say about it."

"Ken, anything at all you can remember about Sam's activities before she disappeared may be a big help in finding her. Please know whatever you tell me will be held in confidence." Rachel patted him on his arm. "I'm just trying to help. For you and the girls."

Ken looked at her with despair. "I know. It's hard being in here. I'm used to being in control of these types of situations. To sit here and know there is nothing I can do is tearing me apart." He clenched his fists. "Despite knowing about the affair, I still love Sam. I want us to work through things."

Rachel looked around the room. The one guard in the room was busy picking at his fingernails. Suzette sat at the couch flipping through a *Vanity Fair* magazine.

"There is something you can do." Rachel leaned forward again and whispered, "Something that might help us find her."

Ken looked at her hopefully. "What is it?"

"Tell me what you did with the money."

Chapter Twenty-Nine

Ken leaned back in his chair, crossed his arms, and stared back at Rachel. He seemed to contemplate her question.

"Let me rephrase that. If you did hide the money, which is what the rumors are, did Sam know where it was?" Rachel asked.

"I have no idea what you're talking about."

Rachel switched her tactics. She knew this wasn't going to be easy.

"We're working on a theory here. Someone who knew about the money grabbed Sam, with the hopes of getting their hands on it. We think. If you tell me where the money is hidden, I can get the dogs out there and see if they can pick up Sam's scent. It's worth a shot."

"Who all would be involved in this search?" Ken asked.

"It would just be me and a couple of my volunteers."

He looked at her skeptically. "No police?"

"No police."

"I'm putting a lot of trust in you," Ken said. "If you find any money, what will you do with it?"

"I won't touch the money. I just want to know where it is. We'll search the area and see if we can pick up any clues on Sam's whereabouts."

"Assuming I would hide any money, I wouldn't do it on my property. And Sam wouldn't have any knowledge of it."

"Right. Your property has already been searched. I wouldn't think you'd hide anything there. " Rachel paused. "And Sam might not know about the money, but it doesn't mean someone doesn't *think* she knows where it is."

Ken thought about it for a minute. Then he said, "When I was little, my dad used to take me fishing every Sunday after church. We would go to my dad's favorite fishing hole. A beautiful place called Millers Lake."

"Where is Millers Lake?"

"Just north of here. You can find it on any local area map." Ken paused, and looked over at his attorney. She was still preoccupied with her magazine. He continued, "Anyway, after a hot day of fishing, we'd eat a lunch my mom had packed. Then, while my dad took a nap, I'd climb this tree. It was a big tree—lots of branches—with a nice-size hole in the trunk, about halfway up. I hid little trinkets in there—Matchbox cars, colored rocks, four-leaf clovers..."

Rachel got his meaning.

"I took the girls fishing there once. I let Bella, my older girl, climb the tree and showed her the secret hole. It was still there. I told her the tree was worth a half-million dollars."

Rachel looked back at Suzette, who had apparently gotten bored and was now staring out the window. The guard was still interested in his fingernails.

"Thanks. I'll get back with you and let you know what we find." Rachel got up to leave.

Ken stopped her. "Hey, by the way, what happened to you?" He motioned to her hand.

"I was in an accident. I'm okay." She didn't want to go through the whole story of the fire.

"Okay." He looked unsure. "Take care."

"Suzette, your turn," Rachel said when she walked over to her.

"That was quick."

"Told you it wouldn't take long."

"Did you get whatever information you needed from him?"

"Yes, I think so."

"Okay. Give me a few minutes to speak with Ken, then we'll get out of this dump."

After fifteen minutes, Suzette was done, and they were on their way out.

As Suzette walked her to the car, she said, "Every time I leave here I have to go home and take a shower. The smell of sweat and despair just soaks into your clothes and skin."

"Job hazard. We all have them." Rachel shook her hand. "Thanks, Suzette. I'll be in touch."

Maybe going back to the hotel and taking a quick shower wouldn't be such a bad idea, she thought. Then she could gather the troops and head out to Millers Lake. Today was going to be her lucky day. She just knew it.

Chapter Thirty

After a long, hot shower, Rachel took the time to tend to the burn on her hand. She used the ointment the doctor had given her and applied a clean bandage. Her ankle still hurt, but she didn't want to take any more of the strong painkillers. She needed to think clearly, so she swallowed two ibuprofen with a glass of water and got to work on finding more information on Millers Lake. If she was going out there to have a look around, she'd have to hurry. Only a few hours of daylight were left.

First, she'd have to find out where Millers Lake was. She didn't want to involve Mack or Tammie with this. She still felt unsure about Mack's motives with Sam and she didn't want Tammie to get suspicious.

She hooked up her computer and tried Googling Millers Lake. No luck. Ken had told her it was his dad's favorite fishing hole, so she decided to call a store that sold bait and fishing supplies. She got the phone directory out of the desk drawer and looked for store listings under *fishing*.

She tried the first number. No answer. But someone picked up at the second number.

"Haverty's Bait Shack. This is Stan. Can I help ya?"

"Hi, I'm new in town and would like to try out some fishing spots. I was wondering if you knew where Millers Lake was located?"

"Yes, I do," Stan answered.

"I need directions. I'm staying at the Seaside Inn."

"Why do you want to go over to Millers Lake? There's better fishing over at McCann Park."

"I want to go to Millers Lake. Can you help me?"

"Okay. If you are sure that's where you want to go," Stan said reluctantly. Then he gave her the directions.

She quickly called a couple members of her team and asked them to meet her at the hotel in a half hour.

Rachel knew that going to Millers Lake and finding something that would help locate Samantha was a long shot, but with nothing else to go on, she had to try. The tricky part was going to be honoring her promise to Ken to keep the police chief out of it. That in turn meant also keeping this from Stacy—not something she wanted to do again, but she had no choice. If she told Stacy about the search at Millers Lake, and the search was successful, Stacy had an obligation to report that in her paper. And if she reported the search, the chief would catch wind of it and confiscate any money—if there was any money—and she'd lose Ken's cooperation. She was lucky that Stacy had plans to go to dinner with Mack tonight to wrap up her interview. The important part was to find Samantha—not the money.

Rachel was getting everything ready for the search at Millers Lake when she heard a dog barking in the hallway. *Must be Rankin and Max*, she thought as she opened the door.

"That was quick—" she was beginning to say when a black Lab jumped up and licked her on the face. "Mags!" Rachel was stunned to see her faithful companion, Maggie, and her top investigator at Florida Omni Search, Red, standing at her doorway. "What are you guys doing here?"

"We thought you might need some help. And besides, Maggie was missing you." Red walked in her room.

"I missed her, too." Rachel limped over to the sink and filled up a bowl of water for Maggie.

"You okay?" Red asked, looking at Rachel's bandaged hand and wrapped ankle.

"Oh, yeah. Nothing to worry about."

"Well, too late for that. When I heard about the fire and that you got hurt, I started packing my stuff to head up here. You need somebody watching out for you."

Red sounded like her father. Always worried about her. He'd been the lead investigator on the case when Mallory went missing, and he'd been tremendously supportive. They'd formed a tight bond during that awful time, and ever since then, he'd been like a second father to her.

"As you can see, I'm fine." Rachel eased herself down to the floor and cradled Maggie in her lap. "Last I talked to Janine, she said you were working on a new case."

"Yep, well, the case resolved itself." Red sat down on one of the dining room chairs and watched Rachel interact with Maggie. She knew that his heart still ached for her and all she went through with Mallory.

"Which case was this?" Rachel inquired.

"Wife reported her husband missing when he didn't come home after a dinner meeting. The police gave her the standard 'we can't do anything for forty-eight hours' line, and she freaked out and called us. Long story short, a hotel maid discovered him the next day handcuffed to a bed. Apparently he'd picked up a prostitute after the meeting and they'd disagreed about the fee. So she tied him up, gagged him with her bra, and left. She told the police she'd intended to return later that night and let him go—after he'd learned his lesson—but her son got sick and she had to take him to the ER. She forgot about it until the next morning and then was too scared to go back to the hotel. So she made an anonymous call to the police."

Rachel started laughing. "Oh my gosh, that's hilarious. Was the guy okay?"

"He was when he left the hotel. I'm sure his wife did some damage when he finally got home." Red looked around at all the stuff on the dining room table. "So, what's going on here?"

"You arrived at the perfect time. We're getting ready to go on another search." Rachel brought him up to speed on the case and what they were planning on doing at the lake.

"If you can give me a few minutes to change, Maggie and I will go with you."

"Thanks for looking out for me."

"You sure you're up to this?" Red asked.

"Yeah, I'm good."

Red was a man of few words when it came to mushy stuff, but Rachel could always rely on him to have her back. She had a feeling he would make his way up here to help her even though she'd told him not to. While he went to change, she continued to play with Maggie.

"I missed you, girl. This has been so hard for me. I need to find Sam. Can you help me find Sam?" Maggie answered by licking Rachel's face. "That's a good girl."

A few minutes later, Mike walked in with Rankin Smartz and his dog, Max, and Peter Moore, her forensic specialist.

"Who do we have here?" Mike said as they all walked in.

Mike had never met Maggie. And Maggie had never met a human being she didn't like. Especially if they gave her belly rubs like Mike was doing.

"You think Sam knew where the money was hidden?" Peter asked.

"Ken didn't say it outright, but I think he must have thought Sam knew where it was. Or had an inkling."

"How do we know Sam didn't take the money before she went missing?"

"We don't. But my gut feeling tells me she wouldn't take the dirty money."

"Why not?"

"She was looking for another job. Her mom said that she was struggling to make ends meet," Rachel said.

"It could have been a cover," Peter said.

"No. I don't think Sam would have risked it. Unless someone forced her to find the money," Mike added.

"You're operating on the assumption she was taken against her will?" Rankin asked.

"Yes," Rachel replied.

"So what next?"

"If she was at Millers Lake recently, hopefully Max will pick up the scent and lead us to where she was taken. At least we'll know she was there at some point."

"It's a long shot," Rankin admitted.

"Yes, it is, but it's all we have right now," Rachel agreed. "And you guys know me by now. I check out every lead and don't give up."

They all shook their heads in agreement.

"What are we waiting for? Let's get our asses over to Millers Lake," Red said.

✦ ✦ ✦

After a thirty-minute drive, they finally found Millers Lake. Rachel felt a sense of peace and tranquility when she viewed the surroundings. The lake was spring-fed, which gave the water a pretty cerulean color. Visibility was about six or seven feet. Magnificent tall oak, birch, and pine trees surrounded the lake. A few picnic tables and BBQ grills were scattered around. Rachel could imagine families coming here for Sunday picnics, spending the day fishing and tossing a Frisbee or football, but now, during the weekday, they had the place to themselves. She then remembered Tammie's story about Sam's accident. *This is where it had happened*, Rachel thought. *How ironic.*

While everyone set up and got ready, she walked over to one of the trees. There were so many of them she wished she'd asked

Ken to be a little more specific on where his particular tree was. She looked up, but couldn't see the hole Ken had described.

She started to walk around, checking them. Her ankle was bothering her and she slowed down. *In the fall this would be easier*, she thought. The trees were now thick with leaves, and finding the one Ken had described seemed like it would be hard—if not impossible—to do. But then the fourth tree she checked out had possibilities. She could see what looked like a small hole about halfway up the tree.

"Hey, I think this is it," she called out to her team.

"Want me to climb up and check it out?" Peter asked.

Rachel looked around. Daylight was fading fast. The sun was starting its slow descent, and soon it would be dark.

"Yeah, go ahead."

While he climbed the tree, she helped get Max ready for the search.

"Here's the shirt we used for the last search." She pulled it out of the truck. "Let's see what Max comes up with."

They all walked over to the tree and waited.

Peter yelled down. "I found something."

"What is it?" Rachel said.

"You're not going to believe this."

"Try us," Rachel shot back.

"Matchbox cars. And rocks. And…"

Rachel could barely see him up in the tree.

"Star Wars toys. Old ones."

"Money?" Red asked hopefully, looking up at him.

"If there was any, it's gone now." Peter headed back down the tree and dropped to the ground from the lowest branch.

"It's like a dream toy chest for a seven-year-old up there." He wiped his hands on his jeans. "But no money."

"Either Ken was telling tall tales or someone got it already," Mike said.

"I'm betting that someone else beat us to it," Rachel said. She walked over and sat on the picnic table to rest her ankle. She watched Rankin and Max walk around the perimeter of the lake. After a few minutes of sniffing around, Max started whining.

"Didn't catch anything," Rankin said, walking back to them. "I thought he caught a scent, but it turned out to be nothing. If Sam was here, she stayed in this immediate area and then was driven away."

The team looked disappointed. "We have a few more minutes of daylight left. Let's take another good look around and then we'll head back," Rachel said.

Mike grabbed a flashlight from the truck.

"What are you doing?" Rachel asked.

"I want a look inside the tree. See for myself."

"Might as well," Rachel said. "We'll start packing up."

After a couple of minutes, he yelled out. "Hey, Rach. Looks like we missed something."

Rachel looked up and could see Mike's legs dangling precariously from a branch, his scuffed boots swinging back and forth.

"Looks like someone was here," he called down.

"Well?" Rachel said.

Mike worked his way back down the tall oak. "I'm not sure what this means, but I got something." He handed Rachel a sterling silver necklace with a broken-heart charm.

Peter took a look. "I don't know how I missed that."

"It was hung up on a piece of the tree inside the hole," Mike said.

She turned the charm over and saw the initials engraved on the back. A feeling of elation came over her slowly. Then the feeling of dread when she realized what this meant.

"I think I know where Sam is."

Chapter Thirty-One
Lake Juniper, FL,
Tuesday 7:50 p.m.

Sam was lying on a dirty cot in the cellar, trying to think of reasons why Patrick would want to kidnap her and hold her in this hellhole. He wasn't like the Patrick she first met back in high school, the Patrick she dated for several years. Or was he?

When they'd first met, she was smitten by all the attention he gave her. She was still self-conscious about the scars from the boating accident. Everyone, including Patrick, told her she was still beautiful, but she didn't buy it. All she saw when she looked in the mirror were the angry, pink zigzag streaks that snaked down her face. She wore makeup to cover them up, but you could still see them.

Patrick met her every day after football practice and they'd do their homework together. Most of the time he stayed over for dinner. In the morning, he'd pick her up in his Camaro and take her to school. They'd take off the T-top and turn up the radio, singing "Sweet Child o' Mine" at the top of their lungs, the salty air blowing through their hair.

Patrick wasn't the cutest guy in school, but he was the funniest. He was the class clown and never failed to make her laugh. His red hair and green eyes made him look sweet and innocent, and most of the time he was. But Sam started seeing another side to him.

She saw Patrick lose his cool twice. The first time was during their senior trip to Disney World. The park opened its gates at midnight every year for graduation night. All Florida seniors were invited to play at the parks from midnight to 6:00 the next morning. She couldn't ride some of the roller coasters because of the head injury from the accident. So while Patrick and his friends rode Space Mountain, she sat down at a table and waited.

Kenny, a guy she recognized from a rival high school, offered to buy her a Coke and wait with her. Kenny was also a football player and she thought he was kinda cute. They talked about school, football, and college plans while she waited for Patrick. When Patrick and his buddies got off the ride and he saw her talking to Kenny, Patrick lost it. She'd never seen him jealous before. He started shoving Kenny around. If his buddies hadn't pulled him off, there would have been a fistfight.

She'd been cool to him for the rest of trip. He apologized over and over, but she hadn't given in. He gave her a sterling silver necklace with a broken-heart charm to make it up to her. It had their initials, P+S, on the back of the charm.

"You wear this half of the heart," Patrick had told her. "And I have the other half of your heart." He put the second broken-heart charm on a key ring he always carried around.

The thought of Patrick carrying around a silver heart charm had made her giggle. Patrick thought she'd forgiven him, but the fiasco at Disney World was when it had all started going downhill. She'd seen a scary and possessive side of him. What she'd first thought was cute—Patrick always insisting he take her places, never letting her go anywhere alone—now felt claustrophobic.

She'd been glad when graduation and summer were over. Maybe new goals and responsibilities would settle him down.

They started fire college together in the fall, but while she excelled in all of her classes, Patrick struggled. Her feelings toward him had cooled considerably, but she felt bad that he was having such a hard time with school. So she stuck by him for two years until graduation, when they both received their firefighter certification and associate degree in fire science.

She hadn't realized that Patrick's feelings hadn't diminished at all. Quite the reverse.

The night after graduation, she saw the angry side of Patrick again. He'd wanted to take her to dinner to celebrate, but her family had already made plans. She promised to meet him afterward to celebrate, but she figured it was time to break it off with him. What she hadn't known was that he had other plans.

After dinner, Patrick took her to Millers Lake, where they frequently went to hang out. She willed herself to be strong and tell him how she felt. She rehearsed the words in her head all night. She'd tell him they needed a break, she wanted to remain friends, and they'd still see each other.

Patrick parked the truck and they walked over to the picnic area. He pulled a bottle of champagne and two glasses out of a bag. She'd thought he was celebrating their graduation. She took a deep breath and started to say the words that had been in her head all night. "Patrick, I just want you to know I've really enjoyed our time together—"

He reached over and put a finger on her mouth. "Shhh…I have something to ask you." He got down on one knee and took her hands in his.

Oh shit, she'd thought. Not this. Not now. She should have seen this coming. The champagne, the flowers, his nervousness.

"Patrick, I don't think—"

"Please, Sam, let me finish before I lose my nerve," Patrick pleaded. "I've loved you all my life. I want us to be together forever. We have the same dreams, the same goals, and we're perfect for each other. Will you give me the honor of being my wife?"

She was stuck. She hadn't wanted to hurt his feelings, but at the same time, if she didn't say something now, it would just be harder later on.

She took a deep breath. Now or never. The words came out in a rush. "Patrick, I can't do this. I was going to tell you tonight. I think we need to take a break. This is just too fast for me. I want to get a job and get settled. I'm not ready to get married."

Patrick was crushed. She'd never forget the look on his face.

"What? You want to break up with me?"

She'd nodded her head yes.

"Are you fucking kidding me?" His face got red and flushed. "Who is it?"

"What do you mean?"

"Who are you seeing?"

"There isn't anybody. I just want to take a breather. That's all."

He sat there for a minute, trying to calm down. He took the ring and twirled it around in his hand. The tiny diamond glittered in the moonlight.

"You can still wear this. We can call it a promise ring. We can wait to marry after we get jobs," Patrick pleaded with her.

"No, Patrick. I can't accept it. It's time for us to move on." She forced herself to look directly at him. "We can still hang out as friends." She regretted saying it as soon as the words came out of her mouth.

He started to get mad all over again. He stood up and clenched his fists. "Don't…do…this…Samantha. Please. If there is no one else, then why are we breaking up? Don't you love me?"

She'd shaken her head no. All the things she'd planned to say were gone. "No, Patrick. I'm sorry, it's over."

Patrick took the bottle of champagne and threw it, the bottle giving a satisfying pop and sizzle as it hit a tree. He took the skinny champagne glasses and did the same thing. "I can't believe this!" he yelled at her. "You…will…regret…this…you fucking bitch!"

Patrick was shaking as he got in his truck and left. She sat on the picnic table and cried for a long time. She hadn't been sad; she'd been relieved. She hadn't realized until that moment that she'd felt stressed the whole time she was with Patrick. Now, she felt nothing but sweet relief. She was free.

After what seemed like hours, another vehicle pulled up. It was one of her brother's friends, Blake, and his girlfriend. They'd given her a ride home. After that fiasco, she didn't see Patrick again for a couple months.

They ran into each other at the fire station for tryouts. He acted like nothing had ever happened between them. It had been awkward at first, but then she got used to it. They both ended up getting hired at the same fire department, but thankfully, worked on different shifts. She managed to be civil to him when they saw each other. Eventually the awkwardness went away, and she didn't give Patrick a second thought.

Then she met Ken at a call. She hadn't realized it was the same guy she'd met at Disney World her senior year. Kenny Collins. He looked a little different now. His skinny frame had filled out nicely, and he was taller.

Ken was a police officer and they ran into each other at a domestic dispute call. The husband had tied his wife to a dining room chair and set their house on fire. After they'd rescued the victim and arrested her husband, they all stood outside the house talking shop. Ken asked her out for coffee. She told him no, but said he could take her to dinner instead. She'd been a little unhappy to find out that Ken and Patrick were friends. It didn't seem to bother Ken that she and Patrick had once dated, so she decided to put the past behind her and move on. She'd thought Patrick had done the same. Ken and Sam were married within six months of dating. They had two beautiful girls and everything had been good.

Until she learned Ken and Patrick's secret.

Chapter Thirty-Two
Santa Rosa Beach, FL, Tuesday 11:55 p.m.

Stacy handed Rachel her cell. "This thing has been going off like gangbusters since you've been in the shower. Vibrating all over the counter."

"Thanks." Rachel took the phone and glanced through the call log. "Jeff Stanton called. Probably to let me know the tool impressions have come back." She sat down and put her head on the table.

"Everything okay?"

"It's been a long day."

Stacy sat down at the table with her. "I hear you. The hot lead I got about Pedro Gonzalez turned out to be a dead end. At least the dinner with Mack wasn't a waste of time."

"Mack is a very handsome guy."

Stacy agreed. "Yes, he is. But it's so obvious that he's in love with Sam."

"Really? Why do you think so?"

"You really have to ask?" Stacy laughed. "When he talks about her, his eyes light up. They're in love."

"What happened at dinner?"

"We went to Jack Speight's house. He's a detective at the police department. Even though he's not active on Sam's case, Mack thought he'd be able to give me some insight on the arson cases."

"How did it go?"

"Good, although I don't think any of the information he gave me will help us find Sam. What happened with Ken?"

Rachel told of her visit at the jail and the decision to search around the lake. Since no money was found, she thought it was okay to tell her what happened. "We found a necklace that belonged to Sam."

"How do you know for sure it was Sam who left the necklace?"

"I don't know for sure, but it seems to fit the puzzle. Tammie told me the story about the necklace when we met before the press conference. As far as she knew, Sam didn't wear it anymore. If it had been in the tree for a long time, it would have shown some wear from the weather. The necklace was clean when we found it. I think Sam left it there on the chance Ken or Mack would find it and understand its significance."

"You think Patrick kidnapped Sam?"

"That's a strong possibility. We need to find Patrick and talk to him."

"At dinner, Mack mentioned that Patrick has a cabin somewhere north of here. He's supposed to be there now. Fishing or something."

"Do you know where the cabin is?"

"Not sure. I can call Mack and ask for directions."

Rachel looked through her call log again. "Jeff Stanton called me three times. I better call him back before everyone comes back. Mike went to pick up a pizza for a late-night snack and then we're going to regroup."

"Are you going to tell Jeff about the necklace?" Stacy asked.

"Not yet." Rachel walked into her bedroom to call Jeff. "Hey, Jeff, it's Rachel. Sorry I missed your calls."

"Hi, Rachel. I'm sorry to be calling you so late, but I wanted to let you know this before it comes out in the media." Jeff hesitated.

Rachel sensed something bad was coming down. She instinctively sat down on the bed. No late-night phone calls were usually good ones.

"Mack Dixon was killed in a car accident tonight. I wanted to tell you before it hit the media outlets."

"Oh my gosh! What happened?" Rachel asked.

Stacy could tell something was wrong by the tone of Rachel's voice. She came into the room and sat down next to her on the bed.

"I don't know all the details yet. It happened on Highway 20. From what the state trooper told me, it looked like he lost control of his truck and it flipped over in a ditch. He died on impact."

"When did this happen?"

"About ten o'clock."

Rachel was speechless. She sat numb for a minute, trying to gather her thoughts. "I'm so sorry. Please keep me updated." Rachel clicked off. She didn't know how she was going to tell Stacy. She'd just had dinner with him.

Stacy put her arm around her. "Bad news?"

Rachel nodded her head and whispered, "Mack Dixon is dead."

"What? I just saw him a couple hours ago!"

Rachel repeated what little information Jeff had given her. "He said he'd call me later when he found out more."

"Mack said he was a little tired when we were leaving. Maybe he fell asleep at the wheel?" Stacy covered her face with her hands. "Oh God, I can't believe this is happening."

Rachel rubbed her back. "I know. I'm sorry."

"Mack was fine while we were at dinner." Stacy reflected. She just couldn't wrap her head around the fact Mack was now dead.

"Did he have anything to drink?"

"Yeah, one beer. Maybe two. But we had a huge dinner. I wouldn't let him drive me back if I thought he was inebriated."

"Of course."

Rachel heard some noise in the other room. "Sounds like Mike's here with the pizza. Want something to eat?"

Stacy shook her head. "I'm not hungry. Give me a few minutes, okay?"

"Sure. Take your time." Rachel went to go tell Mike the bad news.

Chapter Thirty-Three

Santa Rosa Beach, FL, Wednesday 9:35 a.m.

Since Jack Speight was close to Mack, Stacy thought it was a good idea to head over there first thing in the morning to talk to him about what had happened. She couldn't shake the feeling that his death had something to do with Samantha's disappearance.

Jack lived in a nice subdivision close to the beach. It was a modest neighborhood dotted with colorful Florida cottages. She drove past the swimming pool, a children's playground, and tennis courts. They parked in front of a pale-blue house at the end of a cul-de-sac. As soon as she rang the bell, dogs starting barking. A petite blonde with hazel eyes and a nice smile answered the door. She was wearing an apron decorated with a daisy design.

"Hi, Jenny. Nice to see you again." Stacy introduced Rachel to Jack's wife.

"Nice to meet you. Please come in," Jenny said.

"Thanks for having us over." Rachel admired the comfortable interior of their home.

It was decorated in a seaside flair with white denim couches, coral-beige clapboard walls, and pale-blue and green accents. The floors were a beautiful blonde bamboo. She could see Jack and the kids tossing a football in the backyard.

"Can I get you some lemonade?" Jenny offered.

They accepted the sweet, tangy drink and Jenny led them outside.

"Hey there," Jack said as they walked out onto the deck.

Jenny handed her husband a drink and took the boys inside. Stacy introduced Jack to Rachel and they all settled on the Adirondack chairs that overlooked the lake.

"I was sorry to hear about Mack. Stacy said you were close," Rachel said.

"Thank you. I think we're all still in shock."

"I appreciate you letting us come over. I'm sure Stacy told you my background and what we're doing to find Samantha. I can't help but wonder if Mack's car accident wasn't planned."

"The thought crossed my mind a couple of times, too. Until we get the coroner's report, I don't want to jump to conclusions." Jack paused. "Why do you think Mack's death wasn't an accident?"

Rachel wasn't ready to disclose what they'd found at Millers Lake. "There's something about Patrick I don't like. I think he has something to do with all this."

"Funny you mention that. Mack said that just last night." Jack looked at Stacy for verification.

"He said he'd gone to Patrick's house a couple of days ago to talk to him about Sam. He said something was bugging him the whole time he was there, but he couldn't put his finger on it," Stacy said. "It finally dawned on him last night."

"What was it?"

"When Mack was leaving, he saw a tool Patrick had just bought," Jack responded.

"A Halligan bar?" Rachel asked.

Jack looked surprised. "Yes. How did you know?"

"I've been working with Jeff Stanton, and he called me early this morning. He said the tool marks left at the scene matched the marks of the other arson cases. He speculated it was some type of crowbar. Possibly a Halligan bar."

"Mack thought the same thing. When he noticed the new one, he asked Patrick what had happened to the old one. Patrick said it had been stolen. Mack asked me to check if Patrick had reported it stolen—like he said he had—but he hadn't," Jack said.

"Why would Patrick lie about his tool being stolen?" Stacy asked.

"He's trying to hide something," Jack answered.

"Because he's the one who started all the fires," Rachel concluded.

"Chief Gladstone needs to know about this." Jack picked up the phone and got through immediately. He outlined their theory to the chief. But then, as he listened, Jack's face got angry. "Chief, I don't think—" he started, but then stopped. "I understand," he said finally, and hung up.

"What?" Rachel asked.

"The chief thinks I'm butting in," he said. "And he's right about that; I'm not on this case. And he doesn't think it's a big deal that Patrick didn't report the Halligan bar stolen. He'll bring him in for questioning when Patrick gets back from his vacation. And then he'll see."

"I don't think we can wait for that," Rachel said. "I think we have to talk to Patrick immediately."

"You know best. You can probably find him at his fishing cabin. I'd check there first."

"Do you know where it is?" Stacy asked.

"Sure. I've been up there a couple of times with some of the guys during hunting season. I can give you directions. It's about an hour from here."

Chapter Thirty-Four
Juniper Lake, FL, Wednesday 12:00 Noon

"Are we sure the fishing cabin is this way? This road seems to go nowhere," Rachel said.

"I think we're right." Stacy consulted the directions Jack had given them. "But this place is so out in the boonies the GPS doesn't even register it."

Just as she said that, the road opened up to a large field with a small cabin beside a lake. The cabin was made of logs and had a wide front porch with two rocking chairs on one side and a wooden bench on the other. Planter boxes that looked like they once had held beautiful flowers adorned the windows.

"Looks like no one's here," Mike said. "I don't see Patrick's truck."

"That's a good thing. We can snoop around a bit." Rachel stepped out of the truck. She walked up to the front door and tried the knob. "It's unlocked."

"Knock first. You don't want to get shot or anything," Stacy said. "Red wouldn't like it if we came back without you." Red had stayed behind to look after Maggie and catch up on some paperwork while they came up to the cabin. He hadn't been happy about it, but Rachel assured him they were just doing a look-see.

She softly knocked on the door. "No answer." She opened the door cautiously. "Hello," she called out.

"Let me go first." Mike stepped inside.

"He must have been here recently. It still smells like breakfast," Rachel said. "Bacon and eggs, I'm guessing." She looked around the room. The place was clean and tidy. A small, worn couch sat in the middle of the room with a La-Z-Boy recliner in front of fireplace. On the coffee table were a few well-read hunting and fishing magazines. Off to the right was a tiny kitchen with a table and chairs. On the left side of the room a hallway led to three closed doors.

"Those must be the bedrooms." Stacy led them down the hallway and opened one of the doors. The room's queen bed had been hastily made with a quilt bunched up and two throw pillows placed by the headboard. There was a half-empty glass of water on the nightstand, along with a bottle of Tylenol.

She opened the next door in the hallway and walked into the bathroom. The sink was still wet and a damp towel hung from the towel bar.

"Someone was just here," Stacy said. "But no sign of Samantha." She pointed to the wet towel and used bar of soap.

The last room was a smaller bedroom with twin beds. "Looks like no one has used this room in a while." The room held a musty smell and the beds were meticulously made.

"Well, we didn't pass Patrick's truck on the way out unless he went the other way," Mike said from behind her.

"Let's take a look around outside." Rachel led the way through the back door off the kitchen. Mike opened up the trash cans by the back door.

"Why are there latches on the lids?" Rachel wondered out loud.

"Raccoons probably. They're smart little buggers and like to get in the trash," Mike said, digging around in the trash bag.

"What are you doing?" Rachel asked, wrinkling her nose at the smell.

"You can learn a lot by looking in someone's trash," Stacy said.

"You sound like you've done that before. Yuck."

"He must have emptied it recently. Just some beer cans and food," Mike said. "No signs of a guest."

They looked around the yard. "Nice little retreat Patrick has here. Let's walk down to the lake," Rachel suggested.

A worn and heavily used path led to the water's edge. From the rise where they stood, the lake was a beautiful emerald-green color with a sandy bottom. They started down.

"Florida has the most beautiful lakes I've ever seen," Stacy said as they walked.

Mike crouched down to the ground. "Lots of footprints. Maybe recent, hard to tell." The sandy path was covered with them.

"Looks like two sets," Rachel said.

"Man and woman." Mike said. "See the size difference? And look at the direction of the prints. The larger one goes both ways."

"And the smaller set of prints heads only toward the lake," Rachel said.

"Patrick had some company. Let's see where they went."

They followed the prints down to the lake.

"Maybe one of you should stay back at the cabin for lookout," Mike suggested.

Stacy nodded. "I'll go back and wait." She pulled her cell phone out of her pocket. "Shit, no cell service."

Rachel and Mike looked at their cell phones. "Same here," Rachel said as Mike nodded his head, too.

"There's a whistle in my backpack, but I left it in the truck," Stacy said.

Mike tossed her the truck keys and laughed. "And if a whistle isn't enough, I have a loaded Glock in the glove compartment. You know how to shoot?"

"Yes, I do."

"Good. Whistle if you need us. Use the gun in an emergency."

"Right. Got it." Stacy turned back and headed toward the cabin.

Rachel and Mike carefully made their way through the thick brush, following the trail and the footprints.

"What do you think about the two sets of prints? Patrick has an accomplice? Or is it Sam?" Rachel said.

"I'd like to think it's Sam."

Rachel nodded in agreement.

The trees were thick and provided shade from the overbearing sun. It gave the effect of approaching darkness and there was a distinct chill in the air.

"We should have brought a flashlight with us. The more we head down this path, the darker it gets," Mike said, brushing a branch out of his way. "How's your ankle holding up?"

"Good, so far. I wonder how long—" Rachel started to say as she slipped on something and landed flat on her butt. "Ouch. What the hell was that?" She reached around and rubbed the side of her hip.

"Whoa. You okay?" Mike held out his hand to help her up.

"Yeah, I'm fine." Rachel looked down at the path. A shiny object protruded from the sandy path. Mike reached down and picked it up.

"A wine corkscrew. That's weird," he said.

"It could have come from the cabin. Let's keep going."

After a few hundred feet the footprints stopped.

"Looks like they go off the path here," Mike said.

A small tunnel cut into the undergrowth led through the dense pine forest. Mike had to hunch down to go through it. Rachel followed him. He came to a standstill. "Is that what I think it is?"

A small structure was almost invisible from the trail because it was covered in thick brush and shielded by all the pine trees. Its wooden door was locked with a heavy latch across the front.

"It's an old cabin," Rachel said. She started to step up to the door when a loud gunshot rang out through the woods. She jumped back in surprise.

"What the hell? Stacy?" She turned around to face Mike.

"I don't know," Mike said. "It could've been a hunter. Hard to tell where it came from."

Rachel turned back to the door. She wanted to go in and take a look, but the thought of Stacy in trouble was too much.

"We can always come back. Let's go check on Stacy," Mike said. "Stay low and follow me." Rachel followed Mike's lead as they made their way back to the other cabin. The thick trees and undergrowth made a great camouflage for them.

"Why do I get myself in these messes? I always wind up with the psychos," Rachel mumbled.

"Shhh. Keep quiet and move faster," Mike whispered.

"Easy for you. You don't have a sprained ankle."

"Sorry, Rach. I forgot."

They came back to the clearing by the lake and Mike stopped suddenly.

"What?" Rachel whispered.

"I see someone. Just stay behind me," Mike said as he reached down and got his pistol out of his ankle holster.

"Wait! It's Stacy." Rachel pointed.

Stacy was running toward them with the whistle in her hand.

"Just stay down. Someone may be following her," Mike said.

It was hard for Rachel not to run toward Stacy. She wasn't sure if she was in trouble or not. In a few seconds she was upon them at the trail.

"What was that?" Rachel asked as Stacy got close.

She was so out of breath it took her a minute to answer. "I don't know. I was just getting back to the cabin when I heard the gunshot. I couldn't tell where it was coming from. I didn't see anyone or hear any vehicles. I hid behind a tree for a few minutes until I could get the courage to come after you guys." Stacy was gasping for air. "I thought maybe someone was after you, so I came looking for you."

"No. We thought the same thing," Rachel said.

"It could have been a hunter," Mike repeated.

"Did you guys find anything?" Stacy asked.

"Yes, an older cabin off the beaten path. It was boarded up. We didn't get a chance to look inside. We heard the gunshot before we could do anything," Mike replied.

"It's getting dark, and I don't want any of us to accidentally get shot by an overzealous hunter thinking we're dinner. Let's come back tomorrow during full daylight," Rachel suggested.

"That old cabin looked deserted, anyway. We'll try again in the morning," Mike agreed.

They quickly made their way to the truck and headed back to the hotel.

"That place is creepy," Stacy said.

"Just like Patrick," Rachel agreed.

"It's a true sportsman's paradise. Remote, hidden from view, with everything a hunter could need," Mike said.

"And a perfect place to hide a body." Stacy shivered.

They rode in silence, each lost in thought. When they finally reached the hotel, Mike escorted them back to their room.

"Want to stay for dinner?" Rachel asked him.

"Why don't I cook dinner for you guys?"

"Sounds great." Rachel looked at Stacy for confirmation.

"Hey, whatever you guys want to do. I thought I'd go over to Jack's house for a bit. He invited me over for dinner again. They're planning a memorial for Mack."

"I guess it's just you and me, then," Mike said. "I'll go change and pick up something from the store."

"What time to you want to leave tomorrow?" Stacy asked him.

"I say we leave around seven. Get an early head start." Mike grabbed his stuff. "I'll be back in about an hour."

"Got it. Bright and early," Stacy said as Mike left. She waited until Mike was gone and said to Rachel, "I'm gonna take a quick shower. I'll hurry so you can get ready for your big date."

"What?"

"You and Mike," Stacy said with a smirk.

"I have no idea what you're talking about," Rachel said, pulling a couple of beers out of the fridge and handing one to Stacy.

"The chemistry between you two is undeniable."

Rachel took a deep pull of her beer.

"Mike? He's not my type."

"Yeah, whatever. The man is fixing you dinner. I'd go for it if I were you."

"He offered to fix dinner for *us*. You're the one who's bailing and going over to Jack's."

"I would've gone somewhere else, anyway. You guys need some privacy. And don't worry, I'll be home late."

Rachel laughed. "I'm so not talking about this right now."

"I want details in the morning." Stacy walked toward the bathroom. "Be out of your way soon."

Rachel took her beer out on the patio. Maybe she would make a move tonight.

Chapter Thirty-Five
Santa Rosa Beach, FL, Wednesday 4:30 p.m.

That was cutting it close, Patrick thought, as he made his way back over the bridge and into town. Thank goodness he'd spotted them first.

He'd just been getting ready to move Sam back to the cabin when he saw Rachel and her friends walking outside. It was perfect that they left the other girl behind. He'd waited until Mike and Rachel started down the trail before shooting his gun. He knew it would spook them and they'd come running back.

But now he'd have to wait until morning to get Sam. She'd eventually come around and see things his way. With Gonzales breathing down his neck, he knew they had little time to escape. First, he had to switch vehicles. Everyone knew he had a black truck, but not many people knew he still drove his father's old pickup. When he got back to town, he'd get everything ready to go. His heart quickened with anticipation. Sam and the girls would finally be his, and they'd start a new life together.

✦ ✦ ✦

Rachel walked into the living room, which smelled of garlic, onions, and tomatoes. It was heavenly. "What's this?"

Mike was stirring something in a pot on the stove. "Spaghetti and meatballs. My mom's special recipe. Guaranteed to heal what ails you." He handed her a glass of red wine.

"Thanks. It smells delicious."

"You look very nice." Mike gave her kiss on the cheek.

"Why, thank you. You, too." Rachel took her wine and sat on one of the barstools, watching Mike work. She'd had a hard time deciding what to wear. She still hadn't bought much to replace what she'd lost of her wardrobe, and her choices were limited. So Stacy had ended up loaning her a simple black jersey knit dress with crochet detail on the cap sleeves and upper back. The dress hit just above the knees and showed off her legs.

It was still hard to brush her hair and put on makeup due to the heavy bandage on her hand. But she felt like she'd done a fairly good job. Her singed eyebrows hadn't grown back yet, so she'd had to take an eyebrow pencil and fill in the bare spots. She'd kept it simple and just put on some mascara to make her green eyes pop and a swipe of strawberry-flavored lip gloss. She'd added mousse to her naturally wavy hair to make it glossy. Rachel thought she looked pretty damn good for working with what she had. A spritz of Bulgari, her favorite perfume, and she was ready to go.

She looked around the room, surprised. It had been magically transformed. Candles sparkled on the table and jazz was playing in the background. *This certainly feels like a date*, she thought. *Very romantic.*

Mike dished some spaghetti on the plates. "Please have a seat." He pulled out a chair for her. "Just let me get the garlic bread from the oven and we'll be ready to eat."

She watched as he finished up, bringing the bread and salad to the table. Rachel thought he looked great in a pair of khaki pants with a polo button-down shirt and his scuffed cowboy boots. She'd never seen him out of jeans and a T-shirt, so this was a treat.

"You clean up nice," Rachel said, teasing.

"Why, thank you."

"Everything looks great. Thanks for doing this." Rachel ate a forkful of spaghetti and savored the taste. "Yummy."

"Mom would be proud."

"Yes, she would. This is delicious."

"I'm sure this is nothing compared to the fine cuisine you're used to in Miami."

"I'd rather eat this than anything I could get in Miami. This is pure comfort food."

"How do you like living in Miami?" Mike reached for a piece of garlic bread to sop up some of the red sauce with.

"It's great. All you can ask for. Great white sandy beaches with emerald-green water. Nice weather year-round. Shopping galore. And an international airport to take you anywhere you need to go."

"Sounds like a nice lifestyle."

"And the Miami Heat. Can't forget my sports team," she said, taking a bite of the salad.

"I never pegged you as sports fan."

"Sure. I love basketball. I even have season tickets. You should come with me sometime."

"I'd love to." Mike took a generous sip of his wine. "Is that an invitation?"

"Yes. Hot dogs, beer, and a basketball game. We'd have a blast."

"What else do you do in your spare time?"

"Well, unfortunately, I don't have a lot of spare time. When I do, I like to shop. I'm an antiques junkie. Also, I have a weird thing for learning different languages."

"I don't think it's weird. How'd you get started?"

"When I was in real estate, I wanted to do all I could to stand out as a top agent. The first language I learned was Spanish, since Miami is home to many Hispanics. Miami also has a large pool of international investors. I had clients from all over the globe." Rachel took a sip of her wine. "I found it easy and fun to learn. After Spanish, I mastered other languages."

"Such as?"

"*La cena è deliziosa.*" Rachel waved her hand over the food and smiled. It was Italian for, *The dinner is delicious.*

"*Grazie.*"

Rachel looked amused. "*Parli Italiano?*" *Do you speak Italian?*

"*Un po. La mia mamma è Italiana,*" he answered. *A little. My mom is Italian.*

"Nice. I love Italian. It's the most romantic language of all."

"It sounds really nice when you speak it," Mike said. "What else do you know?"

"German and French. I was working on Mandarin Chinese before I got called on this case."

"A woman of many talents. Is there anything else I should know?"

"I'm a lousy cook. I have about twenty-five restaurant phone numbers memorized. My kitchen drawers are filled with take-out menus instead of utensils. So this is really a nice treat." Rachel pointed to her plate of spaghetti, which was almost gone.

Mike laughed. "I love to cook. My mom taught me everything I know." He twirled some noodles around his fork. "I was raised by a single mom. My dad was in the armed forces and he and mom had a whirlwind romance while he was stationed in Italy. They had plans to marry, but before that could happen, he died. My mom found out she was pregnant a few weeks after his death. Most of her family had moved to the States, so she packed up and followed them to New York City. I was born a few months after that. We lived with my aunt and cousins in a tiny apartment in Brooklyn while my mom worked three jobs to support us. Soon after high school, I joined the army."

Rachel touched his hand with hers. "Your mom sounds like an amazing woman."

"She is. Tough as nails. You remind me of her."

Rachel smiled. "When did you see her last?"

"She comes and visits every summer. That's when I have Addison. I would love for my mother to eventually move to Florida and live with us."

Addison was Mike's ten-year-old daughter. Rachel knew he was divorced and loved spending time with his daughter.

"That's sweet. So what other special recipes did your mom teach you?"

"Let's see…Besides spaghetti and meatballs, I can make lasagna, pasta carbonara, and a mean steak and twice-baked potato."

"That's more than I can do. I've mastered bacon and eggs fairly well, though."

"Well then, you can make breakfast sometime," Mike said.

Rachel's heart skipped a beat. Breakfast. She thought about what that implied.

They finished eating and Mike opened another bottle of wine. "Let's go sit outside. It's nice tonight." There was a little private courtyard just off the living area. Mike and Rachel sat down at the small table. Her bare leg brushed up against his.

"This is nice," Rachel said. "I'm glad you came over."

Mike reached up and stroked her chin with his finger.

"I've been wanting to do this since the first time we were alone together." He leaned over and kissed her softly on the lips.

Rachel returned his kiss with more urgency. She ran her hand across his chest and down his left arm. He was so strong and hard. She found herself completely turned on.

Mike wrapped his fingers around her hair and tugged gently, kissing down her neck. Rachel's head was spinning from the combination of the wine and the passion that was heating up from inside of her.

"Let's go inside," she suggested in a throaty voice.

And for the first time since her divorce, she opened up and made love to another man.

✦ ✦ ✦

The next morning, Rachel woke up to an empty bed and the smell of bacon and coffee. She grabbed her robe and went out to the kitchen.

"First you cook me a great meal. Then you seduce me. Now breakfast? I thought it was my turn to cook."

Mike turned from the stove, spatula in hand, and smiled. "I thought I'd let you sleep. We have a busy day ahead."

"You sure know how to turn on the charm." Rachel gave him a kiss as he handed her a cup of coffee. "If you keep cooking for me, I'm going to have to up the miles I paddle every day to ward off the pounds."

Mike looked her over. "I think you look fabulous."

They sat down to eat breakfast. Mike said, "So we didn't get around to talking about your visit with Jack."

Rachel finished chewing her eggs and said, "Jack had Mack and Stacy over for dinner the night of Mack's accident. He said that Mack had talked to him a little about the case and he thought Patrick was hiding something, too." She looked around the room. "Where's Stacy?"

"She's already up. Came in for a cup of coffee and then said she was going for a run. She should be back in an hour to get ready to go."

Rachel smiled. She knew Stacy didn't run unless someone was chasing her or there was a big sale at her favorite store. She was just giving them more time alone.

"Jack works for the police department, right? They should be looking at Patrick," Mike said.

"Jack isn't active on Sam's case. But he did say Chief Gladstone isn't looking too hard at Patrick. The chief is pretty convinced the Mafia's to blame for Sam's disappearance and her body will turn up eventually." Rachel finished her coffee.

"You didn't tell him about the necklace we found yesterday?" Mike got up and cleared the breakfast dishes away.

"No. I think we need to keep it under wraps until we check out Patrick's cabin again. Besides, I gave Ken my word about not involving the police with the search at the lake."

"What would Patrick gain from kidnapping Sam?"

"I'm not entirely sure he kidnapped her. Maybe she used him to get away."

"There's only one way to find out."

Chapter Thirty-Six

Lake Juniper, FL, Thursday 10:30 a.m.

"Still no truck," Rachel said. "That's weird. Red drove by Patrick's house several times last night just in case he decided to go home. Red said Patrick wasn't home all night. Where is he?"

"Maybe he hid his truck somewhere. Jack said his cabin was located on forty acres of land. That is a lot of land to hide a vehicle."

"Let's check the inside of the cabin again," Stacy suggested.

Just as they were getting out of the truck, Rachel saw a figure running from the house. She stopped in her tracks and pointed toward the house.

"Look! Somebody just left."

Mike pulled out his gun and motioned for them to stay behind him. As they made their way closer to the house, Rachel stopped. "What's that smell?"

Before anyone could answer, the whole cabin blew up in front of their eyes. No one had time to react. The force of the blast blew them back a few feet. Debris from the impact rained down all around them. Rachel looked at the house as it became a large fiery ball of orange, then thick black smoke filled the air. Her vision was a little blurry and her ears hurt. She could feel the intensity of the heat all around her.

One minute she saw a figure running from the cabin and the next minute there was nothing but a black hole of smoke and fire.

Rachel looked around for Mike and Stacy. Mike was sitting up a few feet away from her. He looked as stunned as she was. Stacy was to her right, propped up against a tree.

"You guys okay?" Mike yelled.

Pieces of black debris floated through the air. Slowly, her hearing came back to her. She checked all over her body. Nothing seemed broken or out of place. "What the hell just happened?"

"Are you okay?" Mike made his way over to her.

"Yes, I'm fine," she said as Stacy crawled over to her. "Let's just hope Sam wasn't in the cabin."

"Did you get a good look at the person who ran out?" Stacy asked.

"No, I didn't get a chance. It could have been anybody."

"We need to get to somewhere with a cell signal and call the fire department," Mike said. "Rachel, you go with Stacy and call for help while I go check out the other cabin."

"No way. I want to go with you. In case we find Sam." Rachel saw the look on Mike's face. He didn't want her to go with him. "Mike, I have to go."

"Okay." Mike tossed Stacy the keys. "There's a flashlight under the driver's seat. Can you bring it back to me before you leave?"

"Sure." Stacy headed for the truck.

"Are you sure you are okay? You look peaked," Mike asked Rachel.

"Yeah. I'm fine. Just a little shook up."

Stacy came back with the flashlight. "I'll be back as soon as I get a signal and call the police and fire department."

Mike took the flashlight. "Be careful."

✦ ✦ ✦

Stacy got in the truck and headed down the long drive that connected to the highway. Even though it was daylight and the sun was shining bright, the dense overgrowth and tall pines shaded the sun and made it hard to see, especially since her eyes were still adjusting from the blast. She flipped on the headlights and spotted someone limping along the side of the road. She instinctively slowed down. The person was obviously injured. *Was this Sam? Did she somehow escape Patrick and get hurt in the blast?*

Stacy tried to get a better look. The figure was dressed in long pants and a baseball cap. It was hard to tell whether it was a man or woman. Whoever it was collapsed as soon as Stacy pulled the truck over. She quickly checked her cell phone. Still no signal. Cautiously, she got out of truck and walked over to the side of the road.

"Are you okay?" She got a little closer. "Sam? Is that you?"

The figure emitted a low moan that reminded Stacy of a cat when it goes in heat. She bent down next to the person and repeated, "Hey, are you okay?"

He shot up so quickly she didn't have time to react. His right hand brusquely grabbed her wrist and pulled her down hard. It was then she looked into a pair of eyes that made her spine tingle. It was Patrick.

He forced her up and jammed the barrel of a handgun into her back. *Shit,* she thought. She was in trouble now.

"Walk slowly to the truck and get in. No funny stuff, or I'll shoot you. And I won't think twice about it."

Stacy thought about her options. She was still a couple of miles away from the highway, and she didn't know the area very well. She tried to remember if Mike had left the gun in the truck or had taken it with him.

Patrick made her get in the driver's seat. "Let's go. Pull out nice and slow."

"Where are we going?" Stacy stole at look at him, meeting his cold blue eyes.

"Just drive. I'll let you know when you need to turn."

Stacy's hands shook as she took the wheel and slowly pulled back onto the road. She wondered how long it would be before Mike and Rachel knew she hadn't called the police.

Chapter Thirty-Seven

"You feel up to going to the other cabin?" Mike asked as he helped Rachel stand.

Rachel got her balance and tested her legs. She felt a little unsteady on her feet and her ankle throbbed.

"We can rest for a bit," Mike offered.

"No, let's go. I'm ready." Rachel knew their time was running out. *Like Sam's time was running out was more like it*, she thought. She found her backpack a few feet away, picked it up, and slung it over her shoulder. Looking back at where the cabin once stood, she said a silent prayer. *Please let Sam be alive.*

They retraced their steps from the day before, carefully making their way around the lake. "Watch your step. Stay close behind me," Mike said as they headed through thick brush.

"What in the world just happened back there?" Rachel asked, still in shock. "Did Patrick have something to do with that?"

"I don't know why Patrick would blow up his own cabin, unless he was hiding something from us."

They moved down the trail as quickly as Rachel's ankle would allow her to walk. Mike tried to hold back the thick branches so they wouldn't whip Rachel in the face and arms as she walked behind him. "You doing okay?" he asked as they got closer to the old cabin.

"Yeah. Looks like we're almost there." Rachel's "spidey sense" was tingling now. She didn't know what they were going to find, but she knew it would be significant.

Mike pushed back the vegetation covering the front of the cabin. The door was secured with a heavy-duty padlock.

"Now what?" Rachel asked.

Mike reached down and pulled the Glock out of his ankle holster. "Step back." He aimed the gun at the lock and pulled the trigger. The lock blew off and left a small hole in the door. He yanked the door open and looked inside.

"It's dark. Hand me the flashlight, please."

Rachel handed over the flashlight as he stepped inside.

"What do you see?"

"Looks like he's using this place for storage." He shined a light around the area. Rachel could see a couple of ATVs and storage shelves that were neatly stacked against wall. They held several rows of storage tubs.

Rachel followed Mike deeper inside the musty cabin. The cabin was one large room with a fireplace and sleeping loft. Rachel figured the room was about six hundred square feet total. The flooring was made of old pine and was scratched and worn. In some places you couldn't see the flooring because it was covered with a heavy layer of dirt and leaves. The ladder to the sleeping loft was missing several rungs.

"I guess this is where Patrick stores all his hunting gear," Rachel said as she walked to the back of the room. "He sure likes everything neat and orderly." She took the lid off one of the boxes and rummaged inside.

"I wonder why they built a cabin so far away from…Hey, wait a sec. Did you hear that?" Mike asked, shining his light near the back of the cabin.

Rachel took a step back and listened.

A faint noise seemed to come from beneath the flooring.

"What is that?" Mike shined the light on the floor where Rachel was standing.

"An animal? It sounds like it's coming from underneath the floor."

Rachel got on her hands and knees and felt around. She brushed away some debris. Her hand felt something rough.

"I think this is some type of cellar." She found a hidden handle and gave it a tug. The door didn't budge.

"That's strange. It's almost impossible to build anything underground in this area because the bedrock is so near the surface," Mike said. "This cabin must have been built into a hill. It's hard to find with all the foliage surrounding it."

"I wonder if this was the original cabin. It looks older."

"And Patrick turned it into a storage space for all his junk. Makes sense," Mike said. "Here, let me help."

Rachel got out of the way and Mike gave the handle a hard yank. It budged a little and Mike pushed harder as the door slowly creaked open.

"Hand me the flashlight."

She passed him the flashlight.

He pointed it down the dark hole. "What the hell…?" Mike let out a sigh.

A small room, no bigger than six by eight, held a small cot, jugs of water, a bucket, and a shelf with canned goods. But it was the smell that turned Mike's stomach. A smell of a mix of sweat, urine, and fear.

Rachel peered into the hole with a sense of dread. Her gaze followed the flashlight's beam. A woman was curled up in a tight ball in the corner. Not moving. Mike quickly climbed down the ladder into the cellar with Rachel right behind him.

She just knew it. They were too late.

Chapter Thirty-Eight

Stacy tried to keep her cool while she was driving. She wondered if Patrick would risk going back to his house. They were headed back toward town and she needed to start thinking about her options. The last thing she wanted was to be held hostage at his house. Maybe she should try and talk to him. Reason with him.

"How long have you lived around here?" she asked.

Patrick sat in silence. She sneaked a peek at him. He was sullen and lost in thought. She tried another tactic. Maybe he didn't want to talk about his transgressions. "My dad used to own hunting land in Alabama. He would shoot anything that moved, from deer to doves to turkeys." She came to a fork in the road. Left would take them to the interstate and toward Pensacola. If they went right, it would take them back to Santa Rosa Beach.

"Take a right." *Okay, so we're heading back to town,* Stacy thought. She tried to look around the truck for a possible weapon without being obvious, but Mike kept his truck so meticulously clean there wasn't a pen or piece of trash in sight.

A police cruiser approached them, and an idea popped in her head. She pushed on the gas pedal ever so slightly and watched her speed slowly increase. She knew police officers loved setting up speed traps on these rural roads and prayed they would get pulled over.

"Keep it within the speed limit." Patrick snapped out of his daze and finally noticed she was going faster.

Stacy silently cursed and eased off the gas pedal. They were getting closer to town. The Clyde B. Wells Bridge, which crossed over the bay, was looming up ahead. They'd be at the beach in a matter of minutes. She wondered what Patrick had in mind once they got to where they were going.

Chapter Thirty-Nine

"It's Sam. She's alive." Those were the sweetest words she'd ever heard.

Rachel limped over to Sam. "We've been looking for you. Are you okay?"

Sam looked up at her with tears in her eyes. She nodded her head yes.

"I'm Rachel Scott with Florida Omni Search, and this is Mike Mancini with the DEA. We're going to get you out of here."

"Can you make it up the ladder?" Mike asked her.

"I think so."

Mike helped her up. "Take it easy. Nice and slow."

Rachel said, "Why don't I go up first, then you can follow with Sam."

When they got outside, Rachel found a blanket in her backpack and wrapped it around the firefighter.

"Where's the asshole?" Sam asked, shivering.

"Patrick? I don't know," Rachel answered her. "We haven't found him yet."

"I wonder what's taking Stacy so long. She should have been back by now," Mike said as they started walking back up the trail.

"How did you find me?" Sam asked Rachel.

"We got a lead and went to Millers Lake. I found your heart charm necklace."

Sam looked shocked. "You found my necklace?"

"Yep. Your friend Tammie told me about the necklace a couple days ago. We just got lucky. I knew you must have left it there on purpose."

"The asshole made me wear it again. It was his half of the necklace. He took me back to the lake to look for the money that Ken hid. I took a chance when Patrick wasn't looking and hid it in the tree." Sam took a deep breath. "He had this silly plan that we'd get back together. I don't know what happened to Patrick. He just cracked and went crazy. I was afraid I'd never see my kids again. I hoped one day Ken would find the necklace and know what had happened. That I didn't leave our kids."

"I think he knows that you wouldn't leave your kids on purpose. After we found the necklace, we came up here to talk to Patrick."

Rachel wanted to prepare Sam for what she was about to witness. "One thing—while we were looking for you, Patrick's cabin exploded and burned." She explained to Sam what happened.

"What? That crazy bastard blew it up?"

Mike nodded. "We don't know exactly how it happened. We'd just pulled up and were walking toward the cabin when it exploded."

"That must have been the noise I heard. The ground shook really hard."

"We saw someone, but we weren't sure if it was Patrick or not," Mike said. "A friend of ours, Stacy, went to call the police after the house went up in flames."

"Hopefully, she's waiting for us there," Rachel said.

They walked slowly back to where the main cabin had once stood. Sam had to stop a couple of times to rest and catch her breath.

When they finally made it back, Sam gasped when she saw the gaping hole where the cabin used to be.

Rachel and Mike looked around. Mike's truck was nowhere to be found.

Chapter Forty

"Stacy should have been back by now. She would've gotten cell service up by the main road. What should we do?" Rachel asked Mike.

"Do you think you'll be okay here? I can start walking that way and call for help as soon as I get service," Mike offered.

The sound of a truck coming down the drive got their attention. It was an old red Chevy. It came to a stop and an older man in blue-jeaned overalls got out. "What the hell happened here? You can see the smoke all the way up at my farm!"

Mike stepped forward and introduced himself. "The cabin exploded as soon as we drove up."

"Huh." The man looked suspicious. "Where's Pat?"

"We have no idea. We saw someone running off toward the woods right before the explosion. It could have been him."

The old man took off his hat and rubbed his hand through his thinning gray hair. "Huh." He seemed to be at a loss for words.

Welcome to the club, Rachel thought.

"Did you call the fire department?" Mike asked.

"Yep. But it will take them a while to get here. Volunteer." He looked over at Sam. She was still huddled up in the blanket. "What happened to her?"

"Long story," Rachel said.

"Did you pass a black Dodge Ram on the way here?" Mike asked him.

"Nope. Sure didn't. I thought—" Sirens howling in the distance interrupted his thoughts. "That was faster than I thought."

They watched as a fire truck and ambulance pulled up to the cabin. The firefighters immediately pulled their hoses and started attacking what was left of the fire.

Rachel directed the paramedics to Sam and waited while they tended to her.

"You'll be okay," Rachel reassured her. "The police will find Patrick."

"I hope so. I'm worried about my kids."

"I'll give your mom a call and let her know to meet you at the hospital," Rachel told Sam as the paramedics loaded her into the ambulance. "She'll be so happy to hear that you're okay."

Sam grabbed her hand. "Thank you for everything."

Rachel smiled. "Take care of yourself."

Mike was giving the police officer the details of what happened at the cabin. After hearing that Patrick had kidnapped Sam, the officer put a call into Chief Gladstone. "We put an APB out for your truck as well as for Patrick Hart," the officer relayed to Mike.

"There's a lot of land to cover here. Patrick might still be hiding out somewhere," Rachel whispered to Mike. "We should go back to the hotel and get the team together to look for him."

Chapter Forty-One

Gripping the steering wheel, Stacy knew she had to come up with a plan quickly. They were getting closer to town and the odds of Patrick just letting her go were slim. He'd obviously gone off the deep end.

"Where are we going?" Stacy asked again.

Patrick let out a sigh. "Don't you ever shut up? We're going to get my money and then I'm taking off."

"Taking off where?"

"That's none of your business."

"Are you planning on letting me go?"

Patrick seemed to think this over. "As soon as I let you go, you'll call the cops. So what do you think?"

"I think you're crazy. That's what I think." Stacy regretted the words as soon as they came out of her mouth. Patrick got red in the face and slammed his fist in the dashboard.

"I think you better shut the fuck up and not say another word, or you'll be swimming with the fishes soon." He hooked his thumb in the direction of the water.

They were just coming to the end of the bridge. Stacy briefly thought about driving the truck right into the bay. "Take your next right. We're almost there." Patrick held the gun at her. "Don't even think about doing any funny stuff."

Stacy knew he lived somewhere off this road. Rachel had mentioned it when she'd asked Red to drive by Patrick's house last night. Maybe she'd get lucky and Red would be staking out the house.

Rachel and Mike might have called the police by now, too. She'd been gone for over an hour.

"Take a left here. Third house on the right," Patrick snarled at her.

She drove up the gravel driveway to a nice brick house. The house was in good shape. *No way of knowing a psycho lives here,* she thought. She shifted the gear into park and waited. "Now what?"

"Shut off the truck and get out. Don't think about running. I'll put a bullet in your back. Don't tempt me."

There were plenty of houses around, although his house was far back from the main street. She didn't want to risk making a break for it just yet.

Stacy got out of the truck and walked slowly up to the front door. She'd wait until the right time to make her move.

Although the outside of the house was nice and orderly, the inside was a complete mess. It was obvious he was remodeling. The flooring was covered in paper, and sheets covered all the furniture. The place still faintly smelled of wet paint. Empty beer bottles and pizza boxes littered the kitchen countertop, and the trash can was overflowing. Stale beer, wet paint, and sweat—the smells made her stomach churn. She wondered why he'd go through all the trouble of fixing up a house if he was planning on skipping town. Something must have happened recently to make him go nutso.

"Nice place. I like the paint color." She tried to make nice again.

"Sit down." Patrick ripped off a flowered sheet that had covered a wooden dining chair. After she sat down, he picked up a roll of duct tape off the kitchen bar. "Put your hands behind your back and sit real still."

She knew he'd have to put the gun down to tape her up. It was now or never. She heard the clunk of the gun hitting the countertop. Stacy took in a deep breath and mentally prepared herself. Her heart was beating so fast she thought it would come out of her chest. As soon as she felt him starting to go down behind her to bind her hands, she sprang up and knocked over the chair, causing Patrick to fall backward into the countertop.

"Fucking bitch!" Patrick slipped on the paper covering while trying to stand back up. Stacy lunged for the gun on the countertop. Her hand hit the cool metal of the gun just as Patrick put his hands around her waist, trying to pull her down.

"Let me go, you motherfucker! I'll shoot your balls off!" Stacy fought like a madwoman while Patrick tried to drag her down. She remembered the defense moves her ex-boyfriend had taught her. Swinging her left elbow back, she connected with Patrick's nose. He still didn't let go, but his grip slackened enough for her to turn around.

She pointed the gun at him and pulled the trigger.

Chapter Forty-Two

Rachel called Nora to let her know Sam was being transported to the local hospital. Nora was overjoyed Sam was okay and profusely thanked Rachel. She told Nora that she would stop by the hospital later to check on Sam.

Just as she got off the phone with Nora, Chief Gladstone and Jeff Stanton pulled up to the site. Chief Gladstone confirmed that an APB was already out for Mike's truck, and an arrest warrant for Patrick was in the works. He said they'd send someone over to Patrick's house to check it out.

Rachel was worried that something had happened to Stacy and conveyed that to Chief Gladstone. She used Jeff's phone, which was the only one that had cell service, to call Stacy, but it went to voice mail. She tried again and got the same result. "Something went wrong," Rachel said.

"The police are out looking for my truck and Stacy. She'll turn up," Mike tried to reassure Rachel.

"That was Patrick who ran. He blew up the cabin as a distraction and he ran. Somehow he got ahold of Stacy when we went looking for Sam. I know it. I can feel it."

"Jeff's giving us a ride back to town. We'll go back to the hotel and get your truck. We'll find her," Mike said.

✦ ✦ ✦

Stacy stared at Patrick, then back at the gun.

Patrick laughed. "The joke's on you! The gun wasn't loaded. Stupid bitch."

Stacy was so stunned she didn't have time to react when Patrick swiped the gun from her hand. He pounded the gun into her temple and she crumpled to the floor.

"Time for a little burn out."

He had to work quickly. He knew he didn't have much time before the cops would be crawling all over the place. Too bad things didn't work out according to plan. He'd really wanted to have a new life with Sam and the kids.

"Plan B," he said out loud to no one in particular.

He hauled a couple cans of gasoline from the garage into the house. He started pouring gas around the furniture, splashing some on all the walls.

"Such a shame. I had big plans for this house." No one would find Sam for a long time—she was hidden away. He thought about letting someone know where she was. But if he couldn't have her, no one else should be able to. Mack was taken care of. Ken was in jail. She'd be all alone, anyway. What was another murder? He'd be far, far away by the time they discovered both bodies.

He grabbed his bag—the one he'd packed over a month ago—and his fake passport. He'd go to his hideout until things cooled down. Then he could make his escape. He was glad he'd put most of his money into an offshore account. Harder to trace. And he had the cash he'd recovered from Ken's hidey-hole. That asshole stole his girl and, if that weren't enough, ratted him out in the marijuana scheme. Patrick had enough of people shitting on him.

He walked back to the garage and uncovered his motorcycle. Everyone thought he was still working on his bike, but Patrick had finished it months ago. No one would suspect he got away on his bike. He'd been on his way to his hidden truck when Stacy had found him. That part was unplanned, but proved to be genius. He made sure everything on the bike was in order and then pushed it up to the side of the house.

When he reentered the house, he took out his matches. Stacy was still out cold on the floor. He lit a match and threw it against the wall. The curtains immediately caught fire. He took one last look around and left. He strapped his backpack to the bike, got on, and took off, never looking back.

❖ ❖ ❖

Rachel called Red once they were on the way back to town. "Take Maggie and head back over to Patrick's house. Chief Gladstone said he was sending a patrol car over there, but I'd feel better if you went, too. I have a bad feeling."

"Sure thing. I was beginning to wonder what was going on. I'll call you when I get there." Red hung up.

"I'd just gotten the call from Jack Speight before I left for the cabin." Jeff looked over at Rachel. "Mack's truck had been messed with. It wasn't an accident."

"I knew it! Stacy did, too. What happened?"

"His brake lines were cut. When he tried to slow down at the big curve, his brakes failed and he ran off the road. When he hit the embankment, his truck rolled over. Mack wasn't wearing his seat belt, and he was thrown from the truck."

"Jack tells me Mack was suspicious of Patrick. And I think Patrick knew it. He must have followed Mack that night and then taken the opportunity to mess with his brakes."

"That fits. Patrick used to work as a mechanic. Tammie told me it's what he did while he was in high school. His dad owned a car repair place in town."

Rachel's cell phone rang. "It's Red. He must be at Patrick's place." She took the call. Immediately, Mike knew something was wrong when she said, "See if you can find Stacy. We'll get there as soon as we can."

"He just got to Patrick's house." Rachel turned around to the backseat and said to Mike, "Your truck is there and the house is on fire." She pleaded to Jeff, "Please hurry!"

Chapter Forty-Three

Stacy felt the heat pressing down on her body before she even opened her eyes. *Oh shit*, she thought as she struggled to come awake. Flames were dancing all around her. She tried to get up, but she couldn't move. *The bastard tied my hands and feet together with duct tape.* A loud popping sound diverted her attention from trying to get free of her bonds. The paint cans in the kitchen were exploding.

She worked faster, rubbing her wrists against each other. The heat was working in her favor. The glue in the duct tape was melting, and she was able to work free of the tape around her hands. She was elated when she got free. But the feeling was short-lived when she realized there was nowhere to go. She was surrounded by fire.

Her throat was so swollen from the heat that she couldn't scream for help. Not that anyone could probably hear her, anyway. The fire seemed to have consumed the room in less than a minute. The situation was hopeless. She was going to die.

She half-crawled to the coffee table and hid underneath it. She knew the fire would find her under there, helpless and vulnerable, but she somehow felt safe. Starting to lose consciousness, her last thoughts were of Mack. As her eyes closed, she imagined him bursting through the door to rescue her, just as he had for Rachel.

Red got to Patrick's house in record time. From the hotel, the trip would normally take about ten minutes. He made it in five, running every red light and stop sign. He saw the smoke before the house even came into view. He quickly called Rachel to let her know what was going on. Parking the car at the curb, he ran up to the front door and threw it open. The intense heat pushed him back. The living room was engulfed in fire and smoke. He stood back and scanned the room. He saw a foot sticking out from under the coffee table.

Red ran back to his truck and grabbed Maggie's blanket. He used the water hose by the front door and soaked the blanket. He heard the sirens and knew help was on the way, but he didn't think there was much time left. He had to act now to save Stacy.

He covered his body as best as he could, took a deep breath, and ran through a wall of flames. Grabbing Stacy by the feet, he pulled her out from under the table and reached down to pick her up. Using a fireman's carry, he threw her over his shoulder, covered both of them with the blanket, and headed back out the front door. He collapsed onto the front yard, still holding on to Stacy.

Chapter Forty-Four
Santa Rosa Beach, FL, Thursday Evening

Rachel walked into the hospital room where Red was lying covered in bandages and hooked up to tubes and wires. The doctor had told her that Red had suffered a mild heart attack while rescuing Stacy. He'd also sustained second- and third-degree burns on his hands and feet.

As soon as she sat down, he opened his eyes.

"Hey, buddy. We have matching bandages." Rachel held up her right hand where she was burned.

He smiled faintly. "Is Stacy okay?"

Rachel nodded. "She's doing just fine. She had some smoke inhalation and minor burns. Stacy is a tough cookie. The doctor said she can probably go home tomorrow." Rachel gently smoothed the sheet over him. "We're both very grateful for what you did."

Red lifted his left hand and waved it away. "It was nothing. I was there at the right time."

"Yes, you were. Any later and Stacy might not have made it."

"Rachel, there's something I need to tell you." Red cleared his throat. "There's another reason why I came here."

"Save your energy. We can talk later."

"No. I need to tell you now."

Rachel felt her stomach tighten in a knot. "Okay. Go ahead."

"We got a lead on Mallory."

Rachel's heart skipped a beat. "What? Why didn't you tell me sooner?"

"Janine wanted to be sure it was valid before we proceeded. I just found out this morning that it might be worth checking out."

Rachel wanted to scream. He should have told her sooner. Whether or not the lead was valid was up to her to decide. But she treaded lightly. She didn't want to add stress to Red's already weakened heart. She supposed they were just trying to protect her.

"What was the lead?"

"Janine got a call about a missing girl. An American couple was on vacation in Mexico when their daughter was kidnapped," Red said. "Her parents were staying at a resort hotel. While their daughter was sleeping, they went for a quick drink at the pool bar. The mom went back thirty minutes later to check on her, and the little girl was gone."

"What does this have to do with Mallory?"

"I'm getting there." Red took his time getting the facts right. The pain meds were making him groggy. "They searched the resort, but didn't find her. They called in authorities and searched the entire island. The little girl wasn't found. The police thought that, since the couple was rich, there eventually would be a ransom, but nothing ever came in."

"When did this happen?"

"A few days ago. Now the FBI is involved. We got a call at the office the day after you left to come here. A maid at the resort came forward and gave the FBI information about a child-kidnapping ring. Her son also works at the resort and she found out he was involved. She'd struggled about doing the right thing and finally turned him in. She told the authorities what she knew. When they busted the son, the FBI raided their house. They took his computer." Red paused and collected his thoughts.

Rachel's heart was beating fast and she started sweating. *Please don't let my little girl be dead. I'll do anything. Just don't let her be dead.*

"They found some information on the computer that led to other people involved in the kidnapping ring." Red took a deep breath. This was going to hurt her. It was the reason why they'd kept the information from her in the first place. Red had wanted to be sure it was true. "Scott Jensen was on that list."

Rachel was stunned. "Janine's ex-husband? That Scott Jensen?"

"Yes." Red knew this would be hard for her to hear. Scott had worked for Rachel's husband for a short time at the car dealership. This was before she even knew Janine. Before Janine's son was kidnapped by his father after not returning him after a scheduled visitation. It was a very odd situation at best.

"Why was Scott on the list?"

"The FBI is investigating that, Rachel. They've talked with Janine, but she claims she didn't know anything about it. So far, the authorities haven't located Scott."

"Scott may have had something to do with Mallory's disappearance?" Rachel put her hand over her mouth in disbelief. Her heart fluttered out of control.

Red nodded his head.

Epilogue

Sam was reunited with her mom and children. She gave birth to a son on April 21. She named him Breck, after the brother and father she'd lost. She has not identified the father, although most people assume it was Mack. Sam filed for divorce, put her house and land up for sale, and returned to work at the fire department.

Ken was sentenced to twelve years in jail for his part in the marijuana operation. He is currently serving his time in the Walton County Jail.

Mack was given a funeral with honors. He was laid to rest in the same cemetery as Sam's brother and father.

Red recovered from his injuries and is back to work at Florida Omni Search.

Rachel is working on her latest lead to find Mallory.

Stacy quit her job at the *Miami Sun* and decided to freelance for a while. This was her last article she wrote for the *Sun*:

Missing Firefighter Found Alive
by Stacy Case

Samantha Collins, a firefighter with the Santa Rosa Beach Fire Department, was found alive yesterday. She'd been held captive by Patrick Hart, also a firefighter with SRBFD.

Acting on an anonymous tip Thursday morning, Florida Omni Search located the missing firefighter on a hunting property owned by Hart. "She was held against her will in an abandoned hunting cabin," said Florida Omni Search founder Rachel Scott.

Chief Gladstone of the Santa Rosa Beach Police Department said that Collins was in good shape at a local hospital. He also commented that Hart is still at large and wanted by the SRBPD for questioning.

Hart had been arrested last February along with Ken Collins, Samantha Collins's husband, for marijuana trafficking.

"Right now, there's no clear motivation on why Hart kidnapped Samantha Collins. We haven't had a chance to question Samantha in depth yet," Gladstone said.

Collins's mother, Nora Prince, said, "This is the best moment in my life," after hearing that Collins was alive. Prince thanked Scott and Florida Omni Search for locating her missing daughter.

"It was truly a miracle we found her. I just hugged her and told her over and over she was safe now," Scott said.

Prince said that her daughter had been through some "really horrible circumstances and was mentally tortured" during her imprisonment. She declined to elaborate due to an ongoing police investigation. She described Collins's mental state as "terrified and extremely anxious."

Patrick Hart has a twisted history with Samantha Collins, according to her mother. "They dated in high school and for two years after that, but Sam broke up with him before she dated Ken. Patrick was also friends with Ken and was arrested as a coconspirator in his marijuana grow operation."

"Samantha Collins is under police protection until Hart can be located," Chief Gladstone confirmed.

There is a $10,000 reward for any information leading to the capture and arrest of Patrick Hart.

Made in the USA
Columbia, SC
25 April 2019